IRISH
MEADOWS

COURAGE TO DREAM
BOOK 1

IRISH MEADOWS

SUSAN ANNE MASON

BETHANYHOUSE

a division of Baker Publishing Group
Minneapolis, Minnesota

© 2015 by Susan Anne Mason

Published by Bethany House Publishers
11400 Hampshire Avenue South
Bloomington, Minnesota 55438
www.bethanyhouse.com

Bethany House Publishers is a division of
Baker Publishing Group, Grand Rapids, Michigan

Printed in the United States of America

Library of Congress Cataloging-in-Publication Data

Mason, Susan Anne.
    Irish meadows / Susan Anne Mason.
        pages cm—(Courage to Dream; Book 1)
        Summary: "At the renowned Irish Meadows horse farm in New York, 1911, sisters Brianna and Colleen O'Leary struggle to reconcile their own dreams with their father's plans for the farm and his demanding marriage expectations"—Provided by publisher.
        ISBN 978-0-7642-1724-1 (pbk.)
        1. Horse farms—New York—Fiction. 2. Sisters—Fiction. 3. Fathers and daughters—Fiction. I. Title.
    PR9199.4.M3725I75 2015
    813'.6—dc23   2014047390

Cover design by Jennifer Parker
Cover photography by Olga Shelegeda

Author is represented by the Natasha Kern Literary Agency.

15 16 17 18 19 20 21   7 6 5 4 3 2 1

*To my Grade 6 teacher, Mr. Guistini,
the first person to encourage me to write a book.
Thank you for planting the seed that eventually took root.
Almost forty years later, I finally did it!*

1

LATE-AFTERNOON SHADOWS chased Gilbert Whelan up the long drive to the O'Leary mansion. The fanciful images seemed to bolster him from behind, giving him the courage to push forward. Even so, his steps slowed as he approached the flagstone path leading up to the house. A wave of homesickness tightened his throat, his suitcase weighing heavy in his hand.

Had it really been the better part of three years since he'd crossed the threshold? Gil swallowed the bitter taste of guilt that plagued him and continued to the foot of the wide, welcoming staircase. He set his battered bag on the ground and took in the familiar view—the wraparound porch, the double front door. He'd come here as a child with his widowed mother, who'd hired on as the O'Learys' housekeeper. Gil still found it difficult to think of the tragic illness that had claimed his mother's life and led to him being taken in as part of the O'Leary family.

Belonging . . . yet not belonging.

Gil ran a hand over the large white column to his left, his touch hesitant, nearly reverent. The red bricks of Irish Meadows had changed little since he'd been gone. If only the same could be said of its inhabitants.

Gil let his hand fall away with a sigh. If he'd had his way, he wouldn't have come back at all—for a multitude of complicated reasons. But he owed the O'Learys too much to avoid them any longer. So, he would stay long enough to repay his debt to his guardians, and then he'd move on to start a life of his own.

Lord, I could really use Your guidance here. Give me the strength to do what needs to be done without hurting anyone in the process.

Behind the ornate doors, Gil knew the family would be waiting to greet him like a long-lost son returning home. Reluctant to face their exuberant welcomes just yet, Gil turned down the stone path and made his way to the one place he felt most at home—the O'Leary stables. When he rounded the corner of the house and spied the enormous barn, a thrill of anticipation shot through him. How blessed he'd been to work on such a top-notch farm, raising and training the best racehorses on the eastern seaboard. At James O'Leary's feet, Gil had learned everything he needed to branch out on his own one day soon.

As he entered the building, Gil breathed in the familiar scent of hay, horse, and manure. He'd missed working with the animals almost as much as he'd missed the O'Learys. Manhattan was an exhilarating city, but Gil far preferred the fresh air, wide skies, and open meadows of Long Island. Especially in the spring when all of nature bloomed anew.

His gaze skimmed the immaculate mahogany stalls with their engraved brass nameplates for each thoroughbred. His ears tuned to the horses' quiet nickering, a sound more beautiful than a symphony. As his eyes adjusted to the dim light, Gil made his way to the one stall he'd be able to find blindfolded. When he raised the latch, Midnight Royalty gave a loud whinny in greeting. In an instant, Gil had his arms around the great black neck, murmuring words of affection for his friend. The horse tossed his head, flicking his nose to send Gil's cap sailing into the straw.

Gil laughed out loud. "I've missed you too, boy. But I'm home now." *For a while anyway.* He stroked his hand along Midnight's sleek flank. "Looks like they've been taking good care of you while I was gone. Your coat's as shiny as I've ever seen it."

"I brushed him every day for you."

Gil's hand froze on Midnight's back, every vertebrae of his spine stiffening.

Brianna. The one person he'd been trying not to think about, trying not to imagine seeing again for the first time in three years. He swallowed hard, and then turned to find her standing in the open doorway of the stall. His lungs seized, trapping his air, while his heart beat an unsteady rhythm in his chest.

The sprite of a girl he'd left behind had matured into a beautiful young woman. Clad in a dress of soft green that showed off her slim figure, Brianna stood quietly, hands clasped against her skirts. She wore her reddish-gold curls swept atop her head, leaving a few strands clinging to her slender neck. Wide green eyes watched him as though trying to gauge his reaction.

"Brianna. It's good to see you. You look . . . wonderful." He wiped his hands on his wool pants and moved forward to kiss her cheek. Her delicate scent, a cross between green apples and roses, met his nose.

A smile lit her features. "Thank you. You look well yourself."

He glanced down at his brown tweed vest and linen shirt. "I feel in need of a bath after the dust from the train and the walk here from the station."

A slight frown knit her brows together. "You should have called. Daddy would have sent Sam to get you."

He gave a sheepish shrug. "I wanted to walk. It felt good to breathe the fresh air after the grime of the city."

She stepped into the stall. "I'm glad you're home, Gil. I . . . we've missed you."

The already tight space seemed to shrink. Gil managed a brief smile. "I've missed all of you, too." *More than you know.* "And look at you. You've gone and grown up while I was away." He hoped his voice conveyed a levity he didn't feel. This mature young woman left him sorely out of his element. Where was the tomboy he'd felt so comfortable with? "Tell me, who's the lucky man courting you now?"

"Who says anyone is courting me?"

He stuffed his hands in his pants pockets. "You're almost eighteen. About to graduate. I assumed—"

"Well, you assumed wrong."

The pinched lines around her mouth told him the subject was not open for further discussion.

She turned away to pick up a piece of hay and shred it between her slim fingers. "So how does it feel to be finished with your college courses?" she asked brightly.

He studied her profile for a moment and decided he'd let her get away with changing the subject. He'd learn all the family news soon enough. "It feels like I'm finally starting my life. Doing something that matters." He bent to retrieve his hat from the floor and brushed the dirt from the brim.

She tilted her head. "Getting your degree didn't matter?"

"It's a means to an end, that's all."

"I think going to college would be the most thrilling thing ever. Living in the city surrounded by all the people and excitement." Her eyes glowed brighter than the stars he'd missed since leaving Irish Meadows.

He shook his head, chuckling. "Same old, Bree. Always dreaming of adventure. Glad to see some things haven't changed."

A slight flush colored her cheeks. Very attractive cheeks in a very attractive face.

He turned to run his hands down Midnight's haunches. "Looks like Sam's been exercising him regularly." The head groom, Sam Turnbull, had taught Gil everything he knew about training horses.

"Of course. Sam always keeps his word." She stepped closer, trapping Gil between Midnight and the wall, and laid a warm hand on his sleeve.

Gil went completely still. If he moved his head, his nose would brush tendrils of her hair. His throat became as dry as the dust that coated the floor, the tight enclosure suddenly too much to bear. He slipped around her and pushed the stall door wider. "We'd best be going. I'm sure your mother's waiting."

"All right." The disappointment in her voice matched the regret that stole the sparkle from her eyes.

Gil had hoped by now her childhood crush on him would have faded. That had been the main reason he'd stayed away, to give her time to mature and find a more suitable male to become interested in. And he'd vowed that when he returned to Irish Meadows, he would do nothing to encourage her. After all, they were practically family.

With a last rub of Midnight's nose, he latched the door behind him. They'd taken a few steps when the sound of a motorcar pulling up to the house echoed through the open stable doors. Brianna stopped dead in the middle of the corridor. She whirled around, eyes huge. "That's Daddy. I have to go."

Instead of heading toward the main doors, she set off at a fast pace toward the back of the barn, the swish of her skirts kicking up a cloud of dust.

"Wait." Gil fell into step beside her, eying her dress that was anything but suitable for the barn. "What are you doing down here anyway?"

She paused to raise slightly vulnerable eyes to his. "I knew you'd come here first. And I wanted to be the one to welcome you home." A car door slammed, and she jumped. "Please don't tell Daddy I was here."

Brianna O'Leary slipped through the back door of her family's home and down a small corridor to the kitchen. It was the only way to reach the back staircase without running the risk of bumping into either of her parents. Leaning against the doorframe to get her bearings, she closed her eyes and released a frustrated breath.

For weeks she'd daydreamed about Gil's homecoming— imagined what it would be like to see him again, to have her best friend back. Yet the reality of their reunion had not lived up to her expectations. Their connection—once so strong and unbreakable—now seemed as fleeting as the afternoon sun that filtered through the barn. Gil had acted awkward and halting around her, as though he felt uncomfortable with her nearness. How would they ever return to their former closeness if he kept an invisible wall around him?

Brianna squared her shoulders in firm resolve. What she needed was a different approach, a new plan to gain Gil's confidence, as well as his help in changing Daddy's mind about her future.

But first she had to reach the shelter of her room. Daddy wouldn't like it if he found out she'd waylaid Gil in the barn. Her father had made it plain he would no longer tolerate her hanging around the stables, and now she only rode her beloved Sophie when he wasn't around to scold her.

Brianna peered around the corner into the busy kitchen. Mrs. Harrison barked orders to the scullery maids, who scurried to do her bidding. Steam whistled from the large pots on the stove. The enticing aroma of freshly baked bread made Brianna's stomach grumble. With dinner preparations in full swing, she hoped she'd be able to slip by the cook unnoticed.

When Mrs. Harrison turned to stir a pot on the stove, Brianna lifted her skirts and tiptoed across the tiled floor.

"Is there something I can help you with, Miss Brianna?" The woman threw an amused glance over her shoulder.

Brianna froze in the middle of the room, then forced an innocent smile. "Mama was wondering how long until dinner."

The plump cook wiped a bead of sweat from beneath her white cap, then fisted a hand on her hip. "You don't fool me for a minute, missy. You've been down to the barn to see Master Gilbert, and now you're sneaking back in."

"How did you—"

"I've known you since you were a babe. You never could hide anything from me."

Brianna's cheeks heated. "I had to see Gil"—*before Colleen gets her claws into him*—"before everyone starts fussing over him."

Mrs. Harrison chuckled. "I've missed that boy almost as much as you have." She winked at her. "Go on and freshen up. Dinner will be ready in twenty minutes."

"Thank you." Brianna let out a relieved breath and dashed from the kitchen to the back staircase.

Once safely in her room, Brianna locked the door and plopped down on her quilted bed, the iron frame squeaking under her. She reached beneath the mattress and pulled out her journal to read the words she'd penned that very morning.

Goal for the summer: Enlist Gil's help in persuading Daddy to let me go to college in the fall.

She sighed and snapped the book shut. Not off to a promising start. She supposed she couldn't expect her relationship with Gil to remain the same as it had been before he went away. In fact, she didn't want it to. Her silly schoolgirl crush was a thing of the past, the passing fancy of an immature fifteen-year-old. Her focus now was on getting an education and seeing more of the world outside Irish Meadows. Romance could play no part in her life for the foreseeable future.

The only thing she wanted from Gil was his assistance with her father. To that end, she would make renewing her friendship with Gil her top priority.

After checking her appearance in the mirror, Brianna descended the grand central staircase to the entry hall below. Her hand slid over the polished mahogany rail as she moved, her ear attuned to the sounds of her family below. She paused for a moment before entering the formal parlor, relishing her siblings' giggles and the snatches of conversation drifting into the hall. She could picture her father sitting in his usual armchair, nose in his newspaper, her mother perched on the edge of the brocade settee. Adam would be standing at the French doors, looking out over the back gardens, and Colleen would be seated beside Mama, trying to ignore the antics of the two youngest O'Learys, Connor and Deirdre.

Taking a deep breath, Brianna entered the elegant room. Her eyes automatically scanned the room for Gil. Ignoring the dip of her heart when she didn't see him, she bolstered her flagging smile and continued forward.

Her mother glanced up from her book. "There you are, Bree. We thought you'd fallen asleep in your room."

"Has Gil not arrived yet?" she asked in what she hoped was a casual tone as she moved toward the marble fireplace.

"Mrs. Johnston said he got here earlier, but of course he went to see the horses first." Mama laughed and shook her head. "I swear that boy loves those animals more than his family."

"He is *not* family." Adam's voice seethed with bitterness.

Brianna gave an inward sigh. She'd hoped her older brother would have gotten over his resentment of Gil by now, but apparently it had as strong a hold on him as ever.

Daddy snapped the paper closed. "Gilbert has been raised in this house as one of us. I will not tolerate any animosity toward him."

"Of course you won't." Scowling, Adam turned back toward the window.

Seconds later, the clatter of footsteps broke the tense silence in the room. Gil burst through the parlor door, straightening the sleeves of his jacket, which he'd apparently donned in a hurry before dashing down the stairs.

He broke into a wide grin. "Hello, everyone."

Brianna stood off to the side as the whole O'Leary clan fawned over him, welcoming him home. Mama hugged and kissed him, then dabbed a handkerchief to her eyes. Daddy shook his hand and clapped him hard on the back, beaming, while Deirdre and Connor clamored for Gil's attention.

Brianna remained in the background, content to drink in the sight of him. His black hair still waved over his forehead in unruly curls despite his attempt to tame them. His eyes, under the dark sweep of his brow, were still the same intense blue that used to jolt her heart like a bolt of electricity. The only change was the breadth of his shoulders and chest, visible beneath the tweed suit jacket. He'd filled out while he was away, looking more man than boy now.

Her pulse quickened. Had he noticed similar changes in her appearance? That she was no longer the tomboy who'd followed him around the barn and the horse track every day? She frowned and pushed away the errant thought. What did that matter since she was only interested in Gil's friendship?

He stepped toward her, and Brianna froze. Would he give away the fact that she'd been in the stables?

"Bree, it's good to see you again." He bent to kiss her cheek as if he hadn't already greeted her earlier.

His amused wink allowed her to relax, confident he wouldn't reveal her secret. She smiled and played along. "And you, as well."

Gil looked past her, his smile freezing in place. "Hello, Adam."

Adam came forward with obvious reluctance to give Gil a quick handshake before stepping back. Brianna stiffened as

Colleen sashayed over, the swish of her silk skirts drawing every eye. Glorious auburn hair accentuated her older sister's flawless skin and vivid blue-violet eyes. Beside her, Brianna's freckled skin, nondescript red-gold hair, and slim silhouette always went unnoticed.

Colleen leaned in to give Gil a lingering hug. "Welcome home, Gilbert," she purred, her cheek pressed to his.

A fierce stab of jealousy ripped through Brianna's midsection. Colleen had worn a low-cut gown that highlighted her assets. With half the county's eligible men vying for her attention, did she have to capture Gil's, too?

As the family moved down the hall into the dining room, Brianna squeezed her hands into fists at her side, determined to keep her feelings in check. Yet an underlying fear rose up to choke her. She'd worried that when Gil came back, he'd become enamored of her sister and totally forget Brianna existed. Gil was *her* friend. They'd shared a bond that had excluded everyone else, even her beautiful sister. Secretly, Brianna had reveled in the knowledge that Gil had never shown any interest in Colleen. But would all that change now that Colleen had blossomed into a voluptuous woman?

Her jealousy, Brianna told herself, had nothing to do with wanting Gil for herself. She was only looking out for Gil's best interest. The fact that Colleen could beguile any man quicker than a spider could snare a fly made Brianna all the more uneasy. She'd have to do something before Gil became the next unsuspecting victim of one of her sister's cold-hearted schemes.

"Gilbert, my boy, it's great to have you home." Her father helped Mama into her seat, and then motioned Gil to take the chair next to his at the head of the table.

Gil smiled. "It's good to be back, sir. I can't wait to get out and work with the horses tomorrow."

Her father frowned. "I thought you'd start on the books first. I'm eager to put that business degree of yours to good use."

The lines around Gil's mouth tightened.

Mama clucked her tongue. "James, let the boy have a few days to rest before you besiege him with bookwork." Her gentle chiding brought a rush of color to Daddy's face. "I'm sure Gil longs to give Midnight a good workout. Besides, he deserves a bit of a holiday. He's worked every summer and never had any sort of vacation." With a flick of her wrist, Mama opened her napkin and laid it across her lap.

Gil shot her a grateful look. "I could use a few days to unwind."

His gaze swung the length of the table, catching Brianna's stare. Those vivid blue eyes she'd missed for so long seemed to look right through her. It used to be that Gil could tell her every thought, every feeling, without her having to say a word.

The servants' door opened, breaking their connection, and the kitchen maids filed in with the covered dishes, placing them on the sideboard with a flourish.

"We're having your favorite tonight, Gil," Deirdre said in a loud whisper across the table. "Mama said we could have my favorite tomorrow." Her seven-year-old cheeks glowed with the good health of outdoors and innocence.

"Thank you, Dee-Dee. I'll admit I've been looking forward to Mrs. Harrison's roast pork for weeks now. My mouth watered at the very thought of it." Gil gave the girl a bold wink, making her giggle.

"And we're having chocolate cake for dessert."

"Only if you eat all your main course, young lady." Mama's attempt at sternness fell short with her light laugh. "And that goes for you, too, Connor O'Leary. No scraping the peas into your pocket to dispose of later."

Eleven-year-old Connor gave their mother an impish grin. "For chocolate cake, I'll even eat extra peas."

Idle chitchat flowed easily while her family ate the scrumptious meal Mrs. Harrison had prepared especially for Gil. Once the chocolate cake had been sliced and served, along with more glasses of milk, tea, and coffee, Brianna started to relax. So far things had fallen back into a familiar rhythm—almost as though Gil had never left.

"Before I forget, I have some news to share." Her mother stirred her tea, the silver spoon tinkling in the dainty china cup. "I received a letter today from my cousin Beatrice in Ireland. You remember her, James. The one whose son is in the seminary."

Her father patted his mustache with a linen napkin. "Yes, of course. Studying in Boston, isn't he?"

"Yes. But he's coming here to Long Island as part of his internship. He'll be assisting at St. Rita's."

"Well, well. What a small world. We'll have to have him over for dinner."

Mama laid down her spoon and cleared her throat. "Actually, that's why Beatrice is writing. She wondered if we could put him up for a while. The rectory is undergoing renovations at the moment, and they have no place for him."

Daddy's eyebrows drew together. "I don't know, Kathleen. I'm not sure I'd be comfortable with a priest under our roof. Bad enough on Sunday morning."

Brianna tensed at her father's disapproving tone.

"He's not a priest yet. And we could put him up on the third floor so Gil won't feel so isolated."

Silence hung in the air, broken only by the scrape of forks against plates as Connor and Deirdre polished off every last crumb of cake.

"He's family, James. And we have plenty of space." Mama's tone became pleading.

Brianna hid a smile behind her napkin, knowing her father could never refuse her mother when she used that tone.

"The connection is distant at best. Isn't Beatrice your third cousin or some such thing?"

"Family is still family."

He gave Mama a look that would have withered most of his business associates, but Mama only smiled serenely, waiting.

At last, Daddy shook his head in apparent defeat. "Fine—as long as he doesn't expect me to attend daily church services."

Her mother clasped her hands together and beamed. "I'll send a telegram tomorrow and let him know."

Across the table, Brianna caught Colleen rolling her eyes. Her sister had little tolerance for anything religious. Only the wrath of their mother made her comply with their weekly church attendance.

Basking in her small victory, Mama leaned back against the plush dining chair, her teacup in hand. "So, Gilbert, tell us about your young lady. How is the grand romance progressing?"

The air tangled in Brianna's lungs. She knew Gil had been seeing a girl in Manhattan, but she had assumed since she hadn't heard anything lately, they had parted ways.

Gil cleared his throat. "I'm afraid my . . . association with Miss Haskell has come to an end."

Mama's cup clattered to the saucer. "Oh, Gil. I'm sorry. I'd hoped that we might expect a wedding announcement in the near future."

Gil's attention shifted to his plate, color staining his neck.

"Isn't her father the professor you worked for at Columbia? The one you spent every holiday with?"

Brianna stopped stirring her tea at the hurt in her mother's voice. How many times had Mama railed against the man who had hired Gil as his assistant, keeping Gil too busy to come home, even for holidays? And Brianna had agreed wholeheartedly. Other than the first Christmas after he left, Gil had not been back once to Irish Meadows.

Lines bracketed Gil's mouth. "One and the same. However, I fear Professor Haskell holds a grudge because of the termination of my relationship with Laura. He, too, hoped for a betrothal."

A minute of silence passed while everyone appeared to digest this latest news.

Then her father clapped Gil on the shoulder, looking decidedly relieved. "Not to worry, my boy. There are plenty of available young ladies in the area. As a matter of fact, I have one in mind for you myself."

The tension in Brianna's shoulders cinched the nerve at the base of her neck. "Really, Daddy. I'm sure Gil doesn't need you to find women for him." The words erupted from her mouth before the thought had fully formed in her head. A streak of fire heated her neck and cheeks.

Her father scowled at her. "That is no concern of yours, missy." He turned to Gil, pushing his chair back as he spoke. "Let's adjourn to the study. I have several important matters to discuss with you."

Gil's soft look of sympathy as he passed Brianna's chair did nothing to lessen the sting of her father's words. With Daddy's usual dismissive attitude, she was once again relegated to the background of her father's existence.

2

GIL SANK INTO ONE OF THE ARMCHAIRS in Mr. O'Leary's study, the scent of leather and pipe tobacco surrounding him like the hug of an old friend. Other than the stables, he'd missed this room the most, with its purely masculine overtones—the stone hearth, the enormous mahogany desk by the window, and the endless rows of books. Gil had shared many lengthy conversations with Mr. O'Leary here, discussing anything from the world of horse-racing to the price of hay. He looked forward to diving back into that aspect of the business.

Mr. O'Leary finished stoking the fire and took a seat in the wingback chair across from Gil. His shoulders slumped as he leaned back heavily on the cushions, his usual fortitude growing ragged around the edges. "I can't tell you how glad I am to have you home, son. This new anti-gambling legislation has me worried. Tracks are closing, jockeys are being dropped. Horse farms are bound to feel the pinch next if we can't get this law overturned." He picked up his pipe from the table beside his chair and tapped it on his palm. "I only hope we can keep our heads above water until this all blows over."

Gil frowned. "Is Irish Meadows in trouble?"

"Not yet. But if they shut down racing for good, it won't take long for things to go south. Especially if our clients start removing their horses from our care."

"Surely they won't go that far?"

"A few already have. I've managed to convince most of them to hold on a while longer." The strain of the last few months showed in the older man's face. Tired lines bracketed Mr. O'Leary's eyes. The light from the fire glinted off threads of silver invading the black hair at his temples. "Tomorrow I'll show you the new horses and let you have a day in the barn before you start on the books. I'm hoping you can recommend some ways to give our cash flow a boost."

Gil repressed a sigh. Seeing as how Mr. O'Leary had paid for his education, the least Gil could do was repay him with some bookkeeping and financial advice. He only hoped James O'Leary didn't expect him to stay at Irish Meadows forever. Gil ached to get out in the world and make the Whelan name count for something. He owed his father that much. Gil released a slow breath. Sooner or later he'd have to tell the O'Learys he planned to leave, but that could wait . . . for now.

Mr. O'Leary lit his pipe, took a long draw on the stem, and blew out a fragrant swirl of smoke. "Gilbert, you're twenty-one now. An adult with no need of a guardian. I have no real right to ask, but I need a favor from you."

Gil's stomach tightened at the grim look on Mr. O'Leary's face. "What kind of favor?"

"You've met Arthur Hastings, haven't you? He's been here for various events over the years."

"The banker?"

"That's right."

"What about him?"

Mr. O'Leary fixed Gil with a long stare. "I want you to begin courting his daughter, Aurora. Your alliance with the Hastings family could tip the balance in our favor when we apply for a business loan."

Gil curled his fingers around the arms of the leather chair until his knuckles ached from the force of his grip. After recently ending things with Laura Haskell, he had no interest in courting another woman.

The logs shifted with a loud *pop* in the fireplace.

"Aurora's about your age and not a hardship to look at." Mr. O'Leary chuckled. "From what I gather, she's had her eye on you since before you went away to school."

Gil strained to remember anything about the Hastings family. "I don't recall meeting her."

"Well, she remembers you. Asked her father to speak to me about arranging an occasion for you two to meet again."

Gil loosened his tie in an attempt to get more air. "With all due respect, sir, I've just broken off one relationship. I'm not ready to begin courting someone new."

"Don't you think it's time you called me James, son? And I understand your reluctance to jump into a new alliance. At least meet the girl and see what you think. We'll invite her family to the welcome-home dinner we're planning next week."

"Mr. O—James—you know I'd do anything I can to help, but—"

"I know you would, son. That's why I'm counting on you to save Irish Meadows from financial ruin."

※

Brianna rose early the next morning, grateful for a day free from school responsibilities. With mere weeks left until her graduation, she was finding school more and more challenging, determined as she was to earn the best grades possible in order to increase her odds of gaining entry into college. How she envied Gil going away to continue his education, experiencing life in the big city. If Gil could persuade her father, she'd follow in his footsteps next fall.

While the morning breeze teased the lace curtains through the open window, Brianna brushed the tangles out of her hair, recalling how her easy friendship with Gil had flourished over the years. As children, both of them spent every spare moment in the stables with the horses. Gil had secretly taught her to ride bareback, a fact that had thrilled Brianna. Gil had always treated her as an equal and not just a girl.

She laid down her hairbrush and moved to the wardrobe, where she fingered the elaborate riding outfit her father insisted she wear. Beautiful, for sure, but dreadfully uncomfortable. Instead, she pulled out her working attire, smiling at the brown wool skirt her mother had fashioned into a feminine version of riding pants. Unlike Daddy, Mama saw no harm in Brianna's love of horses and had finally given in to sewing legs into some of her older skirts.

Too excited to eat breakfast, Brianna hurried outside, her pulse sprinting faster than the horses racing around the practice track. Hooves pounded the soft earth as several riders urged their mounts to greater speeds on the straightaway. Brianna dashed to the white fence and leapt onto the first rung, thrilling to the power of the magnificent animals flying by. She grinned when she spotted Gil hunched over Midnight's neck. What a sight they made—Gil's white shirtsleeves flapping in the wind, his cap slung low over his forehead, and Midnight's sleek muscles flowing in perfect motion. A seamless blend of power and skill.

When Midnight crossed the finish line a full length before the other horses, Gil let out a loud whoop. Standing upright in the stirrups, he pulled off his hat and waved it in the air.

"Great time, Gil." Sam Turnbull's deep voice boomed out over the track as he held up his stopwatch.

Brianna hopped off the fence and ran over to where Gil would exit with Midnight, catching up with him as he reached the stable door.

"Good morning." She hoped she didn't sound as out of breath as she felt.

A smile of pleasure lit his features. "Good morning. I didn't think you'd be up this early."

"Couldn't wait to take Sophie out. It's been ages."

He nudged the door open and motioned for her to precede him. "You don't ride every day anymore?"

She shook her head. "It's not always possible with schoolwork and . . . social obligations." *And Daddy's constant disapproval.*

Gil turned the corner down the main corridor. "What kind of social obligations?"

"Oh, you know Daddy." She managed to keep her tone casual as she ran a hand over Midnight's smooth coat. "There's always some party or business dinner for us to attend."

Gil frowned as he opened Midnight's stall. "Why would that involve you?"

Brianna bit her lip and shrugged. "Seems Daddy's determined to find me a suitable husband." Her mood darkened at the mere mention of a future she didn't want. Why couldn't Daddy understand that marriage wasn't the only aspiration a woman could hold?

But she wasn't prepared to discuss all that with Gil yet. Not until she made sure he would support her decision to further her education.

She ducked past Midnight and slipped down the corridor to Sophie's stall. The chestnut mare whinnied her greeting, her white mane fluttering as she tossed her head over the door.

"How's my beautiful girl?" Brianna crooned, dropping a kiss on her silky nose. "You ready for a ride?"

The mare snorted her enthusiasm. Brianna laughed and moved to the tack room to fetch her riding gear. She scanned the area, but her old leather saddle wasn't in its usual cubbyhole.

Instead she found it suspended from an overhead hook on the wall. She frowned. The new stable hand probably didn't realize she needed it stored at a lower height. With a grunt, she pulled a wooden stool over and climbed up, stretching on her toes to reach it.

"Why is your father so intent on you getting married?"

Brianna turned her head sharply. Gil loomed in the doorway of the small room, a scowl darkening his face. She teetered, almost losing her grip on the leather. Gil moved quickly to steady her with a hand on her arm, then reached to take the heavy saddle from her. Without a word, he lowered the saddle to the ground and held out a hand to her. She stepped down, ending up much too close to him. His masculine scent—a mixture of sweat, horse, and sandalwood soap—swirled around her, making her senses spin. She stared at the buttons on his shirt, not quite daring to look up. If her eyes met his—got lost in those crystal blue depths—her misplaced crush might flare back to life.

"Is your father trying to find a husband for Colleen as well or only you?"

She made the pretense of brushing a piece of straw from her clothing, hoping to calm her erratic heartbeat. "Colleen's always got a string of men after her. She doesn't need Daddy's help." Without meaning to, the bitterness she couldn't quite conquer slipped out.

Gil lifted her chin with one finger. "I think you need to fill me in on everything that's been going on around here."

Her gaze strayed to the hint of stubble covering his jaw and the beloved cleft in his chin. When at last her eyes met his, the blue intensity, focused with singular purpose on her face, erased every thought from her head.

"After one night back, I can tell you're not getting along any better with your sister. And there's a great deal of tension between Adam and your father."

She wanted to say something—anything—but no words

would form. All she could do was stare at his handsome face and the enticing lips so near to hers.

His gaze moved to her mouth and lingered. She swallowed hard, her heart thrumming against her ribs. Suddenly, his eyes widened, and he dropped his hands. With a jerk, he stepped back, kicking over a pail in the process. The clatter echoed through the tack room.

"I'd better see to Midnight." He looked as spooked as a startled horse.

Equal measures of disappointment and relief coursed through her as Gil charged out the door. She bent to pick up the saddle, her grip unsteady.

Resuming their easy relationship was turning out to be much more complicated than she'd anticipated.

Coming back was a huge mistake.

Gil rubbed the brush over Midnight's rump with a bit more force than necessary. He'd half hoped when he returned that Brianna would be engaged with a wedding in the near future, safely belonging to someone else, so any hint of the inappropriate feelings he'd once experienced would remain safely buried.

Instead they'd roared back to life, bigger and stronger than ever.

No wonder Laura had broken off their relationship. Though Gil had tried to make things work between them, she'd believed his affections belonged to another woman. Deep down, he knew there existed a grain of truth to her accusations.

Gil hung the brush on a hook, swiped at the perspiration on his forehead, and left Midnight happily munching his hay. Pulled by an irresistible force, Gil made his way to the fence surrounding the track. A few of the trainers continued their work with the horses, but one reddish-brown blur claimed his attention. Brianna and Sophie flew around the dirt track, clumps of earth spewing out behind the horse's hooves. Bree's long braid flopped up and down as they moved, her split skirt flapping over her ankle boots. The fierce determination on her face made Gil smile. Though sometimes timid in her dealings with her family, Bree's independent nature shone through when on her horse. If only she could claim that boldness when dealing with her father.

Gil's thoughts turned to James's request concerning Aurora Hastings, and he grimaced. Perhaps Gil needed to take his own advice and stand up to the man who expected his orders be obeyed without question.

But how could he deny his mentor this one favor when the O'Learys had given him everything? Taken him into the heart of their family—provided love, shelter, schooling, even a college education. Didn't he owe them whatever he could give in return?

He certainly owed them more than a misplaced affection for their daughter. He needed to put Brianna O'Leary out of his thoughts—and out of his heart—once and for all.

Gil moved away from the track and headed over to talk to Sam Turnbull. He wanted an update on the horses, to see which ones were top contenders for the racing season in the states where racing hadn't been banned. And to learn which mares were due to foal in the coming weeks.

Two hours later, Gil felt as though he'd never left Long Island. The sheer joy of being with the magnificent animals and working with Sam under the clear spring skies gave Gil a feeling of freedom he seldom experienced. He stopped for a moment to gaze out over the pastures of green meadows, and a renewed sense of purpose filled his chest. One day, he would make the Whelan name a success in this great country and fulfill his late father's dreams. The familiar twist of guilt hit Gil's stomach. Because of Gil, John Whelan had died before seeing his dream realized. If it took Gil's last breath and his last dime, he would achieve it for him.

"Ready for something to eat?"

Bree's voice brought him crashing back to reality. She stood beside him, smiling, a large picnic basket looped over the crook of her arm. At the mention of food, his stomach growled.

"I could eat. What did you have in mind?"

"A picnic. So we can catch up like you suggested." The slight tremor in her voice gave away her uncertainty. "I thought we could sit under the willow by the back pond. It should be shady enough there."

His gut warned him to avoid being alone with her, but at the vulnerable look in her eyes, he couldn't refuse. "Let me wash up and meet you there."

By the time he'd rinsed the dust off his hands and face and made his way across the back pasture to the small pond where they'd loved to swim as kids, Brianna had unfolded a red-plaid blanket under the tree and spread out the contents of the basket.

"That's quite a feast. Did you have to bribe Mrs. Harrison for all this?"

She chuckled. "Of course not. For you, she'd have come out here and served it herself."

He sat on the far edge of the blanket, careful to keep as much distance as possible between them. A breeze off the water teased the tendrils of her hair, now swept up on top of her head. She removed the cloth from the sandwiches and handed him one.

"How does it feel to be home?" she asked.

He took a large bite of the roast-beef-and-cheese sandwich and chewed thoughtfully. "Familiar and strange at the same time."

"I know what you mean. It's as though time stood still around us, but we've grown up."

"Exactly." He reached for a Mason jar and opened the lid. The strong citrus smell of lemonade made his eyes water.

Brianna handed him two cups, and he poured them both some of the pale liquid. Her hands trembled slightly as she grasped her cup. Was it the unfamiliarity of being together again that made her nervous? Or was something more going on in that head of hers?

"So how are you really, Bree?"

She blinked as though surprised by the question. "I'm fine."

Funny, she didn't seem fine. His usually relaxed Bree seemed as high strung as a mare cornered by a stallion.

"What do you do for fun when you're not studying?"

She laid her half-eaten sandwich on the napkin in her lap and shrugged. "I spend time with the horses on the weekends, unless we're entertaining company."

He frowned. "What about friends?" He hesitated as the next word stuck in his throat. "Or suitors?"

Her glance slid away. "There are no suitors yet, though I'm sure Daddy has plans to remedy that. I still see a lot of Rebecca Nolan. And church activities keep me busy."

Her tone sounded wistful, matching the sadness that lurked in her wide eyes.

"Why don't you seem happy, then? Is it your father?"

She didn't answer, only fiddled with the fringe of the blanket.

"Bree, you used to confide in me. You still can, you know."

When she finally looked at him, turbulent emotion made her eyes as vivid green as the waving grass around them. "All Daddy cares about is money. As soon as I graduate, he expects me to marry well and make him proud. But I don't want to get married—not yet anyway."

Gil repressed an urge to smooth the furrow from her brow. Instead he plucked a blade of grass and shredded it. "What *do* you want to do?"

Her expression changed immediately, excitement brightening her features. "I want to go to New York and study, just like you. I've been reading up on Barnard Hall, the woman's college associated with Columbia. It sounds wonderful."

Gil smiled, but the lemonade soured in his stomach. She wanted to leave just when he'd returned. Yet perhaps that was for the best. With Brianna away, he wouldn't have to fight the daily temptation to be near her. He could do his job, and when the time came, leave without regret.

She sighed. "Unfortunately, Daddy thinks education is a waste of time and money for a girl. In his mind, the only thing a woman needs to do is get married and start a family."

He leaned back on one elbow. "You should follow your heart, Bree. Don't marry someone just to please your father. No matter how much you crave his approval."

Her chin dipped. "I wish I didn't care what he thinks."

Gil almost laughed out loud. Caring about James O'Leary's opinion appeared to be the fate of everyone living at Irish Meadows—Gil included.

She studied him a moment as though about to say something important. Instead she looked away and brushed some crumbs from her skirt. "Enough about my problems. What are your plans now that you're back?"

For a moment, he considered confiding in her about Aurora Hastings, but then thought better of it. He needed to make that decision on his own. "I guess I'll be taking over the bookkeeping for your father. At least for a while. I still hope to work with the horses like before I left."

"Of course you do. You'd be miserable cooped up at a desk all the time."

Her vehemence surprised him, as did her immediate understanding of his disdain for office work. The only reason he'd agreed to study business was to obtain a solid foundation for his future horse-breeding venture. From what he'd learned here, it took more than an innate connection with horses to make a business thrive.

"You don't plan on staying here forever, though, do you?" Bree glanced through her golden lashes at him. He couldn't quite decipher what he saw there. Hope, fear, longing?

He shook his head. "No. I still want to buy my own property, start my own farm. Maybe somewhere upstate. Far enough away that I won't be competing with your father."

For a few moments, she remained quiet, looking out over the pond. Only the soft ripples of the water broke the stillness. At last she turned to him, her eyes sad, her voice a whisper. "Mama won't be happy about you moving so far away."

His heart thudded heavily in his chest. "And how will you feel, Bree?"

She lowered her gaze to the blanket, a blush spreading over her cheeks. When she didn't answer, a tense silence hummed between them.

At last, she lifted her head to stare out over the water again, her lips twitching. "Remember the summer you stepped on that nest of yellow jackets? I never saw anyone run so fast in my life. You plunged into the water like a pack of wolves was after you." Her light laugh floated on the air.

He chuckled. "Took days for the swelling of those stings to go away. Lucky for me I had a pretty nurse to tend my wounds."

She screwed up her nose. "I was *not* pretty. Homely and awkward more like."

Annoyance made him straighten on the blanket. He reached out to cover her fingers with his. "You were never homely, Bree. Not to me. And now you've turned into a beautiful woman."

Her eyes widened, and her mouth fell open. The sunlight danced over her hair, glinting the red highlights to gold. The yellow flecks in her eyes mesmerized him, and the desire to kiss her burned as brightly as the hot sun beating down on his head.

But that was one line he did not intend to cross. Ever. Because once he did, he could never go back.

Mustering every ounce of willpower, he moved away from her, getting to his feet. "Come on, Bree. We'd better get back. The horses are waiting."

3

BRIANNA STEPPED OUT of St. Rita's church after the service, grateful for the slight breeze that rustled her skirts. She paused for a moment on the top step and scanned the gathering of people waiting to greet Reverend Filmore. Like a magnet, her gaze was drawn to Gil under the shade of a tall maple, surrounded by a flock of girls, all giggling and vying for his attention. Bree clutched her prayer book tighter. Of course, the handsome Gilbert Whelan, fresh from college, would be the most eligible bachelor in town. Or at least a novelty for the moment.

With studied casualness, Brianna descended the wooden steps. Manners dictated she shake Reverend Filmore's hand and thank him for his inspirational message, then join her parents at the cemetery. Every year on the anniversary of her little brother's death, the family visited his grave to say prayers and remember sweet Danny.

"I'm glad you enjoyed the service, my dear." Reverend Filmore winked at her. "You must be glad to have Gilbert home."

A flush heated her cheeks. "We all are. Especially Daddy."

Reverend Filmore nodded in Gil's direction and laughed. "It appears the young ladies in town are happy to have him home, as well."

Brianna schooled her features so she wouldn't scowl at the man. "So it seems. Excuse me, Reverend. I must find my parents."

"Good day, Miss O'Leary. I'll see you next Saturday for Gilbert's homecoming party."

She inclined her head, hoping her surprise didn't show on her face. "See you then."

Brianna had thought her mother had intended a small dinner with a few friends and neighbors. This sounded like a much grander event, which meant all those silly girls hanging around Gil had likely been invited, too. Brianna pushed away her uncharitable thoughts and instead searched for her mother among the groups of parishioners gathered on the lawn.

"Hello, Brianna."

She whirled at the masculine voice behind her, hand to her throat. "Oh, Henry. I didn't see you there."

Henry Sullivan, immaculate in his brown suit and bowler, took her gloved hand and raised it to his lips. Brianna gave a slight curtsey, grateful the glove kept Henry's mustache from tickling her skin.

"You look particularly lovely today," he said.

She removed her hand as soon as it was polite to do so. "Thank you. How is your family?" The Sullivans had been her family's neighbors since Daddy had built Irish Meadows.

"They're all well, thank you. And you must be happy. I hear good ol' Gil is back."

Brianna didn't miss the edge to his voice. "He is. I imagine your family will be invited to his homecoming party on Saturday."

"I believe I heard my parents discussing such an event." His gray eyes twinkled. "I, for one, am happy to have any excuse to call on you. Perhaps we can share a dance."

Brianna hesitated. Henry was attractive enough in his own way. He wore his blond hair short, his mustache and sideburns precisely trimmed. And he was charming in a quiet way. Yet he made Brianna uncomfortable. Perhaps it was the intensity of his interest in her she found unnerving. Whatever the reason, her reply froze on her tongue.

The whisper of a touch on her back alerted her to Gil's presence.

"Hello, Henry," Gil said. "It's been a while."

If she didn't know Gil so well, she wouldn't have noticed the chill in his voice.

"Gil." Henry held out a hand. "You're looking . . . well."

"Must be the Long Island air." Gil's chuckle seemed forced as he shook Henry's hand. His fingers returned to grip Brianna's elbow, sending shivers up her arm. "Brianna, your parents are heading to the cemetery, if you're ready."

"Yes, of course. Good day, Henry."

"I'll be looking forward to that dance," he called after her.

Aware of Gil's gaze on her, Brianna tried to ignore the heat infusing her cheeks. When she dared peer over at him, one dark brow rose over amused eyes.

"I thought you had no suitors."

She snorted. "Henry's not a suitor."

"Seemed pretty interested to me."

She pulled her elbow free of his hold. "You're one to talk with half the county's girls hanging all over you." She regretted the comment the moment it slipped out.

Gil's laugh only made her cheeks hotter as she stormed toward the cemetery.

Why should she care if Gil flirted with all the unmarried girls in town? She and Gil were friends, nothing more. She set her jaw, determined to remember that fact come Saturday.

Standing at the back of the group huddled around her brother's grave, Colleen O'Leary crossed her arms and tapped a foot on the grass, stifling an impatient sigh.

For pity's sake. Do we have to perform this maudlin ritual every year?

Mama and Bree would cry as usual, and Daddy would try his best to comfort them. Connor and Deirdre, both too young to remember their brother, would fidget while Mama recited the familiar prayers. It's not that Colleen wasn't sad—but Danny had been gone six years now, and Colleen could barely remember his little face.

Colleen turned her head to find Adam leaning against a tall headstone, scowling. He, too, hated this annual pilgrimage to the cemetery. Why they had to drag out their grief, Colleen would never understand.

As the prayers droned on, Colleen peeked under her lashes to study Gil. His handsome profile provided a welcome distraction while she waited for the monotony to end. A prickle of jealousy spread through her system at the way he stood so close to Brianna, as though he were her personal protector. Colleen pursed her lips. Why did Gil find her mousy sister so fascinating when he could be reaping the benefit of Colleen's attention? Instead of friendship, Colleen could offer him the intoxication of her kisses, which so far no man had been able to resist. No man, that is, except Gilbert Whelan.

She tapped a gloved finger to her cheek, a wicked plot forming. Her current beau, Jared Nolan, had become a bit too boring and predictable for her liking. She needed a challenge—a risk—to keep life from becoming excruciatingly dull.

Perhaps seducing Gil was just the diversion she needed. The fact that it would vex her sister was an added layer of icing on the cake.

The prayers ended, and one by one, the O'Leary clan made their way to the front of the church, where one of the stable hands had their carriage waiting. Colleen far preferred her father's new Model T "horseless carriage," but the vehicle couldn't hold the entire family.

Footsteps scuffed on the church walkway behind her. "Good day, Miss O'Leary. I hoped I hadn't missed you."

Colleen groaned inwardly but schooled her features into the perfect smile as she turned to greet Jared. "Mr. Nolan. How good to see you."

As Jared bent over her offered hand, Colleen couldn't help but compare him with Gil. Though attractive in an ordinary sort of way, Jared's brown hair and pale complexion faded beside Gil's black hair and brilliant blue gaze.

Jared smiled. "I understand we've been invited to your house this coming Saturday."

"Why, yes," she said brightly. "A welcome home for Gil."

Jared winked at her. "Any excuse to see you is fine by me." He lowered his voice. "Maybe we can steal away for a private moment or two."

Colleen's pulse skittered at the lurid look in his eyes. Perhaps Jared wasn't as boring as she'd assumed. She placed a hand on his arm and tinkled out her favorite laugh, guaranteed to attract male attention. "I think that can be arranged." Juggling Jared and Gil at one party—what a delicious evening to anticipate!

"Can't keep you away from my daughter, I see, Mr. Nolan." Daddy's voice boomed behind her.

Jared jerked upright. "Mr. O'Leary."

Daddy's laugh rang out, and he clapped a hand on Jared's shoulder. "No need to be nervous, boy. I'm delighted to see you two together. Perhaps it's time we had a private chat." He winked at Jared, whose cheeks reddened.

"Fine by me, sir."

"Good. We'll see you on Saturday, then. Come along, Colleen."

"Coming, Daddy." Colleen tried not to frown as she bid

Jared farewell, wondering what her father meant by that cryptic comment. If it had anything to do with announcing a betrothal, she'd have to do her best to thwart that particular conversation.

She was by no means ready to settle for one man just yet.

4

BRIANNA HAD NEVER been more eager to get home from school than on Monday afternoon—eager to see Gil and convince him to join her for a ride. It had been ages since she'd taken Sophie for a long trek over the back meadows, and with Gil for company, she couldn't think of a better way to spend the afternoon.

When she'd changed into a split skirt, she made her way to her father's office on the main floor where she assumed Gil would be working. She wanted to speak to him today about championing her cause with Daddy. In light of Gil's college experience, she hoped he could convince her father that many intelligent young women were choosing to pursue higher learning these days.

When Brianna found the office empty, she continued outside to the paddocks. A childish squeal of delight drew her attention to the far corral, where Gil led Deirdre on Twizzle, one of the Shetland ponies her father had purchased for the younger children. Brianna walked up to the fence for a closer view, noting the protective way Gil kept his hand on Dee-Dee's back. He would make such a good father one day. The thought brought a pang of longing with it. What would it be like to have Gil as the father of her children?

She pushed the fantasy to the far corners of her mind. Marriage and children were many years off for her. Who knew where Gil would be by then?

Off to the side, Joe, one of the trainers, worked with Connor astride Sadie, their gentlest mare. Her little brother grinned, bouncing with excitement. "Bree! Look, I'm riding Sadie."

She laughed. "Good for you, honey."

Deirdre twisted in her saddle to wave at Bree and almost slid off Twizzle's back. Gil immediately steadied her.

"Number one rule, young lady," he said with mock sternness. "Never take your attention off your pony."

"Sorry, Gil."

Gil turned to smile at Brianna. "Can you give us a hand? I think this cowgirl is ready to trot."

"Of course." Brianna quickly slipped through the fence rungs to join them, not at all sorry to postpone her outing with Sophie. Spending time with Gil was more important.

Gil handed her the rope. "You take Twizzle, I'll take Dee-Dee."

She grinned. "Hope you can keep up."

Brianna set off at a fast pace, and the pony picked up speed, its chubby legs pumping. By the time they'd gone around the enclosure twice, Brianna and the pony were trotting. Gil barely seemed to notice the quick pace, keeping a firm arm around her fearless sister, who whooped with delight.

At last, Brianna slowed the pony to a walk, out of breath and laughing. "Good work, Dee-Dee. You're a real cowgirl." Some of Brianna's hair had come loose from her pins and now blew freely around her face. She swiped at it with the back of her hand.

"More, please." Deirdre squirmed in the saddle.

"I think we've had enough for today." Gil smiled as he lifted her down. "Time to wash up for dinner."

"I'm going to wait for Connor by the fence."

"All right. I'll take care of Twizzle."

Gil reached to take the rope from Brianna. His fingers skimmed hers, and her pulse skipped. "It was nice of you to do that for her," she said. "You make Dee-Dee and Connor feel special when you spend time with them."

He smiled. "It's no hardship. I enjoy their company."

Brianna wished her father felt the same. Connor, especially, hung on every word Daddy said, on every scrap of attention. Brianna knew exactly how he felt.

Gil tipped up her chin. "Hey, why the sadness?"

She shook her head. "I'm just glad the kids have you."

He gave her a long look. "You'll always have me, too, Bree."

The huskiness of his voice sent goosebumps down her spine. He brushed some strands of hair from her cheek, his fingers lingering on her skin. Brianna's heart froze in her chest at the intensity in his eyes. She dared not take a breath for fear of breaking the spell.

"Are you going to kiss?" Deirdre's giggle floated across the pasture.

Brianna jerked away from his touch as though scalded, a tempest of emotion swirling through her. Gil ducked his head and bent to untangle the reins. Though the brim of his cap hid his expression, Brianna sensed he was as unsettled as she.

In an effort to diffuse the situation, she walked briskly toward her siblings on the fence. "If I catch one of you monkeys, I'm going to tickle you until you can't breathe."

Like a shot, the pair screeched and scrambled down from their perch.

As Brianna let herself out of the gate, she peered over her shoulder and found Gil staring at her with a force that made her breath catch.

If the kids hadn't interrupted them, would Gil have let down his guard and actually kissed her? Brianna shivered, both relieved and disappointed she wouldn't get to find out.

Second.

Colleen sipped a second cup of coffee in the quiet of the dining room on Wednesday morning. This was her favorite time of day, when her siblings had left for school, her father had gone either to the city or out to the stables, and she and her mother planned their day. She tapped a fingernail on the delicate china as she contemplated what her mother might have scheduled for this morning, hoping it was anything other than sewing or knitting.

Perhaps she could convince Mama to go into the city for some well-deserved shopping. After all, they both could use a new dress for Gil's party on Saturday. A tiny thrill bloomed at the idea of an entire day with her mother all to herself—a rarity indeed. They could try on dresses, or look at new fabrics, maybe even have lunch at one of the restaurants on Fifth Avenue.

As if summoned by her thoughts, Mama entered the room, clutching a piece of paper in her hand. "Good morning, Colleen. I'm glad I caught you. I need your help with something."

Colleen tried not to groan as her hopes for the day vanished. "Help with what?"

Mama pulled out a chair at the table and smoothed her skirts under her. "I received a telegram from Beatrice's son, Rylan. He's arriving on the noon train, but I'm afraid I won't be able to meet him. I'm committed to chairing the Ladies' Auxiliary Meeting."

Colleen set down her cup with a clatter. "I'm sure Daddy or Adam could go."

"Your father is meeting with a client in the city today, and Adam has gone with him to see about a job."

"What about Sam or one of the stable hands?" Colleen's voice rose an octave, despite her attempt to keep her desperation from showing. What would she do with a priest all the way home from the train station?

Mama reached for the coffee pot. "I've already asked, and the men are too busy. Besides, I want a family member there to give Cousin Rylan a proper O'Leary welcome." She poured coffee into the cup before her.

"Oh, Mama. You know I hate taking the carriage out. The horses don't like me." Her pout, which always worked with Daddy, got her nowhere with Mama.

"I have absolute confidence in you, my darling. Sam is hitching up the horses for you, so they'll be ready whenever you are."

Colleen sighed. "How will I know this Rylan?"

"He'll be the one in a clerical collar, of course."

An hour later, dressed in her serviceable blue cotton dress and straw hat, Colleen maneuvered the carriage down the main road into town. She turned her nose up at the rows and rows of trees that stretched for miles. Why Daddy had chosen this rural outpost for their home she'd never understand. At least the Hastings family kept only their summer home on the island, with their main estate situated in downtown Manhattan. Now there was a place Colleen would love to live. The excitement and energy of the city called to her like mermaids called men to the sea.

Her future husband, she'd determined long ago, would be rich and powerful and love the city as much as she did. She smiled to herself as she thought of all the wonderful servants they would employ, especially a chauffeur so Colleen would never have to drive any kind of conveyance again. Although trying Daddy's motorcar might be exhilarating . . .

As though offended by her thoughts, the carriage lurched to one side and stopped fast. Her lack of attention had caused her to veer off the road and onto the soft shoulder. She whipped the reins harder, clucking to the horses. The animals strained in their harnesses, but the carriage only leaned farther to one side in a precarious angle that had Colleen sliding along the bench. She peeked over the side to find one of the back wheels bogged down in the soft dirt, made soggy from the overnight rain.

"Oh, for the love of St. Patrick. Now I'll be late to meet the train."

With an annoyed huff, she lifted her skirts and hopped down from the seat. As she performed an inspection, Colleen's spirits sank. She doubted she'd be able to free the wheel from the deep suction of mud, even if she could manage to get the horses' cooperation. She'd have to wait for someone to come by.

Picking up her already dirt-encrusted hem, she made her way out onto the road. Surely some nice gentleman would come by and offer to assist a pretty damsel in distress. Maybe her future husband would come to her aid and fall madly in love with her. She giggled at the notion, content to lose herself in imaginary romantic encounters.

But time dragged on without a single person passing by. Colleen's feet now ached from standing for so long, and the idea of having to walk miles into town made her whimper. Would God listen if she prayed to Him for help after she'd ignored Him most of her life? At this point, she'd try anything.

Lord, if it's not too much trouble, please send someone to help me out of this predicament. As soon as possible.

The thought of her mother's extreme disappointment brought her close to tears. She'd counted on Colleen to do this one thing for her, and Colleen had let her down. Again.

When her feet couldn't take another minute of standing, she pulled a woolen blanket from the back of the tilted carriage and laid it on the ground. She removed her hat before she eased down to rest for a few moments. Maybe if a passerby saw her on the ground, he'd rush to her aid. She took off her shoes, closed her eyes, and sighed with pleasure at the relief to her poor feet. The midday sun warmed the top of her head, while a soft breeze floated over her, keeping her cool. She could almost imagine she was on a romantic tryst.

"Excuse me, miss. Are you hurt at all?" A masculine voice with a decidedly Irish lilt awakened Colleen from an apparent doze.

She shot to a sitting position, amazed and embarrassed to find a very handsome man staring at her, concern evident in the frown lines on his face. Eyes the color of rich chocolate gazed intently at her.

She smoothed her fingers over the bun at the nape of her neck, making sure her stylish appearance was still intact. "No, I'm not hurt. My carriage is stuck, though."

The stranger held out a hand to help her to her feet. "Would you like me to take a look?"

She flashed her most charming smile. "I'd be obliged. Thank you."

While he strode over to assess the problem, Colleen peered down the road to see what mode of transportation had brought him here. But she could see nothing, not even a horse. Then she noticed a suitcase and a discarded jacket by the side of the road.

"It's not good news, I'm afraid." He came around the side of the carriage, wiping dirt from his hands. He wore a white linen shirt under a tweed vest and dark wool pants. He began to roll up the sleeves of his shirt, a grin lifting the corner of his lips. "But if you're game, we can give it a try."

She blinked. "What exactly do you have in mind?"

He moved a few steps closer. "Well, we wouldn't want a lovely lady like yourself getting dirty, so I'll do the hard part. If you'll direct the horses, I'll push from behind."

The wind blew some locks of dark hair from under his cap as he waited for her answer.

Colleen's heart began a rapid patter. "But you might get dirty."

He gave a full-bodied laugh, revealing even, white teeth. "A bit of mud never hurt anyone."

"Very well. I suppose it's worth a try."

He followed her to the front of the carriage and held out a hand to assist her. She remembered then she was in her stockings. "Just a moment while I put on my shoes." She ducked her face to hide the heat rising in her cheeks.

What was wrong with her? She never blushed.

Stumbling in her haste, she sat down heavily on the blanket and snatched up her shoes. She stuffed one foot in and then the other, not bothering with the laces.

"Allow me." Kneeling on the blanket, the man reached over to tie one of her shoes.

Colleen swallowed her surprise and quickly tied the other herself. For a second time, he helped her up, this time holding her hand a moment longer than necessary.

"And where are you off to this fine day?"

Gazing into the brown depths of his eyes, Colleen couldn't remember for the life of her where she was headed. "Into town," she finally managed.

"Let's see if we can get you on your way, then." He picked up the blanket, tossed it into the carriage, and helped her onto the tilted seat. "When I say ready, give the reins a good, hard slap and tell the horses to giddy-up."

Seconds later, he yelled, "Ready."

She whipped the reins and called out to the horses. They lurched forward, and the carriage rocked, but sank back into the same position.

The man appeared at her side. "Let me talk to the horses before we give it another try."

Her mouth fell open. "Talk to the horses?"

"Aye. If I ask them nicely, I'm sure we'll do better next time." He winked at her before jogging over to the beasts.

Colleen watched in fascination as he spoke some foreign

language to them while stroking each on the nose. Then he turned back, touched the brim of his cap in a mock salute, and returned to the back of the carriage.

"Ready."

She repeated her actions, slapping the reins and calling out loudly to the horses. The wagon rocked and groaned, then suddenly jerked forward, up and onto the road. Relief spilled through her tense shoulders. She tugged the reins to stop the horses and turned to thank the stranger for his help.

When she didn't see him, she hopped down from the bench and rounded the back of the carriage. Dismay rushed through her at the sight of the poor man on his hands and knees, dripping in mud. The wheels had spewed filth all over him.

"Oh, dear. I'm so sorry." Without thinking, she rushed to help him, tugging on his arm. Too late she realized her shoes had become bogged in the mire. They squished in the brown sludge as she fought for footing. Before she could react, the man lost his balance and slid backward down the slight incline, pulling her with him into the soft mud.

Colleen shrieked as wetness soaked her backside.

So much for chivalry.

Rylan fought the rise of laughter at the spectacle before him. The striking red-haired young woman sat sprawled in the mud, streaks of dirt dripping from her furious cheeks. He swiped ruefully at his own soaked attire. This was not the type of impression he'd hoped to make when he met the distant relatives who'd been kind enough to take him in. In fact, this whole day had not gone at all as planned.

No one had arrived to greet him at the train station as promised, and he'd had to set out on foot—a fair distance indeed. Then he'd happened upon this young lady sleeping at the side of the road beside a drunken-tipped carriage, and he couldn't very well leave her there without offering his assistance.

He pulled himself to his feet, grimacing at his besmirched clothing. *God must have an odd sense of humor.* Once he regained his balance, he held out a hand to the lady.

"No, thank you. I'll manage on my own." She glared at him as she tried to pull herself up, only succeeding in sliding farther into the mire.

"Please, I feel terrible." He bit his lip to keep from smiling at her comical attempts to rise.

"You *should* feel terrible. This is all your fault." She flailed her arms, flinging muck in all directions.

He couldn't keep the laughter in as he trudged closer.

Her eyes blazed blue thunder. "You, sir, had better not be laughing at me."

"I'm laughing at this whole daft situation." Despite her protests, he put a hand under her elbow and lifted her out of the dirt. "I never expected to spend the afternoon wallowing in a mud pit with a beautiful woman."

She speared him a furious glare and yanked away from his hold, only to lose her balance a second time. Rylan caught her before she tumbled once again. She landed against him with a thud, and the frantic beat of her heart fluttered against his chest. His amusement faded as his gaze locked with eyes the color of spring lilacs. Delicate skin and full lips startled Rylan, sending currents of electricity racing through his veins. He couldn't remember the last time he'd held a woman in his arms. And never one of such startling beauty it robbed him of breath.

The girl seemed as momentarily stunned as he. Taking advantage of her hesitation, he picked her up and carried her to a drier spot, where he managed to navigate the short incline to the road. Once beside the carriage, he set her gently on her feet.

"A fine pair we are." He took out a handkerchief from his pants pocket and attempted to wipe the mud from her face.

"Give me that." She snatched the cloth away from him and dabbed at her cheeks, smearing the dirt even more.

"I doubt you'll be wanting to go into town without a bath first." He tried to joke with her, to ease the lines of worry from her face, but to his dismay, tears bloomed in those amazing eyes.

"I was supposed to meet someone at the train. My mother will be furious with me."

He stopped brushing at the grime on his pants. "You're not by any chance from the O'Leary house, are you now?"

Her fingers froze, her eyes widened. "Yes. I'm Colleen O'Leary. How did you know?"

He shook his head and bit back another grin. God was having a very good time with him today. "I'm Rylan Montgomery. Pleased to meet you, Colleen."

She took a step backward, her hand clutching the fabric at the neck of her dress as she scanned him from head to toe. "You . . . you can't be Rylan Montgomery. You're not a priest."

He laughed again. "Not yet. But one day soon, God willing."

"Oh." The handkerchief fluttered to the road. The misery on her face clutched at him.

"Come now. It's not so bad. You found me after all, and other than getting a wee bit dirty, we're all in one piece."

She huffed out a defeated sigh, and he suddenly longed for a return of the temper he'd glimpsed earlier.

"Let's turn the horses around. I'm sure we can get cleaned up before your mother even knows what happened."

The fluttering of hope in her eyes matched the hint of a smile on her lips. "Maybe we can. Mama's out at a meeting for the afternoon."

"There you go. She'll be none the wiser."

Colleen bent to retrieve a small straw hat from the grass, then primly pinned it on top of her mud-encrusted hair. He hid his amusement as he guided her onto the carriage bench, then hopped up to join her.

She sat, as regal as a muddy queen, upon her throne. "Would you do me a favor, Mr. Montgomery?"

"Don't you think you should call me Rylan? After the adventure we've had, Mr. Montgomery sounds far too formal."

She lifted her chin. "Very well, Rylan. Would you mind driving the carriage back? I think I've had enough of horses for one day."

5

GIL SAT BACK AT THE DINNER TABLE and observed the new O'Leary houseguest. Rylan Montgomery was the most unlikely-looking priest he'd ever seen. The man seemed far too at ease in his own skin and much too charming with his dark good looks and that strong Irish brogue, which seemed to have captivated everyone at the table.

"So, Rylan, what exactly will you be doing at St. Rita's?" Mrs. O'Leary beamed a smile across the table.

"Learning the ways of a parish priest for the most part. Though I will be helping out at an orphanage a few days a week. I won't know all the details until I meet with Reverend Filmore tomorrow." He pushed his plate to one side and patted his stomach.

"And why is it you can't stay at the rectory?" Colleen sounded angry, though Gil couldn't fathom why.

Rylan only chuckled at her rude glare. "The rectory is undergoing renovations. Reverend Filmore is staying with his sister until the work is done." He turned to Mrs. O'Leary. "Which is why I was ever so grateful to learn my mother had a distant cousin here in Long Island."

"Well, we're more than happy to have you." Mrs. O'Leary passed a platter of pastries down the table. "You didn't say how Colleen found you at the station this afternoon. I trust everything went smoothly."

"Smooth as mud, Mrs. O'Leary."

Colleen choked on her tea, then quickly pressed a napkin to her mouth. Gil noted with interest the bloom of hot color in Colleen's cheeks. Something had the girl off kilter—a rarity indeed.

"Forgive me for saying so," Gil said, "but you don't look Irish."

Rylan grinned. "That's my Italian blood showing. My grandmother on my father's side was Italian. Hence the brown eyes and ruddy skin. The dimples, however, are all Irish."

Deirdre and Brianna laughed at his exaggerated facial expression, while Colleen scowled at the tablecloth.

Maybe having Rylan Montgomery around wouldn't be such a bad thing. Especially if the good reverend-in-training kept the eldest O'Leary sister duly preoccupied for the near future.

Colleen tapped an impatient foot on the floral carpet in the parlor. If she had to listen to one more story from Rylan Montgomery about growing up in Ireland, she'd scream. He was the most infuriating man she'd ever met. And it was criminal the way he went around in ordinary clothing, charming everyone with his dreamy eyes and dimples. He should be forced to wear his priest's garb so unsuspecting girls wouldn't think . . .

She pulled herself upright against the cushioned back of the settee. The white-and-gold clock on the mantel chimed nine o'clock. She shot to her feet, smoothing out the silk skirt of her lilac dress and feigned a deep yawn.

"If nobody minds, I think I'll head up to bed early. I'm especially tired tonight." She moved to kiss her mother, trying not to notice Rylan's gaze following her.

Mama patted her arm. "The carriage ride into town must have worn you out."

Rylan's laughter rang out over the room. "More than you'll ever know, Mrs. O'Leary."

Colleen stumbled, her foot catching in the hem of her dress. By sheer willpower, she righted herself.

A frown crossed her father's features. "What do you mean by that, young man?" He turned his attention to Colleen and pinned her with a withering stare. "Nothing happened to the carriage, I hope."

Colleen gritted her teeth while planting a kiss on her father's cheek. "It was nothing, Daddy," she fibbed smoothly. "The horses gave me a bit of trouble, that's all. Cousin Rylan drove on the way back, and everything was fine."

She kept her gaze averted from the side of the room where Rylan was seated, sure he was mocking her with his trademark grin.

Her mother rose from her seat. "Tomorrow I'd like your help collecting some items to give Rylan for the orphanage. Maybe you could accompany him to the church if we're ready in time."

Using all her self-control, Colleen smiled sweetly at her mother. "Of course, Mama."

She bid the room a cordial good night, and on the way upstairs, silently planned to develop one of her famous headaches in the morning.

⁂

Rylan whistled on his way down the grand central staircase of the O'Leary home the next day. Cousin Kathleen, as she insisted he call her, had surely done well for herself. His gaze swept the tiled marble entranceway and the crystal chandelier suspended high above the ornate railing. This mansion was indeed a far cry from his family's thatched cottage back in County Cork.

At the bottom of the stairs, Rylan stopped to peer into the gold-framed mirror and make sure his clerical collar wasn't crooked. In honor of his first day as an intern with Reverend Filmore, he figured he should dress the part. Truth be told, he was having trouble adjusting to the tightness of the collar, as well as the drabness of the black shirt and pants that made up his uniform. He supposed he'd get used to it eventually. The most important thing was witnessing his dear mother's tears of pride the first time she'd seen him in his priestly attire. Her joy made every itch of the uncomfortable cloth bearable.

"Good morning, Rylan." Kathleen appeared from the direction of the dining room. "I hope you'll take some breakfast before you leave."

He smiled at the handsome woman, so fresh in her white blouse and rose-colored skirt, auburn hair swept up on her head. "Ah, yes. I'm a firm believer in a good breakfast to start the day off right."

Kathleen laughed. "Well, go on in and enjoy. I'm on my way to get those things I promised you for the orphanage." She glanced at a small watch pinned to her blouse.

"I'll be sure and check with you before I go, then." He paused. "Will anyone be joining me for breakfast?"

"I'm afraid not. Brianna and the children have left for school. James and Adam are out on business, and Gil is already working in the study." Her eyes narrowed as she looked up the stairs. "Only Colleen is unaccounted for, but that will be rectified in short order."

His lips twitched. "Does she always sleep this late?"

"Only when she's trying to avoid work. But don't worry, she'll be ready when you are."

He didn't even try to hide his amusement. "Really, Cousin Kathleen, I can find the church on my own."

"Nonsense. That girl needs something to occupy her time and keep her from plotting against the unsuspecting male population. Thank goodness she's safe with you."

As Kathleen swept up the staircase, Rylan wondered if *he* would be safe with Colleen.

Half an hour later, after a fortifying breakfast, Rylan picked up one of the boxes of clothing Kathleen had left in the foyer and made his way outside to the waiting buggy. When he'd hefted the last box into the back and brushed the dust off his hands, he turned to find Kathleen marching across the lawn, her hand firmly around Colleen's upper arm. "Oh good. You haven't left. Here's Colleen now."

The girl wrenched herself free and crossed her arms in front of her. Her vibrant red hair was pulled back with some type of ribbon that matched her dress. "I'm only staying long enough to give Reverend Filmore these boxes." She shot Rylan a dark look. "You'll have to find your own way home." Chin raised, she flounced by him, ignoring his offer of assistance into the buggy.

Kathleen stormed over, her face thunderous. "Colleen Elizabeth O'Leary, you will treat Cousin Rylan with the respect he deserves. I've not raised any child of mine to be rude. For penance, you can ride back out to pick Rylan up before dinner."

Mother and daughter glared at each other, but Kathleen's withering stare won out. Colleen lowered her eyes. "Yes, Mama."

Rylan bit the inside of his cheek to keep from chuckling. He wanted to say he could walk home but didn't dare interfere with the power play in progress. Instead, he bid his cousin good-bye, hopped up on the bench seat, and guided the horses down the road. He and Colleen rode in silence for some time, with Rylan asking directions only when necessary. Finally, conscious of the anger shimmering off Colleen in waves, he decided he'd best smooth things over if they were to live under the same roof in some semblance of peace.

"I'm not sure what I've done to incur such loathing, but please let me offer my sincerest apologies for any offense I may have committed." He slid a glance sideways to gauge her reaction.

She stared straight ahead, her back as rigid as the plank seat beneath them.

"What have I done that's so unforgivable?" he asked in a soft voice.

She lifted one shoulder. "I don't know. You just rub me the wrong way."

"I see."

She whirled to face him then, her expression murderous. "First, you drag me into the mud and ruin my dress. Then you make fun of me for it. And now I have to waste my day as your escort—to the church of all places."

Rylan made sure his lips didn't curve even a little. He kept his eyes trained on the road ahead, letting her anger roll off him. "I've apologized at least three times for the mud. If you recall, I was only trying to be a gentleman and help get your carriage free."

Colleen shifted on the seat, paying a great deal of attention to the flow of her skirts around her knees. "Yes, well, you enjoyed the situation entirely too much."

His stomach shook with the laughter he could no longer contain. "I'm afraid I tend to see the humorous side of most things. It's a character flaw that confounds my calling to be a priest, since for the most part, clergymen are pretty serious fellows." He glanced over at her, still chuckling. "You have to admit, we must have looked rather silly, wallowing in the mud that way."

Her lips twitched before she pressed them into a firm line. "I suppose we did."

"As for your mother, I'll speak with her tonight and let her know I can manage without you as my personal escort."

"That would be . . . appreciated. Thank you."

"So we can be friends?"

She clutched the side of the buggy as they hit a bump. "I guess so."

A small concession at best, but he would take it. "Good. Now, maybe you can tell me more about your family. Exactly where does Gilbert Whelan fit in with the whole O'Leary clan?"

Colleen took a moment to let her emotions settle, while she determined how she should act with Rylan. Somehow, she couldn't stay mad at him, yet it seemed wise to keep an emotional distance. Something told her he would dig out all her secrets if he could. Talking about her family, however, seemed safe enough.

"Gil's widowed mother worked for us as a housekeeper. When she became ill, she asked Mama to take Gil in if she didn't survive. They had no other family here, and she didn't want him going back to Ireland on his own."

Rylan gave a low whistle as he guided the horses over a dip in the road. "An orphan, poor lad."

"Not really. We're his family now."

One dark eyebrow rose. "So he's like a brother to you, then?"

She sent him a saucy smile, one that turned most men to putty. "Oh no, he's far too handsome for that."

Rylan opened his mouth as though to challenge her, but stopped. A few seconds later, he asked, "And what does Adam do?"

"He recently started a new job in the city." A stiff breeze came up, and Colleen clutched her hat to keep it from blowing off.

"So he doesn't work for your father?"

"No. He and Daddy don't agree on most things."

"And Brianna? She seems the quiet type—more content to watch the goings-on around her."

Colleen raised one eyebrow. "You're very observant."

He smiled. "It's an advantage in my profession." He slapped

the reins to make the horses keep their pace. "I noticed there's quite a gap between Brianna and your younger siblings."

Sorrow squeezed Colleen's heart before she lifted her chin. "We had another brother, Danny, but he drowned several years ago."

"I'm ever so sorry. That must have been difficult for your family."

"It was, especially for Mama. She's never been the same since."

"So Gil works for your father. And Brianna is almost finished with school. What will she do then?"

Irritation prickled Colleen's neck. "You ask a lot of questions."

"Best way to get answers."

"I think it's my turn to ask the questions."

He grinned at her, a dimple appearing in his cheek. "Ask away. My life is an open book."

It took all her concentration to keep her expression unchanged, as if those dimples didn't affect her at all. "Do you come from a big family?"

"Big enough, though in Ireland we're considered average. I've three brothers and a little sister. My father died in a mining accident years ago, so my brothers look out for my mother and Maggie."

"I'm sorry. It must be difficult to lose a parent."

"Aye. My father was a hard man. But he loved my mother something fierce."

"Sounds like Daddy." She glanced sideways at him, admiring his profile, his full lips and strong jaw. Despite every effort to remain aloof, Rylan aroused a strong measure of curiosity in her. Why would such a charming, handsome man throw away his life to hide in a church? "What made you want to become a priest?" she asked before she could check herself.

His features softened. "My own dear mother. She'd always

hoped one of her sons would enter the religious life. It happened to be me."

"But don't you want to marry and have a family?"

"That's not what God has planned for me," he answered quietly. His eyes held hers for several moments.

She swallowed and tore her gaze away to focus on the road ahead.

"The rest of your questions will have to wait. There's the church up ahead." A few seconds later, Rylan pulled the horses to a stop in front of the building and jumped lightly to the dirt path below.

Before Colleen could move, he jogged around and reached up to help her. Strong hands gripped her waist as he swung her easily to the ground. When she looked up into his face, she forgot to breathe.

"So tell me about Reverend Filmore. What's he like?"

She blinked to clear her thoughts. "He's all right—for a priest."

He pinned her with a pensive stare. "Sounds like you don't have much use for the clergy. Is that why you've taken a dislike to me?" Though his tone was glib, a glimpse of hurt crossed his features.

"I haven't taken a dislike to you." She pushed by him. "But I don't have much use for religion."

"And sorry I am to hear it, Miss O'Leary." Reverend Filmore stepped out of the church.

Colleen bit back an unladylike word and forced a smile. "Reverend Filmore, I've brought your new assistant, Rylan Montgomery. Rylan's mother is a distant cousin of ours."

"Indeed? That works out quite well now, doesn't it? Welcome, Mr. Montgomery." The paunchy man descended the stairs to shake Rylan's hand.

"It's grand to meet you, Reverend. I'm honored to be under your tutelage." He grinned and pointed to the buggy. "Mrs.

O'Leary sent some used clothing and other items for the orphanage. Where would you like the boxes?"

"We have a storage room in the basement. Let me give you a hand."

Rylan lifted one of the cartons out of the buggy, broad shoulder muscles straining under his dark shirt. Colleen bit her lip and forced her gaze away. Why couldn't he look more like Reverend Filmore? Older, with thinning hair and a stomach that protruded over his pants.

While the men hoisted the rest of the boxes onto the grass, Colleen climbed onto the bench seat, ready to depart as soon as the back was empty.

"I expect Mama will send me to fetch you later," she said to Rylan when they'd finished.

He paused to wipe the sweat from his brow with a handkerchief, and then looked up at her. "Tell your mother I'll be fine to walk home. The exercise will do me good, and it will save you the trip back."

She nodded to him, chin high. "That's very . . . thoughtful of you. Good day, gentlemen."

With a flick of the reins, she clucked the horses into motion and set off, using all her willpower not to turn around and see if Rylan Montgomery was watching her.

6

SEATED AT HER DRESSING TABLE on Saturday afternoon, Brianna hummed to herself as she prepared for Gil's welcome-home party. Nerves danced an Irish jig in her belly as she imagined Gil's reaction to seeing her dressed in all her finery—her green silk gown that showed off her shoulders and neck, her curls piled high in a most intricate fashion, with a few tendrils left loose around her face.

Would he be impressed, or would he even notice?

She pressed a palm to her stomach to quell the butterflies within. Ever since the afternoon at the corral, something significant had shifted in her relationship with Gil. A certain *awareness* had sprung to life on both sides, and she had no idea what to do about it.

If she were smart, she would fight this attraction with everything she had, since it could come to no good end. Even if Gil felt the same about her, what right did she have to claim his heart and then abandon him while pursuing her education? Was it fair to expect him to wait for her? After all, he was twenty-one and ready to begin his life. Soon he would leave Irish Meadows and strike out on his own. Could she give up her dream to follow him?

Sighing deeply, she gave herself a stern internal talking-to. Falling in love with Gil would only lead to heartache. Tonight she would enjoy Gil's company, perhaps share a dance or two, and if the opportunity arose, she would speak to him about advocating her cause with her father.

Brianna startled as Colleen breezed through the door connecting their bedrooms.

Colleen stopped and took in Brianna's reflection in the mirror. "My, won't Henry be impressed tonight."

Brianna blinked. She hadn't given Henry a single thought. But better her sister believe she had dressed for Henry than for Gil.

Colleen preened in front of the mirror, adjusting the bodice of her lemon chiffon dress, which showed off far more skin than their father would deem suitable. Her auburn curls fell into one perfect roll over her left shoulder, bangs swept off her forehead to showcase her amazing violet eyes.

"I, for one, am looking forward to this evening," she said with a sly glance at Brianna. "I intend to make Gilbert fall madly in love with me."

Brianna stiffened on the plush stool, her fingers curling around the handle of her hairbrush. Despite her racing heart, she kept her expression cool. "Have you forgotten about Jared Nolan? I don't think he'll be too pleased."

A scowl marred Colleen's perfect features. "Frankly, I don't think Jared and I make a good match." She threw Brianna a smug look. "I do believe Gilbert would suit me much better."

Brianna fought the urge to wipe the smile from her sister's face. Calmly, she laid the brush on the ornate table in front of her. Whether she knew it or not, Colleen had just declared war.

For most of her eighteen years, Brianna had played second fiddle to her older sister's beauty and confidence. But no more.

Tonight Brianna would cast off her usual timid nature and stake her claim—before Colleen ruined Gil's life.

Gilbert adjusted the cufflinks at his wrist as he paused to collect himself in the grand hallway. He checked his tie in the gilded mirror and patted down a wayward curl that wanted to spring across his forehead. He cut quite the dashing figure, if he did say so himself.

The murmur of voices, punctuated by the light laughter of his family and friends, drifted out from the dining room. Knowing they awaited the guest of honor, he took a fortifying breath. Gil hated being the center of attention, but to please Mr. and Mrs. O'Leary, he'd put up with an evening of social frivolity. Especially if it meant he might capture Brianna later for a waltz.

With a flourish, Gil stepped into the dining room. All heads swiveled in his direction, followed by whistles and light applause.

James rose from his position at the head of the table. "Gilbert, my boy. We were about to send out a search party."

A collective chuckle erupted from the guests.

"Come and take your seat so we can eat." James patted the chair to his right.

Farther down the table, Adam glared at him. Gil held back a sigh. He couldn't blame Adam for his jealousy. James had never attempted to hide his preference for Gil over his eldest son. Gil hoped for an opportunity soon to reassure Adam he need have no fear of Gil usurping his rightful position in the family.

As Gil made his way to the far end of the room, he greeted the Nolans and the Sullivans, longtime friends of the family, and his tense shoulders began to relax. For the most part, the guests were familiar. He saw no evidence of the banker or his daughter. A reprieve until another time, thank goodness.

He stopped behind the chair pulled out for him and made

a point of looking at each person. "Thank you, everyone, for coming tonight. I have missed all of you during my time away and am quite glad to be back."

When his gaze came to rest on Brianna, he fought to keep his jaw from dropping. Dressed in a gown of deep green silk, her eyes stood out like glittering emeralds. Her hair had been swept on top of her head, save for two long swirls that teased her bare shoulders. Her skin gleamed like smooth ivory, highlighting her long, slender neck. He cleared his throat and tore his gaze away. "Tonight is not only a homecoming for me, but a welcome for our houseguest, Cousin Rylan. Now, let's all enjoy this wonderful feast Mrs. Harrison has prepared."

As the maids uncovered the silver serving dishes, the enticing odors of roast beef, fresh bread, and gravy filled the air. Gil took a seat on the plush chair, spreading his napkin on his lap. Seated to his left, Rebecca Nolan, Jared's younger sister, smiled at him.

"Hello, Miss Nolan. How are you this evening?" He gave her a saucy wink.

She giggled and blushed. "Gilbert Whelan, you haven't changed a bit."

Gil smiled. As Brianna's best friend, Rebecca had spent a lot of time at Irish Meadows, so he felt very comfortable with her. He peered down the table as the maids served the soup. Henry Sullivan's fair head bent close to Brianna's, their hair almost touching. Gil's fingers tightened on his spoon. Did Brianna not see Henry's blatant interest in her? He'd have to keep an eye on the situation as the evening progressed.

After dinner, the men retired to the study for cigars and brandy while the ladies freshened up. Gil endured the male posturing with ill-concealed irritation. Adam's boasting of secret financial deals sounded anything but legitimate, and Henry's attempts to impress Mr. O'Leary soured Gil's stomach almost as much as the cigar smoke burned his eyes.

It was a relief when they joined the ladies in the parlor. The center of the room had been cleared for dancing. Chairs provided seating around the walls, where the ladies perched like lovely plumed birds.

Mrs. O'Leary clapped her hands as the men took positions around the room. "I hope everyone is in a dancing mood. I have several pieces picked out I hope you'll enjoy."

With that, she took a seat at the piano and began to play a lilting waltz. Gil immediately searched for Brianna, but his gut tightened as he watched Henry lead her out to the dance area. How long had Sullivan been pursuing her? Did Brianna approve of his suit, or was she as unaware of his intentions as she claimed? Gil frowned. Perhaps he needed to have a chat with Henry and find out where things stood.

"What's the matter, Whelan? Jealous?" Adam's tight voice behind Gil's shoulder startled him from his thoughts.

"Not at all," he covered smoothly. "Just wondering about Henry's intentions toward Bree."

"I think it's fairly obvious. He intends to marry her. Sorry to put a damper on your romantic daydreams."

The sneer in Adam's tone fueled a sudden urge to punch him. Gil swallowed the bitterness on his tongue and reminded himself of his intent to repair their relationship. "All I want is Bree's happiness. If she chooses Henry Sullivan, then so be it."

He turned to face Adam, whose high color indicated an over-indulgence in his father's brandy. "Look, Adam, can we not put our differences aside and be civil to each other—for your parents' sake if nothing else?"

Adam's harsh laugh was anything but humorous. "Forget it, Whelan. I know you only came back to worm your way into my father's will. I intend to make sure that doesn't happen."

With supreme effort, Gil controlled his rage. If he said anything else, this conversation could escalate into a most unpleasant scene, something Adam would enjoy to no end. Gil clamped his jaw tight and focused his gaze out over the couples dancing.

The fact that Adam assumed him so low as to manipulate James in order to inherit his money hurt Gil's pride. Did everyone else believe the same thing? If so, maybe coming back had been a mistake on all counts.

Gil turned to find James headed toward him, flanked by a shorter man with two ladies behind. Though the man looked somewhat familiar, Gil could not recall having met the women before.

James clapped Gil on the shoulder. "Gilbert, allow me to introduce you to Arthur Hastings."

The stout man with a handlebar mustache stepped forward to shake Gil's hand. "A pleasure to meet you, Gilbert. Sorry we couldn't make the dinner. Another engagement, I'm afraid."

"It's good to meet you, too, sir."

Mr. Hastings stepped aside, and a tall woman with soft brown hair smiled at Gil.

"This is my wife, Dorothy, and my daughter, Aurora."

Gil greeted the older woman, then stopped short at the beautiful young woman beside her. With a cloud of golden hair and startling blue eyes, Aurora Hastings was breathtaking. He bowed over her hand. "A pleasure, Miss Hastings."

She blushed to the roots of her hair. "Likewise, Mr. Whelan. I've heard so much about you."

"All good, I hope." He winked in an attempt to dispel her obvious embarrassment, remembering what James had said about her request to meet him.

"Heavens, yes. Brianna has nothing but wonderful things to say about you."

"You're a friend of Bree's, then?"

"More of an acquaintance. We worked together on the Christmas play at the church."

Mr. O'Leary nudged him from the side. "Why don't you ask this lovely young lady to dance, Gilbert? I'm sure she doesn't want to sit with us old folks." He boomed out a hearty laugh.

"Of course. Would you care to dance, Miss Hastings?"

"I'd love to."

He led the way to the middle of the room, where several other couples swayed to the music. Gil held out his arms, and Aurora placed her gloved hand in his. Soon they were gliding in time to the melody. She was a tiny thing, barely reaching his shoulder. He prayed he wouldn't trample her toes. Thankfully, the song ended soon, but as he slowed to a smooth halt, he caught Brianna's frown over Henry's shoulder. She didn't seem at all pleased to see Aurora in his arms. He dipped his head at Brianna with a grin.

"Excuse me, Miss Hastings. There's someone else I've promised a dance to." He bowed over her hand once again, ignoring the disappointment on her lovely face, and made his way to find Brianna.

Flushed from dancing and from watching Gil with Aurora Hastings, Brianna took a seat on one of the chairs and pushed a drooping curl off her forehead. She'd thought Colleen would be the only thorn in her side tonight. Now she had Aurora to contend with, as well.

Out of the corner of her eye, she became aware of Henry hovering at her side, as he had all evening. If only he'd leave her alone for five minutes.

She flashed him a smile. "All this dancing has me parched. Would you mind getting me something to drink? The refreshments are in the dining room."

"Of course." He gave a slight bow. "Don't go anywhere."

She let out a huge sigh of relief as he retreated through the crowd. Many more guests had arrived after dinner for the evening's entertainment. She hardly recognized half the people here.

A shadow fell over her chair.

"Good evening, Miss O'Leary. May I have this dance?" The familiar lilt, exaggerated as Gil often did, made her pulse sprint.

She looked up into the dazzling blue eyes of the most handsome man in the room. In his charcoal-gray suit and striped cravat, Gil took her breath away. He waited with his hand outstretched.

She ran her tongue over her parched lips, half wishing Henry would return with her drink. Why was she hesitating? Isn't this what she'd been hoping for?

"Of course," she said at last and placed her hand in his.

When she stumbled slightly, he caught her elbow to steady her. "Th—thank you."

"You're welcome."

Gil guided her onto the floor, one hand to the small of her back where the tiny covered buttons of her bodice ended. The tempo of the music changed to a much slower song as they joined the rest of the dancers. She turned to face him and placed a tentative hand on his shoulder. Gil caught her other hand in his large, warm one. She almost jumped as he wrapped his left arm around her waist and pulled her close. With his face so near to hers, she didn't know how she'd remember any of the steps to the waltz. Every coherent thought seemed to have flown from her mind.

"I haven't had the chance to tell you how beautiful you look tonight." His breath tickled the wisps of hair near her ear.

Her heart raced. That was the second time he'd called her beautiful since he'd come home. "Thank you. You're quite handsome yourself." She struggled for something to say, something to take her mind off the warmth of his splayed fingers on her back, the scent of his cologne filling her senses with each intake of breath. "Are you enjoying all this attention?"

He chortled. "What do you think?"

She gave a light laugh. "I think you hate it, but you're putting up with it for Daddy's sake."

He pulled back to look at her. "I forget how well you know me. I can never hide anything from you, can I?"

Her mouth went dry at the heat of his scrutiny. "You sound as though I can read your mind. Sometimes I wish I could."

"Really? What is it you wish to know?"

The noise of the room faded into the background. Did she dare ask the question that plagued her—the nature of his feelings for her? Better not to tempt fate, for if he admitted to having more than brotherly affection for her, what would that do to her plans for the future?

The music stopped, and the couples around them slowed to a halt. Brianna's gaze remained locked with Gil's, his arms still firmly around her. How she wished she could stay in this position for the rest of the night. She bit her lip and took a reluctant step backward. "Thank you for the dance."

"The pleasure was all mine, Brianna." He took her gloved hand and pressed it to his lips, his eyes never leaving hers.

"There you are, Gilbert." Colleen's falsely sweet voice raised the hairs on Brianna's neck. "Brianna, you mustn't monopolize the guest of honor. I believe it's my turn to dance with him."

Sending a sharp glance her way, Colleen squeezed in between Brianna and Gil and captured Gil's hand. Brianna fought the rising tide of her temper. If there weren't so many people nearby, she'd have shoved Colleen into the potted plant behind them.

Gil threw her a silent look of apology as the music started and they swept off around the perimeter of the room.

Brianna set her chin and returned to the seating area. She kept a discreet eye on the pair, thankful to note that Gil did an admirable job of holding Colleen at a respectful distance. No matter what, Gil did not deserve to be a pawn in her sister's romantic games.

※◆※

Colleen pouted as her waltz with Gil ended. Despite her attempts to press her body close to his during the song, he'd shown no reaction whatsoever. Never once had his gaze strayed to her low-cut décolletage, nor had he tried to flirt with her. What was wrong with the man? Maybe Gil was better suited to become a priest than Rylan Montgomery.

"Thank you for the dance." Gil gave a mock bow, then leaned close to her ear and whispered, "Try to behave yourself for the rest of the night—if that's possible."

She wanted to stick out her tongue, but instead she gave a small curtsey. "Your loss, Mr. Whelan." She whirled around to seek her next dance partner, bemoaning the lack of wealthy men in attendance tonight. Mama must have invited every single girl in the area—but had sadly under-invited the gentlemen.

"There you are, Miss O'Leary." Jared Nolan pushed his way through the crowd to reach her. "I've been trying to catch up with you for a dance all evening."

Tonight, dressed in a dark suit, his brown hair swept back off his forehead, Jared cut a very appealing figure. Gold cufflinks glittered at his sleeve as he held out his arm for her. Colleen gave an inward sigh. If only his family were richer. Yet, moving in the Nolans' social circles would mean the opportunity to meet other, more wealthy men. She needed to make the most of every connection available to her.

"Would you mind terribly if we postponed our dance and got some fresh air instead?" She peered at him through her lashes.

A sly smile slid over his features. "Even better."

She took his arm, and they made their way to the French doors leading onto the balcony. On the way past a group of guests, the bold grin of Rylan Montgomery caught her eye, making her very glad to be on the arm of such an attractive man. Rylan nodded at her, and she raised her chin as they sailed past.

The cool evening breeze was a welcome relief after the crowded interior. Colleen led Jared along the balcony to a more secluded area where a low, stone wall overlooked her mother's famous rose gardens. An almost full moon beamed subtle rays of light over the grass and shrubs, giving ghostly illumination to the marble statue of a woman in flowing robes, arms extended over a birdbath. Colleen breathed in deeply, hoping the soothing scent of her mother's flowers would calm the unrest in her soul.

As though sensing her tension, Jared draped a casual arm around her shoulders. "Are you enjoying yourself, my dear?"

"Of course. It's a wonderful evening." The practiced line slid off her tongue. In truth, things had not gone at all as she'd hoped. She wasn't actually planning to marry Gil, but sharing a few kisses in a dark corner could prove exhilarating.

"You look so beautiful in this lighting." Jared's husky voice whispered over her ear, sending shivers down her back.

The adventure she'd craved all evening became a sudden possibility. She half turned so that her face almost met his, giving him an open invitation. With a low growl, he lowered his mouth to hers. No longer the restrained gentleman, he pulled her tight against him and deepened the kiss. A thrill tickled Colleen's belly as the taste of whiskey filled her senses. At last, here was a man who took her seriously. This was no schoolboy kiss. This kiss hinted at dark pleasures she could only imagine. His hand roamed up her ribcage to brush her bare arm. She jumped, sudden panic seizing her limbs as awareness of just how secluded they were infiltrated her dazed mind. She wiggled to ease out of his embrace, but Jared only tightened his grip.

"I'm thinking Mr. O'Leary might not like you manhandling his daughter that way." The Irish lilt held an undercurrent of steel.

Jared jerked back, releasing his tight hold on her. "Who the devil are you?"

A wave of relief washed over Colleen, so intense it left her knees weak, followed just as quickly by a flare of annoyance. Grateful for the darkness to hide her flaming cheeks, Colleen pulled herself upright, her head high. "This is Rylan Montgomery, a cousin visiting from Boston." Before she could continue the introductions, Rylan moved closer with the stealth of a leopard.

"And who might you be, sir?" His dark brows met in a frown.

"Jared Nolan, Colleen's future husband."

Colleen started at Jared's bold claim. Since when had they discussed marriage?

"I'm thinking the key word here is *future*." Rylan pinned Colleen with a hard stare. "Some of the guests are leaving. I believe your parents are looking for you."

She swallowed and dipped her chin. "Of course."

Rylan waited for Jared to precede him into the house. He raised one eyebrow at Colleen as she smoothed her hair and dress. "I won't mention this to your parents—this time."

Raw anger pulsed through her veins at the nerve of the man. "Aren't priests supposed to be nice?" she hissed.

His low laugh only irritated her further.

She needed to find a way to get this meddling priest out of their home—and, more importantly, out of her life.

7

"GILBERT, THE HASTINGSES are leaving," Mr. O'Leary called to Gil from the doorway of the parlor. "Come and walk them out with me."

Gil stiffened at the clipped words. As usual, James issued an order then disappeared, expecting absolute compliance.

"Excuse me, Miss Miller," Gil said to the brunette at his side. "It's been a pleasure speaking with you."

Ignoring the disappointment on the girl's features, Gil pushed past a group of women near the doorway and made his way into the corridor. He released a long breath, grateful for an excuse to leave the over-warm room containing too many young ladies vying for his attention. At dinner, he'd assumed the evening would be quiet, with only a few friends and neighbors, but Mrs. O'Leary must have invited every eligible girl from two counties tonight.

Pasting a smile on his face, he approached Mrs. Hastings standing beside her husband. "So lovely to meet you, Mrs. Hastings. I hope you enjoyed the evening."

"Very much, Mr. Whelan."

He turned to Aurora and bent over her offered hand. "Thank

you for the dances, Miss Hastings. You are a most accomplished dancer."

Her cheeks reddened. "As are you, Mr. Whelan. You must come and visit us at Belvedere now that Mother and I are here for the summer. Papa comes home on weekends, but during the week, we're quite lonely." She nudged her mother slightly.

"Oh, yes. Of course. We'll call with a lunch date."

Tension banded Gil's shoulders, but he fought to keep his expression unchanged. "That would be"—*dreadful*—"delightful, I'm sure."

Arthur Hastings took his wife by the arm. "Dorothy, Aurora, please wait for me in the auto. I need a word with Gilbert."

Now what?

Once the women left, Mr. Hastings turned to him. "James tells me you've recently obtained a Business degree from Columbia."

"That's right, sir."

"We could use a young man with your talents at our bank. Would you consider coming to work for me in the city?"

Gil blinked. He'd assumed the man wanted to speak to him about his daughter.

James stepped forward. "Sorry, Hastings. Gilbert has agreed to take over the books here. Between that and his work with the horses, I'm afraid he won't have a spare moment."

The edge to Mr. O'Leary's voice surprised Gil. From the sound of it, his mentor expected him to dedicate the rest of his life to Irish Meadows. Gil would have to start dropping hints that this was a temporary position.

Mr. Hastings reached out and gave Gil's hand a firm shake. "Our loss. But if you ever want a change, please think of me. I can offer you a substantial salary. Not to mention that working in the city could be advantageous to your career."

Gil swallowed. "I'll keep that in mind, sir. Thank you."

Gil stood with Mr. O'Leary on the porch until the Hastings family's automobile drove out of sight.

"The nerve of the man—trying to steal you out from under my nose." James scowled as he leaned against one of the white columns. "If I didn't need to be on his good side, I'd have had a few choice words for the rotter."

Gil frowned. "I thought you liked him."

James pulled a pipe out of his jacket pocket, followed by a box of matches. "Not particularly. But I respect his business sense." He lit the pipe, drew in a long breath, and blew out a cloud of smoke. "Which brings me to the next order of business. It's obvious Aurora is smitten with you. I need you to begin a formal courtship as soon as possible."

The evening breeze snaked the smoke across the porch. Gil shoved his hands in his pockets and tried to think of what to say.

"What's the matter? You've seen how attractive the girl is."

"She's very attractive."

"So? What's the problem? I'm not asking you to marry her—at least not yet." He boomed out a hearty laugh. "We'll wait and see how much money I need first."

Gil couldn't make himself laugh at the joke. Surely James didn't expect him to marry Aurora for financial gain. Gil loosened his tie and undid the confining top button of his shirt.

James sobered. "All kidding aside, we really need your help." His stare bored into Gil. "I know you'd never want to see us lose our home."

The last shred of resistance leeched away, and Gil's shoulders sagged. How could he refuse this man who'd given him so much? He sighed. "They've invited me to Belvedere. I'll make a point of going soon."

The relief on Mr. O'Leary's face erased the worry lines from his forehead. He squeezed Gil's shoulder with a beefy hand. "Thank you, son. I knew I could count on you."

Rylan clapped with all the other guests as the music ended. Cousin Kathleen was indeed accomplished on the piano. Right now, flushed with pleasure at the applause, she resembled a girl of twenty instead of a woman twice that age. In fact, if Rylan could picture her as a young woman, he imagined she'd look just like Colleen. He wondered if Kathleen had been as precocious as her daughter, or if she'd always been the devout, focused woman she was today.

Rylan frowned, picturing that beast, Jared Nolan, pawing at Colleen. Though she'd hissed like an angry cat when he'd broken up their little tryst, Rylan hadn't missed the relief that had crossed her features when Jared first released her.

Rylan pushed away from the wall, intent on finding another glass of delicious punch. As he made his way past the couples, he thanked the heavens above he didn't have to worry about such things. Being a priest had the advantage of making him unavailable and therefore un-noteworthy to the single females. He fingered his white collar, worn tonight for that very reason.

Rylan ducked into the dining room, happy to find it empty for the moment, and headed straight for the crystal punch bowl on the sideboard. He used the ladle to pour the beverage into a ridiculously small cup and swallowed it down in one gulp. How was a man to quench his thirst with these thimblefuls?

The tap of heels on the tiled floor made Rylan glance at the door, just as Colleen swept inside. She stopped cold upon seeing him.

"Hello again, Miss O'Leary." He raised his empty cup in a salute.

"Hello." She moved swiftly past him and chose a glass.

"Allow me." Rylan picked up the ladle and poured the cherry-colored liquid into her cup, thankful he didn't spill a drop. "And where is your *future husband* at now?"

She sliced him with a glare of blue ice. "That's no concern of yours."

He set the ladle back in the bowl. Something about this woman affected him on a deep level. His intuition told him that her prickly nature was a mask for some hidden pain, and everything in him wanted to ease that pain. He watched her take a quick sip, her hands unsteady.

He moved a step closer until their arms almost brushed. "It seems to me," he said slowly, "that a man should treat his intended bride with far more respect than Mr. Nolan was showing you. You're an upstanding young woman from a good Christian family. I don't see why he'd be thinking it acceptable to behave in such a forward manner."

She jutted her chin out. "Maybe I wanted him to."

"Do you love him that much?"

"I don't love him at all." Her eyes widened as she realized the mistake of her admission. She slammed the glass onto the table, red liquid sloshing over the sides to stain the white tablecloth. She glared at him, a mixture of pain and anger.

"Just leave me alone, Rylan Montgomery. I don't need any more interference in my life."

Thank the Lord the guests had gone home and Brianna could finally head up to bed. Her feet ached in the new shoes she wasn't used to wearing. She couldn't wait to take them off and lie down.

At the foot of the daunting staircase, she paused to gain the fortitude to climb it. Or perhaps she was secretly waiting for Gil to say good night before he retired. Disappointment settled on her shoulders. Other than the one dance they'd shared, they hadn't had another chance to talk all night. Probably because he'd been too busy entertaining all the unmarried women who'd arrived.

Frustration pinched her heart as surely as the shoes pinched her toes. It seemed likely that Gil would never consider her as anything but a little sister. Yet the look in his eyes while they'd danced—one that had made her pulse leap—led her to hope he might feel something more.

She scanned the hallway, and with no sign of Gil, took one last peek into the parlor. Only the maids remained behind to clean up. Perhaps he was with her father in the study. She tiptoed to the doorway and listened outside for voices. Only a thin sliver of light shining under the door told her someone was inside. Should she go in? Would she find Gil there and be able to share a few moments alone with him? The notion made her heart gallop in her chest.

At the sound of footsteps crossing the room, Brianna jumped back from the entrance.

The door swung inward, and her father appeared. "I thought I heard someone lurking about. What do you want, Brianna?"

She raised her chin with a forced smile. "Only to say good night, Daddy. It was a lovely evening."

The lines on his forehead eased a fraction. "I'm glad. You and Henry seemed to enjoy yourselves."

"Henry was very . . . attentive." *More like smothering.*

"I was going to wait to speak to you about this, but now seems as good a time as any." He motioned her to follow him inside.

She groaned inwardly. Why hadn't she just gone up the stairs? She could've been lying in the comfort of her bed with her feet raised in blessed relief. Instead, she stepped into the study and waited for her father to speak.

"Brianna, I think it's time we discussed your future."

The soles of her feet throbbed. She lowered herself to one of the leather chairs facing her father's desk. Did she dare broach the subject of college? Or should she wait for a more opportune time, once Gil had had a chance to soften him toward the idea? "Yes, Daddy?"

"Tonight I gave Henry official permission to court you. It will make me very happy to join our family with the Sullivans."

Brianna gripped the arm of the chair until her fingers ached.

The desire to please her father warred with the unfairness of his demand. "What about what I want?"

Her father's thick brows crashed together. "Why wouldn't you want to marry a fine man like Henry?"

The familiar shiver of dread skittered down her back. "It's just that I didn't intend to get married so young."

He blinked, seeming thunderstruck. "What else would you do?"

She bit her lip. "I . . . I . . ."

"Don't stammer, girl. If you have something to say, spit it out."

She stiffened until her spine felt as rigid as the poker standing beside the fireplace. "I want to continue my education and . . . go to college."

His mouth dropped open. "Why on earth would you need to go to college? You have a bright young man interested in a future with you. Surely you wouldn't throw away such a fine opportunity."

Brianna shot to her feet and paced to the large hearth. "There's plenty of time for marriage, after I finish college. Henry could still court me if he wishes."

Her father slapped a palm on the desktop. "Court you long distance for two or three years? I've never heard of anything so ridiculous."

Under the glare of her father's indignation, Brianna wanted to crumple. But she would not give him the satisfaction—not this time. "It might sound ridiculous to you, but not to me. I want to live in the city, see more of the world than this island. Expand my mind—"

"No woman needs to expand her mind."

Brianna shoved her resentment aside and grappled for a compelling argument. "What about Aunt Fiona? Your own sister went to college and now teaches at one."

He rolled his eyes. "Fiona always went against the grain. She made poor choices, and now she's a bitter old maid living alone with her birds. Not the type of life you should aspire to. You need to focus on becoming a suitable wife to Henry. Learn wifely duties from your mother, as Colleen is doing."

A harsh laugh escaped Brianna before she could check it. "Is that what Colleen is doing?"

Her father took an intimidating step toward her. "I'll thank you to show your sister more respect, young lady. Colleen is the epitome of beauty and grace. You'd do well to try and be more like her."

Brianna bit down hard on her quivering lip. There it was—out in the open. Her father's blatant preference for his oldest daughter. The beautiful one who could do no wrong. Words of reply stuck in her throat, held prisoner by the lump of emotion she could not dislodge.

"We'll have no more talk of this nonsense. I've told Henry he may court you, and you *will* accept his suit. Now I bid you good night." He resumed his seat at the desk and turned his attention to the papers on his blotter, dismissing her like always.

A tidal wave of hurt threatened to crush her. Before her tears could betray her, Brianna fled the study—her dreams as battered as her aching feet.

8

GIL LED THE EBONY STALLION into the barn. He'd given Morgan's Promise a good workout this morning and hoped his owner would be pleased with the horse's progress. One of the wealthiest men in the country, Mr. Morgan paid Irish Meadows well for their services. He intended to race Morgan's Promise in the states that still allowed the sport, and he expected his animal to be ready.

"Here you go, boy. You deserve a treat after your hard work." Gil pulled a small apple from his pocket and held it out to the stallion. Velvet lips tickled Gil's palm as Morgan took the offering. Gil stepped out, closed the stall door, and bent to retrieve a bucket of water to refill the trough. A sense of peace washed over him as he watched the magnificent creature slake its thirst.

This was where Gil belonged, working with animals that held no judgment, that loved him unconditionally despite his impoverished parents and his orphan status. Animals loved you for who you really were, not for the money you had or the social circles you graced.

Gil moved down the corridor to check on Georgina. The gentle mare was due to give birth any day now. Gil loved the spring, when new life filled the stables. Georgina's head hung over the door as though she expected his visit. She neighed and tossed her head, eager for his greeting. Georgina held a special place in Gil's heart. He and Bree had helped bring her into the world four years ago. With her gentle spirit, the lovely lady had captured both their affections.

Gil entered the stall, running his hands over Georgina's swollen side. "How's my girl? Any sign of that baby yet?"

Big hopes were pinned on this foal. Mr. O'Leary had paired Georgina with one of the best racehorses around in hopes of breeding the next Kentucky Derby winner. Gil patted Georgina's rump and sighed. Over the years, he'd learned the folly of attaching such importance to one horse. Mother Nature often had a way of thwarting expectations.

He checked Georgina's feed and water and let himself out of the stall. As he latched the door, the stomp of angry footsteps echoed through the barn. Footsteps that sounded decidedly feminine. Gil rounded the corner to the main aisle but couldn't see anyone in the corridor. Puzzled, he pushed outside into the bright morning sun and shaded his eyes against the glare to see if Brianna had taken Sophie out for a ride. But except for Joe exercising Starlight, the track was empty.

As Gil turned to head back, the determined figure of Brianna emerged from the double doors. Clad in her usual riding attire, her cinnamon-streaked hair coiled up on her head, she led a horse down the path toward the opening in the fence. His momentary pleasure at seeing her turned to apprehension the minute he recognized which horse she'd taken.

"What do you think you're doing?" He fought to keep the anger out of his voice as he jogged toward her.

Hot eyes pinned him to the spot. If he'd been a piece of hay, he'd have ignited where he stood. "I'm going for a ride."

"Not on that horse, you're not." At the best of times, Major Selection was hard to handle, but according to Sam, since the horse had injured his back hoof two months ago, he was more unreliable than ever. It took a strong hand to keep him in line, and like it or not, Brianna didn't have the physical strength to handle him.

Ignoring Gil, she flung herself into the saddle and gave the horse a vicious kick. Alarm leapt through Gil's veins. Bree had never acted in such a reckless manner with an animal.

"Brianna, stop!" He made a wild dash to catch the bridle, but she jerked Major's head away from his grasp.

Two more kicks and the horse sprinted off to the right. Instead of leading the animal onto the track, Brianna veered around the fence and bolted toward the open pasture beyond the barn.

Alarm escalated to panic, choking the breath from him. Was she trying to kill herself? It was hard enough to control the animal on a groomed track. Heaven only knew what the beast would do in open fields—especially if his back foot turned on the uneven ground.

Gil charged over to Joe, who'd pulled Starlight to the side of the track. "Joe, give me the reins. Quick!"

Surprised brows tented over his eyes, but Joe hopped off and held out the leather strap.

"Tell Sam that Bree's gone out on Major. I'm going after her." Gil swung easily into the saddle and jabbed the horse's side, a prickle of remorse setting in at his rough treatment.

He only hoped Starlight had enough speed to catch Major.

Leaning straight out over his neck, Gil urged the horse to give it his all. As one, they flew over the grassy surface and crested a hill. In the distance, Gil made out the black speck of Major with—thank God—Bree still on his back.

He pushed Starlight hard, promising him every manner of reward if he managed to catch the other horse. Gradually they gained ground until Gil came within shouting distance.

"Brianna, slow down! That horse is injured." He hoped her concern for the animal would make her ease up.

Her head whipped around. She peered over her shoulder, her hair streaming out behind her, but instead of stopping, she forged onward.

Gil's stomach clenched in dread. *Please, Lord, make her stop before someone gets hurt.*

Why did Gil have to follow her?

Brianna wanted to swipe the angry tears from her eyes but didn't dare take her hands off the reins. She gripped them so tightly she felt grooves forming on her palms. Why hadn't she taken the time to put on her gloves? She'd wanted so badly to be alone, to live life on the edge for a few moments, with no one telling her what she could and couldn't do, that she hadn't taken the proper precautions.

Her vision blurred until she had no real sense of where Major was headed. She held on for dear life, clinging like a bur to his mane as he took the lead.

Shouts from Gil barely registered in her consciousness as the ground flew by. A branch whipped her cheek, the sting making her aware of how close to the wooded property line they'd come. Summoning her strength, she yanked the reins as hard as she could to slow Major down. If he veered into the trees, he could trip on a tree root and break a leg. Daddy would never forgive her if she ruined one of his client's thoroughbreds.

She gave thanks to God as Major slowed to a more normal pace, while inwardly steeling herself for Gil's fury when he caught up with her.

A flash of movement from the trees claimed her attention. Seconds later, a hare darted into their path. Major gave a startled trumpet as he skidded to a halt. Fear slicked Brianna's palms with sweat. She clamped her knees hard into the horse's side and clutched the reins in a desperate attempt to stay in the saddle. But the momentum proved too much.

A scream ripped from her throat as the thrust hurtled her over Major's head and into the air.

Brianna had only a moment to brace herself for the impact as she plummeted headfirst toward the ground below.

9

RIANNA!"

Gil's heart stopped pumping at the sight of Brianna's slim figure flying through the air. With a sickening thud, she landed in a crumpled heap on the hard ground. He jerked his mount to a treacherous sudden stop and threw himself out of the saddle. In seconds, he raced across the grass, reaching her just as the spooked stallion reared up in alarming menace over her inert body.

"Easy, boy. Easy." Gil attempted to keep his voice calm, despite the anxiety clutching his chest. He had to keep the animal from bludgeoning Brianna to death with its hooves.

Gil gave a desperate leap and managed to grab the reins. He yanked the skittish horse away from Brianna to a nearby tree, where he quickly tied the reins around the trunk. His pulse pounding in his ears, he dashed back to Brianna's still form, lying facedown on the grass, hair splayed out around her.

Please, God, let her be all right. The frantic prayer repeated over and over in his mind as he dropped to the ground beside her and placed a finger on her neck. The faint pulse he found there eased his tension a fraction, but thoughts of broken limbs, punctured lungs, and paralysis haunted his imagination.

What had possessed her to take such a foolish risk?

Inch by tortuous inch, he rolled her onto her side, alarm spiking at her lack of response. Even a moan would have been better than such stillness. Dampness from the grass seeped through his pants as he searched for damage. The beginning of a bruise bloomed on her cheek along with several deep scratches. Blood trickled from her lip and nose. He cradled her head in his lap and smoothed the waves of hair away from her eyes.

"Bree. Can you hear me? Wake up, please."

He ran swift hands over her arms and legs, as he would when checking a horse for injuries, relieved to find no broken bones. Still, she needed immediate medical attention.

As gently as possible, he lifted her limp form in his arms and somehow managed to mount Starlight with Bree in front of him. He cradled her against his chest, one arm wrapped tightly around her, the other guiding the horse. He'd send one of the hands out for Major as soon as he got back.

Halfway to the house, she began to stir, a low moan oozing from her throat.

"Shhh. I've got you," he murmured into her hair. "Stay still until we get home."

Her whimpers of pain caused answering spasms of helplessness to wash over him. "Hang on, honey. We're almost there."

Sam ran to assist him the moment Gil reached the stable. "What happened?"

"Major spooked and threw her." Gil handed Bree down to Sam while he dismounted.

"What the deuce was she doing riding him?"

"I have no idea." Gil reached to take Brianna from him. "Put Starlight away for me. And have one of the hands go out to get Major. He's tied to a tree in the west pasture."

"Right away. Let me know how she is."

Gil nodded and set off at a brisk pace across the lawn toward the house. His arms strained with her dead weight as he pushed into the foyer. He headed straight for the parlor and laid her gently on the sofa.

Almost immediately, Mrs. Johnston appeared in the doorway. The housekeeper let out a gasp, her hand covering her mouth. "What happened to Miss Brianna?"

"A horse threw her. Put a call in to the doctor, then get a cloth and some ice."

"Yes, sir." The woman practically flew out the door.

Gil knew he should find Kathleen, but he didn't dare leave Bree alone for a minute—certain if he did, something terrible would happen. As long as he stayed with her, she'd be all right.

"Bree, can you hear me? Open your eyes." He caressed her unmarred cheek with rough fingers, noting the velvet smoothness of her skin. The few freckles she so detested stood out in stark relief against the pallor of her complexion. Not even an eyelash flickered.

What if she'd suffered a brain injury?

Dear God, please let her wake up and talk to me.

In that instant, he would have promised God anything to guarantee Brianna's well-being. Gil lowered his forehead to hers, tears burning behind his lids. He blinked hard to keep them at bay.

He stayed like that, breathing soft prayers in her ear for what seemed like an eternity, until at last her lashes fluttered, and her eyes blinked opened. She stared blankly at him for a few seconds, and then recognition slowly dawned in her eyes.

"Gil."

He heaved a huge breath of relief. That one word was the sweetest thing he'd ever heard.

Thank You, Lord Jesus.

"Take it easy, honey. Just lie still."

"Head . . . hurts." She raised a hand to her forehead.

Gil grabbed it and held it captive. "The doctor's on his way."

Mrs. Johnston appeared with a bowl of water, ice, and a wet cloth. Gil wrapped some ice in the cloth and laid it on her forehead, glad to note the slight easing of pinched lines around her mouth.

Mrs. Johnston hovered by the sofa. "Dr. Shepherd will be here soon, Mr. Whelan. And Mrs. O'Leary is on her way down."

"Thank you, Mrs. Johnston."

Bree's frame tensed, and she grasped his arm with steely fingers.

"What is it? Are you in pain?" he asked her.

"Don't . . . tell . . . Daddy." Each word took great effort to get out.

"Your father's not home. Don't worry about him right now."

The tension seeped out of her, and she closed her eyes, seeming to fall back into unconsciousness.

Mrs. O'Leary rushed into the room, her skirts flying out behind her. "Gil, what happened? Is she all right?" She knelt on the floor beside the sofa and placed a hand on Bree's arm.

As much as he wanted to reassure her, Gil couldn't lie. "She was riding one of the stallions. He spooked and threw her."

Instant tears moistened her blue eyes. "My poor baby."

"The doctor should be here soon."

"What was she doing on a stallion? Why wasn't she riding Sophie?"

"I don't know." Guilt wound its way through Gil's system. Could he have tried harder to prevent her from going? "I tried to stop her, but she wouldn't listen. By the time I caught up, she'd been thrown."

Several minutes later, Mrs. Johnston appeared in the doorway. "Dr. Shepherd is here."

"Show him in, Alice." Mrs. O'Leary pulled herself up tall and patted her hair into place. "Good morning, Doctor. Thank you for coming so quickly. Brianna's had a fall from a horse."

The older man removed his hat and set it on the table by the chair, then stepped forward with his medical bag. Gil and Mrs. O'Leary moved aside to let him have access to Brianna, who lay immobile, the cloth still on her forehead.

"Tell me exactly what happened," he commanded as he focused his attention on his patient.

Gil explained what he'd witnessed while Dr. Shepherd examined Bree's eyes, shining a tiny light into each one. Then he felt around her head, his ministrations rousing Brianna. Gil jerked each time she winced in pain.

At last, Dr. Shepherd rose, his expression grim. "She's a lucky young lady. She could have easily broken her neck or been paralyzed." He turned his gaze to Bree. "You've escaped with only a concussion, though you'll probably feel like you've been kicked by that horse tomorrow."

He picked up his bag and faced Mrs. O'Leary. "You'll need to make sure she doesn't fall into a deep sleep. For the next twenty-four hours, wake her every hour, make her stay awake long enough to take some sips of water or tea, and ensure she's coherent. If at any time she appears worse, or you can't wake her, send for me immediately."

The relief on Mrs. O'Leary's face mirrored Gil's own. Though serious, a concussion wasn't life-threatening.

Once again the doctor addressed Brianna. "I'd advise you to keep off horses for at least a week. And after that, if you do have to ride, try to stick with the gentle ones." He softened the chiding with a wink.

"Thank you so much for coming, Dr. Shepherd." Mrs. O'Leary accompanied the man out of the parlor, leaving Gil alone with Bree. He pulled one of the footstools over to the sofa and sat down, his eyes almost level with her wary ones.

He watched her for a moment, trying to quell the urge to scold her further. "Mind telling me what that little adventure was about?"

She turned her face toward the back of the settee—but not before he saw tears forming. Words of chastisement died on his lips. She didn't need anyone to tell her how foolish she'd been. The regret on her face told him that much.

He put a gentle hand on her shoulder. "Bree, you can tell me anything. You know that, don't you?"

She didn't answer him, but ripples of her distress trembled under his hand. If he didn't expect Mrs. O'Leary back any moment, he'd have pulled her into his arms to comfort her. Instead, he settled on rubbing her shoulder in silence, hoping his presence helped. After several moments, when it became evident she wouldn't speak to him, he reluctantly rose. "You need to rest. We'll talk about it when you're feeling better."

Why did it feel like she was mad at him?

After a long look at her back, he strode out of the room. In the entranceway, he met Mrs. O'Leary coming back from seeing the doctor out.

He gave her a quick nod. "If you need me for anything, I'll be in the barn."

"Gilbert, wait." She put a detaining hand on his arm, concern in her eyes. "What really happened out there?"

He shook his head. "I wish I knew. She was riding that horse like the devil himself was after her. I couldn't catch her in time . . ." He stopped, unable to go on with the guilt closing his throat.

She squeezed his arm, her features alight with sympathy. "It's not your fault. I just wonder what set her off, and why she would choose such a wild horse."

"Give her time to feel better, Mrs. O. I'll get to the bottom of it—one way or another."

Kathleen O'Leary gave a brief smile. "If anyone can, Gilbert, it's you."

The next morning when she awoke, Brianna did indeed feel as though she'd been kicked by a dozen horses. Every muscle ached. Even breathing was an effort. A wicked pounding, like a blacksmith's anvil, besieged her temples. Because the brightness of the daylight hurt her eyes, she squeezed them shut again.

"I hope the pain reminds you of your foolishness." The harsh voice of her father made Brianna groan. "You almost got yourself and that horse killed."

She squinted one eye open. Which would he be more upset about, she wondered?

He stood at the foot of her bed, eyebrows pulled into a scowl, hands stuffed into the pockets of his suit pants. The tapping of his foot made the chain of his pocket watch dance against his vest buttons. It seemed safer to focus on that little movement than to confront his anger head on.

"What on earth were you thinking, girl?"

"I'm sorry, Daddy. Is Major all right?" Maybe he'd accept her apology and drop the whole thing.

"His injured foot took a beating, but he should be fine. What sort of insanity made you take him out in the first place?"

She closed her eyes again, willing him to hug her and tell her how worried he'd been. That he was glad she was all right. "I guess I wanted some excitement." The glib answer rolled off her tongue, knowing she'd never tell him the real reason.

"Excitement?" He practically shouted the word. "You endangered an expensive animal for excitement?"

Brianna jerked under the covers, wincing at the throb of pain that rushed through her body, and forced her eyes open again.

Her father took a step toward the bed, his face a mottled red. "Of all the foolhardy, immature things to do." He shook a finger at her. "Until you show better judgment, young lady, you are banned from the stables."

Brianna's hand fisted in the blankets as she fought to contain her rising anger. Banned from the stables? He might as well ban her from breathing.

The urge to lash out overwhelmed all reason. "Maybe I wanted some attention, Daddy. *Your* attention. Maybe I got tired of being the unnoticed daughter—the one you can't wait to marry off to the highest bidder." She bit her bottom lip, an instant rush of regret stemming the flow of words. The last thing she wanted was her father's pity.

He stared at her as if she had grown two heads. "What on God's green earth do you mean by that?"

"Never mind." Brianna let her eyes drift closed, hoping he'd leave her alone with her bruises, both internal and external. She would not cry in front of him.

"I'll never understand females if I live to be a hundred." Heavy footsteps crossed the room, and the loud bang of the door told her he'd left.

The breath she'd been holding whooshed out of her lungs, followed by a gush of tears that burned beneath her closed lids.

Her father would never change. Why did she always hope he might? That one day he'd smile at her, call her his darlin', say he was proud of her . . . A harsh sob escaped as she buried her face in the pillow.

Please, God, take away this constant hurt and disappointment. Let me be content with Your love and need nothing else. Grant me Your peace and remove this pain.

Before I do something else I'll regret.

10

GIL LEANED AGAINST THE WALL in the upstairs hallway, his stomach aching with dismay. James had rushed out of Brianna's room so fast, he hadn't even noticed Gil standing beside the door.

As much as he respected James, Gil didn't understand his attitude toward his second daughter. Over the years, Gil had seen the toll James's constant criticism and dismissive manner had taken on Bree's confidence. Gil had hoped as she got older, things would change. But it looked like their relationship had only gotten worse.

Gut-wrenching sobs drifted out into the hallway despite the closed door. Gil splayed his fingers over the wooden surface and let his forehead drop against it. If he went in there now, he'd be hard-pressed to control his emotions. He never could stand to see Brianna in pain, be it emotional or physical.

With a loud exhale of air, he straightened. No, he'd best keep his distance. Let her calm down before he attempted to talk to her. In the meantime, he'd try to smooth things over another way.

He found James in the barn, hovering over Major's stall door while Sam did a thorough examination of the injured hoof. Though not a veterinarian, Sam's knowledge and skill with the animals rivaled that of Dr. Phelps. Many a time, they'd relied on Sam when Dr. Phelps was unavailable.

Gil stood beside James and peered into the stall. "How is he?"

A muscle in James's jaw ticked. "Sam says the ride gave his injury a bit of a setback but no permanent damage. Thank heaven."

Gil waited in silence until Mr. O'Leary seemed ready to leave. "Could we talk outside for a minute?"

James pushed away from the stall. "What about?"

"I'd rather not get into it here."

Together they exited the rear door and, as if by mutual consent, headed toward the white fence surrounding the track. Gil leaned a booted foot on the bottom rung and hung his clasped hands over the top.

James took his pipe from a pocket inside his tweed jacket and held it to his lips. "What's on your mind, boy?"

"It's Brianna, sir."

An immediate scowl appeared on James's leathery face. "I don't understand that girl. Should've tanned her hide more when she was young. Kathleen never did let me discipline the children the way I wanted."

Gil took a slow breath before speaking. "I think Brianna feels you ignore her, that you favor Colleen over her." He glanced sideways to gauge Mr. O's reaction.

James's eyebrows shot together. "Where would she get such a notion?"

Irritation throbbed in Gil's veins. How could the man be so blind? "Maybe from the way you dismiss her opinions and interrupt her when she's trying to tell you something. Or the way you praise everything Colleen does, but you barely notice

Bree." Gil forced a halt to his tirade and worked to contain his emotions.

James slowly removed the pipe from between his teeth. "Is that how she sees it?"

"I only know how it appears from my observations."

James slumped against the fence, as though the air had left his lungs. "Colleen has never given me a moment's worry, but Brianna . . ." He shook his head. "I never knew what to make of her tomboy ways. She spent all her time with her nose in a book. Or with you and those horses. Didn't seem natural for a girl."

Gil fought to hide his irritation. "Well, as you can see, she's grown up just fine."

"Except for this fool notion of going to college. What does she need with an education? It won't help her land a husband."

So Bree had told her father about wanting to go to school. Sounded like his reaction wasn't what she'd hoped. Could that be the reason behind her wild ride yesterday? "Maybe Brianna wants more out of life than to just be someone's wife."

"Not you, too." James threw him an annoyed glance. "You've always been her defender, haven't you? Lord knows you're a better brother to her than Adam ever was."

Gil jerked as though the word had hit him square between the eyes. "Brother" did not describe what Gil felt for Brianna. If he'd had any doubts about the matter, seeing Bree's body crumpled on the ground, not knowing if she were dead or alive, had chased away any notion of sibling affection. As complicated and unwelcome as they were, Gil's feelings for Brianna were what a man felt for the woman he wanted to someday marry. He stiffened his spine. "What harm would there be in letting Bree go to college for a year or two?"

"Wasted money and, more importantly, wasted opportunity. Henry Sullivan has asked for her hand. I don't think he'll wait around while Brianna dabbles in academics."

So it was official. Henry and Brianna would be betrothed in the near future. Gil gripped the fencepost until his knuckles ached. "Bree's not even eighteen yet. Colleen's a year older, and you're not pushing her to marry." The defiance in Gil's tone hung between them.

James bristled like an angry rooster. "Colleen is a highly sought after young woman. I'm biding my time, waiting for the right man for her."

"You mean the right offer."

James puffed out his chest. "What's wrong with that? A beautiful daughter is one of a man's greatest assets."

Bile churned in Gil's stomach at the way James used his children as pawns instead of cherishing each one as a blessing. And wasn't that what he was doing with Gil, as well? Using him to better his finances by courting the banker's daughter? Disillusionment settled over Gil's shoulders like a yoke. If James pushed Bree too hard, he'd lose her altogether.

Gil's shoulders sagged farther as another reality hit home.

James wasn't the only one losing her. Once Brianna became Henry's wife, Gil's relationship with her would never be the same.

⁂

Two days after her accident, armed with her Bible and a book from her father's library, Brianna reveled in the sunshine pouring in through the parlor windows at her back, bathing her aching body with welcome heat. Escaping into her story world, she hoped to avoid thinking or talking about the problems that plagued her—her father's refusal to let her attend college, Henry's unwanted courtship, her confused feelings for Gil . . .

Voices in the hallway startled her from her reading. Her shoulder muscles tensed as she waited to see who would enter. She half-hoped, half-dreaded to see Gil again, knowing he would try to discern the reason behind her reckless ride. She could admit to the fight with her father, but she could never tell him the other reason she was so upset that morning.

The parlor door opened. Mrs. Johnston entered and gave a slight bow. "Mr. Sullivan to see you, Miss Brianna. Are you accepting visitors?"

Brianna nodded. "It's all right. You can let him in."

Henry handed his hat to the housekeeper and rushed into the room. His blond hair swept neatly off his forehead as he bowed over her hand. "Brianna, my dear. I was distressed to hear of your accident. How are you feeling?"

"Much better, thank you. Though still a little sore." She gestured to a chair. "Please sit down. Can we get you any refreshments?"

"No, thank you." He took a seat beside her on the settee instead. "What exactly happened? All I heard is that a horse threw you."

She kept her demeanor calm. "I was riding in the pasture, and a hare spooked my mount. It all happened so fast."

"That's terrible. How did you get back?"

She dropped her gaze to the book on her lap. "Gil found me and brought me back." She didn't need to see Henry's face to picture his displeasure.

"Of course. Good ol' Gil to the rescue."

Brianna bristled at his sarcasm. She'd never understood Henry's dislike of Gil, except that perhaps he was jealous of their friendship. "Henry, you must try to put aside your animosity toward Gil. He's part of my family, and I . . . we . . . are all very fond of him."

The hardness left Henry's features. "You're right. I suppose I owe him a debt of gratitude for taking such good care of you. Now that we're practically engaged, though, that job should be mine." He reached out to take her hand in his.

Brianna stiffened in her seat, not ready for such an open

declaration of his intentions. Would he feel free to take liberties with her now? Steal kisses when they were alone? The thought sent a flood of panic through her body. The only kisses she wanted were Gil's.

With the pretense of moving her book, she slipped her hand free. "Thank you for dropping by, but I fear I tire easily."

"Of course. I'll come back when you're feeling stronger." He pressed a quick kiss to her cheek, then rose, gazing at her with a curious expression before letting himself out of the parlor.

The air whooshed from her lungs the moment the door clicked shut. "Thank goodness." She leaned back on the sofa and closed her eyes.

"Is that any way to treat your intended?"

"Gil." Brianna jerked upright, and a moan escaped her lips at the pain that shot through every muscle with that sudden movement.

A soft breeze blew in from the open French doors. Gil stood inside looking down at her. Irritation settled over her at his smug expression.

"What are you doing? Spying on me now?" She snapped her book closed and shoved it aside.

"I had the same intention as Henry. To see how you're feeling."

"As you can see, I'm fine." She brushed the material of her gown with unsteady fingers.

Gil crossed to the settee and knelt in front of her. His amused expression changed to one of concern as he took her hand in his. "You don't know how many years you took off my life with that stunt."

She made the mistake of staring into the blue intensity of his eyes. A pulse beat wildly in her neck. "I . . . I never got to thank you for bringing me home."

"You can thank me by telling me what really happened. What made you take Major out on that crazy ride?"

Heat infused her cheeks, making her wish for a fan. She lifted her chin. "Like I told Daddy, I wanted some excitement."

Gil tightened his grip on her hand. "Nice try. But I saw you before you left. You weren't looking for a thrill. You were angry, and I want to know what upset you so much that you would risk your safety, as well as the welfare of that animal."

Her bottom lip quivered as the guilt she'd pushed back for two days rose to the surface. Not only had she risked her own life, she'd endangered poor Major, who was already dealing with an injury. If he'd hurt his leg any worse . . . well, she couldn't begin to think of what might have happened.

"Bree?"

She dragged her attention away from his hypnotic gaze and gulped in a breath. "I had a fight with Daddy after the party on Saturday. He said he'd given Henry his blessing on our court-ship. I told him I didn't want to get married, that I wanted to go to college."

Gil moved up beside her on the sofa. "I imagine he didn't take that news too well."

"No."

Gil sat with his hands clasped over his knees. When he glanced over at her, a confused frown creased his brow. "But why were you still so angry the next morning? Did something else hap-pen?"

Her heart banged against her ribcage, and she turned her face away. He knew her too well.

"Brianna, look at me. What else happened?"

"Nothing."

"You always were a terrible liar. Was it Colleen?"

"No."

He reached out to grasp her chin between his fingers. "I want to know what upset you."

She wrenched away and pushed up from the settee. The pain

shooting through her stiffened muscles nudged a moan from her and she stumbled, catching herself before she fell.

Instantly Gil was at her side. When he wrapped strong arms around her, she wanted nothing more than to lean into his warmth for even a moment.

"Tell me." His breath stirred the tendrils of hair around her face.

She pushed away from him and limped to the fireplace, knowing he'd never stop badgering her until she gave in. "Fine. I'll tell you the ugly truth. I overheard my father informing Sam we had nothing to worry about now that you were going to marry Aurora Hastings. We'd be guaranteed unlimited bank loans since we'd be part of the Hastings family soon." Helpless anger washed over her. She leaned against the mantel, willing him to leave before she further humiliated herself.

She sensed Gil approaching behind her. "I'm not going to marry Aurora." His quiet voice sent shivers along her spine. "I only said I'd consider courting her until your father acquires his loan."

She whirled around so fast, he stepped backward in surprise. "You think it's acceptable to trifle with a girl's affection in order to gain financial favor with her father? How would you feel if someone treated me like that?"

A flush crept up his neck, giving her a brief jolt of satisfaction.

"I thought you were an honorable man, Gil. But it appears even *you* are willing to forgo your principles to win my father's approval."

"That's not fair." An angry scowl slashed his forehead. "After everything your father has done for me, how can I deny him the one thing he asks of me?"

She crossed her arms. "Easy. Just say no."

He stepped closer, his outrage swirling in the air between them. "If it's so easy, why don't you tell your father no? Refuse Henry's suit."

Her self-righteous anger faded, leaving her limp. The idea of defying her father in such a manner made her break out in a cold sweat.

"Not so easy after all, is it, Brianna?"

Before she could think of a suitable reply, Gil strode out through the open French doors, leaving her more unsettled than ever.

11

SLEEP ELUDED GIL once again. It seemed insomnia had become a way of life since he'd moved back to Irish Meadows. In the stuffy heat of his third-floor bedroom, Gil felt the walls closing in on him, suffocating the air in his lungs. He flung off the bedclothes, pulled on his trousers, shirt, and boots, and let himself into the hall. He'd go for a walk in the cool evening air and check on Georgina. Today the mare had seemed restless in her stall, often a sign of impending labor. Something told Gil tonight might be her time.

He crept down the back staircase and out the side door. The immediate blast of cool air relaxed the tense muscles in his shoulders. He breathed deeply, enjoying the scent of newly blossoming lilacs. In the light of the almost-full moon, Gil ambled along the path beside the racetrack, relishing the stillness of the night as he made his way to the stables.

Inside, the corridor was dark until he turned the first corner and noticed a dim light in the distance. Right about the location of Georgina's stall.

He quickened his steps. A lantern swung from a hook above the mare's enclosure. Gil's heart rate jumped at the sound of Brianna's soft voice crooning to the animal. Steeling himself to see her again for the first time since their fight, Gil peered over the stall door.

Seated in the straw, the mare's head in her lap, Brianna looked up when his shadow crossed her. "Georgina's in labor." Her anxious eyes shone with concern.

Gil opened the door and entered the stall. He moved past Brianna's skirts, which spread out over the straw, and knelt beside Georgina. Swiftly, he ran his hands over her distended abdomen and nodded as a contraction rippled under his palm.

"How often are the pains coming?"

"About every five minutes." Brianna continued to stroke the horse's head. Wisps of hair escaped her braid and curved onto her cheek. "Should we call Dr. Phelps?"

"There's no need to disturb him at this hour unless it's an emergency." He sat back on his haunches as the mare relaxed. "Are things progressing normally?"

"I think so."

Gil rose and plucked a piece of straw from his pants. "What are you doing out here at this hour, anyway?"

She shrugged. "I couldn't sleep. And since Daddy's banished me from the stables, this is the only time I can come without getting caught."

Gil chuckled. "I should have known you couldn't stay away." He leaned a shoulder against the wooden wall. "Could be a long night. You sure you're up for it?"

She flashed him an indignant glare. "Aren't I always?"

"Yes, you are." A smile tugged at the corner of his mouth.

Her expression softened. "Do you remember the night Georgina was born? How we stayed up all night to help Sam deliver her?"

"Of course I remember. It was one of the most amazing

experiences of my life." The memories of that night came flooding back, making him suddenly aware of the intimate space and the lantern shedding a romantic glow over them. He pushed away from the wall and cleared his throat. "I'd better go wake Sam. We might need him if things don't go as planned."

She lowered her eyes, but not before he caught a flash of disappointment. It would have been nice to share the experience alone, but Gil didn't trust himself. After Georgina's birth, Brianna had thrown herself into his arms in an exuberant hug of celebration. It was the first time his feelings had shifted to something other than friendship, the first time he'd had to fight not to kiss her. A situation he did not intend to repeat.

Gil made his way to the building they called the "working barn," where the work horses were housed. Sam's quarters lay shrouded in darkness. At Gil's knock, a grunt sounded, followed by the creak of bedsprings. Sam opened the door, took one look at Gil, and reached for his plaid shirt on the hook beside the door. "Georgina?"

Gil nodded. "It's time."

They walked in comfortable silence back to the stables, where Sam joined Brianna in the stall. Gil waited in the corridor while the older man made a thorough examination.

"Shouldn't be much longer now," Sam said as he wiped his hand off on a towel. "We'd best get her to the birthing stall, where there's more room."

But several hours after they'd moved the mare to the larger enclosure, Sam's optimistic prediction proved wrong. Georgina lay bathed in sweat after straining repeatedly with no success.

"What's wrong, Sam?"

The fear in Brianna's voice tore at Gil's composure. He placed a comforting hand on her shoulder.

Sam scratched his head. "I'm not sure. This foal should've been born long ago. I'll do another exam, and we might have to call in the doc."

When he'd finished, the expression on Sam's face told Gil the situation wasn't good.

Sam let out a long sigh. "Brianna, you'd best go up to the house and call Doc Phelps. Tell him to come as quick as he can."

Tears bloomed in Brianna's eyes as Gil helped her to her feet. "I don't want to leave her."

Gil brushed some pieces of straw from her skirt. "She'll be fine until you get back. I'd go, but Sam might need me. And you'll be quicker."

"All right. I'll be back as soon as I can." With a last whispered word to Georgina, Bree hurried out of the stall.

When her footsteps faded, Gil knelt to rub the mare's head. "What's wrong, Sam?" he asked quietly.

Sam planted his hand on his hips and shook his head. "I don't like to speculate, knowing how set Mr. O'Leary is on this foal being a champion." His shoulders slumped, and he expelled a long breath. "I can't be sure, but this foal might be lame."

Gil swallowed the lump of dread in his throat. Not only would James be upset, but Brianna would be devastated. "I hope you're wrong, Sam."

"You and me both, son."

The sun had started its morning rise by the time Doc Phelps arrived. A grizzled man of undetermined years, he'd been the vet on call for as long as Gil had lived at Irish Meadows. Both Gil and Sam breathed easier when he took over in the stall, knowing the mare was in capable hands. Doc would do whatever he could to ensure the health of the mother and the foal.

Gil and Brianna stood together in the corridor, watching through the open door. When Brianna shivered in the cool morning air, he saw she wore only a thin blouse. "Where's your wrap?"

She shrugged. "I think I left it at the house."

He stepped closer and put his arm around her to share his warmth. "Did you wake your father?"

"No." She lifted weary eyes to his. "He'd only yell at me for being here, and I didn't want him to ruin this moment." On a sigh, she let her head fall to his shoulder.

A fierce wave of protectiveness rose in Gil's chest, and he tightened his arm around her. He wanted to be the one to shelter her from every worry, every disappointment in life. If only James would agree to let him court Brianna. But that was never going to happen—for many reasons.

A flurry of activity drew his attention back to the stall.

"Easy, girl. Whoa." Sam soothed the mare, who was trying to rise. "You're not quite finished."

At the other end of the horse, Doc Phelps had his arm up inside Georgina, his face contorted as he struggled to assist the straining animal. The horse gave a loud whinny followed by the sound of liquid gushing onto the floor.

Brianna jerked as though ready to fly inside the stall, but Gil held her back with firm hands. "Give them a minute."

Sam moved back as the mare lurched to her feet. Doc Phelps worked to free the foal from the birth sac. An oath escaped him as he straightened, hands on his hips, staring down at the straw.

The smile on Brianna's face slid away. "What's the matter? Is the baby all right?"

Doc Phelps raised his head. The sorrow on his face said it all. "I'm afraid not. He's got a malformed back leg."

Gil's heart sank to his boots. Sam had been right, after all. He shuddered to think what this would mean to James.

Brianna pushed into the stall. Gil followed, prepared to carry her out if need be. Despite the oddly shaped back leg, the colt struggled valiantly to get to his feet as his mother licked away the fluid from his coat. Brianna knelt on the straw beside him, whispering words of encouragement. Gil knew she longed to touch him but would wait until he'd gotten his footing—if that were even possible. At last, the colt made it to a standing position, and Brianna clapped her hands.

"Oh, he's a beauty. A chestnut like his mama. And he's got white socks. What will we call you, little one?"

Gil's chest squeezed with pain, knowing what was to come. Gently, he lifted her to her feet, keeping a hand under her arm. "We won't be naming him, Bree." The unfairness of life rose up to choke his words.

"What do you mean? Of course we'll name him."

Loud boots thundered in the corridor. Without looking, Gil knew James had arrived. His foul mood was about to get a whole lot worse.

"Brianna O'Leary, what in tarnation are you doing in this barn when I expressly forbid you—"

The dark scowl on his face turned to shock as his gaze landed on the deformed leg of the new colt. "Sweet mother of Job." All color drained from his cheeks.

Sam, who was standing nearer to the door, reached out a steadying hand. "I'm so sorry, James."

Doc Phelps had wiped his arms and hands on a large towel and was packing his bag. "There's nothing we could do. A real shame, because he would have been a beauty."

Brianna's brow puckered. "You act like the foal is dying. He's got a turned leg, but otherwise he's healthy." She looked from the doctor to Sam, to the grim face of her father, then finally to Gil.

As he stared into her wide, uncertain eyes, the words froze on his tongue. Maybe they hadn't done Brianna any favors, sheltering her from this cruel side of the horse-breeding business. Gil couldn't bear to be the one to inform her of the colt's fate. He shook his head, silently pleading for understanding.

James seemed to rouse himself. "Take him out back, away from the mother. I'll get the gun."

Gil tightened his grip on Brianna's arm, prepared for her to either bolt or faint.

"What are you talking about?" The words shrieked from her as she strained to get free.

James didn't acknowledge her question but strode away from the stall. Brianna wrenched out of Gil's grasp to race after him.

"Daddy. Wait."

Dear God, give her the strength to bear this. The silent prayer formed on Gil's lips as he darted after her.

Brianna threw herself at her father, catching him by the arm. "You are not going to kill that baby!" The hysteria in her voice rang throughout the barn.

As Gil reached them, James twisted to face his daughter. Pain etched in the lines around James's eyes, and Gil realized how much this was costing him.

"Don't argue with me, girl. The colt has to be put down. He's useless with a lame leg."

"He's not useless," she shouted. "He may not be a champion racer, but he still has value."

Red blotches marred the big man's cheeks. "I'm not paying to house an animal that will be nothing more than an overgrown pet. He won't be any good as a work horse. And no one will buy him as a racehorse. We can't afford to keep him."

James continued down the corridor toward the locked cabinet that housed the hunting rifles.

Gil followed him. "Surely there's another option. I'll put out feelers to see who might be willing to take him. Maybe someone needs a horse for their child."

James shook his head. "No one will buy him. Trust me."

Brianna pushed past Gil and ran to her father. "I won't let you do this. You can't murder an innocent animal." An unholy sob tore out of her. "Daddy, please." The wail erupted, keening with such grief that it nearly cracked Gil's heart in two.

When James ignored her, she turned wild eyes to Gil, clutching his shirtfront. "Gil, do something. Don't let him do this." She sank to her knees on the dirt floor as sobs overtook her body.

"Just because he's not perfect doesn't give Daddy the right to kill him."

Her agony became his, fisting around Gil's lungs to squeeze the breath out of him. He knelt beside her, his arm around her quaking shoulders. "Come on, Bree. Let me take you inside." He had to get her out of range before James fired the fatal shot.

Her head jerked up, her face ravaged with tears. She seized his arm in a vise grip. "Please, Gil. Make him stop."

Gil's brain whirled at a dizzying speed, searching for some way to prevent the disaster about to happen. He couldn't bear to let Brianna down, as her father always had.

Lord, show me a solution. How can I fix this for her?

James had unlocked the closet and taken out one of the rifles. He leaned it against the wall while he searched for the bullets. Did he not see his daughter falling apart on the ground? Did he even care?

Gil lurched to his feet as James reached for the gun. "I'll take him."

James stopped dead and fixed Gil with a dark stare. "What?"

"I'll buy the foal from you."

James snorted. "Don't be stupid, boy. You couldn't afford it anyway." He went to grab the rifle, but Gil blocked his path.

"I have money saved. I'll give you a fair price. Better than any other offer you'd receive."

James stopped to stare at him. "Are you insane? What will you do with a lame horse?"

He must be insane. A good portion of the money he'd saved for his own farm would be wasted on an animal who'd be more of a liability than asset. But it was the right thing to do. His gut told him so. And it would be worth every penny to see Brianna smile again. "I'll find a use for him."

Shaking his head, James blasted out a sigh. "If you're fool enough to pay for him, as well as his upkeep, then who am I to turn down good money?"

A flood of relief spilled down Gil's spine. His legs wobbled as the tension drained away.

Muttering under his breath, James snatched the gun, returned it to the closet with the bullets, and locked the door. "Meet me at the house, and we'll discuss the terms." With an odd look at his daughter, still kneeling on the ground, James turned and stalked out of the barn.

The moment he'd gone, Brianna leapt to her feet and launched herself into Gil's arms, laughing and crying at the same time. Tension seeped out of his body as he wrapped his arms around her and buried his face in her hair. Her shaking shoulders told him she was weeping, most likely from relief. He held her until the trembling subsided, taking the time to relish the sweetness of her in his arms.

At last, she wiped her face on her sleeve and pushed back to gaze into his face. Her hair sat in disarray around her shoulders, damp pieces clinging to her cheeks and to the lashes surrounding her puffy eyes, yet she'd never looked more beautiful. His fierce avenging angel, fighting for a helpless animal.

"Thank you, Gil," she whispered, wide eyes brimming with emotion. "You have no idea what this means to me."

He managed a half smile. "Oh, I think I do." With one finger, he brushed a strand of hair from her face, fighting the power of emotions swirling through his system like a drug.

The truth—something he'd repressed for far too long—could no longer be denied. He was irrevocably in love with Brianna. Probably always had been—and always would be.

Before he did anything he'd regret, he took a deliberate step back, away from her magnetic pull. "It's been a long night. Let's go check on the foal before we both get some rest."

As Gil moved away, Brianna's breath hitched in her lungs. She may be delirious from lack of sleep and overwrought from the onslaught of emotions she'd just been through, but she knew what she had just witnessed. The unmistakable hunger in Gil's eyes matched her own longing. And after what he'd done for her, she was more than certain. The evidence was as plain as the sun rising over the back meadow.

Gil loved her.

He knew what destroying the colt would do to her, and he'd bought the horse to save her from pain. A tidal wave of love rose up inside her. "Oh, Gil."

Leaning forward on her tiptoes, her hands against his chest, she followed her heart's desire and pressed her lips to his.

At last, her mind sighed. He tasted just as she'd imagined. Masculine and warm—intoxicating. It took her a moment to realize he hadn't moved a muscle. His body, no longer soft and comforting, went as rigid as the wooden support beam beside them. She opened her eyes to see his horrified expression. Surely he couldn't be that shocked by her behavior.

She pulled back, despair flooding her body. Maybe she'd gotten it all wrong. Maybe the thought of kissing her filled him with revulsion.

Mortification burned her cheeks. "I . . . I'm sorry."

She tried to step away, but his hands clamped around her upper arms. With a groan, he hauled her against him and pulled her mouth back to his.

Like a caged bird trying to take flight, her heart soared and bumped against her ribs. She melted into him and kissed him back with every ounce of emotion in her, relishing the feel of his hands in her hair, which now tumbled around her shoulders. A second groan rumbled up through his chest, followed by a rush of cool air that blasted between them as he pushed her away.

"Brianna, no. We can't do this."

Stunned and swaying slightly, she fixed her gaze on his face, alarmed by the tortured agony shining in his eyes. "What's wrong?"

He stepped back and leaned against the stable wall, as though his legs wouldn't support him. "It's not right. Your father thinks of me as a son, as your brother."

Hurt welled up and turned into boiling anger. Once again her father had ruined a beautiful moment in her life. She clenched her hands until her nails bit into her palms. "I don't care what Daddy thinks. You are *not* my brother."

Gil plunged his fingers through his hair, dislodging his dark curls. "I'm sorry, Bree. After everything he's done for me, I can't betray his trust like this. Please, let's forget this ever happened." He jerked away from the wall and strode down the corridor, kicking up dust and straw in his wake.

Brianna bit her lip, checking her initial urge to chase after him, to convince him he was wrong. He needed time to come to grips with what had happened between them. She wrapped her arms around her waist to hold on to the warmth of his arms and the delicious knowledge that now burned in her heart.

She was in love with Gil, and he loved her, too.

Despite his rejection, a trickle of happiness wormed its way into her heart. She'd kissed Gil and he had kissed her back—in no uncertain terms. Finally she had her answer. Gil did care for her as more than a sister, even if he couldn't admit it. She held a finger to her slightly swollen lips and allowed the thrill of his kiss to wash over her anew. As far as she was concerned, it didn't matter that his conscience had intervened and he'd pushed her away. Their feelings for each other would win out in the end. After all, Daddy already thought of Gil as a son. Why not make him a son-in-law?

The thought of her desire for a college career gave her a momentary twinge of concern, but she stiffened her spine. Gil knew how important her education was to her. Surely he would wait for her. It would give him time to save more money for his farm, as well.

She floated on a wave of happiness back to Georgina's stall, needing to assure herself the little fellow and his mother had bonded. Sam was the only one left outside the stall when she approached.

"How's he doing?" she asked, peering into the enclosure.

Sam gestured toward the mother and the tiny foal who suckled from her. "As you can see, he's doing great."

Her heart swelled. "Isn't he gorgeous? To think Daddy was going to get rid of him."

Sam turned to study her. "What changed his mind?"

She smiled tenderly at the wondrous thing Gil had done. "Gil offered to buy him."

"Well, if that don't beat all." Sam scratched his head, a bemused expression on his weathered face. "That boy is something else."

A rush of laughter bubbled out. "That he is, Sam. That he is."

12

GIL WALKED BLINDLY along the country lanes that weaved between the different estates on Long Island, too aggravated to do anything but keep moving. He must have hiked several miles before he'd turned and headed back, his emotions no more settled now than they'd been two hours ago. He kicked viciously at a stone in the path and sent it hurtling into a grove of trees. How had his life spiraled out of control so quickly? In a matter of hours, he'd bought a lame horse and kissed Brianna O'Leary—the one thing he'd promised himself he'd never do.

And now he could never *undo* it. Never forget the taste of her sweet lips, the smell of her hair, the feel of her warm body in his arms. He'd kissed a few girls in his day, all enjoyable enough, but nothing had come close to this life-altering experience. The moment her lips touched his, he knew his world would never be the same again. No other woman could ever compare to that soul-stirring sensation.

I am ruined.

Gil crested a hill, and the O'Leary mansion came into view. His shoulders slumped. No use putting off the unpleasant task of facing Mr. O'Leary. His body, now as weary as his soul, longed for the oblivion of sleep.

He trudged into the house and found James seated at the desk in his study. Gil breathed a sigh of relief that Bree was nowhere to be seen.

James looked up from the ledger when he heard Gil enter. "There you are, boy. I thought you'd changed your mind."

"No, sir, I haven't," he said quietly.

James put down his pen in a deliberate manner, replaced the cap on the bottle of ink, and folded his hands on the now-closed ledger. "Have a seat, Gilbert. I think we need to talk."

Gil had rarely seen James this serious. Dread pooled in his gut as he reluctantly chose one of the leather chairs across from the desk. "About the foal . . ."

"That's only part of it. The more important part has to do with your feelings for my daughter."

Gil stiffened. He struggled for something to say, but when nothing seemed appropriate, he remained silent.

"Tell me, Gilbert, just how long have you been in love with Brianna?"

Gil jerked as though the man had slapped him. White knuckles gripped the leather armrests. "I don't know what—"

"I'm not blind, boy. I saw what happened in that barn, and I know why you agreed to buy the foal. You wanted to fix the situation for Brianna, to ease her pain. A noble gesture, really. The act of a man in love."

Gil wanted to argue, but his tongue stuck to the dry roof of his mouth. The clock on the desk ticked into the silence.

James leaned over the desktop. "Don't bother to deny it. I recognize the signs because it was the same way with my Kathleen." His expression softened as it often did when he spoke of his wife.

A small glimmer of hope bloomed in Gil's chest. Might James be sympathetic to his cause? "I . . . I don't know what to say, sir."

James's eyes narrowed. "I need you to answer a question for me. And I need the truth. Have you . . . acted on these feelings?"

Gil fought to keep the heat from his face as he recalled their kiss—not something he would share with her father. "I have never said anything to Brianna about my feelings."

"So you haven't been carrying on a secret affair behind my back?"

Outrage slammed through Gil. "Of course not."

James blew out a long breath. "Thank God. It's not too late."

Too late? What does that mean? Gil swallowed and got to his feet. "Mr. O'Leary, I know I don't have many assets, but I have big plans for the future. In a year's time, I should have enough money saved to buy my own property."

A shutter came down over James's face, and he pushed his chair back, holding up a hand. "Let me stop you right there." He moved slowly, as though weighing his words, and came around the desk to stand beside him. "Gilbert, I raised you in the bosom of my family. I consider you another son, and for all intents and purposes, a sibling to my children. I've even named you in my will. It would feel slightly incestuous for you to have a relationship with Brianna."

Gil's hands fisted in helpless frustration. "But we aren't related—either biologically or legally, sir. I don't see why—"

James pulled himself up to his full, imposing height, arms crossed tight over his chest. "In light of these new developments, Gilbert, I believe it might be wise for you to take Arthur Hastings up on his job offer at the bank."

Bile rose at the back of Gil's throat. He sank back onto the chair, speechless.

"You could move back to the city and begin the formal courtship of his daughter. In the meantime, Brianna will continue seeing Henry Sullivan. I expect to announce their betrothal at her eighteenth birthday in two weeks' time." He gave Gil a long look. "Some distance will do you both good."

Gil's head spun with sudden vertigo. "So I'm good enough to inherit your money, but not good enough to marry your daughter?" The words came out sharper than he'd intended.

"Nothing personal, son. I need the wealth and social status that the Sullivan family can bring us. You understand." He clapped Gil on the back, then rounded the desk to resume his seat. "If you're still bent on buying that colt, I'll give you more than a fair price." He took the cap off the ink and dipped his pen, effectively dismissing Gilbert.

Gil rose on unsteady legs, attempting to come to grips with everything that had just been said. As much as it pained him to admit it, James had a point. Gil couldn't imagine being around Brianna after what had transpired between them. "I'll speak with Mr. Hastings, but I'd like to stay until after Bree's birthday. It would kill her if I left before then."

"Fine." James glanced up for a moment. "No hard feelings, I hope, son."

Gil clamped his lips together, fighting the sensation of his world spinning out of control. Morning light seeped through the window to illuminate the rigid lines on James's face. Gil blinked against the harsh glare of reality that had effectively destroyed any lingering delusions he may have had about his place in this family.

He swallowed back his bitter disillusionment. "No, sir. You've made your position very clear. I know exactly where I stand."

Brianna pushed into her father's study without knocking. "Daddy, have you seen Gil? I can't find him anywhere."

It had been three days since the foal's birth, three days since they'd shared their amazing kiss, and Brianna hadn't seen Gil for more than five minutes. She was determined to speak to him today and find out exactly where things stood between them.

Her father looked up from his paperwork. "I believe he went into the city to meet with Arthur Hastings."

A prickle of foreboding raced along her spine. "Why would he do that?"

Daddy removed his spectacles and rubbed the bridge of his nose. "Didn't he tell you? Arthur offered Gil a job at his bank in Manhattan. I suppose they're working out the details."

The room swirled around her. She clutched the back of the chair to keep from stumbling. "That can't be true. Gil would never work in a bank."

"He's an ambitious young man, Brianna. We can't expect him to stay cooped up here forever. Arthur recognizes Gil's talent and wants to groom him in his business. It makes sense—now that Gil is courting his daughter."

Momentary shock paralyzed Brianna's lungs. Then ripe anger rose within her, loosening her tongue. "Gil is *not* courting Aurora Hastings."

Her father flicked her a disapproving glance. "He made it official yesterday. Apparently the whole family is thrilled."

Brianna tugged at the neck of her blouse, which had become unbearably tight. "You're wrong. Gil is not interested in Aurora."

He huffed out a loud breath. "Aurora is a beautiful young woman from a wealthy family. What better match could he make?"

"But Gil loves me." The words burst forth in a torrent of desperate indignation.

Her father frowned. "Quit imagining things, Brianna. Gil loves you as a brother would. Nothing more."

A toxic mixture of anger and jealousy surged through her veins. "You're wrong," she repeated. "Gil kissed me the way a man kisses the woman he loves."

His head snapped up, giving Brianna a small thrill of victory.

"That's right, Daddy. Gil loves me, and I love him. We're going to have a future together. You'll see."

Her father's features turned to stone. He slammed a palm to the polished surface of the desk. "I will hear no more on the matter. You need to forget these nonsensical notions and concentrate on Henry, your future husband."

Brianna's fingers tightened into fists, her nails biting into her palms. She wanted to smash something. To break one of her father's precious trophies. To hurt him as he always hurt her. Instead, she bit her bottom lip until the taste of blood brought about a measure of sanity.

Once she sorted out this misunderstanding with Gil, she would prove to her father that their love was something pure, sanctioned by God, something Daddy's greed would never touch.

Love would triumph in the end. She'd make sure of it.

Avoiding Brianna was slowly killing him—a fate Gil surely deserved. He wiped the sweat from his forehead with his shirt sleeve, silently berating himself as the worst sort of coward. The uncomfortable truth sat like a sharp blade between his shoulders. He just didn't have the courage to face her after that kiss.

Or the courage to tell her he was leaving.

After twelve long hours of work with the horses, followed by an exhausting ride over the O'Leary property—none of which did anything to relieve Gil's guilt and frustration—he now finished brushing Midnight's coat, furious to find that nothing could erase Brianna from his mind.

He exhaled loudly, making the dust motes dance in the air around him, his thoughts turning to the conversation he'd inadvertently overhead the day after James all but banished him from Irish Meadows. Gil had been trying to avoid Brianna by sneaking into the kitchen through the servants' entrance when he'd heard voices on the back porch.

"I suppose you think me an ogre for not letting Brianna continue her romantic daydreams." James's baritone had been clearly audible from where Gil stood, back pressed to the brick wall.

"Not an ogre, my love. But I would like to know what you have against Gil courting Brianna."

"The boy was raised in our home as a sibling to our children. It feels like incest, Katie. It feels like betrayal."

Gil flinched as though James had struck him.

"You make it sound like they created some insidious plan calculated to hurt you. Sometimes love catches you off guard. Have you forgotten how it was for us?"

"I remember." James's voice was husky. "I also remember my father clawing his way up from the dirt of poverty, fighting discrimination at every turn for being a poor Irishman. You know how long it took for us to achieve respectability, Katie."

Heavy footsteps had thumped the porch, and Gil had pictured James pacing like a caged lion.

"I vowed that my children would never know that type of hardship. That our daughters would marry well-respected, wealthy men with good standing in society. Like it or not, Gilbert is the son of a destitute laborer, doomed to a lifetime of struggle. I don't want that for Brianna."

"What about what Brianna wants?"

Gil had held his breath, his fingers scraping the bricks at his back.

James snorted. "The girl is a dreamer. She wants to go to college to 'expand her mind.' And then to marry a penniless boy. Where does she get such notions?"

Mrs. O'Leary's footsteps crossed the porch. "Our children are bound to make mistakes, James, and choose different paths than the ones we want for them. We can guide them, but we can't force our views on them."

"Oh, really? Are you not forcing your religion on them?"

"That's different. I'm trying to save their souls."

"You save our souls, Katie. I'll look after the rest. My decision stands. Brianna will marry Henry Sullivan."

The last thread of hope had drained away then, leaving Gil limp. Mrs. O'Leary was the one person in the world who might have changed James's mind, but she had failed.

Fortunately or unfortunately—Gil wasn't sure which—Arthur Hastings didn't appear to share James's pessimistic opinion of the Whelan name. He'd been thrilled at Gil's change of heart and had eagerly offered him an entry-level position in the Hastings Bank and Loan Company. He'd also granted him permission to court Aurora. Apparently, Arthur didn't share James's reservations about having Gil as a potential son-in-law, perhaps due to the fact that he had no son to follow in his footsteps.

To that end, the Hastings family had invited Gil for dinner tonight at Belvedere, their summer estate. Mr. Hastings was sending an automobile for Gil promptly at six, which meant he needed to get cleaned up soon.

Gil shrugged off his useless ponderings and exited the stall, closing the latch with a soft clink of metal. Overcome with the need to hurry, he failed to see Brianna standing in the main corridor until it was too late. Gil's heart chugged to a stop, his feet rooted to the spot as he braced himself for the inevitable confrontation.

She stood blocking the exit, her arms crossed in a battle stance. Behind her, the wind whipped the dirt and straw in a swirling pattern past the open doorway. Ominous clouds scuttled across the sky, framing her like a picture.

"Why are you avoiding me?" Her words rang through the hollow space.

The speech he'd been practicing for just such an eventuality flew from his mind. "I've been busy." He bent to pick up a coil of rope and loop it over a nail on the wall.

"Is it true?" Raw emotion swirled in the depths of her eyes.

He steeled himself to inflict the blow. "It is."

Her hand shot to her mouth, muffling her cry. A shaft of pain hit his chest as surely as if she'd taken aim and shot him with an arrow, but he held himself rigid.

Her hand fell away, fisting against the blue fabric of her dress. "I want to hear you say it out loud."

He wet his dry lips, careful not to blink. He needed to be strong, to convince her this was the only course open to them. "I have accepted a job at the Hastings bank. And I am courting Aurora."

She swayed for a moment, but steadied herself. "Why, Gil?" Her tortured whisper hung in the air between them.

"I think you know why."

"My father." She spat the word with a venomous sneer.

He nodded. "You may not agree with him, but he's only looking out for you. He wants a better future for you, more than I can offer."

She took several quick steps forward and threw out her hands. "Don't you understand? I don't care about money or social status. None of that will make me happy. Being with you will."

Dear God, how do I fight such naivety, such passion? He yearned to gather her to him and never let her go. Instead, he had to make her accept the reality of the situation.

"Going against your father's wishes won't make you happy, Bree. It will rip your family apart. Create a rift that can never be mended. I can't do that to them—or to you." He took a deep breath. "So unless your father changes his mind, this is the way it has to be."

He knew the truth had hit home when her shoulders slumped and the light dimmed in her eyes. With an unbearable ache in his heart, he shoved his hands in his pockets to keep from reaching for her. "I'll stay until your birthday, then I'm moving to the city for good. It will be better for everyone."

He ducked his head to hide the moisture blurring his vision, then pushed past her out of the barn. The rain had started to fall, fat drops soaking his shirt in seconds. Halfway to the house, Brianna's wail of anguish shattered the last of his control. His grief broke loose in a torrent that mingled with the rain streaming down his face.

He'd lost Brianna and he'd lost Irish Meadows—all because he couldn't resist the temptation of her kiss.

He deserved to be unhappy for the rest of his life.

13

COLLEEN TAPPED A TOE in time with the music, trying to pretend she was enjoying Brianna's birthday celebration. Not that her sister would even notice. Brianna had never looked more miserable in her life. Probably pining over Gil's impending departure—a surprising turn of events, to be sure.

Too bad Colleen had never gotten the chance to steal a kiss from Gil.

Colleen fanned her cheeks, which had warmed at the thought. She'd been fending off offers to dance all evening. After two uncomfortable dances with Jared, she'd claimed a leg cramp and moved to the chairs for the remainder of the night. Jared's indulgence in spirits, as well as his wandering hands, made her want to avoid his company altogether.

The fact that Jared had spent the last twenty minutes holed away with her father in his study had only added to Colleen's foul mood. Their private meeting could only mean one thing—Jared had asked for her hand in marriage. Waves of nausea twisted

Colleen's stomach. At one time, she'd actually entertained the idea of marrying him, but lately Jared's behavior had become more and more alarming, and she was no longer sure she wanted anything to do with him.

But Daddy would never turn down the chance for a union with their well-to-do neighbors. Colleen needed to come up with some indisputable way to get out of this relationship, once and for all.

She scanned the crowd, relieved that for once the knowing eyes of Rylan Montgomery were not aimed at her. Her gaze moved down the room and lit on Gil, standing in the corner with Aurora Hastings at his side, looking as depressed as she'd ever seen him. He hadn't gone near Brianna all evening—a curious event in itself. Normally on her birthday, Gil would lavish all sorts of attention on Bree. Perhaps the rumors were true and Gil had indeed started courting Aurora. If so, maybe the girl had put a stop to Gil's ridiculous fawning over her sister.

"What's wrong with Bree tonight?" Adam sprawled on the seat beside her. "She usually loves her birthday."

Colleen glanced over at her brother, pleased to see that for once Adam hadn't overindulged in alcohol. His eyes were sharp, his speech clear.

Adam nodded toward Gil. "I'm guessing it has something to do with Whelan. Am I right?"

She shrugged. "Possibly. He's working for Mr. Hastings now and is moving to the city."

"Hallelujah! There is a God."

"Adam." She swatted his shoulder. "Don't let Mama catch you talking like that."

Adam's retort was interrupted by Daddy stepping forward and clapping his hands to get everyone's attention. The crowd ceased their chatter to focus on him.

"I want to thank all of you for coming tonight to help celebrate Brianna's eighteenth birthday." Applause rippled through the room. Daddy motioned for silence. "In addition to that momentous event, I have another happy announcement to make."

Colleen stiffened on her chair, her heart pounding an uncomfortable rhythm.

"Any idea what this is about?" Adam whispered.

"None." She gripped her fingers together on her lap. It had better not have anything to do with Jared Nolan.

"I am delighted to announce Brianna's betrothal to Mr. Henry Sullivan, son of our dear friend and neighbor, Mr. William Sullivan."

Colleen sagged in relief as a surprised murmur wound through the crowd, followed by more applause. Her sister moved forward, unsmiling, to stand beside Daddy and Henry, her gaze fused to the floor. Never had Colleen seen such an unhappy-looking bride-to-be. Henry, on the other hand, beamed as he leaned over and kissed Brianna square on the mouth. At that moment, Gil pushed past Aurora and bolted from the room.

Colleen shared an arched look with Adam.

Interesting. Perhaps this betrothal, more so than Gil's upcoming departure, explained the distance between Brianna and Gil. Colleen straightened as a seed of a plan formed. With Gil so distressed, she had the perfect opportunity to take advantage of his pain, and at the same time, free herself from an equally intolerable situation. She just needed to work out the details in short order.

Colleen smiled to herself. Since when had that ever been a problem for the mistress of manipulation?

Gil inhaled the crisp evening air, then blew out a long breath. He'd come out to walk the grounds, hoping the soothing sound of crickets would calm his inner restlessness. Leaning against the top rung of the white fence that surrounded the O'Leary property, he watched the moonlight dance over the fields. Not even such ethereal beauty could soothe his soul tonight.

His heart had shattered the moment Brianna had become officially betrothed to Henry Sullivan.

Though he'd been aware James planned to make the announcement tonight, nothing had prepared Gil for the searing pain that left him reeling when Henry had kissed Brianna right on the lips. Despite Aurora's questioning glance, Gil had to leave the room to keep his emotions in check.

Thankfully, the Hastingses announced their departure soon afterward, and once their motorcar had roared out of sight, Gil refused to rejoin the party and pretend to be having a good time. He craved the darkness, where his black mood matched his surroundings, where he could nurse his pain in private.

From the front of the house, the noise of the last few guests leaving made its way to Gil. The uncomfortable truth sat heavy in Gil's stomach like the overly sweet birthday cake he'd eaten. Tomorrow he would leave Irish Meadows and embark on his new life, away from the O'Learys, away from Brianna. After that, whomever Bree or her father chose for her to marry was none of his concern.

Then why did his fists clench with an overwhelming urge to hit something? To make someone else hurt as much as he did?

With a disgusted grunt, Gil pushed away from the fence and strode down the path toward the stables. He jerked open the door and entered the sanctuary, snatching a lamp from the hook as he went. The horses nickered and stomped in their stalls. Without thinking, Gil headed straight for Midnight's stall, not sure whether he would groom him or take him for a wild run.

The white star marking on the horse's dark head gleamed under the dim glow of the light Gil hung from an overhead hook. He opened the door and stepped inside the enclosure. Midnight gave a low neigh in greeting as Gil ran his hand over the silky coat. Melancholy as thick as morning fog engulfed him at the thought of leaving his four-footed friend once again.

"How are you doing, boy? Better than me, I hope."

"I'm sure *I* can find a way to make you feel better."

Gil jerked at the feminine voice behind him. He whipped around to peer out the door, but the empty corridor mocked him. "Who's there?" He moved out into the open.

"Only me." Soft footsteps rustled the stray pieces of straw on the floor.

His sharp gaze swung to the stall beside Midnight. Had Brianna followed him out here? A combination of dread and anticipation quickened his pulse at the notion of them sharing one last stolen moment together.

Instead, Colleen stepped out from behind the door. Disappointment crashed over him with the force of a hurricane.

"Don't look so overjoyed to see me." She smoothed a hand down the bodice of her lemon-colored gown.

Gil frowned at her obvious attempt to draw attention to her physical attributes. "What are you doing out here, Colleen? You're not exactly dressed for the barn."

Her lips curved up in a smirk. "I'm glad you noticed." She sidled toward him, glancing at him from under her lashes. "I was beginning to wonder if you had blood in your veins . . ." She trailed a finger along the sleeve of his shirt. "Or ice."

Gil forced his gaze to remain on her face and not move down the creamy skin of her throat to the accentuated curves below. "Whatever you're looking for, you won't find it here. You'd best get back to the house before your father misses you." He took a step backward, wincing when the hard scrape of wood bit into his spine.

Colleen moved closer, effectively trapping him against the stall door.

As though reading his discomfort, she let out a low laugh. "I think I've found exactly what I need."

Before Gil's brain could register her intent, Colleen pounced. Her arms locked around his neck as she fused her lips to his. Shock paralyzed his limbs, freezing him to the spot. With supreme effort, he controlled his reaction and allowed anger to take over. He grabbed her wrists and attempted to pry them off, but she clung to him like a bur on a horse's tail.

A sharp gasp echoed through the corridor, followed by the clatter of something skittering along the ground. Gil took advantage of Colleen's surprise to set her firmly away from him.

"That's enough." He glared at Colleen, then swung around to see who had witnessed his humiliation.

Panic ripped through him, stealing his air. Brianna stood in the dim light like a fairy frozen in time. Tears stood out in her horror-filled eyes, her hand clasped over her mouth.

Regret and shame pooled in Gil's gut at the betrayal he saw on her face. He took a halting step toward her. "Bree, this isn't what you think."

She shook her head, curls bouncing as she stumbled backward. "How could you? With my sister of all people?" On a strangled sob, she spun around and fled the barn.

Gil yanked his arm free. "Brianna, wait." He sprinted after her, desperate to make her believe him. He couldn't let her think what she was thinking. Despite her head start, he caught up with her easily on the front lawn and pulled her to a halt.

"Let go of me, you brute." Tears flooded her cheeks as she twisted in his grasp to flail at him with her fists.

He endured her glancing blows, doing nothing to stop them. "Let me explain. Please."

"Explain what? I saw the whole thing." Her chest heaved with rasping sobs.

He stilled her assault by wrapping his arms around her. Though she felt as rigid as a plank of wood in his arms, Gil reveled at the feel of her. The familiar scent of her sweet perfume encompassed him. "Colleen kissed me. I was trying to fend her off."

"Liar." Colleen's voice hissed near his ear. "A gentleman would never say such a thing about a lady." She stood beside them, nostrils flared.

He'd been so consumed with Brianna, he'd forgotten all about Colleen. Now sharp anger rose in his chest. "And a lady would never force herself on a man."

Colleen's hand shot out. The sharp sting of impact with his cheek made his eyes water.

"Don't ever speak to me again, Gilbert Whelan." She picked up her skirts and stalked across the grass in the direction of the house.

His cheek throbbing, Gil kept hold of the still-struggling bundle in his arms. He couldn't let Bree leave believing he'd betray her like that, especially knowing her volatile history with her sister.

"Colleen ambushed me in the barn. Please tell me you believe that," he said quietly.

She kept her face averted, her cheeks pink.

"I did not kiss her back, Brianna. Surely you saw that much."

"You probably wanted to."

When her lip quivered, it took every effort to keep from bending his head and tasting those lips again. The same ones that had haunted him these past two weeks.

He released one hand to cup her chin and raise her eyes to his. "The only O'Leary I have ever wanted to kiss, Brianna, is you."

Colleen marched across the lawn to the stairs leading to the front porch. Her heart beat furiously in her chest. Had her plan worked? Had Jared been waiting for her in the stable as she'd asked and witnessed her little seduction scene? Or had Brianna's unexpected arrival ruined everything? She daren't look around to find out.

"What the devil is going on out here?" Daddy's deep voice

bellowed from the porch, halting Colleen's feet at the bottom of the staircase. His glare swung from Gil and Brianna back to her.

Colleen's fingers froze on the cold railing. She hadn't counted on Daddy becoming involved in her little drama. At least not yet.

"That's what I'd like to know, sir." Jared materialized behind her, sending a cascade of chills up Colleen's spine.

Head high, she turned to face him.

Coldness glittered in Jared's pale eyes. "What is the meaning of this, Colleen?"

She kept her gaze level. "The meaning of what?"

"I want to know," he said, stepping closer, steam rising from his breath, "why you were kissing Gilbert Whelan in the barn—like some common strumpet."

She flinched away from him, her fear quite real at the violence she witnessed on his face. Now, in the heat of the moment, the well-rehearsed lines flew from her mind. "We . . . we got caught up . . . in a moment of passion."

She sensed, rather than heard, the shocked gasp of Brianna's naïve indignation.

Jared claimed Colleen's arm in a grip that made her wince. "You and I are practically betrothed. How could you kiss another man like that?"

With no viable explanation, she simply shrugged.

He thrust her away, disgust curling his lip. "I'm afraid, Mr. O'Leary, that I must terminate our agreement. I can no longer marry your daughter."

Colleen kept her head averted, not wanting to reveal any evidence of her smug satisfaction, and instead tried to appear remorseful.

"Won't you come inside and discuss this in a rational manner?" Her father practically begged the man to reconsider.

"I'm afraid there's no point. My mind is made up. Her beauty is not worth her fickleness." He spared Colleen one more glare before stalking away.

Colleen's breath escaped her lungs in one great whoosh. When she dared peek at her father, her heart pinched. Never had she seen him so angry with her. To make matters worse, Rylan Montgomery stood behind her father on the porch, an unusually somber expression shadowing his face.

"Brianna, you'd best find your fiancé and bid him a proper good night." Daddy aimed furious eyes at her. "Colleen, I will see you in my study immediately."

Like a convicted criminal heading to the guillotine, Colleen followed her father into the house—and attempted to ignore Rylan's pitying stare as she walked past.

14

THE COOL EVENING BREEZE sent tremors racing down Brianna's arms and back. She clasped her arms around her body, whether to get warm or to shield herself from further pain, she didn't know. After the last tortuous two weeks, she thought nothing could add to her grief. But the pain of finding Gil locked in such an intimate embrace with Colleen was too much for her battered heart to bear.

She raised her eyes and lost herself in the depths of Gil's stare. The intensity of emotion visible there made her quiver.

"You must see what Colleen was trying to do. She obviously planned for Jared to catch us together so he'd drop his courtship." Gil raked a hand through his hair, making it stand up in unruly curls. "There's nothing between us, I swear."

Misery made her mute. A gust of wind tore through the gauze of her dress, and her body shivered uncontrollably.

"You're freezing. Come on." He wrapped his arm around her waist and tugged her toward the steps.

As much as she knew she should avoid his touch, her body gravitated toward the warmth that emanated from him. At the top of the stairs, he came to a halt and pulled her close to his chest. In a brief moment of weakness, she allowed her head to rest against him, seeking comfort from his steady heartbeat. This might be the last time she would ever be so close to him, ever smell his aftershave mixed with the smoky scent of cigars and brandy.

The front door opened with a soft squeak. Under the glow of the porch light, she reluctantly stepped back, knowing she had no right to be in his arms.

"I'll thank you to keep your hands off my fiancée." Henry glared at Gil and moved forward to drape his arm over Brianna's shoulder.

Gil flinched, pain alive in the depths of his eyes. Then an expression of desolate defeat settled over his features. "I'm sorry, Brianna. For everything." He ducked his head and dashed down the stairs.

Her every instinct cried out to go after him. She may have even moved in his direction, but Henry put out a hand to restrain her.

"Brianna. It's time you went in. All the guests have left." He paused. "What were you doing out here?"

She halted, her gaze still trained on the stables, where Gil had disappeared. "Just getting some air." *And hoping to see Gil one more time.*

"You'll feel better after a good night's sleep." Henry guided her through the front door and into the foyer.

Numb inside, she didn't even move when he bent to drop a light kiss on her lips. "Good night, Brianna. I'll see you in church tomorrow."

"Good night." She turned to ascend the stairs, acutely conscious of Henry watching her every step, knowing he would remain there until certain she wouldn't try to see Gil again.

The sinking reality seeped into her sluggish brain—she'd

traded one type of prison with her domineering father for another with her future husband.

Colleen perched on the edge of a leather wingchair in her father's study, awaiting his reprimand. Based on past experience, Daddy's temper was mostly bluster and would blow out as quickly as it came up. Especially anything concerning her.

He stood behind his desk, his face as hard as granite. "I have never been so disappointed in you, Colleen O'Leary."

Hands clasped, she lowered her gaze to feign the proper remorse.

"Your behavior tonight was unforgivable and cannot go without consequences."

Sudden nerves rolled in her stomach. Daddy had never punished her for any of her antics before. Still, a temporary penance would be a price worth paying to escape an unsuitable marriage. Besides, how bad could it be?

He pulled out his chair and sat down. "Your mother has always accused me of being too soft with you. Perhaps she's right." He blew out a breath. "You hurt a good man tonight, a man who wanted to give you the type of life you deserve. Not to mention the pain your actions caused Gilbert . . . and your sister."

She hung her head, willing tears to form. Tears often worked on her father.

"I have come to the realization that you have no regard for the feelings of others, or how your actions affect anyone else. You do anything, hurt anyone, to get your own way. It pains me to admit it, but you've turned out to be a vain and selfish young woman."

Colleen's head flew up, her mouth falling open. Never before had her father said such words to her. He'd always considered her pranks amusing.

The tears welling in her eyes became very real.

"I'm so sorry, Daddy. I'll make it up to Bree and Gil somehow." She lifted her chin. "But I'm not sorry about Jared. He's not the man you think he is. Not the man I wish to marry."

Her father shook his head. "Be that as it may, I cannot condone such callous behavior. I need time to think of a suitable consequence for your actions. I'll let you know my decision after church tomorrow."

Colleen's stomach sank to her toes as she took in her father's rigid posture and unflinching features that showed no hint of softening. She swallowed hard as she rose from the chair. "I'm sorry for disappointing you, Daddy. Good night."

As she turned to leave, her father didn't even look up from the book he'd opened on his desk.

After the midday meal on Sunday afternoon, Rylan knocked on the ornate door of James O'Leary's study, trepidation dampening his palms. Although his cousin's rather formidable husband had been nothing but polite since Rylan's arrival at Irish Meadows, James had always maintained an aloof attitude toward him.

So why did the man want to see him now?

The door opened and James smiled, his teeth flashing white beneath his mustache. "Rylan, come in. Please have a seat."

Rylan entered the very masculine room and took the chair Mr. O'Leary indicated by the great stone hearth, while James settled into one beside him. The fragrant scents of tobacco and burning logs filled the cozy area, reminding Rylan of the pubs back home.

James picked up a pipe from the table beside him. "So, Rylan, how do you like Long Island?"

Rylan forced himself to relax. Perhaps the man only wanted to get to know him better. "'Tis a charming spot. Much quieter than Boston."

"That it is. However, my wife tells me you'll soon be working at St. Rita's orphanage in the city." James spoke around the pipe stem now clenched between his teeth.

"Yes, sir. In fact, I'm going there for the first time tomorrow."

"Good. Good." James picked up a box of matches and used one to light the pipe. He took a thoughtful puff before he pinned Rylan with an intense stare.

Rylan imagined not many people argued with James O'Leary.

"I'll get right to the point, son. I need your help with my daughter, and I think this orphanage might do the trick."

Rylan straightened on his seat. "I don't understand."

"I'm not sure how much of Colleen's little drama you witnessed last night. Suffice it to say, I'm less than pleased with her behavior of late."

Rylan raised one eyebrow and waited for more.

James turned his gaze to the flames crackling in the hearth. "I'm afraid I've spoiled my eldest daughter, Rylan, and because of that she's become rather . . . self-centered." He drew deeply on his pipe and blew out a long stream of smoke. "It's time she learned there's more to life than pranks and parties. She'll never make a proper wife unless she learns to think about someone besides herself. Especially if she ever has children."

Rylan couldn't stop his lips from twitching. "I find it hard to picture Colleen with a babe in arms."

"Which is precisely why volunteering her services at this orphanage will do her a world of good."

Rylan stiffened, frowning. "Are you sure about this, Mr. O'Leary? Frankly, I doubt she'd last a day."

James pulled his pipe from his lips, his eyes narrowing. "She'll have no choice in the matter."

Rylan released a long breath, his mind reeling. "Let me talk with the nuns who run the orphanage. If they've no objection, I can take Colleen with me on Wednesday."

"Fine." James stood and shook Rylan's hand. "I appreciate

your help with this. If anyone can help Colleen learn humility, I'm sure it's a priest and the good sisters of St. Rita's."

Rylan left Mr. O'Leary's study more perturbed than before he went in. Somehow he'd gotten roped into being the provider of Colleen's punishment.

Images of her furious, mud-covered face from the first day they met came to mind. Heaven help him, he was going to need a buggy-load of patience and prayer to survive this one.

15

G IL WALKED INTO Hastings Bank and Loan and inhaled the smell of lemon furniture polish and money.
The nerves swirling in the pit of his stomach reminded
him that the newness of the situation would take a few days to
wear off. He squared his shoulders, determination filling him.
No matter how this turn of events had come about, he would
make the best of the situation. The Good Lord had His reasons
for bringing him here, and Gil vowed to do the best job possible,
no matter how much he disliked it.

He took a long look around the interior of the impressive
building. Gleaming dark wood ran the length of the room, di-
vided by iron grills for each teller. Due to the early hour, only
one or two customers were being served. On the opposite wall,
brass nameplates adorned the doors of several offices.

Gil strode down the main corridor to a desk where a receptionist looked up as he approached. He tugged his vest into
place. "Good morning. I have an appointment with Mr. Hastings. Gilbert Whelan is the name."

"One moment and I'll get him for you, Mr. Whelan."

She returned several minutes later with Mr. Hastings behind her.

"Gilbert. It's good to see you. Please come in."

Gil shook the man's hand and followed him to the far end of the building, where Mr. Hastings entered a large corner office. He gestured to a cushioned guest seat while he rounded the enormous desk and claimed the high-back leather chair.

"Once again, let me tell you how pleased I am to have you here. I don't know what changed your mind, and I don't care. I'm only going to congratulate myself on my good fortune."

"I'm glad you feel that way, sir." Gil let his hands rest on the arms of the chair, willing his nerves to subside.

"My goal is to have you in the loans department as soon as possible. Given your excellent education, I'm sure your training will go smoothly."

"I appreciate your confidence."

"Good. Let's take care of the paperwork, and then I'll introduce you to the man who'll be training you." Mr. Hastings rose. "On a personal note, I hope you'll join us for dinner tonight. My wife and daughter are in the city for a few days to do some shopping."

Gil's shoulders stiffened, but he smiled. "Thank you. I'd enjoy that."

They walked out into the main area of the bank. "Did you manage to procure a room at the boarding house I recommended?"

"Yes, sir. Mrs. Shaughnessy had a room available on the second floor. So far it's very comfortable."

"Wonderful. Everything is falling into place nicely."

Gil held back a sigh as he followed Mr. Hastings, thinking how everything had fallen *out* of place and trying not to imagine what Brianna was doing at that very moment.

Bright and early Wednesday morning, Colleen stood on the platform of the Long Island train station, tapping her toe to match the impatience that shimmied through her. What was her father thinking sending her to an orphanage—with Rylan Montgomery of all people? How could she ever hope to meet wealthy bachelors while surrounded by nuns? She huffed loudly, blowing one perfect curl off her forehead. Maybe marriage to Jared wasn't such a bad idea after all, compared to this penance she was being forced to endure.

"Here comes the train now." Rylan jogged down the platform toward her, his dark hair waving in the breeze.

Seconds later, the engine came to a grinding halt in front of them amid a swirl of smoke. Colleen held back, stalling until all the passengers had disembarked and the new passengers had entered.

Rylan took her by the elbow and nudged her toward the open door. "Don't be plotting to miss the train," he said in a low voice. "I've promised your father I'll make sure you do this, and I always keep my word."

She shot him a glare. "I'm sure you do." They mounted the steps and made their way down the narrow aisle, where Colleen chose a seat beside the window. "This whole idea was probably yours to begin with." She arranged her skirt around her with a flare. "It sounds like something a priest would dream up."

Rylan took a seat facing her. "It was your father, trust me. I didn't think Sister Marguerite would even agree to it at first. But my amazing charm won her over." He grinned, creating dimples in both cheeks.

Colleen scowled and turned to look out the window as the train chugged forward. She shuddered, picturing filthy urchins living in a hovel and the nuns who would surely judge her with self-righteous piety. Perhaps she should have given her plan to seduce Gil more consideration.

"So why did you do it?"

Rylan's quiet question brought her attention crashing back to the stuffy interior of the train, with its drab plaid seats and grimy windows. He had leaned forward, his intelligent brown eyes missing nothing. Even dressed in his black priest garb and white collar, he managed to make her pulse sprint.

"Do what?"

"Kiss Gilbert. I thought you had an understanding with Mr. Nolan." He quirked a brow. "Seems to me you couldn't be that committed to him if you were kissing another man."

The fact that his voice held no judgment, only idle curiosity, kept Colleen's temper at bay. The words *loose* and *strumpet* had been bandied about in whispers at church the other morning. It had taken every ounce of pride for Colleen to hold her head high as she'd walked down the aisle to their usual pew. Jared's sister Rebecca's scathing glare had caused Colleen a rare pang of regret for hurting the Nolan family. Maybe Daddy was right. Maybe she was a vain and selfish creature.

Her cheeks flamed as she realized Rylan was still watching her, waiting for a reply. "I was only having a bit of fun." She hoped he'd accept her quip and leave her in peace. She was tired of him trying to peer into her soul.

"You like people to believe you're a tease and a flirt, don't you? With nothing inside that beautiful head of yours but wicked schemes. I'm wondering why that is."

"I have no idea what you're blathering on about."

"I think you do. And I also think you pulled that little seduction scene for Mr. Nolan's benefit, so he'd call off your betrothal."

Colleen's mouth fell open. Did the man have the power to read people's minds? She recovered quickly with a lift of her chin. "How could I have known Jared would happen to be in the barn to catch Gil and me?" She fiddled with the cuff of her blouse, not meeting his eyes.

"You likely arranged to meet Jared in the barn and then ambushed poor Gil, knowing Jared would be waiting for you."

"Ridiculous."

"What I don't understand is why you didn't just tell the man you don't wish to marry him. 'Twould have saved a whole host of problems."

Her temper flared. "You don't know my father. Daddy would never have allowed—" She jerked her head up at the realization that she'd just confirmed his suspicions. He smiled knowingly, and she clenched her teeth together to keep from screaming at him.

Rylan reached over to put a hand on her arm. Heat penetrated through her blouse to her arm as though he'd branded her. "I believe a woman has the right to choose whom she marries, and no man, father or not, should have the power to force her to do otherwise. For what it's worth, I'm glad you're not marrying him. He's nowhere near good enough for you." He gave her arm a light squeeze. "You're worth a great deal more to your family, and to God, than you give yourself credit for."

Once again her mouth fell open. She clamped it shut, astonished to find tears threatening. In an effort to avoid those penetrating brown eyes, she turned her head to the window and pretended a sudden fascination with the passing landscape.

When they reached their stop, Rylan, who had remained blessedly silent for the remainder of the trip, helped her dismount to the platform below.

"The asylum's not far. Only a few blocks from here."

After the stuffiness of the train, Colleen welcomed the fresh air as she kept pace beside Rylan. Right away, the high energy of the city revitalized her. She loved the hustle and bustle of all the people scurrying about, as well as the horses, carriages, and motorcars all jockeying for position on the busy streets. Her spirits lifted for the first time in days.

Rylan guided her across the street to an imposing four-story brown building with a wide cement staircase leading to the main door. An engraved brass sign on the door announced the location as "St. Rita's Orphan Asylum."

As they entered the building, the hushed interior proved a far cry from the noise and bedlam she'd expected. The squeak of the door closing behind them seemed almost a sacrilege in the church-like atmosphere.

A woman at the reception desk peered over her spectacles as they approached. "Ah, Mr. Montgomery. It's good to see you again."

He beamed at the woman. "Likewise, Mrs. Taft. This is Miss O'Leary. She's here to volunteer with the children."

Mrs. Taft smiled at Colleen. "Wonderful. Let me get Sister Veronica for you. Please have a seat while you wait." The plump woman bustled off down the hall.

Colleen took a seat beside Rylan on one of the guest chairs, marveling at the good taste in decorating. The architecture of the building alone inspired awe with its high ceilings, exquisite moldings, and tall windows. Far different from the rundown slum she'd envisioned. Maybe working here wouldn't be as bad as she'd imagined.

Colleen looked up to see a nun, dressed in white from the top of her habit to the white tips of her shoes, gliding toward her on the diamond-patterned carpet. Clasped in either hand was a well-dressed child, each walking with solemn confidence.

Rylan shot to his feet. "Good morning, Sister Veronica."

Colleen envied the nun being the recipient of such a beaming smile. The woman herself couldn't be more than twenty-one or twenty-two, and the purity of her face shone from beneath her habit. Colleen got slowly to her feet, feeling completely out of her element.

"Sister, this is a distant cousin of mine, Miss Colleen O'Leary.

She's the one I mentioned who would be coming to volunteer with the children."

The nun stepped forward to take Colleen's hand. "Welcome, Miss O'Leary. We're so happy to have you here. The children will be delighted, too."

Colleen swallowed hard. What if the children hated her? "Pleased to meet you, Sister."

Sister Veronica indicated the children at her side. "This is Jonathan Feeny and Delia O'Brien. Children, say hello to Miss O'Leary."

The pair, who couldn't be more than four or five, bobbed a curtsey to her. "Hello, Miss O'Leary."

The boy was dressed in short pants and suspenders over a starched white shirt, the girl just as tidy in a yellow dress with a matching bow holding her golden curls in place. Colleen's image of dirty urchins vanished. These children were adorable. She hoped their behavior matched their appearance.

"What will I be doing while I'm here?" Colleen ventured to ask, looking from Rylan to Sister Veronica.

The nun smiled again. "We'll start you off slowly, perhaps in the classroom, helping the children with their spelling."

Colleen fought the dismay that held her breath captive. She never imagined she'd be back in a classroom a mere year after graduating. Still, there'd be no Mrs. Stephens to constantly remind her how brainless she was compared to her brilliant younger sister. Colleen squared her shoulders and attempted to appear confident. How hard could it be to help these little ones with their work?

"Follow me, Miss O'Leary. I'll take you to Sister Marguerite in the classroom."

When Rylan made no move to accompany them, Colleen looked back. "You're not joining us?"

He grinned. "No such luck. Today I'm recruited to paint the dormitories. I'll leave you in Sister Veronica's capable hands."

He gave a mock bow and bounded off toward the wide staircase leading to the upper level.

Instead of feeling relieved to be out of his annoying presence for the day, an odd sense of disappointment plagued Colleen's footsteps as she followed Sister Veronica down the long corridor.

16

BRIANNA REMOVED HER graduation cap and gown and laid them over a chair in the back of the classroom. The chatter of her classmates trickled around her, but she remained detached from the festivities. It had been two weeks since her birthday—two weeks since Gil had left—but it felt like two years. Depression followed Brianna like a fog wherever she went, and today was no exception.

"Come on, Bree," Rebecca Nolan sang out. "Our parents will be waiting for us in the hall for the reception. I can't wait to see the cake Mrs. Stephens baked for us." Rebecca looped her arm through Brianna's and pulled her out into the hallway. "Wasn't that a wonderful ceremony? We are now official high school graduates. We have our whole lives ahead of us."

Brianna winced at her friend's enthusiasm. Had it only been a few weeks ago that she'd looked forward to her graduation with such excitement? She pulled herself up straight and drew in a long breath, giving herself a stern lecture. She needed to stop moping over Gilbert Whelan and get on with her life.

Brianna forced a bright smile. "So, what big plans do you have for the future, Becca?"

The girls' shoes tapped over the tiled floor. "I'm going to wait until the summer's over before I make up my mind." She bent her blond head closer to Brianna's. "I'm still hoping Ben Walters will ask to court me. He's been hinting at it, but I think he's too afraid to approach Papa."

"Ben's crazy about you. I can't believe he's taking so long to speak up."

Rebecca sighed. "If he doesn't act before the fall, I guess I'll head off to college. Maybe I can catch myself a college man."

Brianna pressed her lips together to keep a silent scream from coming out. She'd give anything to be in Becca's shoes and have the support of her father to go on to college. But Becca was merely waiting around for Ben.

Why did a woman's life always seem to hinge on the whim of a man?

They came to the room where the principal and the teachers had arranged a reception for the graduates and their families. Somehow Daddy had managed to invite Henry along—a fact that irked Brianna to no end. After all, he wasn't a member of the family, and . . .

It should have been Gil.

She'd always imagined Gil's proud face in the audience when she accepted her diploma. Not Henry's.

Brianna swallowed the ball of emotion that seemed permanently lodged in her throat since Gil's departure. For her mother's sake, she attempted to pull herself together and pasted on a smile as she crossed the room to greet her family.

"Congratulations, darling. We're so proud of you." Her mother hugged her tight, surrounding Brianna with the comforting scent of her perfume.

"Very proud," her father repeated, pressing a quick kiss to the top of her head.

For once, her father seemed pleased with her. Of course he was, since she was doing exactly as he wanted. That wisp of truth stole her fleeting happiness.

Henry came forward and pulled her into an awkward hug. "The next celebration will be our wedding."

Brianna freed herself, shock wiping the smile from her face. "But that won't be for a long time yet."

Her father raised a bushy brow. "Why wait? The sooner the better, I say."

Mama patted Daddy's arm. "James, darling, don't forget how much preparation is involved with a wedding. Especially the type of event you're talking about. Why, the invitations alone could take weeks."

Unease slid along Brianna's spine. "I don't want a big, fancy wedding. A simple ceremony at St. Rita's will suit me fine."

Henry frowned at her. "Between all the O'Learys, the Sullivans, and our combined business associates, it has to be big."

Mama glanced nervously at her and squeezed her arm. "There's no need to discuss this right now. Tonight is about Bree's graduation. Let's all go over and get some of that cake before it disappears."

By the time Brianna returned to Irish Meadows, her nerves were strained to a high pitch. All she wanted was to escape to her room and hide under the quilt until everyone forgot all about wedding plans.

Her parents, however, left her to say a private good night to Henry on the porch. Now that they were officially engaged, her father afforded them a lot more freedom to be alone—a turn of events Brianna did not welcome.

Henry led her to the side of the house where the porch wrapped around the brick wall like a hug. They each took a seat on a wicker chair. The summer night was the perfect temperature, yet despite the warmth, a chill ran through her.

"I can't stay long, Henry. I'm afraid I'm quite exhausted."

"Of course. It's been an exciting day for you." His condescending tone did nothing to endear him to her. "I'll give you a few days to rest before we begin planning our wedding." He reached over to take her hand in his. "Your fingers are like ice."

He massaged her hand with his own, bringing warmth back to her skin. How she wished Gil were holding her hand instead.

Lord, I know I'm supposed to honor my father, but how can I accept Henry when my heart is crying out for Gil?

As soon as she could, she gently disengaged her fingers. The one thought that had circled her brain these last few days came back with a vengeance. Could she marry Henry and still obtain the education she wanted? If that were possible, maybe she could endure this marriage after all.

She bit her lip and glanced at Henry's profile. "Henry, how would you feel about . . . ?" She hesitated.

"About?" He lifted a brow.

"About me going to college after we're married?"

His thunderstruck expression made her hopes sink faster than a horseshoe in a bucket of water.

"Why would you want to go to college? Shouldn't your priority be our marriage?"

She straightened her back against the chair. "One thing doesn't have to contradict the other. You'll be at work all day, and we'll have maids to take care of the household duties. Why couldn't I continue my education?"

He pushed up to pace the length of the porch. "It would be a waste of time and money. What if you found yourself . . . in a family way? You wouldn't be able to keep attending classes."

Heat blazed in her cheeks at the sudden realization of exactly what being married to Henry would entail. The image, so abhorrent, sent her stomach into a spin.

She rose abruptly, nearly stumbling in her haste. "You're probably right. I really must go in now. Thank you again for coming." Eyes averted, she headed toward the front door. She'd taken two steps when he snagged her hand.

"Wait a minute, Brianna."

She looked up in surprise at the bold intention in his pale eyes.

"I think tonight's occasion calls for a more . . . personal farewell." He swept off his hat with one hand and cradled her neck with the other as he lowered his mouth to hers.

Brianna froze, shock stiffening her whole body under his touch. This was not Henry's usual polite peck. This kiss branded her as his possession, demanding a response she could not give. When he pulled back a few seconds later, his expression radiated disappointment. She stepped out of his arms, trying to force down the anxiety clutching her throat. "G-good night, Henry."

Before he could say anything else, she hurried in the front door, hiked her skirts, and ran up the stairs. Once in her bedroom, she closed the door tight and leaned her back against it, the breath heaving in her lungs.

God forgive her, she could not go through with this. She couldn't pretend to feel things she didn't. If she couldn't tolerate Henry's kiss, how would she react on their wedding night? A shudder shook her from head to toe.

Falling to her knees on the carpet by her bed, she poured out fervent prayers to God, begging for His help and for the courage to plan her escape from the undesirable future that awaited her.

The sun had not even peeked over the treetops on Monday morning when Brianna opened her bedroom door. She poked her head into the hallway to make sure no one was about, and then quietly stepped out, closing the door behind her with a soft click.

Valise in hand, she tiptoed down the main staircase to the foyer below. Swallowing her nerves, Brianna laid two envelopes on the hall table—one for her mother and another for Henry.

After two days holed away in her room, thinking and praying, Brianna had come to a decision. She may have lost Gil, but she could not marry Henry.

No matter how much her father wished her to.

Brianna took one last long look around her beloved home, her gaze caressing every cherished nook and cranny. Then, before she could succumb to the fear that clutched her heart like a cold fist, she slipped out the front door.

The walk to the train station gave her time to review each step of her plan. A mixture of anxiety and excitement churned in her veins. For the first time in her life, she was taking action, taking control of her future. In her letter to Henry, she'd politely broken their engagement and wished him well. Perhaps she'd taken the cowardly way out, but she believed if she'd tried to do it face-to-face, she'd have lost her nerve.

When she reached the station, she purchased a ticket to Manhattan, and not long afterward, the first train of the morning pulled up to the platform. The conductor helped her mount the steps to the car, which was almost empty. Brianna had left early to ensure she wouldn't be on the same train as Colleen and Rylan. She remembered they volunteered at the orphanage most Mondays and Wednesdays, and though Colleen likely wouldn't care what she did, Brianna felt sure Rylan would feel obligated to stop her.

As she took her seat, she heaved a sigh of relief. Phase one of her plan had gone exactly as she'd envisioned. An hour later, when the train pulled into the Manhattan station, Brianna shored up her courage and marched into the depot. The clerk at the main desk gave her directions to the streetcar that would take her to the street where Aunt Fiona lived, assuming she hadn't moved.

The trip took less than fifteen minutes. Brianna got off at the stop the clerk had mentioned and headed west, per his instructions. Two blocks later, she came to West 94th Street. Her spirits lifted at the quaint beauty of the houses lining both sides of the street. Most of the residences were tall and narrow, with a set of wide cement stairs leading to the front door.

At her aunt's address, she paused, doubts drowning her certainty. Perhaps she should have called first, but she'd feared Aunt Fiona might seek Daddy's approval before allowing her to come, and she couldn't take that chance.

Squaring her shoulders, Brianna climbed the stairs to the front door and rang the bell. A big-bosomed woman with graying hair opened the door. From the uniform, Brianna guessed this was her aunt's housekeeper.

"Good morning. Is Miss O'Leary at home?"

The woman looked Brianna up and down. "May I ask who's calling?"

"Brianna O'Leary, her niece."

The woman's eyebrows rose above her spectacles. "Is she expecting you, Miss?"

"No." She hesitated. "It's a surprise."

The woman eyed the suitcase on the ground at Brianna's feet, then switched her gaze to Brianna's face, which burned with humiliation.

"Please come in. I'll see if Miss O'Leary is taking visitors at this hour." She didn't bother to hide the disapproval in her tone.

"Thank you." Brianna stepped inside the door, gripping her gloved hands together. The Victorian-style house oozed warmth and charm, and immediately Brianna felt at home. *If only Aunt Fiona is as welcoming . . .*

In the entranceway, she waited patiently until the murmur of voices met her ears, followed by the sound of footsteps on the narrow staircase. Swishing skirts above high-laced shoes came into view. Brianna found herself holding her breath. She hadn't seen Aunt Fiona in more than five years. Rumor had it she and Daddy had had some type of falling out, and her aunt hadn't visited Irish Meadows since.

The stylish woman stood before Brianna in the hallway, her bright blue eyes so much like Daddy's that Brianna's heart bumped with fear. *Please, Lord, let her be sympathetic to my cause.*

"Brianna? Is it really you?" Aunt Fiona rushed forward and enveloped her in a warm hug. "It's so good to see you." She wiped tears from the corner of her eyes. "The last time I saw you, you were a child with your hair in braids. Look at you now, a beautiful young woman."

Brianna laughed. "I don't know about that." She cast an admiring glance at the tall, willowy woman dressed in a fashionable skirt and a lace blouse. "I'm sorry to arrive on your doorstep without calling . . ."

"Don't be silly. I'm delighted to have company." She looked down, noticing the suitcase. Her thin, arched eyebrows rose in question. "Are you planning to stay awhile?"

Brianna hesitated. "If it's all right with you. I need to decide what I'm going to do with my life, and I'm hoping you can help." She raised pleading eyes to her aunt.

Regret and some other emotion passed over Aunt Fiona's fine features. "Does your father know you're here?"

Brianna's knees shook, despite her will to stay strong. "By now he might. I left Mama a note telling her where I was going." She pushed away the thought of her mother's reaction to finding her gone, lest she break down in front of her aunt.

"Oh, my dear girl. Come into the parlor and tell me the whole story."

17

W ILL YOU HELP ME draw a giraffe, Miss O'Leary?"
Delia O'Brien's big blue eyes widened as she waited
for a response.

Colleen crossed the wooden floor of the classroom with a
ready smile. Though she knew little about giraffes, Colleen would
try her best, just to please the girl. In a little over a week, the imp
had captured her affections, becoming almost as dear as her own
little sister. In fact, Colleen wished she could bring Delia home
for a visit, thinking how much she'd love Deirdre and Connor.

"How is that alphabet coming?" Colleen pulled out a tiny
chair and perched beside the eager pupil.

Delia held the end of the nibbed pen to her lips. "I'm all done."

Colleen scanned the row of crooked letter *A*'s and stifled
a grin. "If you finish one more row of letters, we can draw a
giraffe. I'll find some paper to use."

She smiled at the concentration on Delia's face and checked
on the other children as she moved toward the cupboard that
housed the school supplies.

"Miss O'Leary, did you give ink to the younger children?" The sour nature of Sister Marguerite's voice prickled irritation down Colleen's neck.

She schooled her face into a neutral expression. "Yes, Sister, I did."

"We have to use our resources sparingly. The younger ones are much too clumsy. They always waste the ink." Sister Marguerite's face pinched into a wreath of wrinkles under her wimple, as if the material pulled too tight.

Colleen kept her tone even. "I'm sorry, Sister. I didn't realize."

"Make sure you don't make that mistake again."

Colleen returned to Delia, noting the apprehension on all the pupils' faces. Sister Marguerite was no one's favorite as far as Colleen could tell. How such a strict, dour woman had ended up caring for a group of energetic children was beyond Colleen's comprehension. If only the pleasant Sister Veronica had stayed to help, the atmosphere would have been so much nicer.

The clock in the hallway chimed three o'clock. Soon she would have to meet Rylan to leave for the train station.

"It's time to start cleaning up now, children. Put your work on the teacher's desk and go wash your hands."

A loud gasp made Colleen whirl around in time to see a small river of ink spilling across Delia's desk. The girl stood with the inkpot clutched in her stained hands, panic on her stricken face. Colleen grabbed some loose sheets of paper and rushed to blot the stream before Sister Marguerite could notice it dripping onto the floor.

"I'm sorry." Tears appeared in Delia's wide eyes.

"Don't worry, sweetie. It was an accident." Colleen scrambled to mop up the mess, but two big splats landed on the polished hardwood floor. "Oh, saints alive."

"Miss O'Leary!" The horrified voice of Sister Marguerite screeched across the room.

Colleen froze, wads of crumpled, ink-stained paper in her

hands. She tried to calm the trepidation that crawled up her spine, as though *she* were the child in trouble once again.

"We had a bit of an accident here, Sister. Could you call the caretaker, please?"

Sister Marguerite's beady eyes bored into Colleen. "Who is responsible for this mess?"

Colleen moved to conceal Delia, who cowered behind her out of the nun's immediate sight. "It's my fault for bringing the ink out. I'll pay to replace it."

"Who spilled the pot?" Sister Marguerite peered around Colleen. Her face hardened when she saw the girl standing with the evidence still in her hand. "Delia O'Brien. You know the punishment for wasting supplies."

The girl's tears flowed freely down her cheeks. "I didn't mean to," she whimpered.

"Put that inkpot down at once and get the cane."

Rylan jumped down from the ladder and stood back to survey his handiwork. The girls' dormitory looked much cheerier now, painted a soft yellow. Even better than the boys' room, which he'd painted a bright blue last week. He gathered his supplies and moved them out into the corridor, leaving the ladder against the wall. With quick movements, he retrieved the paint can and the dirty brushes and carried them downstairs to the utility room.

The grandfather clock in the main entranceway bonged out three chimes. He'd have to hurry if he and Colleen wanted to make the afternoon train back to Long Island.

Ten minutes later, hands and face as freshly scrubbed as the paintbrushes, Rylan whistled a tune as he bounded up the stairs to the main floor. Colleen was not waiting for him in their usual spot by the reception area. With a grin, he changed direction and headed toward the classroom, hoping to catch Colleen interacting with the children.

Fortunately, the wooden door stood slightly ajar, allowing him to peek inside. The sight that greeted him, however, wiped the grin off his face. Sister Marguerite stood at the front of the classroom, making angry gestures with a cane before an obviously incensed Colleen. Little Delia, her tiny hands covered in ink, cowered sobbing behind Colleen's skirts. The other children huddled together at the far end of the room, as though fearing the punishment may extend to them, as well.

Colleen fisted her hands on her hips. "Touch that child one more time, Sister, and you'll be meeting Jesus a lot sooner than you expected."

Rylan choked back a half-laugh, half-gasp at the expression of shock on the nun's face, and stepped into the room. "Ladies, what seems to be the problem?" He didn't really need to ask. There was enough ink on Colleen's hands and apron to tell the tale.

She whirled to face him, eyes blazing. "This woman is beating little Delia because of an accident."

Lord, a little help here would be appreciated. Though he tended to agree with Colleen and didn't uphold the beating of small children, he was loathe to challenge the older nun's authority. "Now, Sister, surely we can come up with a suitable consequence that doesn't involve"—he cast a stern look at the instrument in her hand—"caning a child."

Her face turned a mottled purple. "How dare you criticize the way I run this institution."

Rylan pasted on his most charming smile and laid a calming hand on the nun's shoulder. "I see how much responsibility you have here, Sister, and how well you take care of these children."

She relaxed a fraction of an inch, but her mouth remained pinched.

"And I understand the need for strict discipline to keep the asylum running smoothly."

Her shoulder stiffened under his hand as she straightened. "We are doing God's work here, Mr. Montgomery."

"Of course you are." He deftly removed the cane from her hand. "You and the other sisters are doing an amazing job. I'm sure you must find it overwhelming at times. Tell me, do you ever have a day off?"

She blinked like a wizened owl behind her spectacles. "We do not take time off. This is our vocation."

With one hand behind his back, he motioned for Colleen to get Delia out of the way. At the same time, he smiled into the nun's eyes. "What would you do if you had a whole day to yourself with no responsibilities?"

Her mouth fell open, as though she'd never entertained the possibility. "I . . . I suppose I'd spend the day in Central Park."

"Aye, that sounds lovely. I will make it my personal mission to arrange a day off for all of the nuns working here." He smiled at her stunned expression. "Just give me time to line up some volunteers, and we'll make it happen."

She sank onto the chair by the front desk. "I don't see how. Where would you find enough volunteers?" she asked weakly.

"Leave that to me, Sister. In the meantime, if you'd be so kind as to ask the caretaker to clean up the desk and floor, Miss O'Leary and I will be on our way."

"Of course." She rose and headed to the door, then turned back. "Thank you, Mr. Montgomery."

"My pleasure, to be sure."

Seated on the train several minutes later, Colleen stuffed her blackened hands under her skirts. She could hear her father's admonition now. "Ladies never get their hands soiled. And they certainly don't yell at nuns."

She released a weary sigh. She did not regret saving Delia from the punishment Sister Marguerite had begun to inflict. She only wished she'd done it with a bit more grace, without losing her temper in the process.

"Don't worry. That ink will wash off with a good scrub of lye."

Her gaze flew to the amused grin on Rylan Montgomery's cheeky face. He had an uncanny way of always knowing what she was thinking.

She scowled at him. "How do you always stay so calm?"

Amusement softened his eyes to melted chocolate. "The blessing of an easygoing nature . . . and a wagon-load of prayer."

She lowered her gaze back to her lap. He'd been so supportive of her during the whole fiasco, never once admonishing her for her rudeness to Sister Marguerite. Regret sat heavy on her shoulders. "I'm sorry if I caused any problems for you with the nuns."

"What problems?"

She ignored his attempt at a joke. "I suppose they won't let me come back now that I've proven to be an unsuitable volunteer."

Why did that thought make her heart ache? Two weeks ago, she would have plotted just such an incident to get out of going. Now all she could think of was Delia's disappointment when she didn't return. Who would look out for the girl? Keep her safe from Sister Marguerite's dire discipline?

Rylan's warm hand settled on her arm, sending tremors through her body. "It'll take more than one ink spill for them to refuse a volunteer. They're rather short-handed, in case you hadn't noticed." He gave her that cocky grin she'd started to find endearing. "Besides, I need your help with the children on Saturday so the sisters can have the day off I promised."

Surprising tears sprang to her eyes, but she forced them back. What was the matter with her lately? Other than the day her little brother had died, Colleen could count on one hand the number of times she'd cried. Tears were a useless waste of time. Besides, they made her eyes puffy and turned her nose red.

"You will help me, won't you?" Rylan asked. "After all, I did save you from the wrath of Sister Marguerite."

A weak laugh escaped before she could stop it. "I suppose I could spare the time."

Really, what else did she have to do? For some reason, the endless rounds of parties, balls, and social activities she'd been used to now left her cold. Even the lure of rich, eligible men didn't hold the appeal it once had.

She bit her lip, hands clenched under her skirts. "Rylan, could I ask you something?"

"Of course."

"Do . . . do you think I'm going to hell?"

He raised one dark brow. "Well now, I guess that depends on the terrible things you've done. I know you threatened the life of that poor nun today." A teasing glint shone in his eyes.

"I'm serious." She looked away. "I haven't been a very nice person. You know what I did to Jared and Gil. It's not the first time I've used someone to get what I want." Heat spread over her cheeks as the secret she'd never told anyone intruded on her thoughts. Could Rylan absolve her of that long-held guilt? Already she felt changed from her dealings with him and the orphans. What was it about Rylan that made her question her plans for the future?

She heard him release a quiet sigh and glanced up through her lashes. He said nothing at first, simply staring out the window as the train clacked down the line. After a few seconds, he trained his earnest brown eyes on her.

"You're a girl becoming a woman, and you've likely made a few mistakes along the way. You've not done anything so terrible that God wouldn't forgive." In his earnestness, he leaned toward her. "God loves you no matter what, Colleen. Turn to Him, ask His forgiveness, and seek to do better. That's all He wants."

A lump of emotion balled in Colleen's throat. Hot tears burned the back of her eyes. Could it really be so simple? "Will you . . . could you show me how to do that?"

A smile spread over his face. Gently, he reached for one of her stained hands and folded it within the warmth of his fingers. "It would be my pleasure. Why don't we start with a short prayer?"

For the first time since she was a child, Colleen bowed her head and moved her lips in heartfelt words of repentance, followed by praise for God's great mercy.

18

LATE MONDAY AFTERNOON, Gil knocked on the
door to Mr. Hastings's office, trying to keep his trepidation at bay. He prayed he'd not made some terrible
mistake with the bank's money.

"Come in."

Gil stepped inside. "You wanted to see me, sir?"

"Yes, Gilbert. Have a seat. I've had a telephone call from
James O'Leary with a message for you."

Alarm shot through Gil's system as he sank to the chair. The
stuffy air in the room added to the perspiration that trailed down
his back. "Nothing's wrong, I hope."

Lines bracketed Arthur Hastings's mouth. "It's about his
daughter, Brianna."

Gil felt the blood drain away from his face. He was grateful
he was already sitting or his legs would have buckled. "What
about her?"

"It appears she's run away."

Gil's mouth gaped open. A thousand dark thoughts raced

167

through his mind. What would make Bree do something so drastic? "How do they know this?"

"She left a note for her mother saying she'd gone to stay with an aunt in the city. Apparently, James's sister lives here in Manhattan." Arthur pushed a piece of paper across the desk. "He tried telephoning her house, but he only got the housekeeper, who refused to give out any information. James wants you to go and check with the aunt to make sure Brianna is really there. This is the address."

Gil took the paper and tried to focus on the words dancing before him. "Do they know why Brianna left so suddenly?"

Arthur shook his head. "I'm afraid not. James did say the whole family had been at her graduation a few days before and that she'd locked herself in her room all weekend, claiming illness. Then this morning, she was gone." Arthur steepled his hands together. "He also said she left a note for her fiancé, but the man refused to tell them what it said."

Gil jerked from his chair and paced to the credenza. For Bree to leave her family, something serious must have happened. Guilt wound its way around Gil's neck, choking his airway. Did Gil's departure have anything to do with it? He dragged loose his tie and opened the top button of his shirt.

Behind his desk, Arthur rose, as well. "Why don't you leave now, son? I doubt you'll get any work done until you find her."

Gil nodded. "Thank you, sir. I think I will."

Please, Lord, let her be safe at her aunt's.

Twenty minutes later, Gil climbed the stairs to the door at 402 West 94th Street. The walk from the streetcar in the fresh afternoon air had helped ease his nerves. That and the multitude of prayers he'd recited on his way. He knocked and waited until a plump, stern-faced housekeeper opened the door.

"Good afternoon. I'm looking for Miss Fiona O'Leary."

The woman scowled. "Isn't everyone today?" Then she opened the door wider. "Whom shall I say is calling?"

"Mr. Gilbert Whelan."

"Wait here."

Gil removed his cap and scanned his surroundings while he waited. It appeared James's sister had done well for herself despite having never married. The house was tasteful and elegant, with high ceilings and ornate woodwork.

A few moments later, a tall, well-dressed woman appeared in the hall. Gil could see a definite resemblance to her brother in the high cheekbones, blue eyes, and regal bearing. Where James was dark-haired, however, his sister had inherited the trademark Irish auburn hair, which she wore in a loose topknot. He vaguely remembered her visiting Irish Meadows years ago after the O'Learys had become his guardians.

"Gilbert Whelan?" She wore a smile of welcome as she approached him. "Why, I haven't seen you since you were barely out of short pants." She held out a hand to him. "You've grown into a fine young man, I see."

He smiled in return. "Thank you, Miss O'Leary. It's good to see you again."

"Please, call me Aunt Fiona. Won't you come into the parlor?"

Gil bit back his impatience and followed her down the tiled hall, their footsteps the only sound in the house. They entered a warm, Victorian-style parlor furnished with two large sofas and bookshelves filled to capacity. In one corner, a white birdcage housed a pair of colorful birds that darted from perch to perch.

Gil waited for Aunt Fiona to choose a seat and then sat down on the edge of the gold settee. The glow from a lamp created highlights on Aunt Fiona's hair, reminding him so much of Brianna that his chest ached.

"I think I know why you're here," she said without preamble. "James sent you, didn't he?"

"Yes. He's worried about Brianna." Gil leaned forward, hands over his knees. "She *is* here, isn't she?"

"Yes. She arrived early this morning."

"Is she all right?"

"Physically she's fine. Emotionally, well . . . that's harder to determine."

She shot him a piercing look that made Gil squirm on the cushioned seat. Had Brianna told her aunt what had happened between them? Best turn the attention elsewhere.

"Does this have anything to do with Bree's fiancé?"

"That is none of your business, Gilbert Whelan."

The ice-cold fury in Brianna's voice struck Gil like a slap to the face. He shot to his feet and turned to find a very angry female standing in the arched doorway.

"Brianna." His mind went blank at the sight of her. Though it had only been a few weeks, it seemed like months since he'd seen her. She appeared thinner, her eyes shadowed by purple smudges—small signs hinting at her unhappiness.

She marched farther into the room, hands on the hips of her striped skirt. "What are you doing here?"

He swallowed his dismay at her obvious displeasure, wishing for their usual hug of greeting. "Your father asked me to make sure you were here."

She glared at him. "Well, you've done your duty. Feel free to report back to the general."

Aunt Fiona cleared her throat. "Why don't I see about some refreshments?"

When Bree gave a clipped nod, her aunt quietly left the room.

Bree made no move to sit down, so Gil remained standing awkwardly by the sofa. "Why are you doing this, Bree? Running away and upsetting the whole family."

She crossed her arms in front of her and tilted her chin. "I'm taking your advice."

"*My* advice?"

"You told me I should live my own life and not blindly follow what my father wanted me to do." A fierce frown puckered her brow over the vivid greenness of her eyes.

Gil stepped toward her, approaching her as he would an unstable filly. He was not at all sure how to handle this angry, defiant Brianna. "What made you decide to leave? Did something happen at your graduation?"

A wave of hurt passed over her features before her expression hardened. "Nothing happened—except I realized I had my whole future ahead of me—and I did not want to marry Henry."

Shock made him startle. "Did you tell him that in your letter?" Her answer shouldn't matter to him, yet he found a bubble of hope rising through him.

"That's between Henry and me." She stalked across the room to the window and moved the white lace curtain aside to stare out.

The caged birds squawked and flapped their wings, as though agitated by their heated words.

Gil swiped a hand over his jaw. He had no real right to interfere in her life, but he needed to know she was all right. He came up behind her and placed a tentative hand on her shoulder.

She flinched and whirled around, anger glinting in her eyes. "Don't you dare touch me, Gilbert Whelan. You have no right."

His heart sank like a stone. He'd lost her. Lost her friendship and her trust. He'd destroyed everything when he'd left. "I'm sorry." He shoved his hands into his pockets, attempting to push back the tides of emotion raging through him. He had no say in what she did with her life now. Whether she went back home, whether she married Henry, or whether she lived with her aunt. But he couldn't stop himself from asking, "What will you do now, Bree?"

She moved away from him. "I want to enroll at Barnard College in the fall."

So she was going after her dream despite her father's opposition. Her bravery only increased his admiration for her. "What about the tuition? I doubt your father will fund it."

"Aunt Fiona is going to try and persuade him to change his mind. If not, I'll figure something out. I'll get a job if I have to."

He raised a brow. "You're really serious about this?"

"Of course I am."

Gil frowned at a sudden thought. The women's college was only blocks from the bank. Brianna would be close by, a fact he found both comforting and disturbing. He shifted from one foot to the other as a certain awkwardness set in. "Will you at least let your parents know you're all right?"

Her features softened with regret, and she nodded. "I'll ask Aunt Fiona to call. If I hear Mama's voice, I may give in and go home." Her unhappiness shimmered in the air around them like the afternoon sun flickering through the sheer curtains.

The desire to pull her into his arms became a physical ache. "If you ever need me for anything, I'm staying at Mrs. Shaughnessy's boarding house on Amsterdam Avenue, Room 212." He waited until she met his gaze. "Despite everything, Bree, I hope we'll always be friends."

Moisture gleamed in those amazing green eyes. The ones that haunted him each night as he stared at the cracks in the ceiling of his room.

"I hope so too, Gil." She bit down on her bottom lip, and he knew she was trying desperately to contain her emotions.

If only things could be different between them.

He took a deliberate step back. "Take care of yourself."

"I will."

He picked up his hat from the settee, and with a last long look at her, he turned and strode out of the room.

"I spoke to your father last night." Aunt Fiona dabbed a napkin to her lips the next morning at breakfast.

Brianna glanced up from her plate. What little appetite she had left after the shock of seeing Gil yesterday vanished at the mere mention of her father. "What did Daddy say?"

"As you can guess, he wants you to come home." Her aunt

gave a soft sigh. "I don't know why my brother feels the need to control everyone around him. Why he can't just let them live their lives."

Brianna sensed Aunt Fiona wasn't talking only about the present situation. Had Daddy tried to control his sister's life, as well?

"Did you ask him about college?"

Aunt Fiona folded her napkin beside her plate. "Yes. And I'm afraid the answer is still no."

Brianna held back a groan of frustration and took a quick swallow of coffee. The strong liquid helped restore her equilibrium, and determination quickly set in. It didn't matter what her father said. She would find a way to go to school on her own. All she needed was a job to earn her tuition.

"Auntie, would you be able to help me find a position somewhere? I need to make money for tuition, as well as pay you room and board—if you don't mind me staying here, that is."

Aunt Fiona blinked over her raised china cup. "My dear, I think we'd best have a chat before any final decisions are made."

Brianna gripped a napkin between her fingers. What if Aunt Fiona took Daddy's side and refused to help her? All Brianna could do was hear her out and hope to persuade her aunt to see her point of view.

Aunt Fiona drained her cup and rose. "Let's sit in the parlor where we can be more comfortable."

Brianna followed her down the hall. They both took seats on the settee, where the morning sun added a cheeriness to the homey room. Right away the soothing atmosphere put Brianna at ease. Even her aunt's birds dozed quietly in their cage.

Aunt Fiona sat primly, her back straight, hands folded together in her lap. "I haven't told many people about my younger years, but since I can't help noticing a distinct similarity to our lives, I hope hearing my tale will assist you in making an informed decision about your future."

Curiosity spiked Brianna's attention. She turned to face her aunt more fully.

"First I need to ask you a few questions, and I want honest answers." Her normally mild aunt suddenly looked fierce.

Brianna swallowed. "Of course."

"You told me you broke off your engagement because you could never marry someone you didn't love."

Brianna nodded. "Henry is nice enough, but his touch made me . . . shiver—and not in a good way."

A soft smile touched her aunt's lips. "I think I understand." She paused. "What I did notice, however, was your strong reaction to Gilbert when he was here. Am I correct in thinking there are unrequited feelings involved?"

Brianna quickly lowered her head. How she wished she could keep her emotions contained—like her sister who never blinked an eyelash without complete control. She supposed there was no reason to hide the truth from her aunt. "I'm in love with Gil, Auntie."

There. She'd said it out loud. And the roof hadn't caved in.

"Does he feel the same?" her aunt prompted, eyebrows raised.

"I think so. But he won't act on it because of Daddy." She swallowed hard to push back a wave of hurt.

Her aunt pursed her lips. "I see. Your father doesn't approve of Gil as a match for you."

She shook her head. "Daddy's only concern is money or social position." She pulled a handkerchief from her pocket and gripped it in her fist. "He doesn't care about my feelings at all."

Her aunt's features became wreathed in sadness. "I understand more than you know," she said softly. "I had a suitor once when I was young. Because our father was dead, James took it upon himself to act as head of the family, and thus my protector. He deemed Martin unworthy of me and forbade us to see each other."

"What did you do?"

"A very foolish thing. I engaged in a clandestine relationship with Martin, until . . ." Her aunt's voice faltered. "Until I found myself expecting a child."

Brianna gasped. She couldn't imagine her father's reaction to that news. "How awful. Why didn't Martin marry you? Surely Daddy wouldn't have objected with a child on the way."

Fiona smiled sadly. "It turned out Martin was not free to marry me. He already had a wife."

Brianna's heart clenched in sympathy for her aunt's pain. Betrayed by the man she loved. Alone and expecting a child. "What did you do?"

"Something even worse." She took a deep breath. "Seeing no way out, I tried to end my life." Moisture rimmed her aunt's eyes, though her gaze did not falter. "My attempt was unsuccessful. I lived . . . but my baby died."

Tears trailed down Brianna's cheeks. She dabbed at them with her handkerchief, and Aunt Fiona patted her arm.

"It's all right, child. I've made peace with all this many years ago. God has forgiven me, and I finally learned to forgive myself. The hardest thing was admitting James had been right about Martin all along. However, by that time it was too late. I was a fallen woman with no hope for a husband. So I enrolled in college and threw all my passion into furthering women's education."

Brianna admired her aunt's bravery, coming back from such tragic circumstances and making a life for herself as a well-respected teacher.

Aunt Fiona squeezed Brianna's hand. "I've told you all this to show you how quickly life can change. Doors once open to you may close forever. At this point, my dear, you still have all your options open. Are you absolutely sure this is the path you wish to take?"

Brianna twisted the handkerchief in her hand. "I'm sure. I want to study Library Sciences and maybe teach after that, or become a librarian."

"But what about a husband? A family? Surely you want children someday."

Brianna pushed back a clutch of sorrow and lifted her chin. "If I can't have Gil, I don't want anyone. At least not now. Perhaps in time I may reconsider. But I cannot marry a man just to please my father."

Her aunt studied her, and at last she nodded. "Very well. Here's what I propose. You will live here with me, help me with my charity work for the summer, and attend classes at Barnard College in the fall. We'll have to put in your application right away. I will use my connections, if I must, to get your application approved."

"But what about the cost?"

Aunt Fiona waved a hand in front of her. "Thanks to my mother's will, I live a comfortable life. I would consider it an honor to pay your tuition. How wonderful that another O'Leary woman will enter the academic world."

Overwhelmed by her aunt's generosity, the tension drained out of Brianna. "How can I ever thank you?"

"No thanks necessary, my dear. I'm delighted to have you here."

Brianna leaned over to hug her aunt, grateful for an ally who understood her plight. For the first time, Brianna felt she held the power over her future.

She only prayed she was headed down the path God had intended for her.

19

RYLAN WAITED FOR COLLEEN in the parlor early Saturday morning, happy she seemed eager to spend the day with the orphans. Rylan hoped a holiday would go far in softening Sister Marguerite's hostility toward Colleen, who had even arranged to have Mrs. Harrison bake some of her melt-in-your-mouth scones for the nuns to enjoy on their outing. An effort to make amends for losing her temper, he was sure.

Rylan still could not believe the subtle changes he'd witnessed in Colleen over the past few weeks since they'd started volunteering at St. Rita's.

Thank You, Lord, for using me as an instrument in bringing Colleen to know Your saving grace.

Times like this reaffirmed Rylan's decision to enter the religious life, a choice he secretly questioned in rare moments of weakness. Memories of his mother lying ill with pneumonia came back to haunt him. The doctor had told Rylan and his siblings that only a miracle could cure his mother's weakened lungs. Desperate to save their one living parent, Rylan had pleaded with God, offering his life in return for hers. Entering the seminary seemed a small price to pay when his mother regained her health and became well enough to look after wee Maggie. Most days, Rylan felt fulfilled in his choice of career, yet sometimes he wondered what it would be like to fall in love.

Noises in the corridor had Rylan moving to the door of the parlor in time to see Colleen gliding down the stairs, humming to herself. Clad in a lavender-striped gown with a white collar, she stopped at the foot of the stairs to peer at her reflection in the mirror. Rylan stilled, hand on the doorframe, watching as she patted her upswept hair and poked a pin back in place. She turned away from the mirror to tug on little white gloves, still humming under her breath. In that unguarded moment, her inner purity shone in the soft expression of her face, over-powering her physical beauty by far. Rylan started at the sudden realization that most times Colleen wore a polite mask, hiding her true self from those around her. Was she even aware she did so?

He hated to make his presence known and watch the mask slip back into place, but he knew he must. He stepped into the foyer. "Good morning, Colleen. You sound happy this fine day."

She whirled around, hand to her throat. "Rylan. I didn't see you there." Her eyes widened. "Where's your clergy outfit?"

He glanced down at his plaid vest and brown wool pants and shrugged. "Since I'm not visiting in an official capacity today, I thought I'd dress in a more casual manner."

"Oh." A frown tugged her thin eyebrows together.

He tried to imagine what was going through her mind and why she cared whether he wore his collar or not. He actually thought she'd feel more comfortable around him without it, since members of the clergy seemed to put her in an ill humor. "If it bothers you, I can change."

The mask slipped back over her features as she lifted a brow. "Suit yourself. Why would I care what you wear?"

The deliberate chill in her voice sparked the heat of temper in him. He moved a step closer, irritation spiking his pulse. "Why indeed?" He imagined his outdated clothes were not as fashionable as what she was used to. "Are you ashamed to be seen with me?"

She lowered her eyes and flushed scarlet, but she remained silent.

"Don't worry. If anyone asks, you can tell them I'm a poor relation. I'm sure they'll take pity on you for having to put up with the likes of me." He hated the bitterness in his voice. Hated even more the fact that he wished he could be the finest dressed gentleman escorting her about town.

What was the matter with him? As a priest, he would have no need for fine clothing or the pride that went along with owning such items. And he certainly shouldn't be thinking about escorting a woman anywhere.

Without waiting for her, he grabbed his cap from the hook by the door and pushed out onto the porch.

She'd offended him.

Yet how could she tell him she felt safer when he was dressed as a clergyman? That when he looked so handsome and available in regular clothes, she allowed her mind to wander to places it shouldn't?

Colleen stifled a nervous laugh. Of all the irony. She, the girl who'd planned to marry the richest, most attractive man in town, was falling for a poor country priest. Tears gathered in the corners of her eyes. Was this some type of terrible punishment? God's wrath upon her for all the horrible things she'd done in her life?

She swiped angrily at the moisture under her eyes, pinned on her stylish hat adorned with purple ribbons, and followed Rylan out the door. The apology she'd been so desperate to impart a moment ago faded into oblivion. No, best that he remain mad at her. Thought her to be the vain and selfish woman she knew herself to be. That way she could avoid any temptation to fall completely in love with the unattainable clergyman.

Despite the bad beginning to the day and the almost silent train ride, Colleen enjoyed her time with the orphans—especially without the disdainful eye of Sister Marguerite watching her every move. Though Rylan treated her with cool aloofness, he was warm and energetic with the children. Following morning prayers, the children enjoyed packing a picnic lunch with the help of Mrs. Norton, the cook, who, along with Mr. Smith, the caretaker, had agreed to accompany them to the local park.

After a bracing walk, they made their way to the children's playground. The little ones whooped with glee upon spying the recently built swings, slide, and seesaws. Colleen found her spirits soaring as high as the swings. Much to her joy, little Delia insisted on Colleen accompanying her everywhere. She pushed the child on the swing, held her on the seesaw, and caught her as she came rushing down the slide, curls flying behind her. The happiness shining on the girl's precious face made each moment worthwhile.

When they had finished their picnic, the tired group headed back to the orphanage, the older children helping the younger ones. Delia became so weary that Colleen had to carry her most of the way back. The feel of those tiny arms wrapped around her neck and the golden-curled head bobbing on her shoulder tugged at Colleen's heartstrings. Never did she imagine becoming so affected by a child. Most times, she found children loud and annoying. But this imp had wormed her way past all Colleen's defenses.

Colleen carried Delia upstairs to the girls' dormitory and

laid her sleeping figure on the bed. After ensuring the other girls were settled, Colleen returned to Delia and removed her shoes, frowning at the worn soles. Then she tucked Mr. Whiskers, Delia's tattered stuffed rabbit, beside her and smoothed the hair back from her innocent face. A sudden surge of love rose in Colleen's chest—one so strong she had to choke back tears. This darling girl deserved a mother to kiss her good night, to sing to her, to read her bedtime stories. To brush her hair and buy her new shoes and make sure she got plenty to eat. Colleen pressed a fist to her mouth to stifle the sob threatening to burst forth.

God, where are You for these children who need families? Why did You take away their parents in the first place?

She knelt on the floor beside the bed, lay her head on the lumpy mattress, and let her tears fall.

No matter how hard Rylan tried to hold on to his anger, he couldn't stay mad at Colleen. Although he'd kept his distance most of the day, he couldn't help but admire her enthusiasm with the children during their outing. She seemed to enjoy herself immensely, playing like she was still a child herself.

A strong sense of guilt niggled at him, however, because of some information he'd become privy to the previous day. Sister Veronica had told him in confidence that negotiations were underway for Delia's imminent adoption. He huffed out a sigh. What would her departure do to Colleen?

Rylan made sure all the boys were settled in the dorm for their afternoon rest period, then headed to the floor below to check on the girls. Colleen stepped into the corridor before he reached the door.

"Everyone accounted for?"

"Yes." She kept her face averted as she turned in the direction of the stairs.

He placed a hand on her arm to stop her and peered at her face. Her eyes were red-rimmed and puffy. "Is everything all right in there?"

"Everything's fine." She pulled her arm away and continued down the hall.

He stopped her again, not willing to let her get away with the fib. "You've been crying. Obviously something's wrong."

"The wind blew sand in my eyes at the playground. It's nothing." She tried to move past him, but he blocked her path, placing gentle but firm hands on her shoulders.

"Lying to a man of God is a sin, Colleen O'Leary. I want the truth."

She stilled, her eyes cast down at the patterned carpet. He tipped her chin up, and the sorrow shining there stalled his breath.

"It's so sad, Rylan. Those poor children have no families to love them."

The sight of more tears blooming in her violet-blue eyes caused his chest to constrict. Without thinking, he pulled her into a light hug, wanting only to soothe her hurt. "Aye. That's the drawback of helping out in an orphanage. You see a lot of sad cases."

He pulled a handkerchief from his pants pocket and handed it to her. She took it and dabbed her damp cheeks, still standing close enough for her lavender scent to envelop him.

"I wish I could take Delia home with me. Do you think Mama and Daddy would consider adopting her?"

His spirits plummeted even further. Colleen's attachment to the girl was worse than he'd feared. Still, he couldn't break a confidence and reveal that Delia may already belong to another family. Yet he couldn't afford to let Colleen get her hopes up either. "I think your parents may be over the age requirement," he said softly. "They usually place children with younger parents."

He braced himself for more tears. But she sniffed and handed him back the handkerchief. "Do you think anyone will ever adopt Delia?"

Heat scratched the back of his neck. Why did it feel like he was lying by not telling her about the adoption? "I've no doubt some lucky couple will snap her up soon enough."

She let out a long breath. "I hope so. Delia deserves it."

"Aye. I hope so, too."

20

GIL SAT AT HIS DESK in the bank, reentering figures on the adding machine. He jotted the total on the ledger beside him, his head jerking up when he heard Mr. Hastings's office door open. James O'Leary had been in a meeting with the bank manager for almost an hour now, most likely applying for that loan. Gil wanted to speak to James before he left, so he quickly set aside his pen and made his way to the area outside Mr. Hastings's office.

"I hope you can make a quick decision on that loan, Arthur," he overheard James say as he stepped out the door. "Time is of the essence, as you know."

Arthur nodded. "I'll have an answer within the week. In the meantime, I hope to see you at our Independence Day party Saturday night. You and Kathleen will be there, won't you?"

"Wouldn't miss it." James shook Arthur's hand, and then his attention fell on Gil. "Gilbert, good to see you, son."

"Hello, Mr. O'Leary. Do you have a minute before you leave?"

"Of course."

Arthur stepped forward. "Why don't you use my office? I'm taking a short break anyway."

"Thank you, sir." Gil led the way into the office and closed the door with a soft click.

"How is the family doing?" Gil asked after they'd each chosen a chair. It seemed ages since he'd had word of the O'Learys, and he missed them all something fierce.

"Everyone is fine. Except, of course, Brianna." James sighed. "Kathleen is taking this very hard. With you and Brianna gone, she hasn't been herself."

"So Bree is still living with your sister?"

Under his bushy mustache, James's mouth became a grim line. "Unfortunately, yes. Fiona has taken Brianna on as her new cause of the day. The two of them have conspired against me and refuse to do my bidding." He scowled. "Don't think I'm not tempted to swoop in and kidnap my own daughter. If things don't change soon, I may do just that."

Gil shook his head. "Brianna is an adult now," he said quietly. "Though I may not agree with the way she handled this, I do believe she has the right to choose her own life."

James leaned forward. His hard blue eyes pierced Gil's. "You haven't gone back on your word, I hope. You've stayed away from my daughter—now that she's broken her engagement?"

Gil met his stare. "I said I wouldn't go against your wishes, and I meant it."

James huffed. "Thank goodness someone still has the good sense God gave them. I thank you for your loyalty, Gilbert. Speaking of which, I have one more request."

Gil's stomach turned queasy. *What now?*

"I trust you'll be attending the Hastings soirée on Saturday?"

"Yes, I'm escorting Aurora."

"Excellent. I need you to announce your betrothal that night."

The blood drained from Gil's face, leaving him light-headed.

"Arthur is making a decision on my loan application this

week. If you and Aurora become engaged, it will go a long way toward him approving my financing."

James couldn't be serious. Gil had been seeing Aurora for only a few weeks now. "We're nowhere near that point, sir. I . . . we haven't even kissed yet."

"Well, what are you waiting for? Move this romance along. Take her out to dinner tonight. Propose . . . or at least ask Arthur for her hand." He patted Gil's leg. "Time is running out for Irish Meadows. I'm counting on you, son."

Gil ran his tongue over his dry lips. "Are you saying you expect me to marry her?"

James's eyes narrowed. "Once I acquire the funds I need, you can do whatever you like. Though I'd think long and hard before letting a fine girl like Aurora get away."

Sweat beaded on Gil's forehead. He'd grown genuinely fond of the girl and hated that this plan would hurt her.

Turmoil swirled in Gil's gut. Loyalty to James warred with his principles. Brianna had found the courage to defy her father. Why couldn't he do the same?

James leaned closer, as though sensing Gil's misgivings. "I know you wouldn't want to see Kathleen and the children lose their home. The home you grew up in, as well."

Gil met his troubled gaze. "It's that bad?"

"Do you think I'd be taking such drastic measures if it weren't?" Heavy lines crisscrossed James's forehead.

"No, sir." Despite Mr. O'Leary's flaws, Gil had always found him to be a moral man. The finances must be a lot worse off than Gil's few perusals of the ledgers had revealed. Could Gil stand by and do nothing while the O'Learys lost Irish Meadows? He could only imagine Brianna's pain at such an occurrence. It would kill her to lose her childhood home and her beloved horses.

Gil squared his shoulders. He may never become Brianna's husband, but he could do this one thing to help her family hold on to their legacy.

James rose and squeezed Gil's shoulder. "So I'll see you on Saturday?"

Gil swallowed his reservations and nodded. "See you then."

As he accompanied James to the door, Gil tried very hard not to imagine the disillusionment on Bree's face when she heard the news of his engagement.

❧

"Today we are going to volunteer at the orphanage." Aunt Fiona's announcement preceded her entrance into the parlor, where Brianna sat reading her Bible.

Brianna's pulse quickened. Could it be the same place her sister and Rylan visited twice weekly? She hoped not, since she still hadn't forgiven Colleen for the stunt she'd pulled with Gil on the night of Brianna's birthday party. "Which orphanage is that, Auntie?"

Fiona adjusted the angle of the birdcage. "St. Rita's. The nuns there do an excellent job with the children."

Brianna's stomach dropped. She tried to come up with a reason to avoid going, but nothing came to mind. She closed her book and rose. "What will we do there?"

"Usually I help serve the children's lunch and then assist with the cleanup."

Brianna nodded, not wishing to dampen her aunt's enthusiasm. If she ran into her sister, she'd have to deal with it. They moved into the hallway to retrieve their wraps.

"I should tell you that we may run into Colleen and Cousin Rylan. Daddy is making Colleen volunteer there as a punishment."

Her aunt's eyebrow rose above the spectacles she often wore. "Whatever did Colleen do to warrant that?"

Brianna pinned on her hat with unsteady fingers. "She kissed Gilbert to force her intended into breaking their engagement. Daddy decided she needed to learn a lesson about the important things in life."

"Indeed." Her aunt's lips lifted. "I wonder if it's working."

Brianna refrained from snorting in an unladylike fashion. Only a miracle could get Colleen to change her ways.

It didn't take them long on the streetcar to reach the orphan asylum. Brianna was amazed at the size of the building. She'd pictured something much smaller.

They climbed the stairs and entered the front door, stopping at the cloakroom to remove their hat, gloves, and wrap. At a reception desk, Aunt Fiona paused to greet a middle-aged woman seated there.

"Good day, Mrs. Taft. This is my niece, Miss Brianna O'Leary, who is staying with me for a while."

The woman's eyes widened. "My, we are overrun with O'Learys around here lately." She chuckled. "The more the merrier, I always say."

"May I give Brianna a quick tour? She's never been here before."

"Certainly. The children are in the common room right now for a short prayer service. I'll let Mrs. Norton know you're here to help with lunch."

Brianna followed her aunt down the main corridor, their footsteps hushed by the diamond-patterned carpet that ran the length of the hallway. Along the way, they peered into two different classrooms. Brianna was impressed with how well-equipped and tidy the rooms appeared. Near the end of the corridor, Aunt Fiona pressed a finger to her lips and motioned for Brianna to follow her into a large room.

Children of various ages occupied a circle of chairs surrounding Cousin Rylan, who sat with his hands folded, head bowed in prayer. Brianna scanned the assembly until her gaze fell on the back of a familiar redhead, also bowed in a reverent posture. Colleen seemed totally engrossed in the service, her lips moving in time with Rylan's prayer. A small blond girl got up and climbed onto Colleen's lap. Instead of the rebuff

Brianna expected, Colleen gathered the child in her arms and laid her cheek on top of the girl's fair curls, dropping a kiss as she did so. Brianna blinked to make sure she wasn't seeing things.

Aunt Fiona motioned for Brianna to take a seat at the back of the room until Rylan closed his prayer service and released the children to return to their classroom.

In the flurry of activity that followed, Rylan noticed them, and a huge smile creased his face. "Brianna. How wonderful to see you." He strode across the room to kiss her cheek. "And who might this lovely lady be?"

Brianna smiled at his ever-present charm. "This is our Aunt Fiona, Daddy's sister. Auntie, this is a distant cousin of Mama's, Rylan Montgomery."

Rylan bent to kiss Fiona's hand. "Charmed to meet you. Though I must say, you are far lovelier than your brother."

Aunt Fiona actually blushed.

From the corner of her eye, Brianna noticed Colleen approaching, looking beautiful in a simple blue dress. A wave of homesickness washed over Brianna like a physical ache. Colleen set the little girl on the floor, holding her by the hand.

"Hello, Bree. It's good to see you." Colleen stood demurely in front of her.

Brianna hesitated, taken aback by her lack of haughtiness. "Hello, Colleen."

Aunt Fiona moved to embrace her. "Colleen? My, what a beautiful young woman you've become."

"Thank you, Aunt Fiona. You look well yourself." A small frown crossed Colleen's features. "What are you both doing here? Did Daddy send you to check on me?"

"Goodness no, child." Aunt Fiona pulled her short jacket a little straighter. "I like to volunteer here at least once a month. The children bring me a great deal of joy."

Colleen smiled down at the girl beside her. "I know what you mean. This is my friend, Delia. Delia, this is my Aunt Fiona and my sister, Brianna."

Brianna smiled at the girl. "Pleased to meet you, Delia."

Delia tugged on Colleen's skirt. "Miss O'Leary, you have a sister?"

"Yes. I have two sisters and two brothers."

"And a mother and father?"

"That's right."

"You're lucky. I wish I had a family like that."

Brianna's heart squeezed with sympathy at the child's wistful tone. When Brianna looked at Colleen, she was astounded to see tears in her sister's eyes.

Colleen bent and gathered the girl in a huge hug. "I know one day you're going to have a wonderful family, too."

Delia squirmed in her arms. "Could you 'dopt me into your family?"

Moisture shimmered in Colleen's eyes. "I wish I could, sweetie."

Rylan moved in to sweep the child from Colleen. "I'll take Delia back to the classroom. Why don't you visit with your sister for a while?" Rylan's warm voice held a soothing quality.

Colleen nodded, pulling a handkerchief from her pocket to dab at her eyes.

He turned to their aunt. "Miss O'Leary, why don't we let the girls have a moment? We can help Sister Marguerite with the children until lunch."

When Aunt Fiona had left with Rylan, Colleen motioned to the chairs. "Let's sit and talk for a minute."

Brianna nodded and sat down, unsure what to say to her sister.

Colleen twisted the handkerchief in her hands, seeming equally ill at ease. "I want you to know," she said at last, "how sorry I am for ruining your birthday, Bree. It was inexcusable."

Bree straightened her spine against the cool metal. "Shouldn't you be apologizing to Gil?"

"I will as soon as I see him. But I know how much it upset you, as well. Though that's not the reason I did it."

Brianna noted the sincerity on her sister's face and considered the fact that she may be telling the truth for once. "Why did you do it, if not to hurt me?"

Colleen raised her chin. "I needed Jared to break off our relationship, and it was the only way I could think of—for him to catch me with another man. I knew Gil was distressed over your betrothal to Henry, so I used his moment of weakness to my advantage." She paused, crumpling the handkerchief into a ball. "Believe me, I'm not proud of that."

Brianna inhaled and let the breath out slowly. How many times had Colleen repented in the past, only to do something equally hurtful when it suited her? Still, she was her sister, and right now any contact with her family was welcome. "I accept your apology." Brianna managed a slight smile. "Especially since Daddy's not forcing you to say it."

Colleen's lips quirked. "I admit I was angry with Daddy for sending me here, but he did me a big favor." She became serious. "Helping these amazing children has opened my eyes to a lot of things about myself—none of which are admirable. Rylan is helping me turn my life around."

Brianna blinked, too stunned to form a response.

Colleen reached out to take her hand. "What about you, Bree? Mama told me you've ended your betrothal to Henry, and now you're living with our aunt. Are you sure you're all right?"

Brianna couldn't remember her sister ever asking about her well-being. "I'm doing better—now that I'm away from Daddy's constant attempts to control my life. Aunt Fiona is helping me enroll in college for the fall."

Colleen's brows rose. "I had no idea you wanted to go to college." A slow smile bloomed along with the familiar glint of mischief in her eyes. "Daddy must be spinning now that both of us have severed ties with our potential husbands."

Brianna's own lips twitched in response. "He must at that. Right now the only puppet still dancing to his tune is Gil."

On Friday evening, Gil held open the front door of the Belvedere estate for Aurora to pass through, then followed her in. Nerves churned in his stomach. He'd taken Aurora to one of Long Island's best restaurants, and although he'd planned to propose, he couldn't seem to force the words from his mouth. Thank goodness she had no idea what he'd intended. Instead, they'd passed a pleasant enough evening, finishing with a stroll around the grounds of Belvedere. Gil wondered if Mrs. O'Leary had ever had the chance to walk among those amazing gardens. If she did, she would surely envy Mrs. Hastings her abundance of multi-hued rose hybrids.

"Thank you, Gil, for a wonderful evening." Aurora's voice brought Gil back to his surroundings. She paused at the marble entry table to remove her hat and gloves and patted her blond curls into place.

"You're welcome. I enjoyed myself very much."

Her hand fluttered to the neckline of her gauzy dress, as though she were nervous. It hit him then. She was probably anticipating a good-night kiss.

How could he ask for her hand in marriage when he hadn't even kissed her yet? The Independence Day party was the next day, and James expected Arthur to announce Gil and Aurora's betrothal.

"Would you care to come in for a while?" She gave him a shy smile, twisting her hands together in front of her.

"Actually, I do need to speak with your father if he's still up."

A look of disappointment swept Aurora's lovely features before she schooled her expression. "Would you like me to check? He's probably in his study."

Gil took a tentative step toward her. "In a moment." He

reached out to take one of her hands in his, noting the pulse jumping at her wrist. "First, I'll say good night in case you've gone up by the time we finish."

Very slowly, he lowered his head toward her upturned face. He kept the kiss brief, a perfectly acceptable chaste first kiss. She blushed when he pulled back.

"Good night, Aurora. Sleep well."

"Good night, Gil." She ducked her head. "I'll get Papa for you." A moment later, she slipped down the hall.

Gil let out a long breath and squeezed his eyes shut. What manner of fraud was he? That kiss only confirmed how off base this romance was. He felt nothing more than a brotherly affection for Aurora. How could he let her believe he loved her? That he wanted to marry her?

He scrubbed a hand over his jaw.

"Gilbert." Arthur Hastings's booming voice echoed in the marble foyer. "Aurora said you wished to see me."

Gil snapped to attention and pasted a smile on his face. "Mr. Hastings. I'm sorry to disturb you at this hour."

"Not at all, my boy. Come and join me for a nightcap."

Gil followed Arthur down the corridor into the man's private den. A fire crackled in the hearth, giving the room a warm glow.

"Have a seat." Arthur motioned to a wing chair across from his desk.

When Gil had complied, Arthur pulled a flask from one of his drawers and uncapped it. Then he produced two crystal glasses and poured a finger of brown liquor into each.

"Here you go, Gilbert. A little brandy at bedtime keeps a body healthy." He chuckled as he pushed one glass toward Gil.

With some hesitation, Gil wrapped his fingers around the glass and waited until Arthur lifted his vessel in a salute. "To your health." Arthur tossed back the liquid with one smooth motion.

Not accustomed to liquor, Gil didn't dare follow. Instead he took a quick sip, grimacing at the burn as it seared his throat. He counted himself fortunate he didn't choke. The strong smell evoked painful memories of his father, slumped in his wheelchair, an empty bottle at his feet. Gil shook his head to clear the image, and as the warming effect of the drink spread through his limbs, he hoped it would help ease his nerves at the question he needed to ask this man.

Arthur uncapped the flask a second time to pour himself a refill. "Now, what can I do for you, young man? I hope this isn't a business matter that's been weighing on your mind all evening."

"No, sir. Actually it's a personal matter."

Arthur's hand stilled. "Is everything all right between you and Aurora?"

The man apparently had no clue what Gil intended. He swallowed his nerves. "Everything is going well, sir. That's why I wanted to speak to you." He took another sip of courage from his glass and set the empty container on the desk. "I wish to ask permission for your daughter's hand in marriage."

Arthur's mouth fell open for a brief moment, followed almost immediately by a broad smile. "You're serious?"

Gil pictured James's desperate expression when he last saw him. "Very serious." He swallowed. "I know I don't have a lot to offer . . ."

Mr. Hastings waved a hand in the air. "There are more important things than money, my boy. I place a far higher value on a man's integrity and his work ethic. You have both of these admirable qualities. After watching you at the bank, I have no doubt that your ambition and intelligence will carry you far." The older man stood and came around from behind the desk. "Even more important is the respect you show my daughter. I'd be honored to have you as a son-in-law." He beamed, pumping Gil's hand in an energetic handshake. "I've been hoping for this, but I never dreamed it would happen so quickly."

Gil's conscience pricked at him like the small hairs on the back of his neck. "Thank you, sir. That is indeed a compliment." The image of his own father came to mind once more. Before the accident that left John Whelan crippled, his father had oozed integrity. What would he think of his son now?

Arthur's face brightened. He slapped a hand to the desktop. "We can make the announcement at the party tomorrow. The timing will be perfect with all my friends and associates in attendance."

"That sounds fine." James's plan was coming together just as he'd hoped. Gil swiped a hand across his mouth to remove the stickiness of the brandy. "I'll . . . I'll propose to Aurora tomorrow, before the party begins."

"I'm sure we don't need to speculate about her answer." He winked at Gil. "She's made her feelings fairly obvious."

Gil strained his mouth into a smile. "That she has." He moved toward the door, suddenly desperate to be out of this house, away from his lies. "Thank you for everything, sir. I'll see you tomorrow."

Seconds later, Gil left the mansion, but no matter how fast he walked down the long country lane, he couldn't outdistance his conscience.

His lies followed him home.

21

COLLEEN PRIMPED IN FRONT of her mirror one last time in preparation for the Hastings family's Independence Day party. It had been some time since she'd gotten so dressed up, and she had to admit she missed it—a little. She smiled at her reflection, satisfied with the way her violet dress made her eyes appear almost purple. The bodice of the gown was tight enough to be attractive without being too revealing. That one detail alone proved how much Colleen had changed. Normally her chief concern had been to appear as seductive as possible in order to attract the richest, most handsome bachelors. Now she wished only to make her parents proud.

Her hand stilled on the lace collar. Not entirely true. She wanted to make Rylan proud, as well.

Her heart fluttered against the casing of her corset. What would Rylan be wearing tonight? Part of her hoped to see him clad in an expensive suit, while the other more practical part wished he'd wear his clergy clothing, so that she, as well as all the other eligible young ladies, would know he was off limits. She needed that very physical reminder to keep her treacherous heart from feeling things it shouldn't.

Colleen grabbed her wrap and floated down the main staircase, discounting her nerves as normal for such a grand occasion.

The hallway below sat shrouded in shadows with no evidence of her parents. Perhaps they were waiting for her in the parlor. Her feet made no noise as she tripped across the entryway to the parlor door. Inside, a lone male figure stood with his back to her, studying the gardens through the French doors.

Colleen hesitated in the doorway, her usual confidence eluding her. She didn't know how to behave around Rylan Montgomery, charming rogue and pious clergyman all rolled into one. She was about to sneak away when he turned, and his penetrating gaze met hers.

Dressed in a dark tuxedo—one she recognized as belonging to Adam—Rylan was the most handsome man she'd ever seen. A crisp white shirt and black bow tie set off his firm jaw and fascinating cleft chin.

Her mouth went dry, and try as she might, she could not get out a single word.

"You are absolutely beautiful." His reverent whisper made the fine hairs on her neck rise.

"Th—thank you." She couldn't seem to tear her eyes from the burning intensity of his.

He took a few steps forward. "Your parents went on ahead. They asked me to accompany you over to Belvedere."

That showed how much Daddy trusted Rylan. But did she trust herself?

"Well," she said brightly, "I suppose we should be off, then."

"I suppose so." He offered her his arm.

After a slight hesitation, she placed her hand on his arm and tried hard to ignore the furious sprint of her pulse. Her breath came in shallow pants, as though the oxygen had thinned out of the room. Beneath the voluminous skirt of her dress, her knees shook.

God help her, she was falling in love with a priest.

Gil had spent most of the evening plotting ways he could escape before his betrothal became public knowledge. None of his imaginings, however, proved the least bit plausible. Now, as the minutes ticked by and Mr. Hastings's announcement loomed before him, Gil suffered a severe attack of nausea. In desperate need of some fresh air, he moved toward the balcony doors. He'd taken several strides when he spied James heading his way.

"There you are, Gilbert. I haven't had a chance to speak to you all night." James hooked his thumbs in his vest pockets.

Gil managed a feeble smile. "I've been busy meeting an endless stream of people. This is quite the party."

They stepped together onto the stone balcony. Thankful for the cool evening breeze, Gil inhaled deeply as he looked out over the darkened gardens embellished with dozens of candles and a lit fountain at the center.

"Is everything in place that we talked about?" James's urgent question jarred Gil's brief moment of tranquility.

Gil nodded. "Our betrothal will be announced right before the fireworks display."

The tension seemed to drain from James's stiff frame. "I knew I could count on you, Gilbert. I want you to know your loyalty means the world to me, and I will find a way to repay you."

"No need, sir. Consider this my thanks for everything you've done for me."

This man had been his surrogate father through Gil's most formative years. He deserved Gil's respect and allegiance. Would a son do any less for a father?

"I'm very proud of you, son." James's gruff voice hinted that he was experiencing the same swirl of emotion as Gil.

Gil closed his eyes and pictured Irish Meadows in all its glory—the magnificence of the sun shining over the meadows, the beauty of the horses thundering around the track. He needed to remind himself just what was at stake here. If he could help the O'Learys keep their beloved home, as well as the source of their livelihood, then he would do whatever was necessary—no matter the sacrifice.

James cleared his throat. "Looks like Arthur is gathering the guests. We'd best go inside."

Gil almost wished he had some of that brandy right now to dull his senses for the upcoming speech. Aurora materialized out of the crowd like a ray of sunshine in her bright yellow gown. His thoughts went back to earlier in the day when he'd fumbled through the worst marriage proposal ever. Aurora hadn't seemed to notice. She'd thrown herself into his arms with happy tears. And she'd been smiling ever since.

Guilt squeezed Gil's insides, creating spasms in his stomach. If only he could forget about Brianna, perhaps he'd have a chance at a happy life with Aurora.

He wanted to pray for help, for deliverance from this path he'd chosen, but his conscience wouldn't let him. He didn't deserve God's help. Not when Gil was about to perpetrate such a terrible deception.

With quiet dignity, Aurora led him to stand beside her father as he gave a rousing speech to his guests. Finally, when Gil feared his legs wouldn't hold him a moment longer, Mr. Hastings announced the betrothal of his daughter to Mr. Gilbert Whelan.

Gil pasted on a smile so brittle he thought his cheeks would crack as he shook his future father-in-law's hand and then bent to kiss Aurora's cheek amid the polite applause of the audience. His gaze swung out over the sea of people who blended together in one massive blur, landing first on James's beaming features, then moving on to Mrs. O'Leary. In direct contrast to her husband's jubilation, stark sorrow shone from her eyes.

Eyes so similar to Brianna's that Gil's insides froze.

Perspiration beaded on his forehead as the nausea intensified. With a quick apology to Aurora, Gil turned and dashed out the patio doors. He raced down the balcony stairs and fell to his knees in the grass, where moments later his stomach heaved. His own body could not tolerate his treachery.

"Forgive me, Bree," he whispered, but his only answer was the wind singing its disapproval through the trees.

❧❦❧

"May I have this dance, Miss O'Leary?"

Lost in thought after Mr. Hastings's unexpected announcement, Colleen barely noticed the gentleman in front of her. She blinked as she took in the handsome face before her. She hadn't danced much all evening, being very picky about whom she accepted as a partner. Finding herself with no excuse at hand, she nodded. "Very well, Mister . . . ?"

"I'm sorry. I assumed you knew me. The name is Charles Sutton. Our fathers are business acquaintances." He gave a low bow, then reached for her hand.

They slipped into the mix of couples already gliding to the music. At one time, Colleen would have been thrilled to be remembered by the son of one of Daddy's wealthy associates, but tonight all she could think about was Rylan.

Colleen forced her lips into a smile, wishing Rylan would ask her to dance. He hadn't graced the floor with anyone other than her mother and some of the older ladies, seeming to purposely avoid the younger girls so as not to encourage any wrong notions. Colleen scanned the crowd as they twirled, hoping for a friendly face, but not many girls her age wanted to befriend her, fearing she would attempt to steal their suitors.

A small sigh escaped her. Even Brianna's presence would be welcome right now.

Brianna. A pang hit Colleen as she imagined the devastation this betrothal would wreak on her sister. Colleen wanted to ask Bree why she and Gil had never pursued a relationship. Had her father forbidden it?

A wandering hand at Colleen's lower back brought her attention crashing back to her dance partner. She frowned into his bland face, which revealed nothing save for a heated gleam in his eyes. Annoyance flickered through her as she shifted in his grip, trying to make him move his hand, but it only inched farther down. They had come to a near standstill in the far corner of the dance floor, and she realized he'd maneuvered her there on purpose.

"I beg your pardon, sir," she said through her teeth, "but you had best move your hand to a more suitable location unless you wish to lose your fingers."

A scowl brought Mr. Sutton's fair eyebrows together. "There's no need to pretend innocence with me, Miss O'Leary. I'm well aware of your reputation among my peers."

Shock had Colleen's mouth agape. Her footsteps faltered, and she would have stumbled if a hand hadn't gripped her elbow from behind.

"I believe you owe Miss O'Leary an apology."

The steely voice of Rylan behind her sent a wave of relief surging through her. She stepped closer to Rylan, and his arm came around her like shelter from a storm.

Mr. Sutton stared at Rylan, and his face contorted into an ugly sneer. "It's obvious, sir, that you don't know Miss O'Leary very well at all."

❧❦❧

Rylan glared at the man who had been groping Colleen. In an attempt to control his temper, Rylan flexed his fingers, trying not to imagine punching the man's pasty face.

"I know her far better than you ever will. Now if you'll excuse us . . ." He gathered Colleen to him and spun her away from the louse's leer.

When he had put some distance between them, Rylan peered down at Colleen. Her features were pinched, her skin blanched of color. In the circle of his arms, her frame trembled.

"Are you all right? He didn't hurt you, did he?" Hot curls of anger wound their way through his chest.

"No." Shame surfaced in her gaze. "I'm only sorry you had to hear that," she whispered.

The sorrow on her face tore at him, adding to his fury at the man who caused her to feel this way. "You've nothing to be sorry about. That lout is the one who needs a lesson on how to treat a lady."

She shook her head. "Not many people think I deserve to be treated as one. It appears I have a"—she gulped—"bad reputation." She bit her lip and turned her head away.

The music, something sad and haunting, seemed in keeping with her mood. Rylan longed to see her return to her spirited self, filled with confidence. Even anger would be better than this apparent self-loathing. He pulled her closer, as if to protect her from the gossip and disapproving stares while they danced. "Perhaps I should have let you break the man's fingers," he teased.

That coaxed a slight twitch of her lips. "Perhaps." She sobered. "I want you to know something, Rylan. Besides a few kisses—ill-advised as they may have been—I have done nothing to warrant—"

"You don't have to explain yourself to me, Colleen."

"But I want to." Tears gathered in her eyes, creating two twinkling pools of violet.

Rylan tightened his arm around her waist. "I know you're not that type of woman. And no one should treat you as anything less than the good person you are."

A single tear dislodged to trail down her cheek. "But I'm not a good person, and I don't deserve—" She broke off in a stifled sob and lowered her head to his chest.

He needed to get her away from the stares of curious onlookers until she'd gained control of her emotions. Discreetly, he led her off the dance floor, through an open door, and onto the balcony. Once outside, she broke away from him and rushed to the stone railing, gripping it with both hands. Rylan moved quietly beside her and handed her his handkerchief. The cool night air blew tendrils of her red hair about her cheek and fluttered the folds of her dress. She didn't seem to notice the chill in the air or the fact that she had no wrap.

Help me to get through to her, Lord. To convince her of her worthiness. Of Your great love for her.

He stood near her at the railing, not daring to touch her. "Did you not believe me when I told you God loves you unconditionally and that nothing you do can keep His love from you?"

She sniffed, dabbing her cheeks with the handkerchief. "I want to believe that, Rylan. It's easy for you. You don't do anything wrong."

"I've done my share of disreputable things in my youth, before entering the seminary."

"Nothing like what I've done."

Something in the devastation of her voice told him there was more to her story than a few stolen kisses. "What could be so terrible you think God won't forgive?"

"I can't tell you." She glanced over at him with tortured eyes. "I don't want to ruin your opinion of me."

Rylan ached to comfort her, but other guests had come out to the balcony for some air. In order to avoid prying eyes, he took her hand and led her down the nearby steps to walk in the candlelit garden. After a few moments, they came to a stone bench situated between two large bushes, and he motioned for her to sit. He lowered himself beside her, careful to keep a respectable distance between them, then shrugged off his jacket to drape around her shoulders.

They sat in silence for several minutes.

"I promise," he said at last, "that nothing you tell me could ruin my good opinion of you. Not even if you told me you'd murdered someone."

She twisted his handkerchief in her lap, not looking at him. "I think murder would be easier to confess."

She'd done something worse than murder? For a moment, doubts crept into Rylan's certainty. He petitioned God for guidance and forged on. "Have you never told anyone of this great sin?"

She shook her head. "No one."

"Not even your priest?"

Her eyes grew wide in horror. "Especially not a priest."

He was about to remind her of his intended profession but thought it wiser to let it go. Colleen had something eating at her soul, and the only way to remove the power it held over her was to confess it. "Don't you think it's time to get this off your conscience?"

"Not if I lose your respect." She met his gaze. "Your opinion matters to me, Rylan."

He couldn't help it. He took her hand in his. "I promise you won't lose my respect."

Her eyes searched his a moment longer, then she dipped her head and pulled her hand free. He could almost sense the battle raging within her.

Finally, she released a weary sigh. "I made a priest break his vows."

Rylan jerked on the bench, barely keeping from falling onto the grass below. He swallowed hard to hide his dismay. "How exactly did you . . . accomplish this?"

Her hands shook on her lap, and he forced himself not to touch her again.

"I didn't mean to. I had no idea what he was thinking."

"Was it Reverend Filmore?" he dared to ask, praying it wasn't.

"No. It was another priest many years ago."

A host of emotions rioted through Rylan's chest. "Many years ago? How old were you then?"

"Thirteen."

It took all his willpower not to scream his outrage. Whatever had happened between Colleen and this priest, it could not be the fault of a thirteen-year-old child. "Tell me everything," he whispered, not trusting his full voice.

The blue intensity of her eyes stood out in her pale face before her lashes swept down to shutter them. "He was at the school for a prayer service. I . . . I was in trouble with the teacher and had to stay after school to clean the chalkboards. He told Mrs. Stephens she could leave. That he would make sure I did my job and then escort me home."

Nausea curdled in Rylan's stomach as he imagined the rest of the scenario. "What did he do?" He dreaded hearing the rest of the sordid tale but knew for her sake he must.

Her hand fluttered like an injured bird. He caught it in his and held on tight.

"He told me I was a tease and I deserved to be spanked." She gulped as a sob tore from her throat. Her shoulders slumped as she collapsed toward her knees in a storm of weeping.

Rage, more violent than he'd ever known, shook Rylan's frame. He would learn this monster's name and make sure he could never harm another innocent girl again. He took her shoulders gently in his hands, forcing her to meet his gaze. One more question had to be asked. "Did he . . . violate you?"

She was crying so hard she could barely answer. "Not that way, no. He started kissing me, touching me . . ." She shuddered. "I didn't know what to do."

Rylan pulled her near and closed his eyes. God may preach forgiveness, but Rylan doubted he could ever forgive this man for betraying a child's trust. Right now his heart felt as cold and hard as the stone bench beneath him. "It wasn't your fault, Colleen. He was the one who sinned."

"But he said it was my fault for being so bewitching. For flaunting my wiles, I think he called it."

"And ever since then you've been trying to live up to his description," he murmured, almost to himself.

She stiffened in his arms and began to pull away, but he held her tight.

"Not on purpose. That's not what I meant. But he made you feel that you were the guilty party when he knew he was to blame." He tilted her chin to force her gaze to meet his. "Colleen, love, you did nothing wrong. Not a thing. That man lied and made you out to be the temptress, but you were a child. He was a man of God, in a position of trust. He abused that trust in the worst possible way."

"You really believe that?" she whispered.

"It's the truth. You did nothing wrong. I'll keep saying it until you believe me."

She sagged against him once again, and he held her until her sobs quieted, his heart breaking for her misery. In direct contrast to her pain, the sound of laughter drifted out from the open door to the ballroom.

"Why did you not tell your parents?" he asked. "Surely they would have believed you."

She exhaled slowly. "I couldn't add to their burden. My brother, Danny, had just died a few weeks before . . ." She trailed off.

"I see. There was already enough grief in the house, and you didn't want to make things worse."

She nodded against his chest.

"Which only proves how unselfish you really are, Colleen O'Leary." He let out a long sigh. "It seems I have my work cut out for me to make you see your true worth. Your value in the eyes of God, in the eyes of your family, and . . ." He paused. "And in mine."

She lifted her head to look into his face, her eyes liquid pools. "So you . . . you don't think badly of me now?" The vulnerability on her face made him want to weep.

"Never." A fierce wave of emotion enveloped him. His heart began a slow, heavy thump as the reality he'd been trying to avoid for weeks now hit him hard.

Heaven help me! I'm falling in love with this girl.

Intense guilt crashed over him as heat flooded his neck and face. He shifted on the bench, purposely putting some distance between them, except for her small hand, which he kept tucked in his.

"I could never think badly of you. Especially not for something like that." He paused, searching for words of wisdom. "You must let go of the guilt you've been harboring all these years. And if you're able, try to forgive the sorry excuse for a man who robbed you of your innocence. Only then will you truly be free. Only then will your heart be able to heal."

"I'm not sure I can," she whispered, "but I'll try."

"God will help you if you let Him. And so will I."

She leaned forward and pressed a kiss to his cheek. "Thank you, Rylan."

He cleared his throat and rose. "We'd best be getting back before we start any new rumors. Especially since I'm not wearing my collar tonight."

The sadness and longing in her eyes twisted his insides. He only prayed she wasn't falling in love with him, too.

For he was not free to love her as she deserved to be loved.

22

WITH BRIANNA NO LONGER living at home, Gil felt free to spend the night in his old room at Irish Meadows, even though being there after announcing his engagement to Aurora seemed like an added form of betrayal. Sleep eluded him most of the night, and in the pre-dawn hours, he dressed quickly and left the house.

His burdened soul required solace, and the one place he hoped to find it was at church. He'd been leaving God out of his life too much lately—making decisions without the guidance of prayer, ashamed because in his heart he knew his actions were wrong.

Now, in the early morning hours, Gil sought the silence of the large church he used to attend with the O'Learys, hoping for answers, hoping to find a way out of the impossible predicament he found himself in.

The wooden door creaked open as he stepped into the dark interior. Knowing the inside of St. Rita's as well as the Irish Meadows stable, he had no need to illuminate the space. Waiting a minute for his eyes to adjust, he made his way to the front of the church and entered the first pew, lowering himself to the hard wooden kneeler. Hands clasped so tight his knuckles ached, Gil bowed his head and willed peace to descend on his troubled soul.

The treachery of his actions ate at Gil's conscience like a deadly disease. How had he, a man who prided himself on his integrity and principles, fallen so far away from them?

He moved his hand, surprised to find wetness there, unaware of the tears that had fallen.

"Can I help you with anything, Gilbert?"

The sympathetic voice of Reverend Filmore startled Gil from his thoughts. He swiped a sleeve over his eyes and pushed up to sit on the wooden bench. Reverend Filmore stood at the end of the pew, a concerned expression on his lined face.

"Is everything all right at the O'Learys'?"

"The O'Learys are fine, sir."

"But evidently you are not."

Gil opened his mouth to reply that he was fine, but the added lie would not leave his tongue. "No, I'm not."

The priest moved to sit beside him on the pew. "I'm a good listener if you want to get something off your chest."

Gil bent his head over his knees. Could it hurt to hear a minister's opinion, or would it forever taint the reverend's view of him?

"There's nothing I haven't heard before, son. No sin is so terrible it can't be forgiven." His soothing tone gave Gil confidence.

They sat side by side, each man gazing ahead at the simple altar.

"I've got myself into a situation I don't know how to get out of." Gil's voice, a mere whisper, seemed to echo in the silent space.

"This situation . . . does it involve a woman?"

"Not in the way you're thinking, but yes. I've allowed myself to become betrothed to a woman I don't love. Not the way a husband should love a wife." He shook his head sadly. "I knew it was wrong, but I allowed myself to be talked into doing this . . ." He trailed off, not willing to besmirch James's reputation. "I can't go into all the details."

"I understand. What's important is that God knows the motivation in your heart."

Gil squeezed his hands into fists on his lap. "When I break off the engagement, it will cause great pain to the girl and her family."

"I presume you had strong reasons to agree to this. But by doing so, you haven't been true to yourself, and that's what's causing you such misery. That and knowing you're going to cause this poor girl heartache."

"Yes."

"The important thing is you've realized your mistake, confessed it here to God, and asked His forgiveness."

"Do I even deserve forgiveness?" The question he'd asked himself so often in the past now resurfaced.

"Everyone who repents of wrongdoing deserves forgiveness, Gilbert. Ask for God's help. Seek His will in making amends to right the wrong you've done. It may take some time, but I'm sure the young lady in question will forgive you eventually."

Gil released a weary breath. "Thank you, Reverend. I'll do my best."

"Good to hear. Remember I'm always available if you need to talk."

"I'll keep that in mind, sir."

"Now, I'd best be preparing for my service in a few hours." He stood slowly, his knees creaking like the wooden floor beneath him. "I hope to see you back here later."

Gil nodded. "I'll be here."

Gil sat in the silence for several more minutes. At last, some of the burden seemed to lift from his shoulders. Now that he'd involved God in his decisions, as he should have all along, a certain clarity cleared the fog of guilt from his mind. He left the church, praying for the strength to follow through on his decision—as soon as the verdict on the loan came through.

Colleen hummed on her way up the stairs to the front door of the orphanage on the morning after Independence Day, eager to see Delia and hear her account of the parade the children had attended.

In the cloakroom, she removed her hat and gloves, feeling lighter than she had in years, as though a huge burden had been lifted from her soul. Her conversation with Rylan on Saturday night had had a cathartic effect on her in ways Colleen could never have imagined. For the first time since she could remember, she'd looked forward to attending Sunday service with her family and had actually enjoyed Reverend Filmore's sermon. The usual anger and sting of guilt had dissipated from her like the smoke drifting over the church candles.

The fact that Rylan didn't despise her for her secret shame was in itself the best gift she'd ever been given. Total and unconditional acceptance. Affection and friendship based not on her looks, her family, or her wealth, but on the true person she was inside. Rylan knew every dark corner of her soul and liked her anyway.

Dare she hope he might love her?

What a foolish notion. He'd never once indicated he felt anything romantic for her, though she'd mistakenly imagined he might kiss her the other night. But then he'd moved away, and she realized she'd misinterpreted his reaction. She was nothing more than a person he'd helped through a spiritual crisis. She would have to be content with his friendship and keep her true feelings buried deep.

This morning, she'd missed his charming presence on the train ride into the city. He'd said he had something to do at the church before he could join them at the orphanage, so Colleen traveled in alone.

But nothing would dampen her spirits today. She had a new outlook on life, a new joy, a new truth about herself, and she felt all-powerful. Full of love for her fellow human beings. Not even Sister Marguerite's dour countenance could daunt her today.

Smiling, she marched into the classroom, full of purpose. The children had not yet come in, so only Sister Marguerite occupied the room, seated at the head of the class.

"Good morning, Sister," Colleen called out to the nun. "How did you enjoy your holiday?"

The woman blinked, then inclined her head. "I enjoyed it very much. I will thank Mr. Montgomery when I see him."

Colleen ignored the attempt to minimize the part she had played in the nuns' day off. "I'm glad." She smiled as she took a handful of children's readers from the bookshelf. "We had fun with the children, as well."

"Believe me, we've heard about nothing else since."

Colleen tried to curb her annoyance. Sister Marguerite managed to take such an enjoyable occasion and still find something to grouse about. Colleen decided not to take her negativity personally.

The door opened, and Sister Veronica led the children into the classroom. Colleen paused from her task to greet them as they entered, eager to see Delia's face light up in welcome.

When all the children had taken their seats and Delia had not appeared, Colleen crossed the room to peer into the corridor, thinking the girl had lagged behind the others. The hallway remained empty.

"Sister Veronica, where is Delia this morning? Is she ill?" If so, Colleen would go and check on her.

The usually serene face of the young nun turned sorrowful. She placed a gentle hand on Colleen's arm. "You haven't heard?"

Alarm skittered up Colleen's spine as her gaze swung over

the heads of the children to the smug expression on Sister Marguerite's face. "Heard what?"

"Delia is gone," Sister Marguerite snapped.

"What do you mean gone?"

"It's good news, really." Sister Veronica's soothing voice did little to calm Colleen's anxiety. "Delia's been adopted. Her new family came to pick her up yesterday."

The floor swayed under Colleen's feet. "Adopted? Why didn't I know about this?"

"I thought Mr. Montgomery would have told you." Sister Marguerite removed her glasses and set them on the table. "He helped arrange the whole thing."

Colleen's legs wobbled beneath her, and the room spun. Rylan knew this was happening and hadn't said a word? How could he have kept this from her—especially when she'd asked him about the possibility of Delia being adopted? She reached out to grasp the wooden doorframe, willing her legs to hold her.

"I didn't even get to say good-bye." Tremors started in her knees and moved up her body.

"Maybe you should come to the kitchen," Sister Veronica said, her tone kind. "I'll get you a glass of water."

"No, thank you. I just need a moment . . . alone." Colleen lifted her skirts and fled down the hallway. She charged up the stairs and pushed through the door into the girls' dormitory. Her breath came in great gasps as her gaze flew to the little bed at the far end of the room. Right away Colleen noticed the difference. Delia's special quilt was gone. In its place, a standard-issue wool blanket covered the bed.

Colleen moved across the floor as if in a trance and sank onto the mattress. Snatching up the pillow, she pressed it to her face as though she might be able to smell a trace of the little girl left there. Nothing but the freshly laundered odor of bleach met her nose. Tears blurred her vision. She sat rocking on the edge of the bed, the pillow clutched to her chest.

Dear Lord, I know I should be happy for her, but I'm so very sad. Please let Delia have a wonderful family with the kindest of mothers to love her. As I would have loved her.

She brushed at the tears that spilled over and streamed down her cheeks. *Oh, Delia.* How Colleen wished she could have sent her off to her new home with good wishes and lots of kisses. What must Delia think of her, that she never even bothered to say good-bye? Did she think Colleen didn't care about her?

Her watery gaze landed on the polished hardwood floor where a scrap of fabric stuck out between the bed and the night table. Colleen reached down and pulled out Delia's worn rag bunny. A cry escaped her as she caressed the cherished toy.

How would Delia sleep in a new house without Mr. Whiskers?

Colleen grasped the tattered toy in her arms and curled up on the bed as sorrow gutted her. She felt the loss of the little girl in every fiber of her being. Never again would she see those blue eyes light up, never again feel those arms hug her neck.

Colleen's world would never be as bright again.

Rylan trudged up the stairs from the utility room in the basement of the orphanage, the metal toolbox in his hand as heavy and black as his soul. He'd lied to Colleen this morning, told her he had something to take care of at the church, so he wouldn't have to endure the torturous train ride in with her.

How could he face her, knowing how he felt about her, and not have her guess the inappropriate nature of his affections? He needed time to school his thoughts, and his emotions, before being alone with her again. He needed time for God to change his heart and return him to the feelings of friendship he'd started with.

To make matters worse, today he'd have to break the news of Delia's adoption and tell Colleen the girl would be leaving by the end of the week. He sighed as he reached the main level and set the toolbox on the floor with a thud. Though Colleen would be happy for Delia, Rylan was certain she would also be devastated by the loss of the wee girl. Rylan's heart already ached with sadness at the thought of no longer seeing the tot's mischievous grin and bright eyes.

Footsteps pounding on the carpet pulled his attention down the long corridor.

"Oh, Mr. Montgomery. Thank goodness you're here." Sister Veronica rushed up beside him, face flushed, out of breath.

"Sister, what is it?" Concern for the woman banished all thoughts of Delia for the moment.

"It's Miss O'Leary. You need to come with me."

Alarm shot through his midsection, curdling his morning tea. "What's wrong with Miss O'Leary?" He took long strides to keep up with the petite woman's furious footsteps. "Is she ill?"

She looked over her shoulder as they climbed the stairs to the second story. "Sick at heart. She found out that Delia's been adopted."

Rylan's stomach sank to his boots. Someone had told her before he'd had the chance. Would Sister Marguerite stoop so low just to hurt her?

"Why are we going upstairs? Isn't she with the children in the classroom?"

Her white headpiece wobbled as she shook her head. "Once she realized Delia was gone, she came up to the dormitory. I can't get her to leave."

At the top of the stairs, Rylan reached out a hand to halt the nun's movement. "Are you telling me Delia's already gone?"

Regret shone in the nun's large eyes. "Yes. The family's plans changed, and they came yesterday to pick her up." She nudged open the door to the girls' dormitory and pointed to the bed in the far corner.

Muffled sobs came from the figure curled in a tight ball on top of the bed. Sorrow banded Rylan's heart until the pain radiated out over his chest. He put one hand there to rub the ache. "Leave it with me, Sister. I'll see what I can do."

A wave of relief passed over her features. "Thank you."

Like a man heading to his execution, Rylan made his way across the room to the tiny bed. Colleen's back faced him, her shoulders shaking with silent weeping. What he wouldn't give to take away her pain. The last thing he ever wanted was to see her hurting like this.

Gingerly, he sat beside her on the cot and placed a tender hand on her arm. "I'm so sorry you found out this way, Colleen."

She wrenched up to a sitting position, her eyes wild with . . . fury?

"You lying, treacherous, hateful man." Palms fisted, she attacked him, striking his upper torso with angry blows. In her vehemence, her hair shook loose from its pins to cascade around her face and shoulders. She didn't seem to notice as she hurled further insults at him.

He accepted her wrath for a few moments, knowing he deserved it, before capturing her hands in his. "Are you finished?" His calm voice finally seemed to penetrate the haze of her anger, for she stilled and really looked at him, tears streaking her cheeks.

"How could you not tell me? I asked you about adoption and you said nothing." The betrayal and hurt shone in her eyes, searing his heart like a brand.

"I wanted to tell you, but I wasn't at liberty to say anything. I'd given my word."

The fight went out of her then, and she sagged toward him, as limp as the rag doll in her hand. He caught her against his chest and felt the tidal wave of emotion rise up through her body. Once again he found himself comforting her while she wept, her pain ripping through him like a hot poker. Warm tears soaked his shirtfront while he stroked the fall of auburn curls that curtained her face, murmuring soothing words.

"I . . . I didn't even get to say good-bye."

"I'm so sorry." He repeated it over and over, leaning down to kiss the top of her head. The fragrant smell of her shampoo enveloped him.

Huddled in the dim corner of the room, they seemed cocooned in their own private sanctuary. He reached into his pocket to pull out his handkerchief and lifted her face to dry her tears. Devastated not only by her grief, but by his own sense of loss, his eyes grew moist as he pressed a kiss to her forehead.

Colleen fingered the worn toy. "She forgot Mr. Whiskers," she whispered. "Delia can't sleep without him." Fresh tears hovered on her lashes.

"I promise I'll find out where she is so we can send it to her."

"You will?"

"Yes. And we can include a letter and a wee gift to remember us by."

"I—I'd like that."

Her lids fluttered closed. Long lashes, spiky and wet, lay against her cheeks.

"Please don't cry anymore. My heart can't take it."

Her eyes flew open, and he stared into the pools of her soul, recognizing the stark longing on her face.

His gaze strayed to her full bottom lip, which quivered with emotion. As though drawn in by a force beyond his power, Rylan slowly lowered his mouth to hers. When their lips met, a burst of love coursed through him, as bright and charged as a surge of electricity—like nothing he'd ever felt before. As he feasted on the sweetness of her mouth, Colleen's arms came up and wound around his neck. He tightened his grip around her in a fierce wave of protectiveness. He wanted to hold her like this forever, shelter her from every pain, every disappointment in life.

The sudden sound of approaching footsteps and the hushed murmur of voices penetrated the passionate haze surrounding Rylan's brain. He jerked upright, realizing they were almost reclining on the bed, locked in an ardent embrace. Both their reputations, as well as his career, would be ruined if they were caught. He bolted off the bed, swiping a hand across his mouth as though to erase the invisible evidence of their kiss.

Her eyes widened as she stared at him, confusion and sorrow mixing in their depths.

"Forgive me, Colleen," he whispered, and then he raced across the room to reach the door just as Sister Veronica arrived with another nun.

"I think Miss O'Leary is feeling better now. Please excuse me. I have an emergency back at the church."

He dashed down the hall before they could ask any questions and force him to tell yet another lie.

23

WAS I WRONG to leave home?

Brianna picked at the eggs on her plate as the question that had haunted her all night burned in her brain.

Over the past few days, she'd suffered from a terrible case of homesickness, spending her first Independence Day ever away from her family. She couldn't help but remember the wonderful gatherings of friends and neighbors at Irish Meadows over the years, the food, the laughter, the fun times she'd shared with Gil . . .

This year, Brianna had accompanied Aunt Fiona to the house of a colleague, and they'd shared a sedate meal with a group of professors and talked of college programs and politics. *Bored* didn't even begin to describe how Brianna had felt all afternoon. The fact that one of the men's sons had followed her around like a lost puppy only added to Brianna's discomfort. She'd cried herself to sleep that night, wondering how her family had spent the day, wishing for Mama's comforting presence.

"Brianna. There's a telephone call for you."

Brianna looked up from her uneaten breakfast to see Aunt Fiona in the doorway, an almost apologetic look on her face.

"Is it Daddy?"

"I'm afraid so. He insists on speaking with you."

Brianna sighed. She'd known she'd have to face her father eventually. Better to do it over the telephone than in person. She'd half expected him to arrive on Aunt Fiona's doorstep one day and haul her back home.

Brianna crossed the hall to the small study and picked up the earpiece lying on the desktop. She took in a breath and let it out, steeling herself to be strong. "Hello, Daddy."

"Brianna." A loud blast of air hissed through the earpiece. "This nonsense has gone on long enough. I want you home."

Her heart gave a hiccup. Had her father just admitted to missing her?

"You've caused your mother enough grief with this little drama of yours. It's time to start acting like an adult."

Immediately Brianna's back went up. "I'm quite happy here with Aunt Fiona. *She* doesn't tell me what to do every minute."

"I am still your father, and you will obey me." His bellow caused her to pull the phone piece away from her ear.

Brianna could picture Daddy's face turning red on the other end. "I love you, Daddy, but I am not coming home."

With shaking fingers, she hung up the earpiece and sagged onto the nearby chair. She took a few deep breaths, unable to believe she'd just defied her father that way. And she'd done it without insults, tears, or hysterics. A lightness spread through her limbs. Perhaps it wasn't so hard after all to stand up for herself. To stake a claim on her future happiness.

Her thoughts automatically turned to Gil. Could she take her bravery one step further? Could she confront Gil one more time and try to make him see reason?

Filled with newfound purpose, she pushed all doubts out of

her mind, knowing she had to try . . . or she'd regret it the rest of her life.

An hour later, dressed in one of her best gowns, Brianna approached the intimidating door to the Hastings Bank and Loan Company. She clutched her handbag tighter and pushed through the entrance. The elegant surroundings took her breath away. Still, she found it hard to picture Gil working here. Stifling her nerves, she walked up to the receptionist.

"May I speak with Mr. Whelan, please?"

The woman smiled. "Do you have an appointment?"

Brianna hesitated. The temptation to lie gripped her, but she shook her head. "No. It's a personal matter."

The woman's eyebrows rose. "One moment and I'll see if he's free."

Brianna fought the urge to pace the area while she waited. She clasped her hands together to keep them from shaking. Why did it feel like everyone was staring at her?

At last, she heard footsteps and Gil appeared, a frown creasing his brow. "Brianna. Is everything all right?"

She gulped in a breath. He looked devastatingly handsome in a dark suit and matching vest. Like a real banker. "Everything's fine. Could I speak with you for a minute?"

Gil looked at the clock on the wall, then back at the receptionist, who had resumed her seat. "Mrs. Gilmore, if anyone is looking for me I'm taking a ten-minute break."

"Yes, sir."

Gil put a hand to Brianna's back and motioned to the door. "Let's take a walk."

The fact that he hadn't smiled once or said he was glad to see her sent off little flares of alarm through Brianna's system. Maybe he sensed her nerves and figured something was wrong. If only she could figure out how to start this conversation . . .

They exited the bank and walked down the sidewalk. He

turned a corner, led her to a bench in front of a barber shop, and motioned her to sit down.

"What is it, Bree?" His face remained serious as he sat beside her. Something Brianna couldn't quite define hovered in his eyes.

She twisted the strap of her bag in her fingers. "I . . . I spoke to Daddy today."

Gil went still, his back ramrod straight. She glanced at his face. The anguish there stunned her.

"So he told you?"

Confusion clouded Brianna's thinking, and all the words she'd prepared flew from her mind. "Told me what?"

Gil's gaze slid away to some spot on the ground. He ran a hand over his jaw.

She noticed the dark circles under his eyes then, and the slightly hollow look to his cheeks. "What is it, Gil?"

He seemed to pull himself back with some effort. "Never mind. First tell me what you came here for."

It was now or never. Brianna shored her courage and wet her dry lips. "Daddy demanded I come home, but I said no. I stood up to him, Gil. And it felt good."

The lines on his forehead eased. "That was very brave of you." He gave a slight smile, but his expression remained sad.

"And now I'm going to do something else equally brave." She looked him square in the eye. "I'm going to fight for you, Gil. I refuse to let Daddy dictate our lives. We need to follow our hearts, and in the end, when Daddy sees how happy we are, he'll come around. He can't stay mad at us forever."

Pain leapt into Gil's eyes before he closed them on a groan. "Oh, Bree . . ."

She reached out and laid a hand on his arm. "If I can be brave, you can, too, Gil. Please say you'll try."

He jerked off the bench, away from her, and stood staring across the street, his back rigid beneath his jacket. "I'm so sorry, Bree, but it's too late."

The cold grip of fear clutched her midsection. "What do you mean?"

When he turned toward her, his face looked haggard. "I'm engaged to Aurora. We announced it at the Independence Day party at her father's house."

The air rushed from her lungs. The scenery blurred before her eyes. "But you barely know her. How could you possibly . . . ?"

"I'm sorry, Bree," he repeated. "It happened quickly. Some . . . courtships move faster than others."

She lurched to her feet. "What are you saying? That you're in love with her?"

A muscle twitched in his jaw. He swallowed. "Yes."

Searing pain like nothing she'd ever experienced shafted through her heart. He turned his head as though looking at her was too awful to bear. How could she have been so wrong about something? Had she deluded herself into believing what she wanted to believe?

She pulled herself up to her full height, willing her limbs to cooperate. At least now she had her answer. Once and for all. "I see. Well, I'm sorry to have bothered you. I wish you and Aurora every happiness."

Before her tears could betray her, she walked quickly down the sidewalk, away from Gil and away from any ties to the past. Her future had become clear. She would follow in her aunt's footsteps—forgo any foolish notions of romance—and dedicate her life to something that would never cause her this type of agony again.

Slumped at his desk the next day, Gil rubbed his hands over his eyes, trying to dislodge the grittiness that blurred his vision. After another near-sleepless night, haunted by visions of Bree's devastation, he could barely see straight.

He suppressed a groan. Had he done the right thing—lying

to Bree about his feelings for Aurora? It was the only way he could think of to convince her to give up on him once and for all. Despite her talk of bravery, Gil just couldn't betray James or risk tearing the O'Leary family apart. Bree may not realize it, but without her father's approval—something she'd been craving her entire life—she could never be truly happy.

Gil raised his coffee cup to his lips and grimaced at the cold, bitter brew left in the bottom. How many cups had he already consumed today? No matter. He'd need another if he was to get through the afternoon.

Perhaps he'd take a walk to Amsterdam Avenue and buy a coffee from the deli at the corner. The fresh air might do him as much good as the caffeine. With a swipe to the back of his chair, he grabbed his suit jacket and pushed out the wooden gate into the main area of the bank.

Arthur Hastings emerged from his office at the same time, a frown creating furrows on his brow. "Gilbert, may I have a word with you?"

"Of course, sir." The coffee and walk would have to wait.

He followed Mr. Hastings into his office.

"Is anything wrong?" Gil took one of the guest chairs.

Arthur sat down and pushed a familiar blue folder across the desk. The anonymous loan application he'd asked Gil to examine.

"Is there a problem with the file?" Perspiration dampened the back of Gil's shirt. Had he made a grave error?

"You declined this application." Mr. Hastings's flat tone gave away nothing.

"Yes, sir. After calculating and recalculating the figures, I didn't feel the client warranted the loan." Gil frowned. "Did I miss something?" He was still learning the ropes. Had he over-looked an important element?

Arthur ran a hand over his mustache and sighed. "No. You made the right decision. It's the same one I have to make."

The air in the stuffy office became even more suffocating as a sudden suspicion dawned on Gil. "This is Mr. O'Leary's application, isn't it?"

The grim look Arthur gave him told him the answer. Deflated, Gil sagged back against the chair. "This is going to crush him."

"I know." Arthur pushed to his feet and stuffed his hands in his pockets. "But I cannot in good conscience approve the loan. To make an allowance for a personal acquaintance is no way to run a bank."

Gil rubbed a hand over his jaw "Is there no other option?"

"I'm afraid not."

Bile rose in the back of Gil's throat as a horrible thought hit him. He'd agreed to marry Aurora believing it would further Mr. O'Leary's cause, and now it appeared he'd done it all for nothing. The image of Brianna's stricken face when he'd told her of his engagement burned in his mind. The collar of his shirt choked off his air supply like a hangman's noose tightening around his neck. Gil wet his dry lips. "When will you break the news to him?"

Arthur glanced at the clock on his desk. "It's getting late. I think I'll wait until the morning. I feel it only right to tell him in person. I'll have James come in tomorrow." Arthur exhaled loudly as he resumed his seat. "You did good work on that case, son. I'm sorry the answer couldn't have been different."

"You and me both, sir."

In the shadows of the setting sun, Rylan walked down the road toward the home of Reverend Filmore's sister. He'd spent countless hours at the church on his knees in prayer, and still he couldn't shake the guilt that ate at his soul. He'd betrayed a sacred promise to God.

What he needed was absolution—to confess his offense to a priest and receive a clergyman's counsel. It was the only way to make up for his sin and find a way to move forward.

Anna Filmore Brookes and her husband lived in a modest dwelling on the outskirts of town. Their two grown children now lived in homes of their own, granting them the space to put up the good Reverend until the repairs on the rectory were complete. Rylan had met Anna at Sunday services, but never her husband. He was relieved when the plump, gray-haired woman answered his knock at the front door.

"Good evening, Mrs. Brookes. I'm sorry to bother you, but would Reverend Filmore be in?"

Her weary face broke into a smile. "He is. Please come in, Mr. Montgomery."

The delicious smell of fresh bread and some type of cooked meat met Rylan's nose as he removed his cap and stepped inside, and he realized it might be the supper hour. "I hope I'm not interrupting your meal."

"Not at all. We finished moments ago, and the men are having coffee in the parlor. Can I get you a cup?"

"No, thank you. I just need a private word with Reverend Filmore, please." The desperation in his voice must have been evident, for she gave him a curious look before she nodded.

"I'll tell him you're here."

She disappeared down a short hall and into another room. Murmuring voices reached him, and seconds later Mrs. Brookes reappeared followed by a man Rylan presumed to be her spouse.

"This is my husband, Albert," the woman said.

He shook the man's hand, noting his tall, thin frame and stooped shoulders, the opposite of his wife's short, round stature.

"Pleased to meet you, Mr. Montgomery. I understand your sermons are a big hit at St. Rita's." Mr. Brookes chuckled. "Sad to say, I'm not much of a churchgoer, but Anna has told me how good they are."

"That's kind of you to say."

"Please go on into the parlor. My brother-in-law is expecting you."

"Thank you." Rylan made his way to the cozy room and found Reverend Filmore seated in a large armchair by the fire.

He stood as Rylan entered, a look of concern on his face. "Rylan. This is unexpected. Is there an emergency?"

"Not in the way you mean, sir. But I have a personal matter that can't wait." Nerves dampened Rylan's palms.

"Of course. Please come and sit down."

Rylan took the end of the well-worn settee, across from the chair that Reverend Filmore now reclaimed. The glow of the fire cast a rosy hue in the small room, giving the space an intimate air. Though desperate to speak a moment ago, Rylan now found the words wedged tightly in his dry throat. He ran the rim of his hat through his fingers and stared into the flames.

"You seem troubled, Rylan. What is the matter?"

Rylan raised his eyes. "I never meant for this to happen. You must believe me on that, Reverend."

Reverend Filmore frowned. "I believe you. What has you so rattled?"

Rylan clenched his molars together, as though saying the words out loud would change the course of his life forever.

"Whatever it is, son, you can tell me. In all my years of ministry, there's nothing I haven't heard." An air of empathy surrounded the older man.

Rylan stared at the braided carpet. "Have you ever heard of a priest falling in love?" His voice was so low, he wasn't sure he'd actually spoken aloud. When he raised his head, he saw raw sorrow etched into the lines of Reverend Filmore's face.

"Yes, I have," he said quietly. "In fact, I've lived it."

Rylan stared. "You were in love once?"

The pastor folded his hands across his ample midsection and sighed. "Sadly, yes. It happened many years ago, in my first parish. She was a troubled young widow who came to me for counseling. Before I knew it, I'd developed all these feelings for the woman. Feelings I didn't know what to do with."

Relief bubbled through Rylan's tight chest, loosening the bands of tension. If Reverend Filmore had gotten through it and survived, then surely he could, too. "That's exactly what's happened to me, Father. But what did you do about it?"

The man shook his head. "The only thing I could. I requested a transfer to a different parish . . . and never saw her again."

A slash of intense pain hit Rylan like a physical blow. The mere notion of never seeing Colleen again was too excruciating to bear. But the thought of abandoning his vocation was worse. "Did the feelings ever go away?"

"Eventually—after a lot of time and prayer."

That didn't make Rylan feel any better. He lowered his head again. "Something happened today, Father. I . . . I kissed her. I never intended to—it just happened." Misery seeped through every pore as he pictured the disgust that must be evident on the older priest's face.

"And the kiss changed everything." Reverend Filmore said it in such a way that Rylan knew he'd experienced the same thing.

"Yes." He met the priest's gaze, sure his tortured soul must show in his eyes. "What am I to do, Father? I've been praying for hours at the church and nothing's helped."

Reverend Filmore leaned forward in his chair, his hands folded over his knees. "Well, son, this is not a decision you can make lightly. Since you haven't yet taken your final vows, your situation is different than mine. Theoretically, you still have the option to leave the seminary, if that's what you decide."

"Leave?" The dazed question hung in the air. He hadn't let himself truly consider that possibility until this moment, afraid the temptation to make such an impulsive decision might overtake his good sense.

"I believe the wise thing to do now is take time to reflect— seek God's counsel on His will for your life. Return to Boston and take a private retreat to pray for your vocation. I'm sure the clergy there will help you discern your true calling."

Go back to Boston? Why did that feel like such a failure? The image of his mother's beaming face on the day he'd left for the seminary came to mind. What would it do to her if he abandoned his vocation?

"Rylan, may I ask what made you want to become a priest?"

For the first time since Rylan had left the orphanage, tears formed. "My mother had fallen ill with pneumonia. With my father dead, she was all we had, my brothers and my sister and I. We sat by her bedside night after night and prayed for her recovery. Finally I made a bargain with God. If He spared her life, I would dedicate mine to His service." He smiled weakly. "God came through with His end. Now I'm keeping mine."

Reverend Filmore said nothing for several seconds, then tapped a finger on the arm of his chair. "While that's admirable, I'm not sure it's the best reason to become a priest."

Shards of resentment pricked at Rylan. Why would one reason be better than another to give one's life to God?

"The only way to discern whether you have a true calling or not is to step away from the situation, away from the woman who evokes these strong emotions. In the silence of the sanctuary, listen for God's purpose for your life. He will provide the answers you seek."

Rylan hung his head. "I'm so sorry I've let you down, Father."

A large hand squeezed his shoulder. "Don't be too hard on yourself, lad. It's not your fault—as I well know. Give it some time and prayer, and things will fall into place the way God intended."

As Rylan made his way back to the O'Learys' later that night, he wondered how he was going to break the news to Colleen that he was leaving, and he prayed his departure wouldn't be too much to bear after already losing Delia.

24

A T PRECISELY TEN O'CLOCK the next morning, James O'Leary arrived at the Hastings Bank. As Gil watched him enter through the main double doors, his stomach clenched into knots. He would give anything to spare James the devastation the next few minutes would bring. Losing this loan would effectively toll the death knell for Irish Meadows. Sorrow swept over Gil at the idea of losing the stables and the beloved horses. He could only imagine how distressing this would be for Bree and the rest of the family. He straightened his back against the wooden spokes of his chair and vowed to spend every spare moment over the next few weeks trying to come up with viable ways to keep Irish Meadows afloat.

For fifteen minutes, Gil stared unseeing at the work before him on his desk, his whole focus tuned to Mr. Hastings's office. From the corner of his eye, he'd be able to see when James came out. At one point, heated voices became audible through the closed door. Gil's fingers tensed on his pencil, ready to interfere if need be. But less than five minutes later, the door crashed open and James stormed out. He looked neither left nor right but strode straight out of the bank.

Gil grabbed his jacket and immediately raced after him, determined to ensure the man was all right before letting him go. On the crowded walkway, Gil dodged pedestrians, as well as a newsboy and several vendors, while trying to keep James's broad shoulders in sight. When James sprinted across the street in front of a streetcar, narrowly missing a horse and carriage, Gil held his breath. Gil waited for the streetcar to pass before he could make his way across. He swiveled his head, trying to catch a glimpse of James, but the crowd had swallowed the man.

Gil scanned the storefront windows until he came to O'Malley's Pub. He recalled James mentioning the drinking hole a few times. He'd just received bad news, so maybe he'd gone there.

Gil stepped inside the door of the pub, stunned to find so many people at the bar this early in the day. Squinting to see better, he moved farther into the gloomy interior, hazy with smoke and reeking of spilled beer. He dodged a couple of scantily dressed women and kept his focus on the end of the bar, where James sat slouched on the last barstool.

Lord, help me get through to him.

Gil approached with cautious footsteps. He pulled himself onto the stool beside James, taking note of the amber liquid he swirled in a low glass.

A bartender with a stained apron over his large belly wielded a dishrag over the surface of the bar. "What'll it be, mister?"

"A ginger ale, please."

At the sound of his voice, James jerked his head up to pin Gil with a hard stare. "What the devil are you doing here?"

Gil didn't blink. "Making sure you don't do something stupid."

James downed the contents of his glass in one gulp and crashed the tumbler onto the polished surface of the bar.

"Another round," he barked at the man behind the counter. "In fact, bring the bottle."

"You don't want to do this. It won't change anything."

"No, but it'll sure take the edge off."

The bartender arrived with Gil's ginger ale and the bottle of scotch, which he placed in front of them. James took several bills from his wallet and thrust them at the man. "For the both of us. Keep the change."

"Thanks, pal." He slid the money into his apron pocket.

Gil fingered the glass in front of him, searching for the right words to reach the man who was like a father to him. He eyed James swilling back another shot of scotch. Gil couldn't help but remember his own father slumped over a bottle of Irish whiskey more nights than he cared to count. For that reason alone, Gil rarely drank anything stronger than soda pop. He took a small sip of his drink and set the glass back down.

"I'm sorry the loan didn't go through."

James stopped in the middle of refilling his glass. "How hard did you try to persuade Arthur to change his mind?"

Gil let the initial wave of guilt ride over him before he hardened. "I'm a new employee at the bank. I don't carry a lot of clout."

"As the man's future son-in-law, you surely do. How hard did you milk that connection? Or did you even bother?"

The arrows shooting from James's already bloodshot eyes hit their mark, igniting the burn of anger in Gil's chest. How dare he say that? After all Gil had sacrificed for him?

Every ounce of hurt and resentment that Gil had repressed for months boiled up into a fine rage, leaving him powerless to stop the words that poured forth. "Do you ever listen to yourself, to the things you say that wreak pain and havoc on those you claim to love?"

James jolted on his stool, his hand sloshing the liquid over the side of his glass.

"Adam and Brianna have left home because of your bullying tactics. My leaving is your doing, as well. If you hadn't been so opposed to me courting Bree . . ." A sudden thought wisped through his brain. "Or was it because you needed me to do your dirty work with Mr. Hastings? My betrothal to his daughter was your trump card. Is that why you destroyed your daughter's dreams and my integrity? All for your blasted money?" Gil's hands shook as he let loose the bitterness that had been building since the day he'd returned from college. "Do you care about anyone but yourself?"

James jerked up from the bar, his stool toppling over as he rose. He grabbed Gil by the front of his shirt and raised him off his seat with one hand. "How dare you question me after I took you in and raised you like my own son?" Red blotches bled over James's cheeks. His eyes held a type of wildness that shot a streak of fear through Gil. Was the man so desperate he'd resort to physical violence?

The bartender approached. "Keep it civil, lads. Or take it outside."

Gil realized then their voices had escalated to the point that the other patrons were staring. He yanked himself free from James's grasp and stepped back, adjusting his clothes. "Take some advice for once. Go home to your wife and children and be grateful for what you've got, instead of wallowing in what you don't." With one last glare at James, still puffing like an overheated steam engine, Gil stormed out of the pub.

***

Colleen poked her fork into the mashed potatoes on her plate, one eye on the door to the dining room, wishing Rylan would come breezing in with his familiar grin and apologize to her mother for being late for dinner. Wishing he'd come in and act as though nothing were wrong and tease her about something she'd said to Sister Marguerite, or tell one of his silly jokes.

Maybe then her fears would be put to rest. Maybe then she could breathe normally again.

Ever since he'd kissed her with such passion yesterday and then promptly bolted from the room, she hadn't seen a trace of him.

For one brief moment, Colleen allowed herself to relive the thrill of his kiss, an embrace so intense it seemed she'd given up part of her soul. In all the kisses she'd shared with other men, she'd never experienced anything close to that type of bliss.

Her insides roiled with confusion, swirling like the mess she'd made of her mound of potatoes. How in the world had she fallen in love with a priest? With a sigh, she pushed her plate away, turning her attention to the few remaining family members at the table.

Deirdre and Connor chatted away to her unusually sullen mother. Lately Mama hadn't been herself. Colleen noted the deep shadows under her eyes and remembered overhearing heated words coming from her parents' bedroom the night before. She could never remember her parents fighting like that. What was happening to their family?

"Where's Daddy tonight, Mama? Working late?" She tried to keep her tone casual.

The little bit of color in her mother's cheeks drained away. She sent Colleen a nervous glance. "I'm sure that must be it." A frown marred her features. "What about Rylan? This is the second night he hasn't come home for dinner."

Colleen attempted a casual shrug. "I wondered the same thing a few minutes ago."

Mama laid down her napkin. "Deirdre and Connor, you may be excused."

The pair scrambled down from the table and tore out of the room.

"Remember to wash your hands." Her mother's admonition

echoed through the room, and she shook her head. "Those two will either keep me young or make me gray before my time."

Colleen couldn't muster a smile. Deirdre reminded her too much of Delia.

"Did something happen at the orphanage?" Her mother's sharp gaze missed nothing.

Colleen tugged at a curl hugging her shoulder. "One of the children left unexpectedly yesterday. Rylan and I were both very fond of Delia, but we didn't have a chance to say good-bye." She used every ounce of willpower not to break down in front of her mother. The raw hurt ran deep over the loss of the little girl. She couldn't help but wonder—if she had broached the subject with her parents, would they have considered adopting Delia?

"I'm so sorry. That must have been difficult."

"Very difficult."

Her mother stirred a spoon of sugar into her tea. "When you volunteer at an orphanage, you have to be prepared for children to leave. It's best not to become too attached."

"I'll remember from now on."

Mama frowned and gave her a long look. "I think this punishment of your father's has gone on long enough. Do you want me to speak to him about it?"

Colleen startled. "No, Mama. I enjoy working at the orphanage. It's not a punishment at all."

Mama's eyes widened. "I must say I never expected this reaction." She gave a slight smile. "If you're enjoying it, then I suppose there's no harm in continuing."

Colleen sagged with relief. "Thank you, Mama. I promise I'll still find time to help you with your charity work."

"I know you will, dear."

Colleen bit her lip, debating whether she should tell her mother about seeing Brianna. She decided it would be selfish not to. "I've seen Bree, Mama."

Her mother's head flew up. "You have? When?"

"She came to the orphanage with Aunt Fiona."

"How is she? Does she look ill?"

"No. She seems . . . happy."

A flicker of hurt crossed her mother's features. "Happy?"

Colleen shrugged. "Maybe *content* is a better word." She watched her mother. "I don't think Bree will ever be happy until she gets Gil out of her system."

Her mother's expression became pensive. "I'm afraid you're right."

Colleen gave a soft sigh. It seemed she and Brianna were caught in the same predicament. For Colleen feared she would never be truly happy until she got over a certain dark-eyed priest.

25

THAT NIGHT A SMALL BREEZE stirred the cotton
curtain in the window of Gil's stuffy room in the boarding house. Stretched out on the ragged quilt atop his
bed, he could feel no cooling effect. He lay there, hands folded
beneath his head, staring at the cracked ceiling, wishing he knew
what to do with all the guilt he was feeling. Why had he added
to James's misery with his angry accusations? And why hadn't
he insisted on taking James home? At least then he'd know the
man was safe. For all Gil knew, he could still be slumped over
the bar at O'Malley's while poor Mrs. O'Leary paced the floor
with worry.

When sleep wouldn't come, Gil sat up and peered at the face
of his pocket watch under the light of his bedside lamp. Nearly
midnight. He hung his head, wishing the room were big enough
to pace. With all his restless energy, he needed somewhere to
expend it. If he were home, he'd go out to the barn and saddle
up Midnight for an evening ride. The thought of country air and
lush meadows made Gil's throat burn with sudden homesickness.

Bree. He could never think of Irish Meadows without thinking of her. How he missed her face, their easy communication, her rich laughter whenever he told a silly joke. A selfish part of Gil wondered if losing Irish Meadows would change James's mind about Gil being good enough for his daughter. Or would it only make him more determined than ever that she marry a wealthy man?

Loud rapping on his door jerked Gil up from the bed. "Who is it?"

"Mrs. Shaughnessy. There's a telephone call for you in the parlor."

His heart raced as he yanked on his shoes and grabbed a shirt. Who would be calling him at this time of night? "Be right there."

"Some time of the night to be getting telephone calls." Mrs. Shaughnessy grunted as her footsteps shuffled off.

By the time Gil reached the parlor, there was no sign of his landlady. He picked up the receiving end of the phone and leaned in toward the mouthpiece on the wall. "Hello?"

"Gilbert? It's Kathleen." The high-pitched hysteria in her voice sent shivers of alarm down Gil's spine. Had his worst fears come true and James hadn't made it home? Another sickening notion made his stomach lurch. Had something happened to Brianna?

"What's wrong?" His tone came out harsher than he'd intended.

"Oh, Gil. It's James. He's . . ." Sobs drifted through the end of the phone.

Icy talons gripped his chest. "He's what?"

"He's in the hospital. They think it's his heart."

Gil clutched the edge of the piano beside the phone. His mouth became as dry as the dust that coated the instrument, and he had to swallow before he could get a word out. "Where are you?"

"I'm outside the waiting area. The doctors are examining him." Her voice broke. "They don't know how bad it is."

Gil took a breath and forced a calm he didn't feel. "Everything's going to be all right. Which hospital are you in?"

"Long Island Memorial. Gil, I need you to come. I can't find Adam. Colleen and the younger ones were asleep, and I didn't want to wake them." The frailty of her voice shook Gil to the core. "Rylan's here, trying to get some information . . ." She trailed off.

"I'll leave right now. Just hold on a while longer." He paused, hesitating to bring up the subject but knowing it was the right thing to do. Rylan wasn't a priest yet, and Mrs. O'Leary would want the man she relied on for her family's spiritual well-being. "Do you want me to contact Reverend Filmore?"

More sobs fractured her response. "Y-yes, p-please."

"I'll get there as quick as I can."

"Thank you, Gilbert."

With unsteady hands, he hung up the receiver and ran back to his room. As he threw on his suspenders and a jacket, and stuffed his wallet inside the pocket of his pants, his thoughts turned to Brianna. She would never forgive him if he didn't take her with him.

He placed a quick phone call to Arthur Hastings before letting himself out the front door and onto the darkened street.

It was going to be a very long night.

Brianna stirred from her sleep, not knowing what had woken her. She lifted her head off the pillow, listening. In the chill of her room, she shivered and pulled the quilt more firmly under her chin.

"Brianna, dear. It's Aunt Fiona." The door creaked open, and her aunt stepped inside.

Brianna sat up, rubbing her eyes in the darkness. "What time is it?"

"It's after midnight. Gilbert is downstairs asking for you."

She moved to the side of the bed, frowning. "It seems there's a family emergency."

Alarm chased all notion of sleep from her brain. She swung her legs off the bed. "What's the matter?"

Please, Lord, don't let it be Mama.

"He wouldn't say. He's waiting to tell us both at once."

Brianna tugged on her slippers and dressing gown, belting the waist tight, and followed her aunt down the narrow staircase to the parlor below. As she entered the room, she became conscious of the untidy state of her hair and ran a hand over her head to smooth the stray pieces that had escaped her long braid. Her heart thumped a crazy beat, half from nerves at the news to come, half at seeing Gil again.

He stood by the unlit hearth, his shoulders hunched. A candle flickered on the mantel by his head, casting a glow over his dark hair. At the sound of their footsteps, he turned to face her. His curls stood in disarray, as though he'd been running his fingers through them as he often did when agitated. A faint shadow of stubble hugged his jawline, accenting the beloved cleft of his chin.

She clutched the lapels of her robe with icy fingers. "Gil. What's wrong?"

His bleak expression told her the news would be grim.

He crossed the carpet to where she stood and reached for her free hand. The warmth from his skin radiated through her palm and up her arm.

"Sit down, Bree." His tender gaze moved from her to her aunt, who hovered by the doorway. "You, too, Aunt Fiona."

A sob rose in Brianna's throat, fighting for release, but she pushed it back. "Please tell me no one has died."

He guided her to the sofa. "No one has died . . . but your father is in the hospital."

She gasped. Gil sat beside her and reached for her again. She clung to his fingers like a lifeline.

"I'm sorry to spring bad news on you like this."

Aunt Fiona lowered herself to the edge of her chair. "What's wrong with my brother?"

"The doctors are trying to determine that. They think it might be his heart." He turned back to Bree. "Your mother telephoned and asked me to meet her at the hospital. I figured you'd want to come. That's why I'm here."

Brianna shot to her feet. "Yes, of course. Give me a minute to change." She faced her aunt. "Will you come, too?"

Aunt Fiona shook her head sadly. "I don't think I'd be welcome. I'll do more good here by praying."

"You're sure?"

"Yes. Go on now. Don't keep Gilbert waiting."

Brianna dropped a kiss on her aunt's cheek before rushing back up the stairs. In the midst of dressing and twisting her hair into a quick knot, she murmured constant prayers for God to keep her father safe and to give her mother the strength to bear whatever was to come.

She snatched her shawl from a hook on the door and rushed downstairs, not allowing a full thought to form in her head.

Gil waited in the entry hall, cap in hand. Aunt Fiona came forward to embrace her. "Let me know how your father is when you can. I doubt I'll sleep a wink until I hear he's all right."

She squeezed her aunt. "Of course. As soon as there's word, I'll call."

Gil tugged on his cap and offered Brianna his arm, which she accepted, grateful for his steadying presence as they stepped outside. "Which hospital is Daddy in?"

"Long Island Memorial."

She stopped short. "But how will we get there? There's no transportation at this time of night."

With a sheepish shrug, he pointed to the black Model T parked at the curb. "I called Mr. Hastings, and he lent me his chauffeur."

Brianna stiffened at the blatant reminder of exactly where Gil now belonged—and to whom. "Of course. I forgot." She descended the stairs, forcing him to follow.

"Bree, I'm sorry." Sorrow laced his voice.

She couldn't look at him, afraid her emotions, so near the surface at the moment, would overflow. "Please don't. Let's just get to the hospital."

The chauffeur held the door open for them, and Gil helped her into the car. The touch of his hand at the small of her back was almost more than she could bear. She moved as far over on the seat as possible, unwilling to risk any contact.

The stillness in the car stretched into an uncomfortable silence. Brianna kept her eyes fixed out the window, concentrating on prayers for her father's welfare until the need for physical comfort became all-consuming. How she wished she could lay her head on Gil's chest—feel the shelter of his arms around her. She bit her bottom lip to keep it from quivering. She had to be strong for her mother. Mama would need everyone to rally around her now.

"There's something I need to tell you." Gil's quiet voice broke the silence.

Her throat, thickened with emotion, would not allow any words to pass.

"It's about your father."

He had her attention then, and she glanced over at him. A look of grief haunted his eyes.

"This morning, Mr. Hastings had to turn down your father's loan application. James left the bank very upset, and I followed him."

"Followed him where?"

He sighed. "To O'Malley's Pub. I tried to get him to go home, but he became almost violent. I had to leave him there alone. It was either that or get into a brawl."

Brianna bit her bottom lip. Though Daddy enjoyed his after-

dinner brandy, he was not the type to frequent drinking estab-
lishments. Mama wouldn't allow it.

"I don't know what happened after that. But I think the stress
of losing the loan caused his collapse. He was counting on that
money."

"Is Irish Meadows really in that much trouble?" She kept her
eyes fixed on his, willing him not to lie.

He nodded. "Things aren't good at all."

Thoughts flew through her mind, swirling like the debris on
the street below. They could lose their home, their farm. What
would they do then? "What's going to happen to us, Gil?"

His arm came around her then to pull her close. She leaned
her head on his shoulder.

"I promise I'll do everything in my power to make sure Irish
Meadows stays afloat."

Though her eyes remained dry, she accepted the handkerchief
he pressed into her hands.

"Please try not to worry. Maybe I shouldn't have told you, but
I thought you had a right to know what may have contributed
to your father's illness."

She nodded against his chest, her emotions beginning to
steady from the rhythm of his even heartbeat beneath her ear.
He pressed a kiss to the top of her head, and she closed her eyes,
pretending for one brief moment that he still belonged to her.

26

AT SEVEN THE NEXT MORNING, Rylan let himself into the O'Leary house, careful to keep his movements quiet so as not to rouse the occupants. A bone-deep weariness weighed him down, leading him to hope he'd be able to sleep at last.

He'd put his foot on the first stair when he heard the high-pitched voice of little Deirdre coming from the direction of the dining room.

"But where is Mama? I want Mama."

"Hush now, sweetheart. Mama is with Daddy at the hospital. She'll be home as soon as she can."

Rylan closed his eyes at the sound of Colleen's voice, his chest constricting with pain. How could he leave here, knowing he may never see her again?

God, please grant me Your strength, for I am weak.

His hand on the polished rail, he went to take a further step but stopped. He owed Colleen news about her father. With another quick prayer for guidance, he headed for the dining room.

No one noticed him in the doorway at first. Connor sat at the table, pushing the scrambled eggs around his plate, a scowl on his freckled face. But the sight of Colleen, holding Deirdre in her arms, brought an ache to Rylan's chest. With the morning light playing over the loose curls on her shoulders, and her eyes closed, her chin on top of her sister's head, she reminded him of a Madonna. She rocked the child back and forth, and for an instant, Rylan allowed himself to imagine her as his wife, rocking their child, an expression of such love on her face that his throat tightened against the emotion pushing upward. For the first time since he'd decided to become a priest, he mourned the loss of the children he would never have.

"Rylan!" Connor pushed away from the table and raced over to throw his arms around Rylan's waist.

He patted Connor's back, the boy's simple affection adding further pressure to his chest.

"My dad's sick." Connor's voice sounded muffled against Rylan's shirt.

He laid his hand on Connor's head. "I know, lad. But the doctor thinks he's going to be fine."

He sensed Colleen's attention riveted on him. Shoring his courage, he met her eyes. The impact sent jolts of electricity streaking through his body. He swallowed. "I've just come from the hospital."

She rose with Deirdre in her arms. "You were there with Mama?"

"Yes."

"Why didn't either of you wake me?"

The hurt on her face twisted his insides. "Your mother wanted you to be home for the little ones when they woke up."

She moved toward him, anxiety evident in her tense posture. "How is Daddy? Mrs. Johnston said he collapsed, but that's all she knew."

Rylan longed to embrace her and tell her everything would be fine. But he couldn't do that. For more reasons than one.

He looked from Connor to Deirdre, then back to Colleen, hoping she'd understand his message. He didn't want to scare the wee ones by describing the frailty of their father's condition. "The doctors are working hard to make him well."

Without taking her eyes from his, Colleen lowered the little girl to the ground. "Dee-Dee, you and Connor go and get dressed. I'll be up in a minute to help you."

When Deirdre started to wail a protest, Rylan bent to whisper a promise of treats in her ear. The girl beamed a smile and took off out the door after Connor.

Rylan straightened and cleared his throat, conscious of Colleen standing mere feet away, looking so beautiful it hurt. There were so many things he needed to say, but his mouth seemed glued shut. Before anything else, though, he owed her the truth about Mr. O'Leary. "Your father has suffered what the doctors feel is an angina attack, a fairly serious condition of the heart."

She clutched the back of a chair, instant tears welling in her eyes.

Rylan pushed his hands deep in the pockets of his pants to keep from reaching for her. "The fact that he made it through the night is a good sign. The doctors are optimistic he'll recover. It will take some time, though."

Colleen brushed at the tears on her cheeks. "Mama's not there alone, is she?"

"No. Gil and Brianna have been there most of the night, as well as Reverend Filmore. Your mother sent me to let you know what was happening. I tried to persuade her to come home with me for a rest, but she won't leave him."

Colleen pushed away from the chair and crossed to the doorway. "I have to go, too. I want to be there when Daddy wakes up."

Rylan caught her arm before she could go any farther. "What about Deirdre and Connor?"

"Mrs. Johnston will watch them."

"Those children need the comfort of their family." He gave

a rueful shrug. "I'd do it, but I haven't slept in two days, and I'm afraid I'm about to keel over."

She grew very still, her head averted. They remained like that, not moving for several moments. "It's because of me, isn't it? Because of the kiss. That's why you haven't been home. Why you haven't slept."

The steady beat of the clock on the mantel matched the rhythm of his heart beating in his chest. He dropped his hand from her arm and took a step away. "Yes."

***

Colleen's pulse pounded in her ears, muffling all other sounds in the room, except Rylan's shallow breathing. What would he say now about that wonderful, terrifying moment when he'd kissed her and changed her life forever? Did he regret it so much he couldn't look at her?

"I owe you a most sincere apology, Colleen." His voice, a mere whisper, raised the hair at the nape of her neck.

"No, you don't." She turned her face toward him.

"I do. I took an unfair liberty with you at the orphanage. Unfair to both of us. It's even more reprehensible when I think of what that priest did to you when you were a child."

Her whole body trembled with the significance of this moment. She'd have one chance to tell him how she felt, and she needed to do it in a way that didn't send him running for the sanctuary of his church. "I don't see it that way at all." She took a step closer, grateful he didn't move away.

The stubble on his face, the dark circles under his eyes, told her of the depth of the suffering he'd been through. She longed to reach out and brush the hair off his forehead. To smooth the lines of worry from his face.

"Please don't feel guilty," she whispered. "I don't regret it for one moment."

He shook his head, sorrow shining in those warm brown eyes.

"I had no right to kiss you like that. Not when I've committed my life to God."

"Our feelings for each other gave you the right." She kept her eyes trained on his as though he'd disappear if she blinked. Tentatively, she reached out to lay a hand on his arm. He flinched but didn't retreat.

Did she dare tell him she'd fallen in love with him? Or would that only make matters worse?

"I'm going back to Boston."

She jolted as though he'd stabbed her. "Rylan, no. You can't leave."

"I must. I told Reverend Filmore what happened, and he's sending me back."

Her mouth fell open. A film of tears blurred her vision. "You told Reverend Filmore?" Why did that feel like a betrayal?

"I didn't mention your name, if that's what's worrying you."

Relief loosened the grip on her lungs. She should have known he'd never compromise her reputation, but what about him? Concern shot through her. "What will happen to you now?"

A ghost of his endearing grin hovered on his lips. "Don't worry. They won't torture me or anything. I'll have to do a solitary retreat with a whole lot of prayer and penance, I suppose."

"Penance? For comforting a friend?"

He lifted one eyebrow. "You and I both know it was far more than that." He placed the palm of one hand against her cheek, sending warm shivers through her body. "I think I've gone and fallen in love with you, my beautiful Colleen. And I need God's grace to help me figure out what to do about it. If it's still His desire that I continue as a priest, then I'll have to live with that."

She could no longer contain the hot tears that spilled down her face, rolling over his hand. "What about me? What do I do?"

Compassion and regret played over his handsome features. "Pray, love. Pray hard. For both of us."

She'd need a lot more than prayer to survive this. Her world was unraveling around her, the earth shifting beneath her feet. How would she ever regain her footing?

She reached up to clamp cold fingers over his warm hand. "You won't go before we know if Daddy will be all right? I couldn't bear to lose Delia and you and Daddy, too."

He gazed at her with ravaged eyes and sighed. "Very well. I'll stay a few more days—until we're sure your father's on the mend."

"Thank you." She closed her eyes for a brief moment, until he gently disengaged his hand.

"Now I'd best get some sleep before I keel over." He moved past her into the hallway.

She straightened and took a deep breath. As he started to climb the stairs, she rushed after him. "Just so you know, I'm praying that God's changed His mind and doesn't want you after all."

Rylan's low chuckle warmed her battered heart.

27

SEATED ON ONE OF THE uncomfortable chairs in the hospital waiting room, Brianna leaned her head against the wall behind her and stretched in an effort to relieve her aching back muscles. It seemed they'd waited an eternity to hear anything from the doctor. A middle-aged man with a stethoscope had finally come to tell them that her father had likely suffered an angina attack—a fairly serious one that had left him greatly weakened. The staff had been working diligently to make sure he stayed alive, and for now they had deemed him stable. They had allowed Mama to go into the room to see Daddy, even though he was still unconscious. The misery on Mama's face when she'd returned to the waiting room had brought Brianna to the brink of despair. How could this have happened to her strapping father who'd always seemed as strong as a lumberjack?

Brianna glanced over at her mother standing at the open doorway, staring down the long, silent hallway as though willing the doctor or nurse to arrive with good news. Mama's back shifted with her huge sigh, and she turned to face them. Seated on the far side of the room, Gil looked up.

"Why don't they bring us another update? It's been hours." Mama's voice quavered, exhaustion taking its toll.

Gil crossed the room and guided her to one of the chairs. "Can I get you anything? Coffee or water?"

"No, thank you, Gil. I couldn't drink another drop."

Gil straightened and plunged his fingers through his already messy hair as he paced the area like a caged lion. Brianna could tell something weighed heavily on his mind, something more than just the waiting.

He came to sit beside her mother, head bent over his knees. "There's something I need to tell you." He raised wretched eyes to Brianna as though asking her permission.

Brianna gave a small nod. She'd asked him not to mention the financial problems to her mother earlier in the night, but now that Daddy had stabilized, perhaps her mother had a right to know what had contributed to the crisis.

"What is it, Gilbert?" Mama's quiet dignity astounded Brianna.

"I think you should know why James was drinking at O'Malley's Pub all day."

Her mother stiffened until her back became as straight as the painted lines running up the wall. She gave Gil a hard glance. "What do you know about it?"

Misery swamped his features. "I followed him there from the bank."

Gil proceeded to tell her the same story he'd relayed to Brianna. Her mother's face grew paler as he went on, despite the fact that Gil downplayed the severity of their financial problems.

"I'm afraid I only made matters worse by losing my temper. I should never have left him there . . ." Gil's voice cracked.

Mama reached over to put a hand on his arm. "It's not your fault. You know how stubborn James can be."

"I suppose you're right. He was in no mood to listen to reason."

Mama patted his arm and sighed. "So Irish Meadows is in trouble. That explains a great deal about my husband's recent behavior."

Brianna hated that her mother was now more distressed than before. She crossed to sit beside her and took her hand. "We'll be all right, Mama. As long as Daddy recovers, nothing else matters."

Mama aimed a searing look at Gil. "This loan doesn't have anything to do with your sudden engagement to Aurora Hastings, does it?"

Gil pressed his mouth into a grim line. The telling way his gaze slid to the ground told Brianna a lot.

The color rose in Mama's cheeks, an indication of her rising temper. "Did James ask you to do this in order to get that loan? Because as sure as I'm living and breathing, I know it wasn't love at first sight."

Brianna's breath caught in a low gasp, and Gil shot to his feet.

Mama rose as well, temper at full boil. "I want the truth, young man. There've been far too many secrets going on in this family, and it stops now."

Gil exhaled loudly. "James asked me to court Aurora."

Her mother moved closer. "And whose idea was the betrothal, which conveniently happened a few days before the loan decision?"

He raked a hand over his jaw, but then dropped his arm, shoulders slumping.

"It was all James's idea, wasn't it? He asked you to propose."

Gil's blue eyes swam with despair. "Yes."

Gil's admission, which pained her mother greatly, caused a tiny bubble of hope to rise in Brianna's chest. Could it be that Gil had lied to her and didn't have feelings for Aurora after all?

The hope quickly deflated. No matter how the engagement had come about, Brianna knew Gil was too honorable to ever go back on his commitment.

Her mother sank back onto the chair. "So help me, when that man recovers, I'm going to kill him."

An hour later, when the doctor entered the stuffy waiting room, Gil rose from his cramped position on the uncomfortable wood chair, wincing against the pain in his stiffened leg muscles.

Mrs. O'Leary and Brianna rose, as well.

Gil prayed the news was good, though the bland expression on the man's face didn't give him high expectations.

"Mrs. O'Leary?" The paunchy doctor, a different man than earlier that morning, peered into the room.

Kathleen stepped forward. "Yes. How is my husband?"

The man gave a wry smile. "He's awake, and from the hard time he's giving the nurses, I'd wager he'll make a full recovery."

Both women burst into tears simultaneously. Gil had used up his handkerchiefs long ago but moved to put his arm around Mrs. O'Leary's shoulders.

"I must warn you," the doctor went on, "the recovery process will be arduous. Mr. O'Leary must stay in the hospital for several weeks, and when he does come home, he'll have to take it very easy for several months. Which means avoiding anything that will cause him stress, such as a job or difficult family situations."

Mrs. O'Leary straightened. "I understand. Getting my hardheaded husband to understand might be a different story." She looked over at Brianna. "The whole family will have to pull together and make sure he does as he's told."

"We'll do whatever we have to, Mama."

She gave her daughter a quick nod and turned back to the doctor. "May I see my husband?"

"Only for a few minutes. He's still very weak. Remember to say nothing that might upset him."

She nodded. "I'll hold my tongue . . . for today."

Brianna hugged her mother. "Give Daddy our love."

"I will."

The moment Kathleen disappeared down the hall, Brianna seemed to crumble, as if she'd been holding herself together for her mother's sake. Tired of restraining himself, Gil moved quickly to fold her trembling frame into his arms. She leaned into him, her cheek resting against his chest. A sensation of rightness enveloped him. This was where Brianna belonged. In his arms, where he could provide strength when she needed him. At the same time, Gil fought to ignore the image of Aurora's trusting face, which kept surfacing along with an unbearable load of guilt.

He glanced down at Brianna, the dark smudges under her eyes giving him pause. The long hours of waiting had taken their toll on her, and though Gil longed to take her home, he knew she'd never allow it.

With a sigh, she pulled back from his embrace. "What are we going to do about Irish Meadows? If Daddy can't work for several months, we'll lose the business for sure."

Gil set his jaw, a decision that had been swirling through his mind for several hours now taking concrete form. "I'll come back and handle things until he's ready to work again."

Bree's startled eyes widened. "You'd do that? After all Daddy's put you through?"

"Like your mother said, the family has to pull together to get through this crisis. And I know the business almost as well as your father."

"What about your job at the bank?" She twisted a crumpled handkerchief in her hands.

"I'll have to quit, but to be honest, it will be a relief. I don't think I'm cut out for the banking world."

A slow smile spread over Brianna's face, lighting her eyes with more hope than he'd seen in a long time. "Thank you, Gil. That will be a huge relief for all of us." She reached up to give him a fierce hug. "If anyone can save Irish Meadows, it's you."

He tightened his arms around her, his chest swelling at her simple faith in him. A faith he'd taken for granted all these years but which buoyed his confidence like nothing else. The familiar feel of her unleashed a wave of longing through him. James's brush with death had made one thing perfectly clear to Gil. Life was too short to waste. From now on, he intended to make every precious moment count.

Brianna moved back until her face was mere inches from his. "I've missed you so much, Gil." The naked yearning in her voice matched the need inside him, rekindling the intensity of his feelings for her.

"I've missed you, too," he whispered. "More than you'll ever know."

He longed to kiss her and knew she felt the same way, but propriety forced him to gently disengage. "As much as I hate it, I need to speak to Aurora first."

"What do you mean?"

He met her uncertain gaze. "I should never have agreed to this engagement, and I intend to right the wrong as soon as I can. Once I'm . . . unattached, and once your father is stronger, I will speak to him again about us." He brushed a finger down her cheek. "Living a lie these past weeks has taught me a valuable lesson. From now on I intend to live in truth as much as possible."

She returned his smile with one of her own. Words of love hovered on his lips, but again he owed it to Aurora to break off their relationship before declaring his feelings for another woman.

He'd have to be patient a little while longer.

On Friday morning, Brianna set down her travel bag in Irish Meadows' foyer and inhaled the unique scent of furniture polish mixed with the remnants of Daddy's cigars—the smells of home. The knots in her stomach relaxed for the first time in weeks. A bone-deep certainty told her this was where she belonged.

Aunt Fiona had taken her departure with stoic calm, yet Brianna sensed an underlying disappointment. She assured her aunt she would return in the fall for the start of her first semester at Barnard College, and prayed that by then her father would be much improved.

Footsteps descended the main staircase. Colleen came into view, a surprised expression crossing her face at the sight of Brianna. Colleen rushed forward to embrace her, an action that astonished Brianna. She returned the hug, grateful to be back with her family and happy to see the changes in Colleen were apparently real. All traces of her sister's former animosity had disappeared.

Colleen looked pointedly at Brianna's luggage. "You're moving back?"

"For now. Mama needs all the help she can get."

One perfectly arched brow raised over curious blue eyes. "And it has nothing to do with Gil coming back?"

She lifted her chin. "I'd be coming home regardless. Though I can't deny I'm happy he's here."

"But he's still engaged to Aurora, isn't he?"

Brianna removed her hat and gloves, careful to keep her expression neutral. "As far as I know, he is."

Colleen gave a heavy sigh. "We're a fine pair, the two of us."

Loud footsteps clattered across the tiles. "Is that Miss Brianna

I hear?" Mrs. Johnston appeared, a wide smile beaming across her usually stern features.

"It is indeed, Mrs. Johnston."

"Ah, you've made my day." She gave Brianna a quick hug. "We've missed you around here, that's for sure."

"I've missed everyone, too. Could you have my bags brought up to my room, please? And some tea would be wonderful."

"Make that two, Mrs. Johnston." Colleen linked her arm through Brianna's. "We've got a lot to catch up on."

After listening to accounts of the family's activities over the first cup of steaming tea, Brianna leaned back against the cushioned settee. She'd missed these simple pleasures, spending time with her family in this most comforting of rooms. Memories of how she'd left her home, sneaking out of the house at dawn that fateful day, crept over her, but she refused to give in to those darker emotions. Everything had changed since then, and she was determined to keep a positive attitude.

Colleen poured herself another cup of tea with hands that shook enough to rattle the china. Brianna frowned. Was something other than their father's illness bothering her sister? She had her answer when Colleen raised her head. The sadness shadowing her features took Brianna by surprise.

"Can I tell you something in confidence, Bree?"

"Of course you can."

Colleen moved closer to Brianna on the settee and set her cup on the low table in front of them. "I've had no one to talk to about this . . ." She bit her lip.

Real concern shot through Brianna. "What is it? Something's wrong, I can see it."

Colleen turned to her, tears standing out in her vivid eyes. "Since working at the orphanage together, Rylan and I have become close." She took in a deep breath. "And . . . we kissed." She paused. "I think I'm in love with him, Bree."

Shock pasted Brianna's tongue to the roof of her mouth. Her

sister in love with a priest? What could she say to that? "Oh, Colleen, I'm so sorry." She reached over to squeeze Colleen's hand. "How does Rylan feel?"

Colleen dashed at the wet trails on her face. "He's ridden with guilt, of course. He's going back to Boston to sort through things with his superior."

"Does he have feelings for you, too?"

Colleen nodded, her misery palpable. "I think so. But he's made a commitment he doesn't want to go back on." More tears bloomed. "You've been through this type of pain with Gil. How did you get over your feelings?"

Brianna's heart bled for her sister as she recalled her own agony the day Gil left Irish Meadows. "I didn't," she said simply. "I don't know if I ever will. But putting my energy into something else helped take my mind off the grief."

Colleen sniffed. "Will you pray for me, Bree? That I can overcome this."

Another shock rippled through Brianna. Whatever had happened between Rylan and her sister, he'd at least succeeded in bringing her back to God, a huge accomplishment in itself. "Of course, I'll pray for you. As I have been for myself. That God will heal your pain."

"Thank you." She gave Brianna a look of regret. "And Bree, I'm sorry for all the hurtful things I've done to you over the years. I realize now I acted out of jealousy."

"You were jealous of *me*?"

Colleen nodded. "You were so smart and perfect. And you were Mama's favorite. Not to mention the teacher's pet." She sighed.

Brianna shook her head. "But I was jealous of you. You were so beautiful while I was the plain younger sister. And clearly you were Daddy's favorite. I could never do anything right in his eyes." She realized bitterness had crept into her voice. "Seems kind of silly now."

Colleen chuckled through her tears. "I can't believe we were jealous of each other." She sobered. "Do you know how often I wished people would see me for who I am inside, instead of just the pretty outer package? I guess that's what first drew me to Rylan. He didn't seem affected by my looks at all."

Her haunted expression returned. Brianna leaned over to embrace her. "Try not to worry. God's plan will work out in His perfect time. He only has our best interest at heart, and much like Daddy, He'll make sure it happens—whether we like it or not."

28

G IL TRUDGED UP THE STEPS to Belvedere, dread dogging his every footfall. He'd just come from the bank, where he'd met with Mr. Hastings and resigned from his position. To say Arthur Hastings hadn't taken the news well would be the understatement of the year.

Now he had to confront Aurora and let her down gently. He felt like the worst sort of heel going back on his proposal, but to continue the lie would be worse.

"Good day, Mr. Whelan." The housekeeper welcomed him into the residence.

Gil removed his cap. "Good day. Is Miss Aurora in?"

"Yes, she is. Please wait in the parlor while I tell her you're here."

Unable to sit, Gil strode to the windows overlooking the vast gardens below. With the bright sunshine beaming over the flowers, Gil found it hard to imagine ruining Aurora's grand hopes for the future.

"Gil. What a nice surprise." Aurora entered the room like a

fresh summer's breeze, so pretty that Gil had to swallow the bile in his throat. How had he allowed this sweet girl to be made a pawn in James's scheme?

"Good afternoon, Aurora." Gil bent to kiss her offered hand. "I'm sorry to arrive unannounced, but I need to talk to you."

A flicker of concern shadowed her bright eyes for a moment. "Of course. Please have a seat." She motioned to the seating area in front of the large marble mantel.

Gil sat on the edge of the settee near Aurora and clasped his hands over his knees.

She frowned as she studied him. "What is it, Gil? I can tell something is weighing on your mind."

He nodded, his mouth tight. "I have something to tell you, and I hope you can forgive me when you hear the whole story."

Her anxious gaze darted to the fireplace and back. "Has this got to do with Mr. O'Leary's illness?"

"In a way, yes. Now that James can no longer manage the farm, I'm needed back at Irish Meadows. So this morning I tendered my resignation at the bank."

Her mouth fell open, dismay darting over her features. "Why is it up to you? You're not even his son."

Gil chose to ignore her insensitivity, keeping in mind this was upsetting news for her. "No, but I was raised by the O'Learys, and I owe them everything. Not to mention the fact that I love working at Irish Meadows—far more than I do banking, I'm afraid." He gave a sheepish shrug.

She tipped her chin up. "I'm sure once Mr. O'Leary is back on his feet, Papa will give you your job back. This is only a temporary setback."

Irritation crept up the back of Gil's neck. Once again Aurora hadn't listened to what he was saying. Like the time he'd tried to explain his dream of owning his own farm and she'd brushed aside his words, insisting her father would allow Gil to use his stable to indulge his "little hobby." Aurora made it clear she expected him to work his way up in the bank and eventually take over for her father.

"Aurora, I won't be going back to the bank."

Her chin quivered as she processed his meaning. "How can you work at Irish Meadows when you'll be married to me? Shouldn't your loyalty be to my family now?"

Gil sighed. "I need you to listen to me." He reached over to take one of her hands. "I'm sure you noticed our engagement came about rather suddenly."

She didn't reply, just stared down at their hands as though willing him not to continue.

"I'm afraid I got swept up in . . . everything . . . without considering the consequences."

Uncertain blue eyes met his. "What consequences?"

He shifted his weight on the dainty perch. "The fact that you might get hurt. Believe me, I never intended for that to happen. You are an amazing woman, Aurora. Beautiful and smart— everything a man could want in a wife." He paused. "But I'm afraid I can't marry you. Although I care for you, I don't love you the way you deserve to be loved by your husband."

Gil braced himself for her tears, but instead, red flags of anger stained her cheeks.

She seared him with a heated glare. "This is really about Brianna, isn't it? You want to be free because she's broken off her engagement."

He jerked upright on the settee. "That's not the reason." Yet the spark of truth in her statement stirred his shame anew.

"Don't lie to me, Gil. I've seen the way you look at her, the way she commands your full attention whenever she's near. You're in love with her, aren't you?"

Unable to hold her gaze, Gil lowered his head, misery seeping through him. "Yes," he said quietly. "I love Brianna. But her father won't allow us to marry."

"You courted me because Mr. O'Leary asked you to, didn't

you?" Outrage trembled in her voice. "Because of Papa's position in the bank."

It sounded even worse coming from her. He wanted to lie, to soften the blow, but found he couldn't. "Yes." He finally looked at her. "I'm so sorry, Aurora. I'd hoped I could get over my feelings for Brianna and make you happy."

She shot to her feet, her features pinched, and for a moment he thought she would strike him. Instead she moved to the parlor door. "I want you to leave. And don't ever contact me again."

The urge to make amends burned in his chest as he followed her. "I'm sorry," he said again. "I never wanted to hurt you."

Frosty blue eyes raked his face. "Good-bye, Gilbert."

Realizing that nothing he could say would help, he reluctantly retrieved his cap from the hall stand and left the house. Aurora needed time to process this unwelcome turn of events. Gil only hoped that when her hurt and anger faded, she could one day forgive him.

❧

Rylan stood at the window of Archbishop Bennett's office on the second floor of St. Peter's Seminary, waiting for his superior to arrive for their intended appointment. As he stared down at the busy streets of Boston below, he thought about Colleen and what she might be doing at the orphanage today. Absently, he rubbed his hand over the scratchy wool cassock in an attempt to ease the permanent ache in his chest.

Only two days ago, Rylan had bid the members of the O'Leary family farewell. Everyone had gathered on the front porch to see him off. It amazed Rylan how these people, mere strangers two months ago, had come to mean the world to him in so short a time. Little Deirdre had sniffled and clung to her mother's leg. Connor tried to keep a stoic face, but tears hovered on his lower lashes. Gil and Brianna, and even Adam, who'd been home more since his father's illness, all bid him good-bye and good luck.

Leaving Cousin Kathleen had been almost as hard as leaving his own mother. She'd clung to him and thanked him for all his help, reminding him he was always welcome back. All he could do was nod, so thick was the emotion coating his throat.

And at that point, he'd turned to see Colleen waiting, gaze cast down at the wooden porch boards. His heart had given a painful lurch as she raised sorrowful eyes to his.

"Good-bye, Colleen. I hope you'll keep up your good work at the orphanage. The children need you." *Just as you need the children.*

"I will."

"And I hope you'll write me from time to time and let me know how the wee ones are faring." He tried to convey the true depth of his feelings with his eyes, since words were impossible.

"Of course."

How he'd longed to take her in his arms for a proper farewell and pour out his feelings for her—but that, too, was impossible. Instead, he'd leaned forward to kiss her soft cheek. "Take good care of yourself."

"And you, Rylan." Her lower lip quivered before she turned her head away.

With a deep intake of air, he stepped back and shoved his hat on his head. "Thank you again, everyone. I've enjoyed my time with you all." He nodded to Kathleen. "Please keep me posted on James's condition when you can."

Kathleen moved in for one last hug. "May God bless you, Rylan."

"Thank you. I'll be praying for all of you, as well."

The creak of the door jarred Rylan back to the present. He swiped at the moisture in his eyes before turning to greet Archbishop Bennett. The large, white-haired man moved into the space, robes swishing over the floor, offering his ring to be kissed. Rylan bent over his hand. "Good morning, Your Grace."

"Good morning, Mr. Montgomery. Please have a seat."

Rylan chose one of the hard wooden chairs across from the wide desk. The fact that the man didn't smile or offer any pleasantries dashed Rylan's hopes for a compassionate discussion quicker than the sun faded from the bleak interior.

"I'm disappointed to see you back here so soon, Mr. Montgomery. I hope you have a fitting explanation for leaving your placement." The archbishop's stern gray eyes bored into him.

Rylan twisted the end of his rope belt. "I don't know if you'd call it fitting, sir. It was, however, necessary." He fixed his gaze on the severe man, who said nothing. Rylan took a breath and prepared to confess. "It seems I have fallen in love with a young woman I met there."

The man's face became harder than stone. "What were you doing spending time with an unmarried woman?"

Rylan bit back a sigh at the judgmental tone. "It was all above board, I can assure you. She was a volunteer at the orphanage where I was assigned. I provided spiritual guidance and supervised her work with the children. I never anticipated . . ." He trailed off and gave his superior time to digest the information.

"Did you sin with this woman?"

Heat flooded Rylan's neck and face. "I did not. Other than one kiss." *One beautiful, life-altering kiss.*

The silence stretched as the man watched him. Rylan grew uncomfortable under his stare but held himself rigid on the seat, determined not to cower.

"What is your intention now?" Archbishop Bennett asked at last. "Do you wish to continue in the seminary?"

The image of Colleen's cherished face came to mind, but Rylan pushed all thoughts of her away. "I've made a commitment to the priesthood, which I don't take lightly," he said. "Before I make any rash decisions, I need to seek God's guidance to discern His divine purpose for me."

The archbishop inclined his head. "Very well. I believe a solitary retreat for the period of one month is in order. You will have no contact with the outside world for the duration. At the end of that time, I will expect your final decision and a renewed commitment before we continue with your internship."

One month. Rylan managed to keep the dismay off his face. "Thank you, Your Grace, for your understanding and patience." He rose and gave a slight bow to the man in the chair.

"Mr. Montgomery."

Rylan paused at the door. "Yes, sir?"

"I'll be praying for you, too."

29

BRIANNA HUMMED AS SHE entered the stables. Cooler air from the interior met her face, defying the dust motes that danced in front of her. She inhaled the familiar scent of hay and manure, and exhaled pure pleasure. Nothing delighted her senses more.

Before she took Sophie out for a long-overdue ride, she wanted to check on little Sebastian. She'd missed the horses more than she'd realized, almost as much as her family, but now that she was back for the duration of the summer, she planned to take every opportunity to come out to the barn. The fact that her happiness came at the price of her father's health caused a twinge of remorse.

Daddy would have to stay in the hospital for at least another two weeks. Her mother spent the better part of each day at the hospital with him, while the rest of the family took turns visiting. Colleen had gone up today and taken the younger ones for the first time. Brianna breathed a sigh of thanks to God for sparing her father's life and for bringing Gil back into hers.

Brianna peered over the stall door at the gangly colt. She laughed out loud at the sight of him, delighted with how much he'd grown since she left.

"Look at you, Sir Sebastian. You are growing into such a handsome young man."

The colt jutted his head over the stall door, nudging Brianna's shoulder. She laughed again and caressed his snout, admiring his gleaming chestnut coat that matched his mother's. She pulled a piece of carrot from her pocket and offered it to the colt, who seized it with relish. "I'll take you out for some exercise later. First I owe Sophie an outing." She pressed a kiss to his nose before jumping lightly from her perch on the stall door.

"Too bad he's lame. He'd have made a wonderful racehorse." Gil's voice sent warm shivers down Brianna's spine.

She hadn't seen much of him the past several days. He'd been holed up in the study, poring over Daddy's ledgers, trying to find a solution to this impossible situation.

More than happy to share some time with him now, she turned and smiled. "He's beautiful, isn't he? With a spunky personality to match."

Gil grinned, his blue eyes twinkling. "Reminds me of someone else I know."

A blush warmed her cheeks. "I'm not spunky. I'm the quiet type, like my Sophie."

"Well, you both have your moments." Gil reached over to rub Sebastian's nose. "Are you going out for a ride?"

"I am. And you?" She deduced from his plaid shirt and work pants that he might be intending to ride, too.

"I was going to take Midnight out to get away from my desk for a while. Care to join me?"

She smiled. "I'd love to. The track or the meadows?"

"The meadows. I want to explore the whole property. Mark the boundaries and inspect the outer pastures."

"I can help you with that."

"Good. It won't seem like work that way."

They moved to the tack room, where Gil retrieved the two saddles and carried them to Sophie's stall. Within minutes, they had their horses saddled and ready to go. They met at the gate to the east pasture and proceeded through, riding in silence, simply enjoying being back in their element. The summer sun was not too hot, and a slight breeze blew the horses' manes, keeping them cool.

"How are things with the finances?" Brianna dared to ask after a while.

He glanced over at her. "I've had to let some of the trainers go, and I've reduced the boarding fees for most of the clients. Better than having them board their horses elsewhere."

When he released a ragged breath, she berated herself for bringing up the unpleasant topic.

"We might have to sell off some of the land," he continued. "That's why I'm inspecting the outer pastures, to see if we can spare any acreage. I spoke to Mr. Sullivan, and he indicated he'd be willing to buy some adjoining land from us."

Brianna frowned. "I don't think Daddy will approve."

Gil reined in Midnight on the crest of a hill and gazed over the land below. "I know he won't, but it's better than losing everything." He turned to Brianna with a pained look. "I'm doing whatever I can to keep from going under."

She became aware then of the lines of fatigue around his eyes and mouth. "I'm sorry, Gil. I know you're doing what's best for us." She paused. "We can all pitch in to do the grooming, if it will help."

He smiled. "Thanks. I'll keep that in mind."

She bit her lip and looked out over the landscape, working up the courage to ask the question plaguing her. "I noticed you haven't been out to Belvedere lately. Does that mean you aren't seeing Aurora anymore?" She gripped the reins tightly, awaiting his answer.

Gil frowned and pulled his mount closer to Sophie. "I told you I intended to end my betrothal—and I have. I no longer have any ties to the Hastings family."

A dizzying wave of relief spread through Brianna's limbs. She fought to keep the giddiness from showing on her face. "How did Aurora take it?"

"Not well. But I'm sure she'll come to realize it's for the best."

Gil reached over to take Sophie's reins. He guided the animal closer until Gil's legs brushed Brianna's. A streak of heat rose from her neck up to her cheeks. She dared raise her eyes to his and gave a sharp intake of breath at the intensity she saw there.

He raised one hand and laid it on her cheek. "I've missed you something fierce, Bree."

Slowly, he lowered his mouth to hers. His warm lips grazed hers, tasting of his sweet morning coffee. Almost of its own volition, her hand slid up to grasp his shoulder as he intensified the kiss. Shivers of electricity ignited her nerve endings, and her knees went weak. Just when she thought she might fall off Sophie's back in a swoon, he pulled away.

"You are one mighty temptation, Miss Brianna O'Leary." He smiled and dropped another light kiss on her lips before moving Midnight away from Sophie. "Let's finish checking the perimeter of the property, then we can head back."

Two hours later, on their way back to the stables, Gil stopped at the highest point of the west pasture to survey the vast spread of O'Leary land. A thrill of pride washed over him. Sacrificing a tract of land would be well worth the price to keep Irish Meadows alive. He prayed he could convince James to sign the papers Gil intended to have the lawyers draw up.

"Are you still planning to move away and buy your own farm?" Brianna's soft question took him by surprise. She sat atop Sophie, staring out over the pastures.

"Yes." His automatic answer didn't match the uncertainty that had crept in and chipped away at his resolve lately. The dream hadn't been on his mind as much, so content was he to be home again.

"Tell me again why you need to do that when you have a perfectly good farm to run here?" A hint of accusation laced her question.

"You know why. I want to make the Whelan name count for something. Because my father wasn't able to."

"Why do you feel you owe it to him? The accident that crippled your father wasn't your fault."

No, but his death was. His hand jerked on the reins, and Midnight tossed his head in silent rebuke. "It's the least I can do. My parents came here to make a better life for me. My father worked hard on the docks trying to make enough money to buy Mum a house and to start his own mercantile. He'd even designed the sign. 'Whelan's Emporium,' it read. I still remember the pride in his voice when he said the name."

He sensed Brianna's gaze on him but couldn't meet her eyes. "When his legs got crushed under that crate on the dock, the spirit went out of him. Mum had to take two jobs to make ends meet. I think that was the part that killed him. He'd lost his manhood." A stiff breeze blew strands of Gil's hair across his forehead.

"Do you think he started the fire that took his life?" Brianna asked.

A shaft of pain seared Gil at the memory of that fateful day. If he closed his eyes he could still smell the stench of smoke and burning wood. He'd never told a living soul the true story of his father's death. Perhaps it was time to finally admit his guilt. Maybe then Brianna would understand his need to do this. "My father wasn't responsible," he said at last. "I was."

Her mouth fell open. "How?"

He turned away from the shock on her face and dismounted,

letting Midnight's reins dangle. Shoulders hunched, he moved to the edge of the incline.

"Every day after school, I had to care for my father while my mum went to work. Most times he would be asleep in his wheelchair, after a few too many nips of whiskey to dull the pain." He heard Brianna dismount but kept his eyes trained on a tree far in the distance. "One day he left his pipe on the table with a box of matches." He shrugged. "I thought it would be fun to try smoking."

"Oh, Gil." She came up beside him and put her arm through his.

"I couldn't manage to light the pipe, and the match dropped onto the sofa. Within seconds the place was an inferno. I tried to push my dad out into the hallway, but he was too heavy. I could only budge him an inch or two." The feeling of utter helplessness washed over him in waves. The suffocating heat, the blinding smoke, the panic. "I ran to get a neighbor, but when we got back, it was too late."

Brianna wrapped her arms around his waist and laid her head on his shoulder. The wind whipped her skirts against his leg. Though he didn't deserve her sympathy, he allowed the warmth of her body to seep into his chilled soul.

She looked up at him, tears standing in her green eyes. "It was an accident, Gil. You were too young for that type of responsibility."

Gil swiped the moisture away from his own eyes with an impatient hand. "I never told Mum. I was afraid she'd hate me."

"It was an accident," she repeated. "You can't blame yourself."

"I do blame myself. And I swore I'd make it up to him by fulfilling his dream. It's the one thing left I can do for him."

She sniffed and rubbed her face with the back of her hand. "If that's what you need to do, then I'll help you. We'll do it together."

He stilled, and then held her away to study her face. "You'd leave Irish Meadows? Leave your family behind?"

"For you I would."

Her simple acceptance floored him. "This doesn't make you think less of me?"

She laid a soft palm against his cheek. "Not at all. It only makes me love you more."

She loves me! His heart took flight in his chest. He'd hoped she felt that way, but hearing her say it with such conviction humbled him. "I don't know if I'll ever deserve you, Brianna. But I love you, too. More than I can ever express."

His mouth claimed hers in a kiss that joined more than their lips. It united their souls.

With Brianna by his side, Gil knew he could make his dream a reality. After another taste of her sweet lips, he silently vowed that once James had recovered, he would do everything in his power to convince him he was worthy of Brianna.

And this time Gil did not intend to take no for an answer.

30

COLLEEN FLUFFED THE PILLOWS and straightened the covers on her parents' bed, then stood back to survey the room. At last, Daddy was coming home, and Colleen wanted everything to be perfect for him. After three long weeks, the doctor had finally relented and allowed him to leave the hospital. For a while, a nurse would come each day—until they were sure Mama and Mrs. Johnston could manage alone. Daddy would have to spend all his time in his room until the doctor gave him permission to tackle the stairs.

Colleen moved to the dresser. A huge vase of fresh flowers from Mama's garden sat silhouetted against the light streaming in the window. She rearranged the carnations and daisies, determined to make the space as cheery as possible—a real treat after the sterile, beige walls of Daddy's hospital room. She gave a small sigh, thankful for her father's recovery and for these simple tasks to keep her from dwelling on Rylan in Boston. Despite the numerous letters she'd sent him, she hadn't received a single word from him. His silence spoke volumes.

A car horn tooted three times. Colleen raced to the open window and moved the curtain aside to peer into the yard below. At the wheel of Daddy's Model T, Sam pulled the vehicle up in front of the house. Colleen yanked off her apron as she flew down the main staircase and out onto the front porch. Gil, Bree, Adam, Deirdre, and Connor all stood at the bottom of the stairs, an eager welcoming committee. She descended the steps to join them.

"Daddy's home! Daddy's home!" Deirdre hopped from one foot to the other, dancing her delight.

Colleen put a hand on her little sister's shoulder, hating to dampen her enthusiasm. "Hush, Dee-Dee. Remember, Daddy needs peace and quiet."

An instant frown creased Deirdre's forehead. "Is he still sick?"

She lifted the girl into her arms, deriving comfort from the feel of her arms around her neck. "Yes, he is. He needs lots of rest to get better, so we all have to help, understand?"

Deirdre nodded solemnly.

"Good." Colleen nuzzled her sister's neck, inhaling her little girl scent of Ivory soap and sunshine. "Now, let's welcome Daddy home . . . quietly."

Deirdre grinned, revealing a gap where one of her teeth had come out. Colleen's heart squeezed as she wondered if Delia had lost any teeth. She wished she knew if Delia had received her package containing Mr. Whiskers, a new doll, and a letter. She'd hoped Delia's new parents would help her write back. Colleen ached for word from the sweet girl.

Gil and Adam moved to help Sam ease Daddy out of the passenger's side door. Together the three men carried her father up the stairs and into the house, while the rest of the family followed them inside.

The trio sat Daddy down on the chair in the foyer to rest for a moment before attempting the stairs. For the first time out of the hospital lighting, Colleen got a good look at her father, and she bit back a gasp of dismay. His normally ruddy cheeks now appeared sallow and gaunt. His blue eyes had lost their sparkle. Even his broad frame appeared shrunken.

Connor and Deirdre stood staring, eyes wide, most likely as shocked as she.

Mama moved up behind the pair. "Give Daddy a kiss. Then we'll let him get settled upstairs."

"Welcome home, Daddy." Deirdre's voice wavered as she leaned in to kiss Daddy's cheek. Connor followed suit.

Daddy gave a wan smile. "Come up and visit after I've had a wee rest." He reached out a hand to ruffle Connor's auburn curls. "You be sure to help your mama around the house."

"Yes, sir. I will."

Colleen kissed her father and whispered, "Welcome home, Daddy."

He gave her a wink, and she smiled at the slight twinkle in his eye. Maybe having his family around him was exactly what he needed to assist his recovery. She took Connor and Deirdre by the hand and led them out to the kitchen to get one of Mrs. Harrison's freshly baked cookies. Soon the two were seated at the table, happily munching treats and drawing a get-well card to take up to Daddy later.

Colleen returned to the entryway, where Brianna stood staring up the stairs, tracks of wetness staining her cheeks. "Daddy looks frail, don't you think?"

Colleen straightened her shoulders. "Of course he does. He's been in a hospital bed for weeks. He needs time to build up his strength again. Now that he's home where he belongs, I'm sure he'll be back to normal in no time."

Brianna smiled. "I hope you're right."

By unspoken agreement, she and Brianna walked into the parlor together.

"So have you heard from Rylan since he's been gone?"

Colleen's heart lurched at the name she'd been avoiding. "Not a word." She sank onto the sofa, feeling as though the air had seeped out of her like a flat tire on Daddy's Model T.

"Maybe he's not allowed outside contact. Especially from you—if he's told his superior about you."

She paused, digesting Bree's theory. "You may be right." Hope dimmed. "But it's been almost three weeks since he left."

Brianna put a warm hand on her arm. "Don't give up. Right now we need to focus on getting Daddy better, and pray that while we work on Daddy, God works on Rylan."

"Come in." James's loud call penetrated the solid wood door.

Gil took a fortifying breath and pushed into the room. He owed James a long-overdue apology, and now that his health had stabilized, Gil could not put it off any longer.

He squinted into the dim interior of the bedroom. Heavy drapes shielded the daylight from entering. James sat up in bed against two pillows propped behind his back. Like the room, the light had gone out of his eyes.

"Good morning. How are you feeling today?" Gil cringed inwardly, thinking he sounded as falsely cheerful as the nurse who came each afternoon.

James glared at him. "How do you think? Stuck here in this bed with everyone mollycoddling me like a newborn infant."

"They're worried about you because they love you."

"Frankly, I could use a little less love." He scowled, his eyebrows shooting together.

Gil dragged a chair closer to the side of the large, four-poster bed and sat with his hands folded over his knees. "James, I owe you an apology. I'm sorry it's taken so long to get around to it." He glanced up and saw regret on James's haggard face. "I followed you into that pub to help, but I only made matters worse. I should never have—"

James held up a hand. "All you did was speak the truth at a time I didn't want to hear it."

Gil shook his head, shame flooding him. "I had no business being so disrespectful after everything you've done for me." Emotion seized his windpipe. He could've lost this man he loved like a father.

James shook his head. "Truth be told, I owe you an even bigger apology, son. I should never have asked you to court Aurora Hastings. I've no excuse except that sometimes desperation makes a man do desperate things."

Some of the weight lifted from Gil's shoulders. "I wasn't entirely blameless. I could have said no. But at least I've learned a valuable lesson from this whole mess." He paused. "You should know that I've called off the engagement."

James nodded, a sober expression haunting his face. "I'm glad. Facing your own mortality has a way of changing your perspective on things." A smile twitched his lips. "Not that I recommend that particular method of self-discovery."

Gil laughed, greatly relieved to be back on better terms with his guardian.

"I want to thank you for coming back to help out. I know it's eased Kathleen's mind a great deal to have you home."

"There's nowhere else I'd want to be. Like you always remind us, family pulls together in the tough times."

"I'm glad someone listens when I talk." James sobered. "So . . . how bad is it?"

Gil straightened on the hard chair. "You know you're not supposed to be talking business. Your wife would have my hide."

James crossed his arms over his chest, some of the fighting spirit returning to his demeanor. "You may as well tell me. I'll only imagine the worst, and the worry won't be good for my health."

Gil grinned and shook his head. "You are incorrigible." He hesitated, considering his options. He supposed a bit of good news wouldn't hurt. "I can say that things are turning around . . . slowly. And don't ask for details because I'm not going to give them."

Lines spread across James's forehead. "So we won't be foreclosing any time soon?"

James's misery echoed in Gil's heart. How must James feel to fail his family? To think his wife and children would lose their home?

"You're not going to lose Irish Meadows. Not while I have anything to say about it."

James sagged back against the pillows, and actual tears formed in his eyes. "Thank you, Gil. I don't know how you've pulled this off, and for now I won't ask." He swallowed and looked straight at Gil. "Just know I'm extremely grateful."

Gil's throat tightened. At last he'd been able to help James in an honorable way. "No thanks necessary. You know I love this place." In fact, he loved Irish Meadows as if it were his own. Could starting another business be any more fulfilling?

James moved under the covers. "I think I'd better rest awhile now."

Gil jumped to his feet. "Of course. I've got work to do anyway."

On the way out the door, he stopped to glance back at James, whose eyes had already closed. Gil offered a silent prayer of thanks for the relaxing of the lines around his mouth and forehead for the first time since that fateful day in the bank. Maybe now James could breathe easier and concentrate on regaining his health.

Once James was back in the saddle, so to speak, Gil would talk to him about Brianna and plead his case for becoming his son-in-law.

31

GOOD MORNING, Sister Veronica." Colleen pulled off her gloves and smiled at the nun standing in the entrance of the orphanage. "It's a beautiful day today."

"It surely is." The young woman beamed at her, and Colleen suffered a momentary twinge of envy for the peace the nun exuded. "I'm so glad you've continued to volunteer here, even after Mr. Montgomery left."

Colleen froze and then forced herself to breathe. "It wouldn't do to lose two volunteers at once. Besides, I love being with the children." She matched Sister Veronica's quick pace as they made their way along the carpeted hallway.

"And they love you, too."

Colleen took a moment to give thanks for these precious children—who didn't give two figs about a person's clothing, wealth, or social status—and who gave their hearts freely, without reservation.

"What's on the agenda for today?" she asked.

"I believe Sister Marguerite has planned an outing to the park."

Colleen faltered briefly, barraged by ripe memories of the day she and Rylan had taken the children to the park. She swallowed hard. "That sounds . . . enjoyable."

"But first, Sister Marguerite asked to see you in her office."

Instantly, a hoard of butterflies swarmed Colleen's stomach. "I haven't done anything to upset her, have I?"

"I don't know. Spilled any ink lately?" Sister Veronica giggled.

Colleen's lips twitched in response. "Not a drop."

The nun leaned in. "Then relax."

Still, when Colleen knocked on the door to Sister Marguerite's office, the butterflies took flight once more.

"Come in."

The door squeaked loudly as Colleen entered. She grimaced, before schooling her features into a calm mask. "Good morning, Sister. You wanted to see me?"

Sister Marguerite looked up from a book on the tidy desktop. "Yes, Miss O'Leary. Please have a seat."

The sparse room contained a desk, one guest chair, and a small filing cabinet. The only decorations on the stark gray walls were a lone wooden crucifix and a calendar with pictures of the saints, plus the orphanage's only telephone. Colleen smoothed her skirts underneath her, glad the nun's tone didn't seem antagonistic. She waited with her hands folded in her lap for the woman to speak.

Sister Marguerite removed her glasses and focused her attention on Colleen. "I thought you'd like an update on Delia O'Brien, seeing as you were so fond of her."

Odd how sorrow and excitement could combine to twist one's insides. "Yes, please. How is she doing?" She'd heard nothing since Delia's sudden departure, and she thirsted for news of the girl.

The nun pursed her lips. "I'm sorry to say she's having trouble adjusting to her adoptive family. Her mother writes that she can't get Delia to smile or to eat much. And the child cries herself to sleep every night."

Colleen's heart plummeted, her mood turning as bleak as the room. "I'm so sorry. Is there anything we can do to help? Perhaps go and visit?"

"Unfortunately, the parents do not wish Delia to have contact with anyone from the orphanage. They believe it would only serve to stir up old attachments and keep her from forming new ones."

"I see."

"Delia did, however, write a note for you. Her mother sent it along." Sister Marguerite picked up an envelope with childish print scrawled across the front and handed it to her.

Colleen bit her lip as she took the precious missive. "Thank you, Sister," she whispered.

The nun fingered another envelope. "There's something else for you." She waited until Colleen met her hard stare. "From Boston, it seems."

Colleen's heart stilled in her chest. Her hand shook as she accepted the second letter.

The nun's chair scraped the hardwood floor as she stood. "I'll expect you in the classroom in ten minutes."

Colleen nodded distractedly, still intent on the two envelopes. "Yes, Sister."

The door closed seconds later with a small click. Colleen ran her finger over the handwriting on the letter from St. Peter's Seminary in Boston—Rylan's handwriting—and bit her lip to still the quiver.

She opened the note from Delia first. Tears misted her eyes at the sight of the large, childish letters.

Dear Miss Oleery: My new familee is nice but I miss you. Thank you for sending Mr. Wiskers. I hope you can come and visit soon. Love, Delia.

Colleen pressed a kiss to the page and refolded it, planning the letter she would send in return. *Lord, please help Delia learn to love her new family, and please let them be good to her.*

Gathering her emotions, Colleen picked up Rylan's letter and traced the shape of her name written by his hand. With a shaky breath, she pulled the seal from the envelope. Inside, she found plain blue stationery filled with several lines of neat script. She frowned as she noticed the date in the corner. July 10, 1911. Four weeks ago. Why had it taken so long to get to her? Her breathing thinned as she read the words.

Dearest Colleen, I am taking a minute to write now, as I won't be able to for some time. I've been 'sentenced' to solitary confinement on a mandatory month-long retreat. I'm to have no contact with the outside world until then. In the meantime, I hope you are keeping well and that your father is much improved. Give my love to the children at the orphanage. Please continue to pray for me as I will for you. Yours, Rylan.

Colleen's shoulders sagged beneath the weight of her disappointment. No words of love for her. No mention of missing her. No message of hope. She reread the note, trying to decipher any further meaning behind his words, but could find none. He might as well be writing to Sister Marguerite.

A tear slid off her cheek onto the paper, blurring the ink below. She gasped and pulled out a handkerchief to dab at the spot. This might be the only letter she ever received from Rylan, and she'd keep it among her precious keepsakes until her dying day. She let out a sigh and rose from the chair. Sister Marguerite would be expecting her in the classroom.

At the door, she hesitated. She walked to the calendar on the wall to quickly count the days since Rylan's letter. If she'd calculated correctly, today marked the end of Rylan's retreat. Her pulse quickened. Had he made his decision? If so, how would he let her know? Would he send another letter that may not get to her for weeks?

With a determined set to her jaw, she tucked both pieces of mail into her apron pocket. She couldn't wait that long to learn her fate. Somehow she would find a way to get to Boston and make Rylan tell her what he had decided—face-to-face.

Brianna balanced a tray of food as she made her way up the stairs to her parents' bedroom. In the long hallway, she set the tray on a narrow table and paused to catch her breath, bracing herself to face whatever lay on the other side of the door. From what the maid had told her, her father seemed docile today, unlike most days when his vile temper had the girls cowering in fear. Perhaps he'd turned a corner and was feeling better. Come to think of it, Mama seemed more herself lately, as well. Brianna prayed they'd found their way back to the happy marriage they'd always enjoyed.

She opened the door to her father's room, then picked up the tray. No matter what her father's mood, she promised herself she would talk to him today about Gil. Ever since she and Gil had toured the property on horseback, she'd been searching for a solution to keep Gil right here where he belonged, and she had come up with an idea that just might work—for all of them.

"Hi, Daddy. I hope you're hungry." Smiling, she swept into the room, determined to keep things cheerful.

To her surprise, he greeted her with an answering smile. "Brianna. You're a life-saver. I need your help."

She set the tray on the dresser and approached the bed. "What is it?"

His coloring looked better. His face had been freshly shaved, his hair combed. And the life seemed to have returned to his eyes.

"I need you to help me downstairs."

Brianna's mouth fell open. She'd love to help him—with anything but that. "Daddy, you know you're not allowed to use the stairs yet. How about I open the window and get some fresh air in here?"

She moved to the window and jerked up the sash. When she turned back, her father had swung his legs over the side of the bed, about to stand. "Daddy, no." She rushed to place a hand on his shoulder. "You cannot get out of bed without the nurse."

"Tarnation, girl. I've been up every night walking the halls when everyone's asleep. I'm getting stronger by the minute." He fixed her with a pleading stare. "I know I can make it downstairs with your help. I want to sit on my porch and look out over the racetrack. I haven't been outside in over a month."

She hesitated, riddled with indecision, desperate to please him but loathe to cause a setback in his recovery.

"Please, Bree."

"How will I get you back up here?"

"We'll ask Sam or one of the hands to help."

She bit her lip, knowing what it cost her father to ask for assistance. "All right. I'll do it on one condition."

"Name it."

"That you listen to an idea I have once you're settled."

He grinned, a glimpse of his old self peeking through. "I'd be happy to."

Ten minutes later, she had Daddy sitting in his wicker rocker on the back porch, grateful that her mother and Mrs. Johnston had been occupied elsewhere. The smile of contentment on his face as he watched the horses run the track made up for the moments of terror on the way down. She only hoped it was worth Mama's wrath when she found out.

Brianna glanced over at her father, startled to find him watching her with a wary expression on his face.

"I need to ask you a question, Brianna, and I want an honest answer."

She sighed, feeling like a child about to receive a scolding. "All right."

"What made you run away like that?"

The hurt in his tone did more to shame her than his anger ever could. She'd never considered that her actions would cause her father pain. She lowered her head. "I realized I couldn't marry Henry. And I knew you wouldn't change your mind. I thought leaving was my only option."

He shook his head. "I didn't realize you were that unhappy," he said softly. "Your mother was right. I was bullying my children."

"Mama said that?"

A half smile softened his features. "That and a whole lot more. She was right, of course. But I was too stubborn and too consumed with business problems to heed her advice. Both you and your sister took drastic actions to end your relationships, all because you felt I wouldn't listen." He shook his head, sorrow etching lines on his face.

"It's all right, Daddy. The only thing that matters now is that you regain your health. Everything else will work out as God intends." A light breeze blew her skirts against her legs.

Her father reached over to place his large hand on hers. "Thank you, Brianna. Your forgiveness is more than I deserve." He cleared his throat. "Now tell me about this idea of yours."

Despite his attempt to lighten the mood, nerves plagued Brianna. She bit her lip and prayed for the words to present her proposal in a favorable manner. "It's about Gil."

"Go on." A note of skepticism crept into his voice.

"You know he's managed to keep Irish Meadows from the brink of bankruptcy."

"Yes, and I'm very grateful to him."

"Don't you think his hard work deserves a reward?"

Daddy huffed out a sigh. "What did you have in mind?"

Brianna took a breath and plunged on. "I thought you could offer Gil a partnership in Irish Meadows." She held up a hand against his instant protest. "Gil's been saving money to buy his own farm. But face it, Daddy. We need Gil here. He's good for Irish Meadows."

"I don't disagree with you there."

She twisted in her seat to face him more fully. "What if you took Gil on as a partner? If he invested his money with us, it would help offset our debts. And I think if we agree to put his name on the sign, it would be enough to satisfy him."

Her father continued to regard her. "Have you discussed this with Gil?"

"No. I wanted to get your approval first."

"So you don't know if he'd agree to it?"

She hesitated. "Not for sure. But it makes sense. He has every-thing he wants here. Why start from scratch somewhere else when what really matters is having the Whelan name on his business?"

James stroked his mustache. "So a title such as 'Irish Mead-ows: O'Leary and Whelan Enterprises' might be the ticket to keeping Gil here?"

Hope swelled and soared like the rays of sun that danced through the clouds. Brianna couldn't hold back a smile. "That has a nice ring to it."

He gave her a long look. "You really love him, don't you?"

She held his gaze, refusing to cower. Not for something this important. "Yes, I do."

He nodded slowly. "Let me give it some thought, and I'll talk to Gil soon." He chuckled then. "You're one smart cookie, young lady. Irish Meadows could benefit from your help, too."

"Thank you, Daddy." She leaned over to kiss his cheek, amazed to find tears threatening. For the first time since she could remember, her father had listened to her opinion and was actually considering her idea.

God had surely answered one of her prayers.

32

GIL STRIPPED OFF HIS SHIRT, threw it on the chair in the corner of his attic room, and flopped onto the bed. The springs groaned a noisy protest as he stretched out on the mattress. Though he was bone tired, his soul was filled with contentment after an evening with the horses. He'd taken Midnight on an all-out sprint over the pastures, letting him take the lead until they were both spent. Perhaps if Gil were lucky, he'd finally get a full night's sleep.

He'd risen up on one elbow, poised to extinguish the bedside lamp, when an urgent rap sounded on his door. Gil frowned. Who would be knocking this late? Would Brianna be so bold? No, not unless it was a matter of some urgency. He tugged his shirt back on, leaving it unbuttoned, and opened the door.

Colleen stood in the darkened hallway, wringing her hands. "I'm sorry to bother you, Gil, but I need your help."

Concern streaked through him. "What's wrong?"

Colleen peered down the corridor, then turned back to him.

"Could we talk inside, please? It's important, and I don't want anyone to overhear us."

He exhaled loudly, unease skittering across his shoulders. "All right," he said reluctantly. "But we leave the door open."

"Thank you."

Gil pulled the wooden chair over for her, while he remained standing, hovering near the doorway. If the girl didn't seem so distraught, he'd have suspected a new plot to get his attention.

"Please sit down, Gil. I have some difficult things to say, and I don't need to crane my neck."

Gingerly, Gil lowered himself to the edge of the bed. "What sort of things?"

She chewed the inside of her lip for several moments before she finally made eye contact. "I need you to take me to Boston."

Gil straightened on the mattress, grappling with her request. "Boston? Whatever for?"

She gave a soft sigh. "I guess Bree hasn't told you."

"Told me what?" Exasperation set in, mixing with his nerves at having one of the O'Leary daughters in his bedroom. He glanced at the half-opened door to make sure no shadows hovered in the hall.

Colleen fingered a fold in her skirt. "While he was here, Rylan and I"—she hesitated—"became quite close."

"We were all fond of him. What's your point?"

Colleen twisted her hands together in her lap. "You don't understand." She took a deep breath. "Rylan and I . . . fell in love."

Thunderstruck, Gil bolted to his feet. He paced to one side of the small area and back, sudden realization dawning. "That's why he left so much earlier than intended."

She nodded, eyes miserable. "He went back to the seminary to pray about what to do. It's been a month now and he hasn't answered my letters . . ." When her voice broke, she struggled to regain her composure. "I can't keep living this way, Gil. I need to find out if he's going ahead with his plans to become a priest. Once I know his decision, I'll be able to move on with my life instead of hanging in limbo."

Gil reclaimed his spot on the edge of the bed, trying to process the enormity of her situation. "I sympathize with your pain, Colleen. But I—"

She leaned forward and grasped his arm. "Please, Gil. I have to find out what's happening. And I can't go by myself. You're the only one I trust to take me." Her chin quivered.

"What about Adam?"

She shook her head, auburn ringlets bobbing. "He's too busy with his new job."

Gil lowered his head, hands over his knees, mind spinning. "Maybe next week I could manage the time off . . ."

"I can't wait that long. I have a bad feeling if I don't go now, I'll never see him again." Tears overflowed and spilled down her cheeks.

Gil groaned and pulled a handkerchief from his pocket. One thing he couldn't seem to fight was a crying female. He blasted out a long sigh while mentally reviewing his schedule for the next day. "I guess I can postpone business for a day or two." He brightened. "Maybe we can talk Bree into going with us."

"Oh, Gil, thank you." Colleen clutched his hand. "You're the best person I know. Besides Rylan, that is."

Gil chuckled. "How on earth did you end up falling for a priest?"

She gave a sad smile. "I'm not sure. I think God must have a very strange sense of humor."

He sobered. "What will you tell your mother?"

"I'll think of something before the morning. I want to leave on the earliest train, if you don't mind." She got to her feet as she spoke and handed him back his handkerchief.

He followed suit. "Good idea. The sooner we leave, the sooner we can get back." And then he'd only lose one day of work.

"How can I ever thank you? You have no idea how much this means to me." She leaned forward to plant a light kiss on his cheek.

He smiled. "Lord, help me, but I can never say no to an O'Leary."

Behind him, the door crashed into the wall. "Maybe you should learn how."

He spun around to see Brianna in the doorway. Her eyes flashed violence, and her slender frame shook as she whirled on Colleen. "Here you are trying to seduce Gil again. I should have known your repentance was all an act. No one can change that much."

Colleen went white, her mouth grim. "I will not stand here and subject myself to your false accusations." With a swish of her skirts, Colleen swept out the open door.

Gil's emotions swung between humiliation and rage. Granted, the situation didn't look good, but Brianna should know them better than that. "You owe us both an apology." The deadly calm of his voice should have given her warning.

Brianna's nostrils flared. "I find Colleen in your bedroom, with you half undressed, and I owe *you* an apology?"

He glanced down at his unbuttoned shirt and winced. "We were only talking." That sounded lame even to him. "If you'll just listen for a minute, I can explain."

He glimpsed stark pain in her eyes, before her features became shuttered. "I'm through listening to explanations." Without waiting for a response, she stalked out the door.

The instinct to race after her filled him with adrenaline. But after two frantic steps down the hall, he forced himself to stop. It was time Brianna learned to put aside her insecurities and trust him. If she turned tail and ran every time she saw him talking to another woman, what kind of life would they have together?

He trudged back to his room and sank onto the squeaky mattress. So much for getting a good night's sleep.

Late-afternoon shadows fell across the simple altar in the seminary chapel. Rylan sat on the first wooden pew, clutching four letters in his hand. One he'd read several times, the other three remained unopened.

Lord, what test are You putting me through now?

Rylan rose and walked to the single candle that illuminated the altar. He blew out the flame, inhaling the familiar scent of sulfur as the spirals of smoke wisped upward. The plan for his life had gone up in a similar puff of smoke, and he was at a loss as to how to get it back on track.

Despite weeks of solitary confinement filled with meditation and prayer, no solid answers had come to him. No clear-cut divine message to direct his path. He glanced at the unopened envelopes in his hand, postmarked Long Island, New York. His hand trembled, battling the desire to rip open the flap and devour every word Colleen had written. Yet reading her innermost thoughts would tear open the wound in his heart that was just beginning to heal. Rylan couldn't afford to let that happen.

The other letter, the one he'd already read, caused a spasm of grief in his chest. Rylan had always imagined having his mother in the front row at his ordination as he took his vows. But her letter said she'd been ill for several months and would be unable to make the journey. Despair simmered beneath the surface of his tightly held emotions. Just how ill was she? By the time he wrote back, would it be too late?

Slowly, Rylan made his way down the darkened aisle to the door. He paused a moment before reentering the bright world beyond the chapel's sanctuary.

Loud footsteps clicked on the tiled floor. Mrs. Burton, the housekeeper, stopped when she saw him. "There you are, Mr. Montgomery. You have a visitor."

Rylan frowned. "Who is it?"

"Says he's your cousin. Mr. Gilbert Whelan."

A chill raced up Rylan's spine. Why would Gil be here? Surely James hadn't taken a turn for the worse. Rylan forced a strained smile, thankful his confinement had ended the day before. "Thank you, Mrs. Burton."

"He's in the sitting room." She gave a grunt and bustled back to guard her post.

Please, Lord, don't let it be more bad news. I don't think my heart could take it.

Rylan smoothed a hand over his brown cassock, re-tied the coarse rope belt, and made his way to the visitors' lounge.

Gil turned from the fireplace as Rylan entered the room. He gave a rather nervous smile and strode forward, hand extended. "Rylan, it's good to see you."

Surprised at the jolt of homesickness that hit him, Rylan shook Gil's hand eagerly. "Gil, this is a great surprise. What brings you to Boston?"

Gil's smile stayed bright a few moments too long. "Helping a friend with a . . . personal matter." He darted a glance to the doorway, then back.

Rylan gestured to one of the sofas. "Please have a seat. Can I get you any refreshments?"

"No, thank you."

Rylan eyed Gil, noting the uncomfortable way he held himself on the settee. "How is everything at home? Is Mr. O'Leary faring better?" Rylan longed to ask about Colleen but held his tongue until it could come up naturally in the conversation.

"Improving all the time. He's been up on a few walks around the room now."

"That is good news. And how is Cousin Kathleen coping with the situation?"

"It's taken a toll on her, but she's managing—as we all are. And how are things with you?"

"Quiet, actually. I've just finished a month-long retreat." Rylan drummed his fingers on the arm of the chair, conscious of Gil's watchful gaze.

"Will you be continuing your internship somewhere else now?"

Rylan's mouth went dry. Why did it seem like Gil was grilling him for information? "My superior hasn't decided yet." The room suddenly seemed too warm. Rylan jumped up and moved to the window to pull up the wooden sash, letting in a blast of fresh air. Turning back to Gil, Rylan searched for a topic of conversation other than Colleen and the O'Learys. "How long will you be in Boston?"

"I'll be heading back on the late train tonight."

Relief and disappointment rushed through Rylan's system in equal measure. Though it was wonderful to see a familiar face, Gil's presence brought back painful memories of his time at Irish Meadows—memories he'd worked hard to banish from his mind.

Gil rose from the sofa, nervously brushing a thread from his coat. "Actually, Rylan, I brought you something from home. Wait here and I'll get it."

Rylan frowned and dropped into one of the armchairs. The lad was acting as anxious as a cat in a kennel. Over what? A batch of Mrs. Harrison's oatmeal cookies?

"Hello, Rylan."

His heart ceased pumping. The blood congealed in his veins, stiffening his limbs into a paralyzed state. Time suspended, as even the ticking of the brass clock on the mantel stilled.

He inhaled and forced his head up to see Colleen standing just inside the door—a vision in a blue gown and matching hat. His breath caught at the magnificent sight of her. Like a man too long in the desert, he drank her in. Fading memories of her could not compare with the vibrant beauty standing before him. Her vivid violet-blue eyes watched him, filled with trepidation.

Gripping the arm of the chair, he pulled himself to standing, his legs as unsteady as his heart. "Colleen, what on earth are you doing here?"

Colleen willed her erratic pulse to settle and took a few tentative steps into the room. Rylan looked so different in his plain brown cassock—almost monk-like. Still, she couldn't tear her gaze away from him—afraid if she blinked, he'd disappear and she'd discover it was all a dream.

Nervous perspiration dampened the back of her dress. "I came to see you, of course."

"Why?" Those chocolate-brown eyes fixed on her with an intensity that left her knees weak.

She prayed for guidance, for the right words to say to the man she loved. "I needed to see you. To find out what you've decided and make my peace with it—one way or another." She came closer, longing to smell the familiar sandalwood soap and peppermint.

An expression of near terror leapt into his eyes. He took a step backward, almost tripping over the base of the lamp beside the chair.

"How have you been, Rylan?"

"Well enough. And you?"

She fought the urge to laugh at their polite trivialities. Instead she leveled him with a long look. "I've been miserable." When his gaze slid away, she wasn't brave enough to close the gap between them. "You never answered my letters," she continued. "So I decided to come and see for myself where things stand." Her hands shook almost as much as her knees. "May I have a seat?"

"Of course. Please make yourself comfortable."

She lowered herself to the sofa, but Rylan remained standing by the hearth, eyes glued to the floor. Her spirits sank. This was far from the joyous reaction she'd envisioned—he didn't seem the least bit happy to see her. In fact, he looked as though he wished she'd march right back out of the room.

"Have you come to a decision?" she dared ask.

He slowly shook his head. "Not yet." A muscle pulsed in his jaw, his expression wretched.

Sorrow clutched her throat. She'd never expected her presence to cause him such misery. Secretly she'd hoped that he'd be overcome with joy and sweep her into his arms with a passionate kiss. Instead, they faced each other like two strangers, trying to drum up conversation, a veil of tension between them.

Gathering her courage, she rose and went to stand before him. "Forgive me, Rylan. I didn't mean to cause you such distress, showing up here unannounced." Another wave of sorrow swept over her. "I needed to know where things stood between us, and I can see the answer on your face." She swallowed back the threat of tears. "I wish you nothing but the best for the future. I will never forget you—or the happiness you brought to my life."

She let her gaze linger on him another moment, wanting to memorize every inch of his beloved face. On a spasm of grief, she turned to leave.

His hand shot out to snag her fingers, and the anguish in his eyes stole her breath.

"My mother may be dying."

"Oh, Rylan." Without hesitation, she wrapped her arms around him. "I'm so sorry."

A tremor went through him as he lowered his forehead to

hers, tears dampening his cheeks. Another thing she loved about him—he was never ashamed to show his feelings. She held him without saying a word until she sensed he'd regained his composure. Then she moved back to see his face. "Are you going back to Ireland?"

He rubbed a hand over the bridge of his nose. "I don't know. I've just found out and haven't had time to think."

A fierce determination came over her. The man she loved was suffering, and she now found herself in a position to offer comfort and counsel, things he'd given her in abundance. She took his hand and led him to the sofa.

"You must go to her, Rylan. You'll regret it for the rest of your life if you don't. The seminary will always be here, but your mother may not." She was glad he made no move to take his fingers from hers. "One thing I've learned from Daddy's illness is not to waste the precious time we have. We never know when our loved ones could be taken away. I'm so grateful I got to tell Daddy how much he means to me." Her voice broke, and she lowered her gaze to their entwined hands.

He tipped her chin up, and for one dizzying moment, she thought he might kiss her. But he merely brushed a tear from her cheek and gave her a very sad smile. "You're right, of course. I must go home."

More tears blurred her vision as the awful truth dawned. "You won't be coming back, will you? You'll want to stay and help your siblings."

He sighed. "I'll have to wait and see. Maybe we'll be lucky and Mum will pull through."

She nodded and took in a long breath for fortification. "Well, I'd better go and let you make your arrangements."

They rose together, hands still joined. His warmth radiated through her palms.

"Thank you for coming, Colleen. It was so good to see you." Longing and misery shone in the dark depths of his eyes.

Her heart threatened to crack in two. How she wished she could embrace him, feel his lips on hers once more—but she would not violate the sanctity of this holy place. She reached up to brush an innocent kiss across his cheek, inhaling his familiar masculine scent, and then she rushed from the room before she fell apart.

33

BRIANNA SAT ON THE BACK PORCH, staring out over the dirt track where Sam exercised Morgan's Promise. The midmorning sun bathed the veranda's floorboards in soft light while the gentle breeze teased her senses with the last traces of Mama's roses.

She fingered the envelope on her lap—the one Gil had left for her yesterday morning—turning it over and over. Though she'd memorized every word of the note he'd written, she still slid the stationery out and unfolded it.

Brianna,

    Colleen asked me to accompany her on a trip today. She needed an escort, and I agreed to take her. She asked me to keep this confidential, so if you want to know more, you'll have to ask her.

    What you witnessed between us last night was completely innocent. I cannot pretend your lack of faith in me is not troubling, not to mention your constant hostility

toward your sister. I'm praying the Lord will heal the bit-
terness between you and Colleen. Family ties should never
be discarded lightly. Take it from someone who has no
family.

Don't wait up, as we will be returning on the last train.
Gil

Brianna folded the notepaper and returned it to the envelope.
It was obvious he was angry with her. Angry and disappointed.
He'd made her sound like a jealous shrew, but no one could
fully understand her toxic history with Colleen. Not even Gil.

Brianna wanted to believe her sister had changed. That she'd
found a new spirituality and that her request for Brianna's
forgiveness had been real. But finding Colleen in Gil's bedroom
so late at night made it almost impossible. Didn't she have the
right to be angry?

The French doors whispered opened, and someone stepped
onto the porch. Brianna stared straight ahead, hoping whoever
it was would carry on and leave her to her brooding. Luck was
not on her side. Without a word, Colleen sat down on the chair
beside her. Brianna bristled, prepared to take her resentment
out to the barn where she could nurse it in private, but one look
at her sister's face riveted her in place. Colleen's usually rosy
complexion was blanched whiter than the paint on the plank
floor, her red-rimmed eyes standing out in stark relief. What
had happened to cause her such grief? Did it have anything to
do with the mysterious trip yesterday?

Before Brianna could recover her voice, Colleen turned bleak
eyes to her. "I owe Gil a favor, so I'm going to explain something
to you."

Unsure how to respond, Brianna waited in silence for her
sister to continue.

"I asked Gil to go with me to Boston yesterday—to see Rylan."
Brianna's stomach dropped. So this wasn't about Gil at all.

"In hindsight," Colleen continued, "it might not have been the most prudent course of action to go to his room, but at the time, I didn't know how else to catch him alone." She paused. "Judging by my past mistakes, I can see how you might think badly of me and jump to the wrong conclusion. But I don't see how you can claim to love Gil and believe him capable of such dishonorable behavior."

Brianna's cheeks flamed with misery. Colleen was right. Gil had never given her any cause to doubt him. *Except propose marriage to a woman he didn't love.* She pushed that treacherous thought away. After all, these circumstances were entirely different.

"Gil made me see that it may take time for you to accept that I've truly changed and that I need to give you another chance." Colleen attempted a smile. "That man loves you more than anything. Don't ruin a good thing, Brianna. If you constantly doubt his fidelity, you'll drive him away."

Brianna bit her lip. "I owe you an apology, Colleen, for assuming you were trying to hurt me. I should have given you a chance to explain."

"Yes, you should have. Gil wanted to invite you to go with us—before you attacked him."

Shame burned hot in her chest. What sort of Christian example was she setting when she reacted with anger and jealousy?

Lord, forgive me for not trusting my sister and Gil, for not trusting You.

She took a long breath. "If I promise to give you the benefit of the doubt from now on, can you forgive me?"

Brianna was relieved to see a softening of Colleen's pinched features.

"I've already forgiven you," she said softly.

Brianna's throat constricted. "Thank you."

"It's the least I owe you after all the times I've hurt you." Colleen rose from her chair and smoothed out her skirts. "Now, if I were you, I'd go and apologize to Gil. He's working in the study, trying to catch up on the work he missed yesterday."

Brianna jumped up. "Wait. What happened with Rylan in Boston?"

Colleen lifted her chin, her hands clutched together in front of her. A wave of hurt crashed over her features. "We spoke. I don't think he's reached a decision yet. In any case, he's on his way to Ireland. His mother is quite ill."

No wonder she'd been crying. Impulsively, Brianna moved to gather Colleen in a hug. "I'm so sorry. The waiting must be intolerable."

Colleen's stiff figure sagged for a moment before she pulled away. "It is. Harder still to know he's so far away, and"—her voice caught—"that he may never come back."

Brianna looped her arm through Colleen's. Her sister needed a distraction in a big way. An idea formed—one that might go a long way toward making amends for her bad behavior and help Colleen at the same time. "Could you use another volunteer at the orphanage? I enjoyed the time I spent there and would love to go back. We could ride together on the train tomorrow."

Colleen nodded as tears filled her eyes. "Thank you, Bree. I'd like that very much."

Gil tried to concentrate on the figures in front of him but found his thoughts constantly circling back to Brianna. He'd had many hours on the train yesterday to rethink the message he'd left for her. If he had to do it again, he'd have toned down his indignation, or at least tempered it with understanding. Had his anger succeeded in pushing Bree away for good?

His pencil snapped in two. Gil bit back an oath. Restless, he got up to pace the carpet, forcing himself not to rush through the house to find Brianna and beg her forgiveness. This time he had to hold out and wait for her to come to him.

He moved to the window and peered out through the lace curtains at the immaculate lawns and the front garden in full bloom. He should be outside enjoying this day instead of glued to a desk chair.

"Gil, may I speak with you for a moment?"

Gil turned from the window to see Brianna standing in the doorway, as bright as a sunflower in a yellow dress. He took a second to recover his equilibrium, then motioned to the chair across from the desk.

"Could we sit by the fireplace? A little less formal." Her hesitant tone led him to wonder if she'd had a change of heart. At least he didn't detect any remaining anger on her part.

"Of course." He moved to sit at the opposite end of the settee, careful to keep a distance, both physically and emotionally.

She seemed nervous, perched on the edge of the seat. At last, she raised her eyes to his, uncertainty swirling in their green depths. "I came to apologize for the other night. I should never have jumped to such horrible conclusions about you and Colleen. I . . . I hope you can forgive me."

As much as he wanted to, he needed further reassurance before he granted absolution. "How do I know the same thing won't happen again if you see us together? Or if you see me talking with another woman? Aurora, for instance." Not that Aurora was likely to speak to him, but Brianna didn't need to know that.

She let out a soft breath, twisting her hands in her lap. "I've promised Colleen—and I'll promise you, as well—that from now on I'll give you the benefit of the doubt before leaping to any conclusions."

He studied her, keeping his gaze steady. "Trust is vital to a relationship, Brianna. I need you to trust me completely if we're to have any sort of future together."

She stiffened on the settee, her back straightening. "In my defense, our relationship has never been smooth, Gil. What with you kissing Colleen in the barn, and then your betrothal to Aurora."

He bit back a stinging retort about her own betrothal. Such sparring would get them nowhere. Instead, he inclined his head. "True enough."

One delicate brow arched as though she sensed the reservation behind his reply. "How would you have reacted if you'd caught Henry in my bedroom with his shirt unbuttoned?"

A surge of heat blast through Gil's system at the mental image she'd created. His hands curled into fists on his lap. "I see your point. I doubt I would have taken time to ask questions."

"Thank you. So can we agree to both work on establishing trust? If a woman comes up to your room again, take her down to the parlor to talk."

He nodded. "Agreed." A sudden question dawned. "By the way, why did *you* come up to my room at that hour?"

A furious blush spread across her cheeks. She ducked her head. "I saw Colleen go up to the third floor and . . . I followed her."

Gil gave a mock scowl. "Spying and eavesdropping are not qualities I admire in a woman."

Her indignant gaze flew to his. "I did not eavesdrop. I saw her go in and waited at the end of the hall—until I couldn't stand it anymore."

Despite himself, Gil's lips twitched, picturing her stewing in the hall as he and Colleen talked. But he sobered at the overall implication of her actions. "Seriously, Bree. If you'd only come to the door instead of imagining all sorts of illicit intentions, we could have avoided this whole misunderstanding. If these types of disagreements keep happening, they'll eat away at the foundation of our relationship."

"I don't want that," she said in a soft voice as she rose. "I promise I'll do whatever I can to regain your good opinion of me."

He stood, too, and crossed his arms over his chest to keep from pulling her into a hug. She looked like a lost child, seeking approval for her efforts. He realized with a start that the crux of her insecurity lay with James's constant criticism. Bree never felt good enough for her father. Perhaps she didn't think herself good enough for him.

Before Gil could verbalize any of his revelations, Bree left the room.

He returned to his desk full of ledgers. It seemed at every turn their tangled relationship hit some type of obstacle. Would God ever help them sort it out, or did their destiny lie in different directions?

Gil promised himself he'd spend a great deal more time in prayer in the hopes of finding the answer.

34

SHIMMERS OF GREEN CRISSCROSSED the meadows that spread out to each side of the country road as Rylan hiked toward the tiny village in Cork where he'd grown up. The familiar scent of fresh-cut grass and sea air infused him with a sense of peace and homecoming. He'd purposely gotten off the bus a mile away from home so he could walk the last way alone, enjoying the peace of the countryside he'd so missed.

Nostalgia for the happy childhood he'd spent here crashed over him like the waves that had barraged the ship on his sea voyage. The tall tree he and his brothers used to climb still reached its gnarled branches to the sky. The old wooden fence bordering Mr. Foster's property sagged in exactly the same spot, and several fat cattle grazed in a shady pasture near the road. Rylan took out a handkerchief and wiped the beads of sweat from his brow. The sun was unusually warm today. That, coupled with the mile-long hike in his tweed jacket, made Rylan feel like he would soon be a grease puddle on the side of the road.

He paused before the low stone fence that surrounded his mother's property, drinking in the sight of his boyhood home. A lump of raw emotion rose in his throat. Nothing had changed since he'd left five years earlier. The same thatched roof sheltered the stone walls, the same green door still had patches of missing paint, and his mother's flower boxes over-flowed with violets. He took a moment to prepare himself for what he might find inside—his mother bedridden, possibly near death.

Please, Lord, let me be in time to see her again.

He pushed open the wooden gate and strode up to the en-trance. Hesitating on the welcome mat, he opted to knock on his own front door, mainly because no one was expecting him, and he didn't want to frighten his mother.

The door opened almost immediately. A lovely young woman in a simple dress and apron stood with an inquiring look on her face. He was about to ask if Mrs. Montgomery was home when the woman's eyes widened.

"Rylan? Is it you?"

He frowned. "Aye."

The woman launched herself into his arms, laughing and crying at the same time. "It's me—Maggie."

Wee Maggie? Could this really be his baby sister? He squeezed her hard, then pulled her back to get a better look at the raven hair and creamy complexion. "You've turned into a beauty while I was gone. Tommy, Paddy, and Gabe must be fighting the suitors off with a stick."

She laughed, a blush staining her cheeks. "Come in, you. Why did you not write to tell us you were coming?"

Rylan dragged off his cap and entered the small living room of the cottage he'd grown up in. The same stuffed sofa and two rocking chairs flanked the stone hearth. The familiar smells of peat moss and homemade soup lingered in the air—smells that cried *home.*

"It was a last-minute decision once I got Mum's letter." He turned his attention back to Maggie, whose dark hair matched his own. "Tell me the truth, how bad is she?" he asked quietly.

Maggie stared at him. "Mum's fine. Why?"

Rylan frowned. "Her letter said she was too ill to travel. It sounded serious."

Understanding lit his sister's features. "Ah, the pneumonia. Mum had a bad bout of it in the spring. Lasted well into the summer, but she's picking up now. Still tires easily, though, and the doctor said the sea voyage wouldn't be good for her."

Relief made his muscles weak. "So she's not dying?"

Maggie laid a sympathetic hand on his arm. "No."

Rylan scanned the room. "Then where is she?"

"Resting. She takes a nap every afternoon. Come into the kitchen, and I'll make you some tea. You can tell me all about America."

He'd just finished his second cup of tea when the sound of his mother's voice snapped his head up.

"Maggie? Whose voice do I hear?"

Maggie jumped up from the wooden table. "I'd better warn her you're home. Don't want to risk her heart with such a grand surprise." She dashed out of the room and down the hall to the bedrooms.

Seconds later, he heard footsteps. His mother appeared in the door to the kitchen, her eyes brimming with tears. "The saints be praised. Is it really my Rylan?"

"It's me, Mum." He stepped forward and caught the frail woman in a tight hug. Her stooped shoulders shook as she wept. Her auburn hair had turned mostly gray now, still worn in a tidy bun at the back of her neck. Gray eyes that matched Maggie's shone with happiness. "I feared I'd never see you again. I thought once the ordination was over you'd be too busy to come back for a visit." She straightened and scanned him from head to toe. "Where is your priest's collar?"

"I haven't been ordained yet, Mum. Come, let's sit in the parlor and we'll talk."

She frowned, her sharp eyes boring a hole through him with a flash of her Irish stubbornness. "We most certainly will talk."

He settled his mother in her favorite chair with an afghan covering her knees. As he tucked the blanket around her, he took note of how much she'd aged in his absence. Though only in her early sixties, Beatrice Montgomery's hard life had begun to catch up with her. Sorrow gripped Rylan's heart as he held her hand, the crippled fingers giving her the appearance of a much older woman.

"How have you been keeping? Your last letter had me worried."

"I'm much better now that the pneumonia is finally gone. But my rheumatism keeps me close to home, I'm afraid."

Maggie bustled into the room with a tray of tea and biscuits for their mother, then discreetly left them alone.

"And how are my brothers?"

"They're all doing fine. Tommy and Eileen are expecting their fourth babe around Christmas. Paddy and Claire are busy with the twins. And Gabe works hard at the fire station. No time for a wife yet, I'm afraid. I thank God every day that my boys stayed close to home. They take good care of me and Maggie." She reached out a hand to pat Rylan's knee. "And my other son, who traveled across the globe, will be doing God's work."

Rylan's gaze faltered under her admiration. He hung his head and studied the braided rug at his feet.

"Don't tell me you've got yourself banished from the seminary with that tongue of yours."

"Not quite," he murmured.

"Something's wrong. I can tell by your face."

"I've been home fifteen minutes, Mum. Let's catch up first.

There'll be plenty of time tomorrow to talk about my problems."

His mother straightened in her chair. "So there is a problem. I knew there was more to this visit than my health."

Her words startled him. Had he really used his mother's ill health as an excuse to come home—to gauge her reaction to the decision he faced? A rush of air left his lungs. Perhaps on some unconscious level he couldn't make his final decision without her blessing. Perhaps that was the real reason holding him back.

Mum set down her teacup on the table beside her. "Come now. Tell me your troubles, and I'll do my best to give you an honest opinion."

Rylan pushed to his feet and paced to the window overlooking his mother's back garden. A profusion of wildflowers coated the yard with color.

"Do you know why I went into the priesthood, Mum?" he asked, his back to her.

"Because you had the calling."

He stuffed his hands into his pockets. "Not exactly." He paused to watch a butterfly flit from bloom to bloom. "I made a bargain with God when you were so sick years ago. That if He cured you, I'd give my life to His service." Rylan turned from the window with a smile. "A price I was more than happy to pay."

"Oh, Rylan." Moisture rimmed her pale eyes.

"Once I made my decision, I never looked back. I was happy in the seminary, happy to devote myself to shepherding God's people."

"What happened to change that?"

Mum always could see right through him. He came to sit on the lumpy sofa again, his hands clasped over his knees as though he were praying. "I met a woman . . . one of Cousin Kathleen's daughters, and without meaning to . . ." He inhaled deeply and released a long breath. "I fell in love with her."

His mother reached over to grip his hands as silent tears coursed down her thin cheeks. She said nothing—only squeezed his fingers in gentle understanding.

"I don't know what to do. I've been on a retreat for a month trying to determine God's will for my life, but nothing is clear. No matter how hard I pray, no answers are forthcoming." He choked back the emotion rising in his throat and looked to his mother, the fountain of his strength. "Why is God silent, Mum? Why am I not hearing His answer?"

She patted his knee. "Perhaps you're trying too hard. What does your heart tell you?"

The simple answer reverberated in his soul. "My heart aches . . . for Colleen. I love her so much it hurts."

His mother's features softened, and a smile trembled on her lips. "I think you have your answer, lad."

"But how can I go back on the promise I made to God?"

His mother placed a gnarled hand on his cheek. "God would never hold you to such a promise if it's the wrong thing for you. There are many ways to serve God without being a priest."

"But what about you?" he asked sadly. "Won't you be terribly disappointed?" Guilt and fear squeezed his lungs. After everything his mother had done for him, he couldn't bear to let her down.

"The only thing I've ever wanted for my children is for them to find joy in whatever they do. If this woman makes you happy, then that's good enough for me."

He slumped back against the cushions of the sofa. "But what will I do with my life if I leave the seminary? How will I make a living? I have nothing to offer her."

His mother chuckled. "One step at a time, my boy. While you're here, use the time to get back to your roots and discover the things you love. Talk to your brothers. Talk to Father Reginald. And we'll all pray for you."

Rylan smiled a true smile for the first time in weeks. He felt lighter, more certain he was coming close to the right decision. He leaned over to kiss his mother's cheek. "Thank you, Mum. With your connection to the Almighty, I know I'll get an answer at last."

Colleen stepped onto the back porch, letting the cool breeze fan her face. She'd finished reading Deirdre a bedtime story and now found herself at loose ends. Not tired enough to go to bed, where endless thoughts of Rylan would chase around her head like squirrels in a tree, she hoped the quiet sounds of the farm at night would soothe her soul.

She descended the stairs and wandered down the path toward the barn, noting how the bright moon illuminated the meadows in the distance. The flare of a match drew her attention to the fence where Gil stood, inhaling a thin cigar—the same type Daddy sometimes smoked.

"Hello, Gil." She came to stand beside him. "Is it okay to share the fence with you? I don't want to cause any more trouble with my sister."

His jaw hardened. "Your sister had better learn not to jump to conclusions every time I speak to a woman."

The evening breeze ruffled her skirts about her ankles and blew some strands of hair across her face. How she wished Rylan were here to share this moment with her. She watched Gil blow out a long puff of smoke. "Since you rarely smoke except when you're upset, I'd say something's on your mind."

"You could say that."

"Business or Brianna?"

He shot a glance at her. "A bit of both, but mostly Brianna."

"She didn't apologize to you?" It had been more than a week since their conversation, and Colleen assumed Bree had taken her advice.

"She did. I'm just not sure I've accepted it." He poked a

boot in the dirt. "Until she gets over her insecurities, she'll never be able to fully trust me. And without trust, we can't build a future."

Colleen leaned over the top rail of the fence, breathing in the night air. "It's mostly my fault, you know," she said quietly. "I'm not proud to admit it, but I've always gone after everything she's ever wanted . . . including you." Regret moved through her at the realization of just how deeply her selfish actions had affected her sister.

He peered at her in the darkness. "Why is that?"

She sensed no judgment, only curiosity, in Gil's tone.

"I guess I was jealous of how perfect Bree was, jealous of her intelligence and how easily everyone loved her." She shrugged. "I've tried to make amends, but I suppose it's hard to believe I've changed."

"I guess falling for a priest would make anyone find their conscience in a hurry."

She gave a reluctant laugh. "True."

"Any advice on how to convince Brianna my feelings for her are real?"

She threw him an arch look. "Other than the obvious?"

"Which is?"

"Ask her to marry you. What better way to prove you love her and make her feel secure?"

He frowned. "I can't do that without your father's approval. The first time I asked, he sent me off to Manhattan."

So Daddy *had* opposed Gil and Bree's relationship. Leaning against the wooden fence, Colleen studied him. "Have you tried lately? I imagine almost dying could change a man's perspective on things."

"I've thought the same thing myself."

"Then what's stopping you?"

He paused, frowning. "What if he still refuses?"

"Will you really let Daddy stand in your way?" She crossed

her arms. "It's plain you two love each other. That's worth a little disapproval, don't you think?"

"Not if your father disowns Brianna. I couldn't live with causing a rift in the family."

"Trust me. Daddy may bellow like a bull, but he's a softy when it comes to the women in his life. And besides, Mama would never let him get away with it."

A ripple of unease ran through her at the possibility of facing the same battle with Daddy over Rylan. Yet she knew in her heart she would do whatever it took to marry Rylan—if she ever got the chance.

35

Y OU'RE HAVING BREAKFAST with us today! What a wonderful surprise." Brianna bent to kiss her father's cheek, happy to see him seated at his rightful spot at the head of the table, his morning paper and coffee in hand.

She stepped over to kiss her mother, who looked better than she had since before Daddy's illness. Color bloomed in her cheeks, and the lines around her eyes had faded.

"The doctor said your father could use the stairs, as long as someone helps him and he takes it slow." She beamed at her husband.

"Did you have to tell them that part?" He growled like a grumpy lion, but Brianna caught him winking at her mother.

Harmony seemed to be restored in the O'Leary house, and Brianna basked in the glow. Connor and Deirdre giggled at a private joke, while Gil attacked his sausage with gusto.

Brianna had taken her first sip of coffee when Colleen entered the room, stifling a yawn. "Good morning, everyone." Her eyes widened. "Daddy! You're here."

"That I am, darlin'. It's good to be back with my family." His smile encompassed the whole table, dimming only momentarily when his glance fell on Adam's empty chair.

Brianna scooped a spoonful of eggs, trying to ignore Gil's gaze. She still didn't know if her father had had a chance to propose the idea of a partnership to him. If so, Gil hadn't mentioned anything to her about it. In fact, he seemed to be avoiding her lately. She thought he'd accepted her apology, but perhaps he'd decided he wasn't able to forgive her after all.

Either that or he was punishing her for her lack of faith in him.

She looked up from her plate to find her father staring at her.

"So, Brianna, I hear you've been accompanying Colleen to the orphanage."

"Yes, and I'm enjoying it very much. The children are a delight."

"Speaking of the orphanage, what has become of young Rylan? Wasn't he supposed to be around for another month or two?"

Colleen's fork clattered to the ground, and she hastily bent to retrieve it.

"He got word that his mother was ill and had to return to Ireland." Brianna hoped her father would let it go at that. Her mother, however, was another story.

"Cousin Beatrice is ill? Why didn't anyone tell me?" Mama looked from Brianna to Colleen, whose face had gone red and then white.

Since her sister appeared incapable of speech, Brianna jumped in again. "I'm sorry, Mama. I thought Rylan told you."

Mama frowned. "No, the last time I spoke with him in any detail was at the hospital, but he didn't mention anything about his mother. He did seem upset. Said something about a crisis of faith and that he was heading back to Boston."

James set his cup down with a thud. "Boston? Brianna said he was in Ireland."

Colleen appeared near tears.

Brianna sighed. "Daddy, it's not such a mystery. Rylan went back to Boston for a spiritual retreat, and while there, he got word about his mother. I'm sure he'll be back as soon as she's better." Brianna's soothing tone seemed to allay Daddy's suspicions.

Colleen had better sort out this mess sooner rather than later. Or at least tell her parents what had happened between her and Rylan.

"Other than helping at this orphanage, what have you girls been doing? Any hope of one of you finding a decent man to marry?"

Brianna glanced at Colleen, who grew paler by the minute.

Mama gave Daddy a stern look. "James, it's your first day back with the family. Don't start badgering everyone."

Brianna took a deep breath. No time like the present to get her intentions out in the open and maybe diffuse the talk of marriage. "I, for one, will be starting college next week," she said brightly. "Aunt Fiona called to say I've been accepted at Barnard Hall."

Silence filled the room. Brianna lifted her head to find her family staring at her in numb surprise. "Why is everyone so shocked? You knew I planned to enroll." She gave her father a nervous glance. His mouth pressed into a disapproving line, but he remained blessedly silent.

Mama blinked. "I thought you'd changed your mind since coming home."

"No, Mama," Brianna said gently. "I came back to help out, but I always intended to return to Aunt Fiona's. I'll be leaving right after Labor Day."

Gil's chair scraped the floor as he pushed abruptly away from the table. "Excuse me, but I have work to do." His jaw rock hard, he strode from the room without looking at her.

Brianna's stomach sank. She pushed her half-eaten plate of

eggs away, no longer hungry. Why was her attending college such a contentious issue for everyone? And why did Gil suddenly seem angry that she was leaving? Hadn't he encouraged her to pursue her dream?

Connor and Deirdre took the opportunity to excuse themselves from the table, scampering out of the room just as Mrs. Johnston bustled in with the morning mail. The housekeeper smiled at Daddy as she set the stack in front of him. "Good day, Mr. O'Leary. We're pleased to have you back in your proper place."

"Thank you, Alice. Is that my mail?"

"Yes, sir." She pulled one envelope from the pile. "All except this one for Miss Colleen."

Daddy's eyes narrowed on the postmark. "Why would Colleen be receiving mail from Ireland?"

Colleen's initial burst of pleasure at receiving any type of correspondence from Rylan faded into terror. How was she going to explain this? She wasn't ready to tell her parents about her feelings for Rylan.

Mama looked wary. "Is it from Cousin Rylan?"

Colleen pretended to study the address. "Why, yes it is. He's probably writing for news about the children. He'll want to know how little Delia's doing."

Her heart thumped painfully in her chest. Did her parents see through her sketchy explanation? It must be painfully obvious from her blush and her stammering that she was hiding something.

"Well, open it, dear." Mama set down her cup. "I want to hear what he says about his mother's condition."

Colleen's fingers whitened around the envelope. What if it was bad news? What if Rylan had written to say he was staying in Ireland for good?

Dear God, how am I going to get out of this?

She bit her bottom lip and broke the seal on the envelope. She'd skim to the part about his mother, then find an excuse to leave the room. Aware of every eye on her, she pulled out the page, unfolded it, and scanned the script. Relief spilled through her. "His mother is much improved, and"—her heart gave an excited leap—"he's coming home."

"Home?"

"I mean back to New York." Colleen held back a cry of joy. "He says he's sailing on the RMS *Olympic* on the first of September." Her eyes widened. "That was yesterday. He's already on his way."

Mama picked up her napkin and patted the corner of her mouth. "It's very good news about Cousin Beatrice. I'm sure Rylan's relieved. Though I don't understand why he's coming back so soon."

"Soon? He's been gone three weeks." Colleen pressed her lips together the moment the words burst out.

Brianna pushed back her chair and rose. "I imagine the seminary wants him back as soon as possible to continue his preparations."

Colleen threw her sister a grateful look as she refolded the letter.

Daddy picked up the newspaper. "Did you say he was sailing on the *Olympic*?"

"Yes, why?"

"I believe I read something about it in today's paper. Ah, yes, here it is." His face wreathed in a frown, he raised troubled eyes to Colleen and then to Mama. "I'm afraid that ship's been in an accident. A collision at sea."

Colleen gasped and clutched the edge of the table as the room swirled in front of her. This could not be happening. Not when Rylan was coming back to her.

Her father scanned the article until the lines on his forehead eased. "Not to worry, everyone on board is all right. It says the captain had to turn around and go back to the nearest port in England. All the passengers disembarked, and the ship is being sent to Belfast for repairs which could take several weeks."

Several weeks? Her first glimmer of hope, and now she'd have to wait weeks more? Tears sprang to her eyes before she could stop them. With a strangled sob, she jumped up, still clutching the letter. Ignoring her mother's concerned inquiry, Colleen sprinted into the hallway and upstairs to the sanctuary of her bedroom.

On silent feet, Brianna left the room, grateful her parents were too stunned about the accident at sea and Colleen's extreme reaction to raise any ruckus about her plans.

At the foot of the staircase, Brianna hesitated. The desire to comfort her sister warred with the need to speak with Gil. Colleen would need some time alone to read Rylan's letter and process the latest turn of events. Bree sighed. She would go to Gil, then.

Brianna imagined Gil had headed out to the barn—his place of refuge when anything troubled him. He may already be out riding Midnight as he often did when working out a problem. No matter. If he wasn't there, she'd visit with Sophie and Sebastian.

Minutes later, she found Gil in the tack room, mercilessly scrubbing one of the saddles, head bent, arm flying. He didn't even look up as she entered.

She leaned against the doorframe, watching him for several minutes. "If you're not careful, there won't be any leather left on that saddle."

Without looking at her, he stilled his hand briefly before he started scouring again. "Were you planning to tell me you were leaving? Or would I wake up one morning to find you gone?"

The harshness of his tone made her wince. But she refused

to back down. "I didn't realize I had to tell you anything. You knew my aunt had registered me at Barnard. I only came home to help Mama until classes start."

He shot to his feet then, anger swirling in his blue eyes. "You came back for your mother—no other reason?"

A flush heated her cheeks, but she held her ground. "There was the added benefit of spending time with you."

Gil threw the scrub brush into a nearby bucket. Water sloshed over the sides. "You told me you wanted to help me achieve my dream. I thought that meant you'd be willing to go with me when I'm ready to buy my property. Or was that all just a whim?"

So Daddy hadn't said anything about a partnership yet. Maybe he'd changed his mind. She straightened, moving away from the door. "I meant what I said, but I assumed it would happen after I got my degree. I didn't think you'd have enough money saved until then."

Water dripped from his hands. "What if I'm ready to go in six months? You expect me to wait another two and a half years?"

Hurt sank into the very marrow of her bones at the realization that he did not consider her worth waiting for. When would she learn that she would never be enough? Not for her father, not for Gil. Her back stiffened as repressed anger swirled through her system. "I didn't realize you expected me to give up my dream for yours."

"That's not fair." He glared back at her.

"You know what's not fair, Gil? The mixed signals you've been sending me since you got back. Kissing me one minute, then punishing me the next for not trusting you."

"I haven't been punishing you."

"You most certainly have. Ever since you gave me that lecture about trust, I've hardly seen you. And don't tell me it's because you were so busy with the books."

He stood, slack-jawed, staring at her, as though trying to

process her words. Maybe he hadn't even realized what he was doing.

"I'm tired, Gil. Tired of fighting for any scrap of attention from my family and from you. Tired of waiting to see what my father—or you—will decide about my future. So I'm putting my trust in God and doing what's right for me. I hope one day you can understand."

She turned and stalked out of the barn, half-expecting, half-hoping for him to rush after her. To hug her and tell her how sorry he was. That she was right after all.

But when she reached the house and looked back toward the stables, Gil was nowhere to be seen.

36

COLLEEN SAT IN THE CUSHIONED seat of her bedroom window, hugging her knees to her chin, questions
plaguing her mind. Where was Rylan now? Stranded
somewhere in England? Would he wait for the repairs on the
ship or would he try and find another boat? She doubted he'd be
able to afford another passage and would be forced to wait until
the *Olympic* was ready to sail again. Which meant she probably
wouldn't see him for at least another month. Another month to
wonder and worry about what he'd decided about his future.

Their future.

She sighed and opened the letter, hoping that reading it one
more time might provide her a clue she'd missed as to his intentions. The fact that he'd planned to come to New York instead
of straight to Boston gave her a thread of hope. But on the other
hand, even if the news were bad, he'd want to tell her in person.

*Dearest Colleen, Being home in Ireland has been like a balm
to my soul. I'd forgotten how much I loved the countryside,*

*the smell of the sea air, and most of all, how much I've
missed my family.*

Her hand trembled. Was he trying to tell her he'd decided to
go back to Ireland once he finished at the seminary?

*I'm happy to say my mother's health is much improved.
She's recovered from the pneumonia, but the doctors don't
want her to risk a harsh sea voyage. I've enjoyed the time
I've spent catching up with my brothers and sister. Coming
home has given me a much-needed clarity about the future.
I need to talk to you when I get back to New York. Which
brings me to the main reason for writing. I've booked passage on the RMS Olympic set to sail on September 1st. The
tentative date for arrival in New York is September 8th. I plan
to come straight to Irish Meadows if it's all right with you
and your family. Until then, God bless you all. Love, Rylan.*

Her dizzy brain seemed to throb in her skull. She'd analyzed
every word in the letter but could come to no real conclusion.
She still had no idea what he'd decided about his future. And
now she'd have to wait another month to find out.

*Lord, thank You for keeping Rylan safe. Forgive my disap-
pointment and grant me the grace to accept Your will for the
both of us.*

A knock on her door broke the silence. She wiped her eyes,
smoothed her hair, and tucked the letter under a cushion. "Come
in."

Her mother entered the room and closed the door with a soft
click. "I think we need to talk." Mama's face was serious as she
approached the window seat.

With a sigh, Colleen moved to make room beside her. "I
suppose we do." She fiddled with the sash of her dress, trying
to find the words to begin.

Mama smoothed the material of her skirt. "Would you care to tell me what's going on between you and Rylan Montgomery? And don't insult my intelligence by telling me it's about the orphanage."

Colleen picked up one of the pillows and cradled it against her as if to cushion herself from the blow of this revelation. "Neither of us meant for this to happen, Mama . . ." She hesitated, hating that something so beautiful would come out sounding sordid or sinful. "But Rylan and I . . . fell in love."

Her mother's sharp intake of breath made Colleen wince. What would her parents think of her now?

"How did this happen? He's going to be a priest, for heaven's sake."

"I don't know. I didn't even like him at first." Colleen's insides quivered with the magnitude of the situation. "I saw how wonderful Rylan was with the children at St. Rita's. How kind he was to the nuns. And he treated me like someone special. He understands who I truly am on the inside and he . . . he values me." Her vision blurred as tears spilled over.

Her mother's arms came around her. Colleen leaned into her, weeping on her shoulder as she hadn't done since she was a little girl.

"Don't we value you?" Sorrow laced her mother's soft question.

"You and Daddy do. But not the men who try to get my attention. They always make me feel like a beautiful, empty-headed decoration. Until I started helping at the orphanage, I didn't know what it was like to contribute to something worthwhile. My work there matters, Mama. The children . . . they love me."

"Of course they love you. You're a warm, wonderful person." Mama held out a handkerchief. "But getting back to Rylan, what business did he have making a girl fall in love with him when he's promised his life to God?"

"Don't blame Rylan, Mama. It's no one's fault. He . . . he was helping me with my faith. I started reading the Bible and praying." She paused. "Rylan helped me make amends for the awful things I've done."

"So he was acting as your spiritual mentor?"

"Yes."

"What happened to change that?"

Colleen balled the handkerchief in her hands. "The day I learned Delia had been adopted, Rylan found me crying. He tried to comfort me and . . . we ended up kissing. It just happened." She savored the moment for a brief second. That one beautiful, terrifying moment when the course of both their lives had changed forever.

Understanding dawned on her mother's face. "That's why he went back to Boston so suddenly."

Colleen nodded.

"But how did you know he'd gone to Ireland?"

"I convinced him to go. He got a letter saying his mother was too ill to travel over for his ordination. Rylan thought she might be dying, so I told him to go to her because he'd regret it if he didn't."

Her mother's eyes narrowed. "When did you tell him that?"

She swallowed. "Gil took me to Boston to see Rylan. I had to find out if he'd decided to continue being a priest or not."

"And? What did he decide?"

Colleen gave a weary sigh. "I still don't know. I wasn't even sure he'd come back once he got to Ireland. But he's coming here now—most likely to tell me his decision in person." She glanced over at her mother, sad to see a frown marring her complexion. "I'm sorry I've disappointed you and Daddy. I know Daddy wanted me to marry a man of means, not a penniless priest." A strangled laugh escaped at the irony of the situation.

"So you'll marry Rylan if he decides that's what he wants?"

Colleen's pulse took flight at the idea. "Nothing would make me happier." She sighed. "But it looks like I'll have to wait quite a while before I find out his plans."

Her mother rose from the cushioned seat. "I told your father I'll have no more secrets in this family, and I mean it, Colleen. I'm very upset that all this was going on without my knowledge." Hurt shone around her eyes. "Why wouldn't you confide in me? Did you think I'd condemn you for your feelings?"

Colleen picked at the lace on her handkerchief. "It happened right about the time Daddy got sick. I didn't want to add to your worries."

"So you tried to handle it all on your own?"

"I eventually told Brianna and Gil. But I wasn't alone." She smiled. "I had God to lean on."

Mama held out her hand, and Colleen grasped it like a lifeline. "Now you have all of us, as well." She pulled Colleen into a tight embrace. "I don't know how I would have gotten through your father's illness without my family. From now on, no matter what Rylan decides, know you have our love and support. I love you very much, sweetie."

Colleen's heart swelled at the words of love long denied. How often she'd sensed her mother's disapproval, felt slighted over what she'd perceived as her mother's preference for Brianna. But now the truth of her mother's love for her shone through. "I love you, too, Mama."

Her mother pressed kisses onto her hair, and at last the scars on Colleen's heart began to fully heal.

Mama sniffed and pulled away, a determined expression hardening her features. "Your father can still pull a few strings around this town. Why don't we have him send a telegram and find out exactly what is happening with that ship?"

37

G IL PAUSED OUTSIDE THE PARLOR to collect his thoughts. He'd done a great deal of soul-searching since the day Brianna had confronted him in the tack room, and reluctantly, he'd decided she'd been right about a few things. Quite possibly Gil *had* been punishing her for not trusting him. Shame burned at the realization that he could be so unforgiving. What kind of Christian example was he living? Not a very good one, it seemed.

She was also right about the mixed messages he'd been sending her. The truth was he should have been man enough to make a decision and fight for her. Instead he'd taken offense at her choosing college over him. He'd worn his foolish pride like a cloak of honor and let the love of his life leave home with only a chilly good-bye.

Faced with Bree's glaring absence in the family pew on Sunday, Gil had come to a moment of clarity. He needed to stop wavering and take action. Step up and make his intentions known to James. He'd told himself he'd been biding his time until

James had fully recovered, when in reality Gil had been afraid to approach James for fear that he would once again deem Gil unworthy.

But all that ended now.

The grandfather clock in the hallway chimed the hour. Pushing all negativity aside, Gil took a calming breath and entered the parlor.

James sat reading the evening paper in front of the fireplace. "Ah, Gil. Just the man I want to see." He folded the paper and laid it aside.

"I need to talk to you, as well." Too anxious to sit, Gil crossed the room to stand by the hearth. Now that he was face-to-face with James, the words wouldn't come. Gil grabbed a poker and jabbed the logs.

"What's on your mind, son? A business problem?"

Gil dusted off his hands and turned. "No, sir."

James studied him. "I hope you've not suffered any bad repercussions from breaking your betrothal to Aurora."

"Not really, except I doubt the Hastings family will speak to me any time soon." He gave a wan smile, but James did not smile back.

He pinned Gil with a serious look. "I should never have taken advantage of you like that. I'm truly sorry."

Gil held his gaze. "I shouldn't have let you."

James shook his head. "Seems we've both come to some interesting realizations the hard way. I know now that I would never risk my health or my family's well-being again for anything."

Gil nodded, hoping this meant James might be more receptive to his plea. "On that note, sir, I have something to ask you." He cleared his throat and moved to sit on the chair opposite James. The question needed to be asked eye-to-eye. "I respectfully wish to ask for your daughter's hand in marriage."

James's gaze remained steady. "I see. And how do you plan to support her?"

Gil's stomach twisted. "Once we get Irish Meadows back on solid ground, I'll look for a piece of land to start my own farm." He tried not to think of how long that might take.

James considered him for a moment, giving Gil time to sweat.

"Actually, I have a proposition for you, Gilbert, and I hope you'll hear me out before you give me an answer."

Gil swallowed. At least James hadn't flat out refused him. "Go on."

"You've done an impressive job here since I've been ill. Brought us back from the brink of insolvency, something I couldn't seem to manage. Now that my health has forced me to curtail my involvement in business matters, I could use a partner in Irish Meadows. There's no one else better suited to run this place. What do you say? Would you be willing to invest your money here and become a full-fledged partner?"

Shock pushed Gil to his feet. He paced the area in front of the hearth, attempting to digest James's offer. Could he give up his dream to join forces with the O'Learys?

James joined him by the mantel. "We have everything here you'd be creating from the ground up. I'd even give you a piece of land when you're ready to build your own house."

A secret part of Gil yearned to accept the offer. He could stay right here where he'd been so happy as part of the family he loved. It would make Brianna happy, too. How important was making the Whelan name count? "It's a very generous offer . . ." he began, dragging his hand over his jaw. "But it's still your creation, not mine."

"That's not entirely true. You've had a big hand in helping build up this business over the years. If not for your talent with the horses, we would never have attracted the clientele we have. In fact, to show my good faith, I'd even be willing to add your name to the deed and the title. How does 'Irish Meadows: O'Leary and Whelan Enterprises' sound?"

A hint of excitement threaded its way through Gil's system.

"Would you be willing to let me have more say in the direction the farm takes? I have some ideas about expanding the breeding side, especially now that racing is on hold indefinitely."

James eyed him intently. "I'd be open to that. I predict if we survive the next year or two, there's no telling what we can do."

One more roadblock came to mind. "What about Adam? He already resents my place in the family. If he finds out about this, it may cause an irreparable rift."

James took a pipe from the stand on the mantel and ran his hand over the stem. A flash of pain passed over his features. "Adam is a complicated issue. My son may be involved in some activities that are . . . not quite legal." His face became grim. "I went to see him the day I applied for the bank loan. Tried to make him see reason, but only succeeded in alienating him further."

"All the more reason not to give him another excuse to leave the family."

James straightened to his full height, a stubborn set to his jaw. "I'm afraid Adam has chosen his path, and I must choose mine. I can't afford to wait for him to come to his senses. This proposal makes good business sense for Irish Meadows and for you. My offer stands."

Gil nodded, realizing the truth of his words. "That still doesn't address my initial question. Do I have your permission to ask Brianna to marry me?"

James laid a meaty hand on Gil's shoulder. "Ever since your mother died, you've been like a son to me. I'd be honored to make it official and have you as a son-in-law. I'm only sorry it took me this long to realize it."

Gil fought to subdue the tidal wave of emotion rising in his chest. "I'd be honored as well, sir. And I accept your offer of a partnership."

"Miss O'Leary, there's a phone call for you." Sister Veronica's head poked around the door to the classroom where Colleen sat filling the ink bottles.

Colleen looked up and smiled at the youthful nun. "I thought you'd agreed to call me Colleen. After all, we're practically the same age."

"I'm sorry. I keep forgetting." Her eyes sparkled with merriment. "You can take the call in Sister Marguerite's office."

"Thank you." Colleen grabbed a rag to wipe the excess ink from the lip of the bottle. As she capped the bottle, she couldn't help remembering the day little Delia had knocked over the inkpot. At that time, the stains on Colleen's hands had shamed her—now they represented good honest work.

She left the classroom and walked briskly along the hall to Sister Marguerite's office. Who would be calling her at the orphanage? A tiny shiver of alarm tried to catch hold, but she shook it off. Nothing to worry about. Daddy's health was improving every day. Most likely it was Brianna calling from Aunt Fiona's.

The office was empty, the only movement coming from the curtain at the window, which danced in the afternoon breeze. A jar of wildflowers adorned the desktop, filling the barren room with color and wonderful scents.

Colleen crossed to the wall, picked up the earpiece of the phone, and bent to speak into the other end. "Hello?"

When there was no response, she repeated her greeting twice. Still nothing. She hung up, a frown forming. Perhaps she should call home just in case.

The soft click of the office door barely registered while Colleen waited for the operator. From the corner of her eye, she caught sight of someone in the doorway. Goosebumps rose on her neck as she turned to see who had entered. The phone piece fell from her nerveless fingers and clattered against the wall, swinging from the cord.

"Hello, Colleen." Rylan stood watching her, his cap clutched in front of him.

"Rylan." Colleen's hand flew to her mouth. Shock rooted her feet to the floor as she struggled to take in the reality of him being here at the orphanage when he was supposed to be halfway around the world.

The trademark grin broke out over his handsome face, creating dimples in each cheek. "You seem surprised to see me."

Instant tears sprang to her eyes and spilled down her cheeks. Without conscious thought, she rounded the desk and threw herself into his arms, burying her face in his neck. She wept against him, breathing in the familiar scent of soap and peppermint, and a hint of smoke from the train. All tangible evidence he was really here—not in England or Ireland.

"Ah, Colleen, how I've missed you," he murmured into her hair, his lilting accent even more pronounced than before he'd left. His arms tightened around her.

If it weren't for the steady thump of his heart beneath her, Colleen would've thought she was imagining the whole scene.

Rylan handed her a handkerchief from the pocket of his tweed jacket. His brown eyes twinkled. "I always seem to be mopping up your tears, now, don't I?"

She dabbed the cloth to her cheeks. "What are you doing here? Your ship was in a collision and needed repairs."

A confused frown crossed his features before understanding dawned. "Ah, the *Olympic*. I didn't end up on that ship. I couldn't wait, so I changed my ticket and took a steamer out a week earlier."

A riot of different emotions coursed through her. "And you didn't think to let us know? Do you know how worried we were when we heard about the accident?"

"I'm so sorry. I only heard about it myself when I reached Boston."

"Boston?" Her heart plummeted to her feet while her head tried to keep up with the dizzying pace of revelations. So he'd returned to the seminary after all. And she'd gone and thrown herself at him. Her cheeks burned at the realization of how brazen her reaction had been. Slowly, she disengaged herself from his hold and took several steps back. Her legs wobbled beneath her skirts as the thought of having him so near, only to lose him once again to the church, shook her to the core.

Rylan moved to cup her elbow. "Are you all right, love? You'd better sit down. This has been a shock."

More like a cataclysmic event. She sank onto the guest chair by the desk, attempting to even out her erratic breathing. She had to get control, to face whatever it was Rylan had come to say. "So you've made your decision, then?"

He nodded. "The best thing I ever did was go home to see my mum. She helped bring clarity to everything in my life."

Colleen twisted Rylan's handkerchief in her hands. "I imagine your superiors are happy to have you back," she whispered, hating to sound so pitiful.

Staring at his shoes on the warped wooden floor, she sensed him grow still. A moment later, he crouched in front of her, his warm hands covering hers. "I went to Boston to give them my resignation," he said quietly. "We all agreed it's for the best."

"You did?" She focused on Rylan's hands atop hers, not daring to look at him, not daring to hope what this might mean.

"Yes. I've decided my calling is elsewhere. I've accepted a new position."

Her head buzzed with a thousand nonsensical notions. "I'm happy for you" was all she could manage to get out.

"Don't you want to know what it is?"

"Yes, of course." Her mouth gave the expected response while her heart erected barriers to protect itself.

"I am the new manager of St. Rita's Orphan Asylum. Sister Marguerite has decided to go into semi-retirement and is in need of an assistant."

A spasm of pain clutched Colleen's midsection. He'd made

no mention of his feelings or sharing his future with her. Only talk of his new career. Where did that leave her?

Rylan tipped up her chin, forcing her to meet his eyes. "I don't think I'm making myself clear. I've left out the most important part." He shifted position, one knee on the floor. "Colleen Elizabeth O'Leary, you stole my heart the first moment we met. I love you more than my own life, and if you'll have me, I'll spend the rest of my days proving it to you."

Her throat convulsed. No words could make it past the blockage lodged there. She simply stared into the earnest brown pools as the room swayed around her.

He raised an amused brow. "In case you're still not understanding, I'm asking you to marry me."

"You are?"

"Yes."

She'd never expected a proposal. After all, they'd only shared one kiss. "Are you sure?"

"More sure than I've ever been about anything. These last weeks without you have been torture. I don't want to spend one more day apart from you. If you'll have me, that is." His earnest eyes searched hers.

"You won't resent giving up being a priest?" Her hands shook as real concern hit her. What if he came to regret marrying her?

"To tell the truth, it's a relief. I realized I entered the seminary to please my mother, instead of having a true calling. I can still serve God—and love you in the process." He winked at her.

She gulped and waved a hand weakly in the air. "But where will we live?"

He chuckled. "Do we have to decide that right this minute?"

Her lips trembled. "Are you certain you can put up with me? According to my family, I'm not easy to live with."

His gaze grew pensive as he studied her. "Ah, I believe I see the problem. You're thinking with your head instead of your heart." He rose and drew her to her feet. With gentle hands, he cupped her face and slowly lowered his mouth to hers.

Her soul gave a surge of joy at the feel of his lips on hers. A whimper rose in her throat and she pressed closer, eager to drink in every inch of him. His love was evident in the tenderness of his kiss and the gentle way he caressed her face with his thumbs.

When at last he released her, she opened her eyes to see him smiling at her. "Now maybe you'd care to answer my question."

Her heart beat a frantic rhythm in her chest. "Yes." The word whooshed out with a rush of air.

"You'll marry me?"

"Yes, I'll marry you." A laugh bordering on hysteria bubbled up.

He let out a whoop, picked her up, and twirled her around until her head spun. Then he took her face in his hands and kissed her soundly once again. "I promise to spend my whole life making you happy, Colleen O'Leary."

Before she could catch her breath, he reached for her hand and tugged her across the room. "Now that you've come to your senses, I have another surprise for you." He pulled open the door and led her down the hall, stopping in front of the common room. "But first, I have one more question. A rather important one. You do want children, don't you?" His broad grin tempered his boldness.

Heat rose in her cheeks. "Of course, I'd like children one day . . ."

"One day? That sounds so far away." Mischief gleamed in his eyes. "I was thinking of something much sooner." He opened the door and motioned her inside.

"Miss O'Leary!" A familiar childish voice echoed in the large room.

Colleen's mouth fell open at the sight of Delia racing toward her. Colleen dropped to her knees and caught the little girl against her, unable to stop another gush of tears from running down her cheeks.

She squeezed Delia so tight she squeaked, then rained kisses all over her darling face, not even minding the sticky candy residue on the girl's lips. "Delia! I've missed you so much. What are you doing here? Did your family bring you for a visit?"

The blond curls shook back and forth. "No. They didn't want me anymore so Mr. Rylan came and got me."

A mixture of indignation and sorrow squeezed Colleen's lungs as she picked up Delia and turned to Rylan. "Can the family give her back like that?" She ached for the child who'd been given the chance of a new home only to be rejected by her adoptive family.

The regret on Rylan's face told the story. "I'm afraid so, darlin'. There's a three-month clause in the adoption contract, giving them time to see if the child is a good fit with the family."

"But how did you know?"

"There was a letter from Sister Marguerite at the seminary, and since the family lived near Boston, I went to pick her up and bring her home."

Delia's small, somewhat sticky hand reached to turn Colleen's face to her. "Maybe now you can be my mama." The trusting blue eyes, so earnest and sincere, twisted Colleen's insides. How could she say no to her after everything she'd been through?

She threw a desperate glance at Rylan, who was smiling now through misty eyes.

"If I'm not presuming too much," he said, "how would you feel about adopting this lovely wee girl once we're married?"

Colleen's heart swelled with an overwhelming cascade of emotion. This man had given her everything she'd ever dreamed of. "I love you, Rylan Montgomery. Almost as much as I love this imp." She kissed Delia's face and squeezed her again, laughing and crying at once. "I would be very happy to be your mama—as long as you can stand Mr. Rylan for a father."

Delia giggled. "I think so."

Rylan stretched his arms around both of them, pressing a kiss to Colleen's temple. "I love you both very much. I'm incredibly blessed to have you in my life."

"Will I have to live at the orphanage?" Delia's nose scrunched as the question came to her.

"For a little while. Until Miss O'Leary and I get married and find a house to live in. But in the meantime, we'll be here every day with you."

"When we get a house, can I have a puppy?" Her eyes flashed with mischief.

Colleen suppressed a laugh. "You're getting a mother, a father, a new house, and you want a puppy, too?"

Her little face fell. "I'm sorry. That's greedy, isn't it?"

Rylan plucked the child out of Colleen's arms. "We can't promise anything right now, until we see where we end up living." He kissed the top of her head and set her down. "Why don't you run up and put your bag and Mr. Whiskers in your room? I have a few more things to discuss with Miss O'Leary, and then we'll take you out for ice cream to celebrate."

"Ice cream!" She squealed and made a dash for the hallway.

The moment she was out of sight, Rylan pulled Colleen into his arms. "Are you sure about this? Taking on a husband is one thing. But an instant family is quite another."

She pressed a hand to his chest. "Oh, Rylan. Ever since Delia left, I've secretly dreamed she would come back so I could adopt her myself. Only I didn't know how I'd manage it on my own. You've made me the happiest woman in America."

She leaned up to kiss him, winding her fingers through his thick hair. As they drew apart, the intensity darkening his eyes sent goosebumps down her spine.

He leaned his forehead against hers. "I'm thinking I'd better talk to your father and get a marriage license very soon if you're going to be tempting me like that."

She laughed, her heart overflowing with pure joy. "The sooner the better, Mr. Montgomery. The sooner the better."

38

B RIANNA DESCENDED THE STAIRS of Barnard College's main building, her arms laden with the books she'd just purchased. She needed to walk the two blocks to the streetcar stop, and her feet balked at the distance she would have to go before she could sit down. After a full day of touring the campus and then standing in line to buy her books, the soles of her feet burned inside her buttoned-up shoes.

The welcome sight of a bench at the edge of the college property beckoned to her. She sank gratefully onto the wrought-iron seat, her feet throbbing in relief. If she missed the streetcar, there'd be another one along sooner or later.

She set the books beside her and closed her eyes for a moment, letting the afternoon sun warm her face. If only the happy rays could lift her spirits as easily. An unshakeable cloud of melancholy had followed her ever since she'd left Irish Meadows. Instead of reveling in the bliss of finally achieving her dream, all she could think of was Gil.

He hadn't even put up a fight about her leaving, just kissed her cheek and wished her the best of luck with her studies. As if she were a passing acquaintance or a little sister. He could have at least pretended to be more upset at her leaving.

"Miss O'Leary?"

Behind her, a male voice brought Brianna's thoughts flying back. She looked over her shoulder to see a tall, vaguely familiar man rushing toward her.

"Miss O'Leary. Thank goodness I caught up with you. You left one of your purchases behind." With a wide smile, he stopped in front of her and held out a thick textbook.

That was where she'd seen him. He'd been working behind the counter at the bookstore. "Thank you so much." She accepted the book and added it to the already teetering pile on the bench beside her.

"I'm Peter McNamara." He held out a hand to her. "My father is a professor here. We met at the Independence Day party you attended with your aunt." His smile stretched wider. "It's lovely to see you again."

Warmth bloomed in Brianna's cheeks at the undisguised interest on Mr. McNamara's face.

"I'm on my way home myself," he said. "May I offer you a ride? My motorcar is parked right around the corner."

Brianna blinked, not sure what to make of this friendly young man. Though tempted to accept a ride, she didn't feel comfortable getting in a vehicle with a man she barely knew.

"I appreciate your offer, Mr. McNamara, but I'll be fine on the streetcar."

He glanced at the pile of books beside her. "You shouldn't have to carry that load all the way home. Please, I'd be honored to help Miss O'Leary's niece. Besides, my father would have my head if I let you walk."

She bit her bottom lip. "Do you know where my aunt lives?"

"I sure do. We've been to dinner there several times over the years. After my mother passed away, your aunt made it a point to have my father and I over more often. I think she feared we poor bachelors couldn't possibly put a decent meal together."

Brianna had to laugh at the image he created, and his grin made him seem like a young boy. If he and his father were friends of her aunt, she supposed he was safe enough. "Very well, Mr. McNamara. I would be grateful for a ride if it's not too far out of your way."

"Not at all. You wait here. I'll be back in a jiffy. And please call me Peter."

Ten minutes later, with the books safely stowed in the rumble seat, Peter guided the open motorcar down the busy city streets. He chatted about his courses at Columbia and his part-time job at the bookstore, as well as his father's long career as an educator. Brianna was grateful for the ride—and for the fact that she didn't have to add much to the conversation.

Soon they pulled up to the curb in front of Aunt Fiona's brownstone. Peter stopped the car and set the brake, then jumped out his side of the car. He came around to open her door for her and lent a hand as she stepped out onto the walkway. The curtain at her aunt's parlor window fluttered. Brianna gave an inward sigh of relief. Aunt Fiona would be out any minute to greet them. Not that Peter wasn't a charming companion, but Brianna longed to go inside and put her feet up.

"Let me help you with these books, and I'll say a quick hello to your aunt before I leave."

"Thank you so much for the ride. I didn't realize how tired I was."

Peter bent over the back of the car to retrieve her packages. When he straightened with his arms full, he gave her a nervous stare. "If I'm not being too bold, Miss O'Leary, may I ask if you're free for dinner tomorrow night?"

"I'm afraid she's busy." Heavy footsteps thudded down the cement stairs from Aunt Fiona's front door.

Brianna whirled to see Gil's scowling face behind her. A rush of heat flooded her cheeks, as though she'd been caught in a secret tryst. "Gil. What are you doing here?"

Her brain tried to make sense of his unexpected presence. Why would he come to the city in the middle of the week when she would be coming home at the week's end?

"I came to see you, of course." His gaze never left Peter.

Alarm rushed through her as the memory of the night her father ended up in the hospital came roaring back. "Is something wrong at home?"

"Nothing's wrong." Gil's terse words hung in the air.

As if sensing the tension swirling around them like the fall leaves on the pavement, Peter juggled the books to one arm and extended his free hand. "I'm Peter McNamara, a friend of the family."

Gil ignored the hand. "I'm Gilbert Whelan, a *very* good friend of Brianna's." The challenge in his voice was unmistakable.

Brianna glared at Gil. "A friend who's being extremely rude at the moment. Peter offered me a ride home. He doesn't deserve your bad attitude."

"Seems to me he's offering you more than a ride."

A flush darkened Peter's high cheekbones as he turned his attention to Brianna. "I'm very sorry if I overstepped in any way."

She laid a hand on his arm. "Not at all. Thank you again for your help."

"My pleasure. I'll take these inside for you." He dashed up the stairs with the stack of books and returned seconds later. "Please give my best to your aunt. I hope to see you again soon."

Despite the temper building steam inside her, Brianna managed a bright smile for him. "I'm sure you will."

He gave a brief nod in Gil's direction before hopping into the driver's seat.

As soon as his car roared away, Brianna marched up the steps into the house. Without looking back, she pulled off her hat and gloves and slapped them on the hall table. The sharp slam of the door told her Gil had followed her inside. Her hands shook with anger that had little to do with Gil's rudeness to Peter and more to do with the resentment that had built up over the last few weeks.

She whirled to face him, hands on her hips. "How dare you embarrass me like that, Gilbert Whelan. The poor man was only being kind."

His eyes darkened to navy. "That *poor man* was ogling you like an entrée on a menu." He pressed forward, his expression thunderous. "Is that what you meant by wanting to experience college life? You want to see other men?"

She tilted her chin at him in a dare. "Dating other less pig-headed men sounds like a fine idea."

She braced herself for a burst of Gil's temper. Instead, a shuttered look descended on his face, one of sorrow.

He pressed his lips together into a firm line and stepped back. "I can see this was a bad idea." Without further explanation, he turned and strode out the door.

Baffled, Brianna fought for equilibrium. She rushed outside and called after his retreating back. "Gil, why did you come?"

He paused to look over his shoulder, then shook his head. "Never mind. It doesn't matter anymore."

Without realizing where he was headed, Gil ended up on Fifth Avenue in front of St. Patrick's Cathedral. He climbed the stairs to the double set of wooden doors and tried the latch, not certain if the building would be open on a Wednesday afternoon. The handle gave way under his fingers. Removing his hat, he stepped into the cool, dark interior and drew a deep breath into his lungs to settle his system.

His eyes adjusted slowly to the dim interior, while the soothing smell of candle wax and sandalwood soap flooded his senses. He pushed his cap into his jacket pocket, his fingers brushing the small, square package hidden there. Another wave of regret swamped him. He'd come to ask Brianna out to dinner, where he'd planned to propose, but seeing her with that dandy in the fancy automobile had short-circuited the wiring in his brain. All his good intentions had vanished in a black cloud of distrust.

Pushing aside his frustration, Gil moved into the main area of the church. The soft glow of votive candles cast a soothing aura over the vast space. Several people dotted the pews on either side of the long center aisle, heads bent in prayer. Gil took a seat in one of the back pews, hoping that the peace of the sanctuary would soothe his troubled spirit.

He'd behaved badly. He didn't need Brianna's furious reaction to tell him that. He'd allowed jealousy to flare like a lit match and overtake all common sense. The numerous lectures he'd given Bree about trust and jealousy flew to mind. What kind of hypocrite was he?

He bent his head over his knees and ran his fingers through his hair.

Lord, I need Your help. What should I do now?

He sat in the hushed interior, hoping to hear the still, small voice of God offering wisdom. Last Sunday in St. Rita's, Gil had been certain God's nudging had been leading him here. Had he totally misread His intention?

A spasm of pain gripped Gil's chest. He couldn't imagine his life without Brianna. More than anything, he wanted her for his wife.

What about what she wants?

The words whispered through his thoughts, causing him to jolt on the hard wooden pew. Was that it? Had Brianna changed her mind about him? Did she want someone like Peter McNamara, an intellectual who could discuss literature and philosophy?

Or perhaps she'd decided not to marry at all. To become a career woman like her Aunt Fiona.

Had he ever really asked Brianna what she wanted for her future? Or had he simply assumed that she would fall in line with his plans for their lives?

"I didn't realize you expected me to give up my dream for yours." Brianna's bitter accusation stung his memory. The truth slammed into him with the force of a lightning bolt. He *had* expected her to give up her dream. When she'd offered to help him achieve his goal, he'd assumed she would abandon the idea of going to college.

With a surge of remorse, Gil fell to his knees on the hard kneeler. He had put his own selfish wishes before the woman he loved. Worse yet, he'd put his own desires before God's will for his life.

He lowered his head over his clasped hands. *Forgive me, Lord, for my selfishness. Show me what You would have me do. Help me to do the right thing—the unselfish thing—for Brianna, and help me to become the man You want me to be. A man worthy of her and of You.*

Gil stayed on his knees until his thigh muscles ached. At last, he rose and faced the altar at the front of the church. A soft prism of light illuminated the area. A sense of love and gratitude invaded Gil's heart. He inhaled a full clean breath and donned his hat.

With a sure and certain knowledge of what he needed to do, Gil left the sanctuary of the cathedral.

A soft knock on her door startled Brianna out of her prayers.

"Brianna? May I come in?" her aunt called briskly from the hall.

She pushed up from her knees and attempted to smooth out her wrinkled skirt. "Of course, Auntie."

There was no time to wash her face or fix her hair. Her aunt would no doubt be able to tell she'd had a good cry.

Aunt Fiona closed the door softly behind her. "Gilbert is downstairs asking to see you."

Brianna's pulse leapt. Gil had come back? Would she find out now why he'd really come here? Or would they just end up arguing again?

She bit her bottom lip. "We had a fight earlier."

Her aunt fixed Brianna with a no-nonsense stare. "Most couples fight from time to time. What's important is how you resolve your differences."

"Oh, Auntie. We used to be so compatible, but lately all we do is disappoint each other. Do you think God is trying to tell us something?"

Aunt Fiona patted Brianna's arm. "I can't speak for the Lord, but I'm sure everything will work out the way He intends. The bottom line is . . . do you still love Gilbert?"

Brianna nodded miserably.

"And does he love you?"

She twisted her fingers together. "I don't know. Everything about our relationship has been so mixed up lately, I'm not sure of anything anymore."

Aunt Fiona draped a warm arm around her shoulders. "Take some advice from someone who doesn't want to see you end up alone like me." She held Brianna's gaze. "Forgive him."

"But he—"

"Forgive him. Just as he forgave you for your mistakes."

Shame washed over her. Her aunt was right. Gil had forgiven her several times for the exact same crime. Surely she could do the same. "Is love always this hard?" she whispered.

"When the two people are both as stubborn as you, then yes. But it will get easier. Trust me." She moved to the door. "Why don't you freshen up and then give that young man a chance to say what he came to say? Do you think you can do that?"

Brianna nodded.

"Good. Come down to the parlor when you're ready."

Alone in her room, Brianna splashed her face with water from the stand on her dresser, patted it dry, and scrambled through the closet for her favorite dress. She undid her messy topknot and brushed her hair until it shone, catching the curls in a ribbon at the nape of her neck.

"That will have to do for now," she told her reflection in the oval mirror. She couldn't help remembering getting ready for Gil's welcome home party at Irish Meadows. So much had changed since then. She hardly recognized herself as that timid girl, scared of her father, jealous of her sister, and terrified of her feelings for Gil.

Not that she wasn't still scared. Scared that Gil would never love her the way she loved him. That he may never have the courage to defy her father and choose her. Or that he might leave Irish Meadows to forge a new future alone. What would she do if that was the news he'd come to tell her?

Dear God, please give me the courage to face whatever Gil has to say. And give me the grace to wish him happiness—even if his future doesn't include me.

With the prayer on her lips, she headed down the narrow staircase, her legs quaking with every step. When she got to the bottom, Gil emerged from the parlor. Butterflies danced in her stomach. Earlier she hadn't noticed his handsome suit and tie—an outfit far too fancy for a mere social call. Nothing about this whole visit made the least bit of sense.

"You look beautiful," he said when she reached him.

"Thank you." She lifted her chin. "But a compliment won't fix things between us."

"I know." Regret laced his voice. He gestured toward the parlor. "Can we talk, please?"

She nodded and preceded him into the room where a fire cast a warm glow over the space. In the cage off to one corner, Aunt

Fiona's two lovebirds hopped from perch to perch in a state of agitation, as though sensing the tension in the room.

Gingerly, Brianna took a seat at the farthest corner of the sofa while Gil went to stand by the hearth.

The silence stretched between them. Her aunt's brass clock ticked loudly in the quiet, competing with the twittering of the birds.

At last, Gil sighed. "I owe you an apology for earlier today. My behavior was completely out of line."

"You're right. It was." Brianna frowned. "Why did you really come here today?"

He fidgeted with the cuff of his jacket. "I had something important to . . . discuss with you."

The deep furrows in his brow made her heart sink. "What is it?" She braced herself for the answer.

His Adam's apple bobbed and a fine sheen of perspiration coated his forehead. "I want to start by apologizing again—not only for today, but for all the times I've let you down lately. I know I've hurt you more than once, and I deeply regret that."

Using all her willpower to contain her emotions, she focused her gaze on her lap and waited for him to continue.

"I've made many mistakes, but I've learned a lot about myself in the process. Like how important it is to stay true to my values." His foot tapped a nervous refrain on the carpet. "You've helped me come to terms with my father's death, and I think I've finally learned to forgive myself."

Her alarm heightened with every word. This was definitely a good-bye speech.

"Because of that, I've been able to accept a business proposition I never would have considered six months ago."

Brianna's stomach dropped. He must be leaving Irish Meadows after all.

He rubbed a hand over his jaw. "This is not coming out how I'd planned."

She dared to look at him, and her heart twisted at the blatant misery on his face. Her aunt's words echoed in her head. *Forgive him, as he's forgiven you.*

Aunt Fiona was right. No matter how hard this was for her, she had to let Gil go. Give him permission to pursue his dream, just as she was pursuing hers. All the fear and resentment drained out of her, replaced with an overwhelming sadness. "It's all right, Gil. I understand."

His scowl deepened. "No, I don't think you understand at all." He came to sit beside her and took her hand in his. Shivers raced up her arms that had nothing to do with the temperature of the room.

"What I'm trying to say is that your father offered me a partnership at Irish Meadows, and I've accepted. The lawyers will be drawing up the papers next week."

Gil isn't leaving! A part of her heaved a huge sigh of relief at the news. Another part questioned his decision. With a gentle tug, she pulled her hand free of his. "What about owning your own farm?"

He stilled for a moment. "I think that idea was all mixed up with guilt over my father's death. Somehow it doesn't seem as important now."

"Well, then I'm happy for you." She hesitated, not sure what else to say. A log cracked in the fireplace, breaking the silence. "Is that all you came to tell me?"

"There's one more thing."

Nerves quivered deep in her belly at the husky tone of his voice. "What is it?"

"I know I've made a mess of things between us. But I think I finally figured out the problem."

She tensed, almost afraid to breathe, her back as taut as the wooden arm of the settee.

"The first mistake I made was putting your father's approval above my feelings for you. No one else's opinion should have mattered more than yours."

Brianna fought to contain the emotions that coursed through her and threatened to fly loose like the birds fluttering in their cage.

Gil moved closer, the spicy scent of his cologne swirling around her. "The other mistake I made was forgetting what is truly important. I didn't keep God in the middle of our relationship."

Tears burned at the back of her throat. "I was thinking the same thing earlier. Trying to discern what He wanted for our lives."

Gil moved to kneel in front of her and took her icy hands in his, forcing her to look him in the eye. "Brianna O'Leary, you are a priceless gem, and if I lose you, it will be my own fault. But I want you to know I've told your father how I feel, and I've asked for his blessing . . . on our marriage."

Her heart stuttered in her chest. She couldn't seem to get any air.

"You should also know I made it clear I would marry you with or without his blessing . . . that is, if you'll have me." His anxious eyes searched hers. "Will you marry me, Bree?"

Tremors shook her body. She wanted to say yes, but niggles of suspicion whispered through her mind. "What about college?" she asked in a voice barely above a whisper. She held her breath, praying for the right answer to her challenge.

His gaze, solid and steady, never wavered. "I'm willing to wait until you finish."

"You'd really wait three years?"

"That and more if I have to. You're worth every minute, Brianna."

Though she tried to contain it, a tear escaped to trickle down her cheek. "Why now? Why didn't you say all this before I left?"

Gil sighed and rose to sit beside her on the settee. "I didn't want you to think I was proposing as a ploy to stop you from going to school. Plus, I hadn't worked up the courage to talk to your father. Once you left, everything changed." He reached out to caress one of her hands. "I love you, Bree, and I know how important your education is to you. I won't stand in your way."

A rush of joy spread through her body. The words she'd longed to hear for years had finally crossed his lips—the love she'd craved shone from his eyes. She hiccupped as more tears blurred her vision. "Oh, Gil, I've loved you for as long as I can remember. I only prayed that one day you could love me, too, as more than a friend."

"Believe me—I do."

His warm lips came down on hers with a passion she'd never known. A long-held tension uncoiled within her as he intensified the kiss, holding her like a cherished treasure. Her soul sang with the certainty that this was where she belonged.

When at last they parted, Gil dried the remains of the moisture from her cheek with his thumb, a tender smile tipping up one side of his mouth. "You haven't actually answered my question, you know."

She smiled through her tears. "Nothing would make me happier than to be your wife."

He let out a huge breath. "Thank you, God." With gentle hands, he cupped her face and once again lowered his mouth to hers, sealing the promise. When he released her, he reached into his jacket and removed a small black box. The gold lettering had long since worn off the top, and the edges were chipped and faded. "This belonged to my mother."

He flipped the lid, and Brianna gasped. A delicate emerald ring surrounded by tiny diamonds sat nestled in the faded lining.

He removed it and slid it slowly onto her finger. "I know she'd be happy for my future wife to wear her ring."

"It's beautiful, Gil." Brianna held out her hand to admire the way it shone. "It fits perfectly." She hardly dared to believe that she would become Gil's wife. "Are you sure you're willing to wait?" She held her breath, needing the extra assurance that he wouldn't back away this time.

"I'm positive. And to prove it, I have a plan for how to pass the time in between." He tugged her up from the settee with him.

"What sort of plan?"

"I think it's high time I started courting you properly—now that you're wearing my ring." He grinned, making his blue eyes dance. "It seems our romance is destined to be somewhat un-conventional."

"I believe I like unconventional." She laughed, a sudden burst of joy infusing her with energy. "Why don't you take me out for dinner, and we can start our official first date?"

A slow smile spread across his face. "That's the best idea I've heard all day."

When he lowered his head for another kiss, the lovebirds, nestled together on the same perch, twittered their complete approval.

Epilogue

I N THE TINY ANTEROOM of St. Rita's church, Brianna settled the tiara on top of Colleen's fiery curls while Mama arranged the lace veil. When Brianna stepped back to see the full effect of her sister arrayed in a sheath of ivory satin and lace, she bit her lip to stop the flood of emotion.

My sister is getting married.

"Do not start crying now, Bree, or I'll cry, too."

Colleen's mock sternness made Brianna laugh. "I can't help it. I'm so happy for you and Rylan." She took another long look at Colleen, then turned to adjust her own attire.

Today, in her satin bridesmaid dress, Brianna felt every bit as stunning as the bride.

"Your turn will be here before you know it," Mama whispered behind her.

"It's all right, Mama. I don't mind waiting until the time is right for me." She picked up a posy of asters from the small table near the door. "I can't believe Daddy is allowing Colleen to marry Rylan so quickly. How did you manage to persuade him?"

Mama chuckled. "I still have a trick or two up my sleeve when it comes to your father. Facing his mortality has allowed James to see the important things in life. Like his daughters' happiness." She reached up to tuck a stray curl into place behind Brianna's ear, where a pearl earring bobbed. "Seeing you in this dress may make Gil reconsider his offer to wait three more years. You look as beautiful as the bride."

"Thank you, Mama." Brianna drew her into a hug.

"God has been so good to us. If only Adam were here, everything would be perfect."

The fact that Adam had ignored Mama's plea to come home for the wedding was the one blight on this happy day.

A knock sounded at the door. Brianna straightened, shooing Colleen to one side. "I'll get this. You stay out of sight."

She cracked the door an inch, enough to see Rylan and Gil on the other side, resplendent in their tails. With their dark coloring and hair slicked back in the same fashion, the two were enough alike to be brothers. "What are you doing here? Don't you know it's bad luck for the groom to see the bride before the wedding?"

"I told you." Gil thumped Rylan on the shoulder.

Brianna opened the door enough to wedge herself through the tight opening.

Gil's eyes widened, and his mouth dropped open. "You are breathtaking." He moved forward to grasp Brianna's hand and bring it to his lips.

Brianna's cheeks grew hotter by the minute. "And you both look very handsome."

She pulled her attention to Rylan, who shifted from one foot to the other, fingers plucking at the cufflink on his sleeve. Her heart softened at his panicked expression. "Is everything okay?"

"Colleen's taking so long. I wanted to make sure she hadn't changed her mind."

Brianna laid a soothing hand on his arm. "I've never seen a bride more certain of her decision."

Rylan's shoulders sagged as a relieved sigh whooshed out. "Praise be to heaven. I don't know what I'd do without her. I love her more than I ever imagined possible."

Brianna smiled. "Just a few minutes more and she'll be all yours. You'd better go. Send Daddy back. It's time for him to walk her down the aisle."

She turned to Gil. "You, too."

Gil grinned and bent to give her a lingering kiss before following Rylan down the hall.

Brianna returned to the anteroom, unable to erase the smile from her face. Gil looked so incredibly handsome in his suit it made her insides quiver. She'd never really allowed herself to believe the day would come when she and Gil could openly declare their feelings for each other, never mind be planning a future together.

"You look more lovesick than I do," Colleen teased from her spot in front of the full-length mirror.

Brianna laughed and came to give her sister a hug. "Wait until you see your groom. He's almost as handsome as my fiancé."

The hug suddenly became tighter as Colleen clutched Brianna closer. "I'm so glad we're finally acting like true sisters. And that you agreed to be my maid of honor."

Brianna squeezed her back. "I expect you to do the same for me in a few years."

"I'd be delighted." Colleen pulled away with a loud sniff and reached for her bouquet of fall flowers.

Another knock sounded in the room, and her father poked his head inside. "Are you two ready? The crowd is growing restless—not to mention the groom and best man."

"I'm ready, Daddy." Glowing, Colleen went to meet him.

The sight of tears standing in her father's eyes almost undid Brianna's control.

"Ah, look at my two beautiful girls. God has certainly blessed this family."

"Yes, He has." Colleen slipped her hand through Daddy's arm and nodded to Brianna. "Come on, Bree. Let's go put our men out of their misery."

A few minutes later, organ music filled the air, and Brianna pressed a hand to her stomach, willing the chorus of butterflies to settle down. She paused at the entrance as every head swiveled to watch her begin her march up the aisle. She took a moment to drink in the details of this sacred event—the familiar wooden pews filled with friends and neighbors, the rich scent of candles and flowers permeating the church, and dear Mrs. Shepherd plucking at the organ. Seated in the first row with Connor, Deirdre, and little Delia, Mama pressed a gloved hand to her mouth, and Brianna knew she was fighting a rush of happy tears. Behind her, a throat cleared—Daddy's signal to get a move on.

As she glided in measured steps down the aisle, her gaze moved to the head of the church where Gil and Rylan stood tall and proud beside Reverend Filmore, love shining on their handsome faces.

At that moment, a bold ray of sunshine prismed through the stained glass window, flooding the altar area with a beautiful array of colors. Brianna's smile widened, thinking that God's happiness had made itself manifest in the sanctuary—His personal stamp of approval on this rather unconventional, yet holy, marriage.

Filled with gratitude for God's great gifts in her life—the blessing of Gil's love, her father's long-awaited approval, as well as Colleen and Rylan's faith-filled union—Brianna sighed with perfect contentment.

Today would indeed be a monumental day!

A Note
from the Author

D EAR READERS,

As I came up with the storyline for *Irish Meadows*, many factors blended together to influence the creation of my fictional world. With Irish roots on both sides of my genealogical tree, I knew I wanted to write about a big Irish family. My great-grandparents on my father's side emigrated from County Armagh in Ireland to New York City in about 1890. My great-grandfather, Stewart Moneypenny, worked as a ship captain based out of New York, but unfortunately he died quite young, leaving a widow and many children behind. My great-grandmother remarried a shipmate of her husband's and, for unknown reasons, they ended up leaving New York to live in rural Quebec—thus contributing to half of my Canadian roots. My grandfather, Harry Moneypenny, met my grandmother, Daisy, a farm girl in a small, rural town, and they went on to have five children, my father being the youngest. (I must give a shout-out to Ancestry.com, where I learned much of my family's history.)

In researching Irish immigration to the United States, I learned that the Irish were not well treated when they arrived in America, and were in fact despised by many. They had a hard time finding work because many employers would simply post signs indicating "No Irish." So the idea of an immigrant family clawing its way up from poverty and discrimination formed the background for James O'Leary's family and provided the motivation for James's actions. Having attained some degree of wealth and respectability in Long Island, James was not about to slide back into the hard times his father had endured as a new immigrant. This is why James is so determined that his daughters marry well, in order to maintain their status in society.

In choosing the actual setting for the O'Leary farm, I found that around the turn of the century, many of the wealthy New Yorkers built grand country estates on Long Island, which came to be known as the Gold Coast. It seemed a fitting place for the O'Learys to raise and train thoroughbred horses for their elite neighbors.

By accident, when researching horse racing in New York, I discovered that racing had been banned in New York for several years right around the time period I had decided on for my story. This provided additional motivation behind James's desperate actions in making Gil court the banker's daughter to save Irish Meadows from financial ruin.

When I wrote about Rylan's voyage to Ireland, one other tidbit of research led me to learn about the RMS *Olympic*, a transatlantic ocean liner similar to the *Titanic*. The *Olympic*'s accident at sea actually occurred on September 20, 1911. However, for the purpose of my story, I took an author's liberty and had the incident occur several weeks earlier, so it could tie in with Rylan's return from Ireland and wreak a little more havoc for my characters!

I hope you enjoyed the saga of the O'Leary family, and of Brianna and Colleen's journey to happiness. If you did, please look for Adam O'Leary's story coming out in 2016!

Blessings and happy reading!
Susan

ACKNOWLEDGMENTS

MANY WONDERFUL PEOPLE and events came together to bring about my dream of one day seeing *Irish Meadows* in print.

First and foremost, I thank God for the gift of this wonderful story that seemed to pour forth from my subconscious. I fell in love with the characters, the setting, and the history—and many times, through divine inspiration, came upon the right research at the right time.

Secondly, a most profound thank you to Dave Long for choosing this story from a contest win, and for loving it enough to take a chance on a new writer. His support and encouragement continue to amaze and humble me. Thank you so much, Dave.

Thank you also to Charlene Patterson for her excellent editorial input that made this story so much better!

My critique partners, Julie Jarnagin, CJ Chase, and Sally Bayless, have been an incredible blessing to me. I am so grateful for their input in making my story stronger and for their friendship and support. Thank you, guys!

Last, but never least, I must thank my family—my husband, Bud, and my children, Leanne and Eric—for allowing me to pursue my passion and for not complaining about the occasional burnt dinners or the crazy amount of hours I spend on my laptop! I love you all.

I am honored to be a part of such a distinguished publishing house and to share this journey with such amazing fellow authors. I feel blessed to be able to do what I love, to write beautiful stories of romance, and to share God's message of hope and love with my readers.

About the Author

Susan Anne Mason describes her writing style as "romance sprinkled with faith." She particularly enjoys exploring the themes of forgiveness and redemption in her stories. *Irish Meadows* is her first historical novel and won the Fiction from the Heartland contest sponsored by the Mid-American Romance Authors chapter of RWA. Susan lives outside Toronto, Ontario, with her husband, two children, and two cats. Learn more about Susan and her books at www.SusanAnneMason.com.

More Fiction From Bethany House

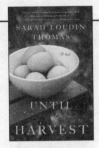

When a family tragedy derails his college studies, Henry Phillips returns home to the family farm feeling lost and abandoned. Can he and local Margaret Hoffman move beyond their first impressions and find a way to help each other?

Until the Harvest by Sarah Loudin Thomas
sarahloudinthomas.com

When a new doctor arrives in town, midwife Martha Cade's world is overturned by the threat to her job, a town scandal, and an unexpected romance.

The Midwife's Tale by Delia Parr
AT HOME IN TRINITY #1

Caroline Taylor has tended the lighthouse since her father's death. But where will she go when a wounded Civil War veteran arrives to take her place?

Hearts Made Whole by Jody Hedlund
BEACONS OF HOPE #2
jodyhedlund.com